SI

BOOK 1 OF THE SINISTER SERIES

TONY
MARTURANO

a Different Angle

Published in the United Kingdom and the rest of the world by
a Different Angle 2022

Cambridge, England

A catalogue record for this book is available from the
British Library

ISBN
978-1-7397694-2-0

This book is dedicated to YOU, my reader. Without you, my words would be nothing but letters arranged on a page.

"Be alert and of sober mind. Your enemy the devil prowls around like a roaring lion looking for someone to devour."

1 Peter 5:8

PROLOGUE

There was no storm outside: no intermittent flashes of lightning, no demon wind screeching around the building, just silence. The deluge of rain had washed away the day's grime, leaving behind only the occasional tap, drip, and gurgle of rainwater.

Inside, the house was still, tomblike, which only heightened the eery squeal of the closet door as it slowly drifted open.

The sound wrenched the little girl out of her sleep to a dark room and the dreaded realisation that it had happened again. Slowly, she turned her head to confirm what she already knew; the nightlight and its silhouette projections of Venice was dead. There were no people floating in gondolas. No stars over Piazza San Marco. Just darkness.

The lamp, a souvenir of her mother's, had sat in her parents' bedroom for as long as she could remember until, one awful nightmare-filled night, her mother had offered it to her with the reassurance that it would always be her beacon in the darkest hours. And it had been, until now.

Now, it was lifeless, almost lost among the many shadows that haunted her room, with the memory of its glow resurrected only by the dirty yellow hue of the streetlight spilling in through the arched bedroom window. On nights like this, these reborn shadows took on the elongated features of a monster with high angry eyebrows and a wide jagged mouth.

She was sitting up in bed now, squinting into the gloom. Eyes wide as saucers, breath coming shallow and fast.

It was in her room again. Hiding in the gloom. She could sense it. The foul malevolent thing was watching her. Plotting. Waiting for the perfect moment to reveal itself.

Her tiny heart was afraid too, for it was knocking on her rib cage, urging her to jump out of bed and flee to the sanctuary of her parents' room. But she couldn't. She dared not move. Instead, she allowed her giant oval blue eyes to flick across the covers to the other corner of the room.

Was she sure it was in there with her? Everything appeared to be in order. Nothing was out of place. She could see the outline of her dollhouse, the chest of drawers, the dressing table, and...what was that? There! In the corner of the room. Something that wasn't there before. A dark shape she did not recognise.

Her heart was hammering loudly in her chest now, begging to be let out, to be set free. Instinctively, her eyes flicked over to the door.

It was firmly shut, but the closet door was wide open, like the gaping mouth of the beast itself. And she knew why. *It* had left its lair and was now stalking her.

Mummy.

But the whimper was in her head. She tried to speak again.

Still, the word resounded in her mind and could not find its way out. It was as if she had been struck dumb. As if *it* had pried her lips apart while she was sleeping and pulled, squelched, and sewed her tongue to the roof of her mouth.

That's when she was struck by the memory. It returned to her in such vivid detail that it felt like it was happening all over again.

Here. In this very room. It was a sleepover night. Her friend was sleeping on the blow-up bed on the floor. She had been roused by a stomach-churning squelching sound. When she dared to peek out over the side of the bed, she felt her body freeze into a horrified paralysis.

There, on the floor, her friend lay, gaping up at her with beseeching eyes, bulging with tears, while *it* used its claws to wrench her mouth wide open into an inhuman gaping black hole and was trying to climb inside...

Movement. In the corner of the room.

Did that shadow just shift?

Mummy.

Again, the cry was silent. She willed her tongue to move but no matter how hard she tried, it wouldn't budge.

Sssss.....oo.....o-phie.

It lingered on the S of her name with a reptilian hiss. Calling. Taunting. Mocking like one of those cruel children in the school playground.

Sophie's eyes flicked over to the bedroom door once more. As she once again considered making a dash for safety, her thoughts were interrupted by the hideous clicking sound of nails on the wooden floor.

It had moved. It was under her bed.

Mummy! Mummy!

Spider legs of terror scuttled down her spine. Was it really under the bed? There was no way of knowing for sure without looking. And the mere thought of that paralysed her with abject terror once more, as it had that night.

She considered hiding under the covers. Plenty of other children did that if scary stories were anything to go by, but she knew it was a stupid idea. *It* didn't care. *It* wasn't afraid. *It* would just crawl over and rip through the covers to get at her.

More scuttling, scraping sounds and her head snapped back to the dark corner once more. It was there, of that she was sure. There was no mistaking the clicky, scratchy sounds of its talons or its guttural wheeze as it breathed in then expelled fetid air back into the room.

Tears of terror welled in her eyes as nervous perspiration, itching like cockroach legs, tickled the roots of her hair.

Do what Mummy told you. Think of good things. Nice things.

She tried to think about Christmas morning, but all she could conjure was the manic grin of that demonic clown she hated, and the dolls that she asked her parents to remove because she could feel their glassy dead eyes following her around the room.

Like Mummy said. It's just your imagination.

It wasn't her imagination. It was real.

Click, scratch. Click, scratch!

This time the sound was much louder. Closer.

It was now or never. *Now* or never.

Jump out of the bed. Race for the door! Jump out of the bed and race for the door! She would run fast, like she did at school. If she ran fast enough, she would be able to outrun it, to get through the bedroom door and to her parents' room. After all, she was a fast runner, a real fast runner, the fastest in her class. She even had the medals and trophies to prove it.

She turned to the door once more. She focussed on it as she had been taught. *Focus on where you want to be and take yourself there. Get yourself there, fast.*

She zoomed her gaze onto the door handle now, focussing on it and sucking in deep lungfuls of air. Slow. Deep. Steady. Ready.

Then she saw it. The door handle was moving, as if someone was rattling it from the other side.

She opened her mouth to scream but nothing came out.

MUMMY! She tried once more but managed to utter nothing but a garbled murmur.

MUMMY! HELP ME!

Now the handle slowly began to arch downwards and knowing she had finally run out of time, Sophie opened her mouth, took a deep breath, and squealed.

"MUUUUUMMY! MUMMY!"

She followed her desperate call with the loudest scream she could muster.

Elena Cooper pushed the door open with such force it slammed against the wall. She reached for the light switch and snapped it on.

"Sophie? Darling?" She rushed over and sat on the bed next to her daughter, wrapping her arms around her. "Sweetheart. What's wrong? Did you have another bad dream?" she cooed, feeling the girl's face, and then brushed a lock of hair from her eyes.

Heart thumping, eyes spilling tears, Sophie was unable to respond, her terror for the moment still with her. It was only after several seconds and a series of unintelligible sounds that she managed to move her tongue to utter, "It...it...w...w...was....h...ere...in...my... my room."

Elena broke their embrace so that she could look into Sophie's wide eyes. She had seen this many times before. Her daughter's night terrors were regular and acute. And this time was no different, judging by the dampness of her daughter's pyjamas.

"Oh baby. You're fine. You're okay. It was just another nightmare, that's all," she said softly, clutching the six-year-old closer in frustration. She wished she could make her better, that she could make them stop. "Just another nightmare."

"N…No, Mummy," the little girl cried, urgently pulling free from her mother's arms, and peering up at her. "*It* was in here. Next to my bed. Just like that night," she cried.

Elena shook her head. "Oh no, darling. No, my baby. That was just another bad dream. You know that."

"It wasn't!" she insisted. "It was here, inside my room, it came from inside of there." Sophie raised a shaky finger and pointed at the cavernous void beyond the closet's doorway.

Elena looked across the room then turned back to her daughter with a reassuring smile. "Did you leave the door open again?"

Sophie leaned in closer and whispered, "No. *It* opened it."

"All right," Elena said. She was used to this routine. "Would you like me to check for you?"

Sophie's only response was the tremble in her body and a reluctant nod while she stared at the black hole across the room.

"Okay," Elena said, rubbing her child's hair, knowing full well that Sophie would never get back to sleep unless she made a show of thoroughly inspecting the place.

Elena left the bed and crossed the room where she pushed the door as wide as it would go. Her daughter could see what she already knew; there was nothing in the closet but the usual clothes and paraphernalia.

She pushed hangers aside so that she could inspect the corners. "See? Nothing in…" but the words died in Elena's mouth when she spotted something peeking out from under her daughter's red coat. Her heart skipped a beat.

Without adjusting her gaze, she reached up, felt for the hanging cord, and tugged on it. Light flickered despondently to life, illuminating a shelf full of board games, dolls, folded blankets, an array of neatly hanging clothing, and then…

"What is it?" Sophie whined from across the room. Elena did not respond. Instead, she slowly pushed dresses, coats, and nighties aside so she could get a better look. As it was revealed to her, she gasped, her mind scrambling to process what she was seeing.

"Mummy?" Sophie called, urgently now. "Mummy, what is it?"

Elena did not turn. Her eyes were deceiving her, surely.

And yet there was no mistaking it. The same tiny toes. Same pink nightie. She was scrunched up into a protective ball in the corner of the closet.

Sophie's imploring blue eyes gaped up at her, a trembling finger held to her lips as she whispered words that shoved an icicle of terror into Elena's chest.

"Shh…don't move. *It's* standing right behind you."

Elena Cooper barely had time to twist her head before she was enveloped by the putrid stench of its breath. Then the thing was upon her, strangling her scream and plunging the room into darkness.

1

JUST ANOTHER DAY

MONDAY EVENING

Sophie bit her lip as she watched them huddle around him. It was only when the pressure started pushing against her temple that she realised she was holding her breath.

Beside her, the man's wife looked on anxiously, clutching her three-year-old to her chest as if his life depended on it. The little boy, oblivious to all the fuss, busied himself with twirling his mother's frizzy brown hair around his chubby fingers.

"Alan? Alan, can you hear me?" one of the paramedics called aloud. He was rubbing the ball of his palm on the man's chest as his colleague placed an oxygen mask over the patient's nose and mouth.

The man had collapsed into a sitting position and was now

leaning up against the side wall of one of the fast-food outlets near the check-in zones. They had managed to move him away from the serving hatch, but the commotion was still putting off customers who were much more interested in gawking than buying.

"That's it, deep breaths for me, matey. Deep breaths," one of the paramedics soothed. He watched the mask fog with each of the man's rasping breaths while his colleague unbuttoned the man's shirt and attached plastic monitor discs to his chest, pushing them through the thick grey hair.

"That's it. Take it easy for me, Alan. That's your name, isn't it?" Sophie had already told the paramedic the man's name, so she assumed he was asking him to measure his attention. Alan nodded. "Good, very good, Alan. That's it, mate, nice deep breaths."

"Control to Alpha 1. Are you there?"

The patient's wife glanced at the radio in Sophie's hand and scowled as if the thing was in some way interfering with her husband's treatment.

Sophie felt an urge to give the woman a hug but opted instead to place a reassuring hand on her arm. "Try not to worry," she said softly. "He's in great hands," she followed with a smile, before exchanging glances with one of the paramedics.

The man with broad shoulders and a buzzed haircut gave her a faint nod, code Sophie interpreted as meaning the patient was going to be fine, although it was obvious the couple would not be travelling today. Sophie made a mental note to arrange a ticket exchange for a different flight.

"Control to Alpha. Alpha 1, please respond," continued the impatient tinny voice. *"Soph, are you there?"*

Sophie gave the woman another reassuring smile before stepping out of earshot.

"Yes, Steve, I'm here."

"*Ah, Soph. There you are. How did it go with the suspected H.A.?*"

Sophie glanced back towards the man. "It's looking good. Paramedics are still with him now. We'll need to confirm baggage removal. These passengers won't be travelling anywhere anytime soon."

"*Right. Okay... Look, Soph, I know you wanna get out of here with it being your birthday and everyfin'...*" Her supervisor's Estuary accent sounded even thicker over the radio.

Sophie looked at her watch. "Go on."

"*Well, it's this sleeper in Departures...*"

"I thought you sent Katy to that."

"*I did, but... ya know, she's still a bit wet behind the ears and all that... think she's struggling, mate.*"

Sophie took a deep breath while her supervisor ploughed on.

"*...and I know your shift is ending soon and everyfin'—*"

"Steve, I have people waiting for me..."

"*Yeah, but you can go once you've done this. As soon as you've done this. You know, just point Katy in the right direction and then you can be out of here.*"

Sophie glanced at her watch again as if expecting something to have changed since a few seconds ago. 18:32. She was going to be late.

"*Departures. On the corner of Perfume Hut and Jewellery. Dressed in black. Red suitcase.*"

Sophie drew a breath to respond...

"*Thanks, babe.*"

She looked across the concourse to see that the passenger with the suspected heart attack was now sitting in a wheelchair and was being prepped for his trip to the ambulance.

The little boy was watching her over his mother's shoulder. She smiled and waved at him, but he didn't respond. Instead, he kept observing her as if she were in some way responsible for all the fuss that had diverted attention away from him.

And so, it was on to the next case.

Sophie's shoes clicked loudly as she made her way past the multi-coloured lines of people queuing with their luggage in front of the first three of the ten check-in desks at London Stansted International Airport. Located almost forty miles northeast of central London, Stansted was known to be the United Kingdom's third busiest airport and today had been no exception. Her feet were sore, she was late, and Steve was always doing this to her.

"Excuse me, miss…" a twenty-something-year-old man said as he approached her. He bent his head slightly to read the name badge affixed to her jacket. "…Sophie. Where do we check in for Ibiza?" he asked, brandishing his ticket.

Sophie looked at the surfer dude with his stereotypical blue eyes and blond scraggy hair, then glanced at the duo of friends behind him. Instantly, they glanced away, suppressing schoolboy snickers.

She glanced at the ticket. "Just over there, sir," she said, sweetly. "Check-in zone C," she added and moved to resume her journey.

But Surfer Dude stalled her further. "I hope you don't mind me saying this, but you're really cute. Is that forward? That's way too forward, right?"

Sophie smiled, heat instantly rising to her cheeks. It irritated her that her body would so readily react to this kind of thing. He obviously wasn't serious. It was banter, or perhaps a dare if the childish giggles of his silly friends were anything to go by.

"Why don't you ditch the job and come away with us?" he continued. "We promise you'll have an adventure you'll never forget."

"Tempting," she said, forcing a smile. "I love the idea of travelling, but I have a birthday party I need to get to," she said, attempting to step away once more only to be intercepted again.

"Yeah? Whose birthday is it?"

"Mine."

"Really?"

"Yes."

"Oh! Happy birthday!"

"Thanks," she said, attempting to move around him.

"So, how old are you today?"

"Twenty-one."

"Twenty-one? You don't look it."

More infantile sniggering from the other two travellers.

"Thanks. Anyway, I really need to get going."

"Listen, if we sing you 'Happy Birthday', will you come away with us?" Surfer Dude was persistent.

The heat in her cheeks had turned into a burn, and the flutter in her chest, a swarm, yet despite this, the trio's childishness, and the continued delay it was causing her, Sophie couldn't help but smile.

Surfer Dude spotted this. "Come on, Sophie. I promise, it'll be the best holiday slash birthday you've ever had." She was about to respond when, "Happy birthday to you... Happy birthday to you..."

Oh no.

Surfer Dude elbowed his friend, who elbowed *his* friend, until a wave of arms travelled the length of the nearby line, and they were all joining in, in chorus.

"Happy birthday to you...."

Before long, the whole crowd had joined in, "Happy birthday, dear [mumble]... Happy birthday to you."

In the two years she'd worked at the airport, Sophie had seen many things, but this was a first, and it only fuelled the burn in her porcelain cheeks. It spread to her ears in a shade of wildfire red.

One of the reasons why she was able to function effectively in her role, despite its requirement that she deal directly with the public, was because the focus was always on the problem and rarely on her. People were never interested in her.

It took all of Sophie's willpower to smile and bow graciously while facing the immensity of such attention.

In stark contrast, Surfer Dude simply shrugged at the flash mob he'd instigated, as the bored travellers in the line broke into raucous spontaneous applause. "See? Just imagine how much more awesome it would be if you came away with us."

Sophie ignored the thudding in her chest and the beads of sweat that had broken out on her forehead and smiled as she handed the traveller's ticket back to him. "Have a safe flight," she said, buoyed by the fact that the birthday well-wishers were already bored again and were slowly resuming their mass zombie shuffle along the queue.

Departures was beyond the check-in area. Sophie held up the identity badge hanging from her neck and smiled. "Hello, Harry."

"You still here, Sophie? I thought you'd be gone by now."

"Me too," she said despondently as she was ushered through.

Beyond security, she made her way past various food and accessory outlets while scanning the crowds. The place was characteristically busy with many travellers eager to flee Britain's deep winter to rediscover the summer sun.

She made her way through the throng while feeling for the plastic container in her breast pocket. She knew it was there. It wasn't the first time she'd sought to reassure herself of its location today. She homed in on the sign for the ladies' restroom and made her way towards it.

Mercifully, the place was unusually empty. Still, she kept her gaze lowered to discourage anybody from reading the identity card hanging around her neck and asking her for assistance.

At the washbasins, she retrieved the plastic container from her pocket, shook out a pill, and swallowed it. Next, she ran cold water over her hands and placed them on her face for several seconds, repeating the process multiple times until the palpitations in her chest subsided.

It's fine. You're absolutely fine. You're fine, Sophie. Fine.

She checked herself in the mirror. The red glow was fading from her neck and cheeks. *See? You're fine. Just fine.* But the freckles that spread out from her pixie nose to her cheekbones were darker, more obvious, as they often were after one of her episodes. They would fade once the heat from her face had dissipated.

The fringe that canopied her large oval blue eyes looked neat and smooth, but that didn't stop her from fussing with it. The rest of her long white-blonde hair had been gathered up at the back into some semblance of a French twist, with wisps strategically placed to spill out of the sides. The look was still the same as it was when she left the house that morning, yet she couldn't stop herself from fiddling with it.

She rinsed her hands with cold water, dried then rinsed them once more before taking a series of deep breaths.

"Sophie!"

The voice startled her, but she swallowed the reaction as she watched the spectacled reflection of a skinny mouse of a girl teeter across the tiled floor towards her.

"I've been looking for you everywhere. Steve said you were on your way over. And I saw you walking towards me but then you came in 'ere. It's bloody Bedlam out there. I feel like I'm being dragged from pillar to bloody post! And now that bloody sleeper, Soph, I'm tellin' ya, she's bloody dead. I mean, I wasn't even sure if I should go near 'er or anyfin'. Or if I should call the police, do you know what I mean? I mean, I'm scared shitless. I ain't never seen a dead body before."

Sophie sighed for a multitude of reasons, not least the fact that every time this girl spoke and dropped the H at the beginning of every other word, she could hear her father's voice in her head correcting her. "It's okay," she began patiently. "It's not that unusual to find *sleepers* in the airport that sleep like the dead. One, I—"

"No, Soph, I'm telling ya, she's dead! She's dead!" The girl flapped her arms and was clearly working herself into a state. She had already drawn the attention of some of the other women who had now entered the room.

Sophie stepped closer and lowered her voice to a calming tone. "It's fine. It's fine," she said, suspending her own emotions to placate the newbie in front of her. "Come on. Come with me," she added, leading the girl out of the restroom and back into the throng of the departure lounge where she took another deep breath before resuming her role. "Okay, listen," she said, eyeing a nearby kiosk and fishing money out of her jacket pocket which she handed to the apprentice. "Why don't you go get a bagel and some water?"

"Thanks, but I ain't hungry," the girl whined. "The last thing I feel like doing right now is—"

"No, Katy, listen." Sophie held the girl's arms firmly with both hands and made direct eye contact with her. "It's not for you."

"But Soph, I told you, I don't think she—"

Sophie cocked her head.

"All right," Katy said with a shrug. She took the money and disappeared into the crowd.

The departure lounge was busy with travellers wheeling luggage, hauling bags, some with and others without face masks.

Sophie moved through them with a series of *excuse mes* and *sorrys* that were lost in the babble of voices, scuffling heels, loud adverts from nearby plasma screens and public-address system announcements.

Her feet were killing her despite her sensible shoes. Katy, on the other hand, insisted on wearing heels to work. She'd told her that she wouldn't be seen dead in anything else. Sophie hated heels and if regulation allowed it, she'd happily wear her trainers to work.

It had been a long shift. And, as much as it made her feel ungrateful, she could do with skipping tonight's celebration meal in favour of some fast food and a hot bath, but her father had made the reservation at PAOLO'S months before and it was notoriously difficult to get a table there. Besides, she was twenty-one, after all. A special birthday needed a special celebration. At least it did according to her father.

But Sophie didn't feel anything special about today. To her, it'd been like any other day so far. She hoped she would feel differently once she got away from work, but that was only going to happen after she'd dealt with this latest crisis.

But then her phone started vibrating. At first, she thought it was a text message but soon became aware of its insistence. She pulled the phone out of her pocket to see her father's scowling face; it was an endearing result of a spontaneous picture Sophie had snapped for his profile.

She looked at the red and green buttons. *Accept* or *Reject*? She vowed not to be long. Smiling, as if the man could see her, she pressed the green button. "Hello, Dad!"

"Hello, sweetheart. Are you on your way?"

"The is the final call for BA flight 301 to Barcelona. All passengers for this flight, please proceed to Gate 9 immediately."

Sophie pressed her phone to her ear and plugged the other with her finger. "Yes, of course," she said, still beaming her smile while transferring her phone to her shoulder and catching the attention of a middle-aged lady.

She had spotted her squinting at the overhead display and back at her ticket enough times to know that the woman was struggling.

She held up five fingers at the woman and mouthed the words *FIVE. Gate 5.*

"You're still at work, aren't you?" Her dad's tone was full of reproach.

"What? On my birthday? No, of course not."

"Easyjet flight 58 to Rome…"

"Sophie, I can hear the public announcements."

Her smile contorted into a pained expression. "Yes, all right, Dad. I'm still here and haven't left yet, but I'm on my way. I promise! I just need to deal with a little emergency and I'm leaving!" she said, patiently waiting for an elderly couple to make their way out of her path.

"You realise I booked this table months ago, Sophie."

"Really? I don't think you mentioned that before."

"Are you being sarcastic? You are, aren't you?"

"No, of course not."

"Oh Sophie. Babe. I really do worry about you."

"Me? Why would you worry about me?"

"You know why. It's all work and no play."

"That's because I'm like you, Dad. I have a very strong work ethic."

"Yes, but there comes a time when even the best of us have to say enough is enough. You know, take a break. I mean you see thousands of people jet-setting off to all kinds of exotic locations every day. Don't you ever feel the urge to join them? Doesn't it make you feel sad?"

"Um no, not until now, Dad. Thanks for bringing it up. Besides, why would I want to go anywhere when I have you? I have everything I need right here. I don't need anything else."

"Yes, flattery will get you everywhere, but it won't get you your youth back. I'm serious. I'm always reading about these kids that get up to all sorts on holiday. Don't you want to experience a bit of that?"

"You want me to go on a Club 18-30 holiday?" Sophie said, distractedly, as she sped around a corner while skilfully avoiding colliding into a young man with a rucksack on his back.

"While you still fit the demographic, why not?"

"Do you know what goes on at those clubs, Dad?"

"Of course I do. It's exactly why I think you should go. Live a little! Have some no-strings fun."

"Ew, Dad! Gross. I can't and I'm not having this conversation with you right now, or ever." Sophie felt that heat rising to her cheeks.

She was now standing at the corner of the Perfume Hut and Jewellery. This is how the PEAs (Passenger Experience Agents) navigated the airport. A general mixture of standard typography and retail establishments. In this case, the Perfume Hut, or its general vicinity, was one of her favourite places as the area was often shrouded in an invisible fog of delicious fragrances. On rare occasions, when she had a spare moment, she'd sneak off for a quick spritz of one of the samplers.

But not today. Today, she was on a mission.

And her objective, as far as she could see through the legs milling back and forth, was lying on the floor of the main thoroughfare.

The human capacity for self-absorption was something that always astounded Sophie. In this case, there was a body lying on the floor. And yet most of the people passing barely glanced down, each wrapped up in their own world. It was a sad but true way of life for most travellers who, like brainwashed cultists, worshipped only the god of time and itinerary. At the airport, nothing else mattered.

"Sophie?"

"Dad, you realise that the longer I'm on the phone to you, the longer it's going to take me to get to the restaurant, right? When are you leaving the house?"

"I'm so glad you asked. Because looking at my watch, I can see that if I don't leave shortly, I am going to be late for the birthday bash of my twenty-one-year-old recluse slash workaholic of a daughter whom I've just learned hasn't even left work yet."

"Are *you* being sarcastic now?"

"Don't be silly. You know your dad doesn't believe in that. Sarcasm being the lowest form of wit and all."

She could hear her father smiling down the phone, and it made her smile too. "I love you, Dad," she said. The expression was as natural as it was spontaneous as she made her way across the stream of people to a battered suitcase that no doubt had started its life fire engine red but was now scuffed and faded to orange. From its erect drag-handle hung a black raggedy shawl as if the body on the floor had staked this patch of the airport and raised a flag to prove it.

"I love you too, sweetheart. You know that, but—"

"I'll be leaving within the next five minutes, I promise," she said, looking down and peering around the case at the body on the floor.

It's an old lady. Wrapped from head to toe in widow's black.

"That's my girl. And Sophie..."

Alan Cooper trailed off here and she knew why. She was always berating him for asking, so now they just exchanged these awkward silences instead. "I'm fine, Dad. Perfectly fine." Sophie could see now that the woman's battered luggage was held together by strands of string. It wasn't tagged in any way, so she was unable to establish anything about the traveller's name or destination.

"Really?"

"Yes. Really. And now I *really* must go if you want me to get there on time."

"Okay, sweetheart. Be careful. It's been throwing it down out there. I'm only telling you because I doubt you've even paused to look out of the window today. I mean, have you even had anything to eat?"

"Bye, Dad," Sophie said. Truth be told, she had forgotten to eat today. "I love you," she threw in again quickly, but the line had already gone dead.

Based on what she had seen so far, Katy was right. Sophie was most likely standing over the body of a dead person.

Sophie had seen it once before. It was a heart attack not so dissimilar to the one she'd attended that afternoon. The man had just keeled over, and paramedics were unable to revive him. There was a moment today when she feared it might happen again, but this time in front of the man's wife and son. Thankfully, it didn't. It hadn't been his time.

There's no escaping fate.

Sophie crouched down and gently touched the body's spindly arm. From her position, she could see a small ear adorned by a simple gold hoop earring and the wrinkled pale skin of a cheek.

"Hello?" she called out over the din, continuing when there was no response. "Excuse me. Hello? Excuse me?" She tried again, tapping the bony shawl-clad arm more forcefully.

Nothing.

The body remained motionless. No sound. No breathing. No life.

A chill rippled through her.

She looked around. The hive of activity continued. Some meandered while others hurried, wheeled cases trailing like umbilical cords behind them. Then there were those who loitered under information screens, watching the changing displays with a rapt focus as if they were the scriptures of digital gods. None seemed interested in her and the other human being that had been lying on this freezing cold floor for God knows how long.

Such ambivalence had shocked her when she first started working at the airport, but not anymore. She could still feel the frustration it caused building inside her, but this feeling was mellowed somewhat by the sound of singing. A choir somewhere in the distance. Something that would probably be deemed unusual in most places, but not at the airport.

As she considered the next steps to dealing with the body with the least amount of fuss, Sophie allowed herself to be momentarily distracted. She turned to the sound to identify its origin but couldn't see much from her crouched position but a blur of legs and shoes.

When she turned back, she found herself looking into a scowling face, craggy and withered with suspicious muddy eyes and a bulbous nose. She recoiled instinctively and lost her balance, almost toppling backward.

She regained her composure. "Oh, I'm sorry. Sorry!" she said with a nervous laugh while clutching a hand to her chest. "You made me jump. Are you alright?"

The old lady didn't answer but simply continued to scowl. Sophie estimated she must be in her eighties and looked oddly reminiscent of the bewildered faces wrapped in headscarves she'd seen on many news reports and documentaries about displaced refugees.

It was this thought that touched her. The old lady must have been sleeping rough in the airport for some time. Was someone missing her? Children? Grandchildren?

"You had us worried there for a second. How are you feeling? Is everything okay?" Sophie asked gently.

Her only response was the blinking of a pair of crepe eyelids.

"Do you speak English?"

Still no response. Instead, the old lady, sitting up now, unravelled the headscarf from her head to reveal a neat plait of long silver hair. Then, she lifted a veiny hand, extended a forefinger and thumb, and rocked them from side to side. She accompanied this with a shake of the head.

"No? No, you don't speak English? Okay, that's no problem. No problem at all," Sophie reassured her. She looked around and wondered what to do next as a nearby digital clock reminded her of just how late she was running.

And yet, a glance back at the old lady told her that she couldn't leave, not without helping her first.

"Do you have your ticket?" She spoke slowly, making eye contact with the woman while signing the air with her fingers. She had no idea why that was supposed to signify travel documents, but she knew that from here on every little thing helped. "Ticket? Passport? *Passaporto?*"

Finally, there was some recognition in the woman's face, and she proceeded to rummage in a nearby plastic bag. It was as she did this that Sophie caught a waft of something that was a far cry from the Perfume Hut and much more akin to something found down a drain.

She waited patiently for the old lady to retrieve a crumpled envelope and hand it to her. Sophie opened it, pulled out a ticket, and read it with interest.

"Oh, Venice!" she said excitedly. Looking back into that wrinkled face, she added, "Venezia?" and elicited a nod. With a big smile, she continued. "Venezia. Bella. I've always wanted to go," she said dreamily, but the blank expression on the woman's face told her she didn't understand. Sophie refocussed on the job in hand by reading the ticket and then checking the woman's passport. "Right. So, your name is Maja. Maja Szymanski? That's a lovely name. Doesn't sound Italian though. More Eastern European? Polish, maybe?"

Guessing traveller's nationalities had become a bit of a pastime and personal challenge for Sophie. She had become quite good at it. But, judging by the vacant look on the woman's face, she didn't appear interested in playing.

Sophie cleared her throat. "So, Maja, can you tell me *how long* you have been here in the airport?" Her words were loud and slow in that tone stereotypically reserved for seniors that were hard of hearing (and, in this case, that didn't speak the same language). The gestures she was making to accompany her words were expressive yet, once again, pointless. "Um... *Qui. Aeroporto. Quanto?*" which was Italian and therefore, Sophie realised, still pointless if the woman was indeed Polish.

She scanned the ticket again. It read that the passenger was due to fly out of England three nights ago. "You've been sleeping like this for three nights?" she asked, incredulous.

The vibration in her pocket told her that she had received a text message. She ignored it and instead looked around. There was still no sign of Katy. And, just to make things worse, when she looked back at the senior traveller, she could see that those muddy eyes had started to well with tears, although her silent demeanour remained the same. She didn't dab or swipe at the runaway tear dribbling down one of the deep lines in her face, irrigating that translucent skin.

"Oh no, no, Maja. Don't cry," Sophie said, reaching out and touching the woman's arm as the vibration in her pocket returned. This time it was constant which meant it was a phone call. She ignored it. "Don't cry. We'll sort this out, I promise."

She looked around again and... finally. "Sorry it took so long," Katy said breathlessly, rushing up to them with a drink and wrapped burger.

The trainee almost skidded to a stop when she noticed the expressionless old lady sitting on the floor, the varicose purple of her veiny legs like tattoos behind her thick black tights.

"Never mind, listen..." Sophie began, but Katy wasn't paying attention. She was busy staring at the woman on the floor. "Hey, Katy, pay attention," Sophie said, switching back to trouble-shooter mode. "Okay, so first, give the food and water to Maja."

"Who?"

"This is Maja," Sophie said, turning to the traveller and smiling. "I have her ticket here. I'm going to need you to call the airline and see if they're willing to comp a ticket change," Sophie continued talking as she retrieved her phone. She ignored the long list of notifications telling her that she'd missed several calls and text messages and began tapping out a number. When she looked up, she noticed that the trainee was gingerly stepping towards the woman as if approaching a snarling dog. She slipped her phone back into her pocket, grabbed the food and drink from Katy, and handed it to the old woman. She accompanied the action with an affectionate grand-daughterly tone to her voice, "Maja, here's some food. I'm going to need you to eat for me. Okay? Eat." She made an eating gesture by putting three fingers to her mouth. "I need you to keep your strength up because we're going to get you home and I don't want you fainting on me, alright?"

The comment was more to herself than to the woman. She'd already concluded Maja most likely didn't understand a word she was saying.

Warily, those veiny, liver-spotted hands reached out and took the food. "Excellent," Sophie said with a smile and then she turned to Katy, who was still gawking.

"Katy." Sophie tried to get her attention, but the girl was busy watching the refugee unwrap the burger and fall upon it like a rabid dog, masticating the food with a toothless washing machine-like mouth.

"Katy!" Sophie hissed, snapping the girl out of her daze. "Can you please focus? I need you to call the airline and…" she trailed off and turned away, unhooking the radio from her pocket. "Steve, are you there?"

The reply came several seconds later. "*Sophie? You still here?*"

"Yep. Still here. Listen, this sleeper, she's a senior who's been stuck here for several days now. I doubt she has much cash, and she doesn't speak English. Someone needs to sweet talk the airline to see if they'll do a complimentary ticket change."

"*Oh no, Soph. You know that stuff takes time and I've already got a bunch of passengers bayin' for blood over the flights that have been cancelled because of this bloody weather. There's no way I've got resource for anyone to get onto anyfin' like that. Not tonight.*"

Sophie sighed. "What about you, Steve? What are you doing?"

"*I'm bloody swamped with bloody paperwork, ain't I? Get Katy to do it. That's why she's here. I mean if she can't sweet talk an airline into changing a bloody ticket then she may as well not be here at all!*"

Sophie looked at the radio's speaker and then at Katy. She had obviously heard the comment and was staring at the device while chewing her lip. She looked as if she was going to burst into tears at any moment.

Sophie's phone vibrated again.

She turned to the old lady who was busy licking discoloured fingernails and then back to the miserable-looking trainee.

"*Soph?*" came the voice over the radio.

"Don't worry about it."

"*Soph?*"

But she was already handing the paper bag and ticket to Katy, pulling out her phone again, swiping away more alerts, and searching through her address book. Then she went through her emails and forwarded one of them. She told Katy that she'd sent her a number earlier, to call it and exactly what to say. "If they agree, which they probably will if you tell them exactly what I told you, they'll ask you to put it in writing. I've forwarded an email to you. Change the ticket number, passenger name and send it on but do not wait for them to get back to you. This won't be a priority to them, so you'll need to progress chase it after a couple of hours and continue chasing until you receive confirmation. When you do, send me a text to let me know. Do you understand?"

Eyes wide and wild, the girl nodded.

"I can't hear you, Katy. This lady's safety depends on this, all right?" She placed a hand on the girl's arm. "Take no notice of what Steve said. If you do this, he'll be so impressed, he won't even remember he said it tomorrow. Okay?"

The girl nodded.

"Okay. Now, I've really got to go." She turned to the old lady who was now busy picking food out of what was left of her teeth. "Okay, Maja." Sophie crouched down so she was at eye level. "WE'RE GOING TO TRY AND GET YOUR TICKET CHANGED FOR YOU, THEN GET YOU HOME. OKAY?" she said, slowly and loudly.

Sophie looked at the old lady's passport. It read POLSKA. She smiled inwardly. She'd guessed correctly. Then she rummaged in her brain for a few seconds. "Um, *zmień, zmień bilet?*" She had no idea how accurate that was but that was the extent of what she had picked up so far. She gestured to Katy. "My colleague here, Katy, is going to do everything she can to make sure that your ticket is changed tonight. Okay?"

Sophie still couldn't be sure the woman had understood anything, but then the words were more for Katy's benefit to ensure she understood what was expected of her.

The old lady stopped rummaging around her mouth with her tongue but still said nothing. She seemed overwhelmed as tears leaked from her eyes once more. Suddenly, a wrinkly hand grabbed Sophie's and the old lady began to kiss it.

"Oh no. No. You don't need to do that. Please… It was my pleasure. And now I really must go." She turned to Katy. "Don't forget to keep me updated."

The girl nodded.

Sophie turned to walk away when she felt bony fingers pull at her arm and spin her around.

The old woman, with clicking joints, attempted to stand, compelling Sophie to assist her until she was back on her feet.

The diminutive woman reached behind her neck and unfastened the gold necklace she was wearing. It was only when the rest of it emerged from inside the woman's cardigan that Sophie could see that a small red amulet dangled from it, shaped like a chilli pepper.

She handed it to Sophie who shook her head. "Oh no. No, I can't take that."

The woman nodded, forcefully.

"I can't. Really. You don't have to. Really. We're not allowed to accept gifts."

But the woman was insistent. She grabbed Sophie's hand with a surprisingly strong grip and placed the chain in it. Then she rasped, as if the fate of the world depended on it, *"Protezione. Dal mallochio."*

Sophie looked at the old lady and smiled. "That... that's Italian, isn't it? So, you do speak Italian?"

The old lady didn't respond but Sophie was sure she spotted a trace of a smile on those chapped lips before she felt her fingers being squeezed shut over the necklace. Then the old woman closed her eyes and started mumbling something that made no sense to her.

"Thank... thank you," she said. *"Grazie.* I've really got to go now but thank you so much. *Grazie* for this." Finally, she turned and hurried away.

As she did, she felt her phone vibrate once more. She hastily plucked it from her pocket, read the screen and smiled before answering. "Yes, Dad, I know, but I'm on my way now, I prom—"

However, it wasn't Sophie's father's voice on the call but a voice she did not recognise. What it said wiped the smile from her face in an instant.

2

ORPHANED

MONDAY. ONE WEEK LATER.

The funeral was every bit as miserable as she'd expected, complete with rain, blustery winds and disgruntled crows loitering in nearby trees.

Sophie counted that there were exactly thirty-one people in the congregation, most of whom were strangers to her. All were huddled around the rain-spattered coffin. It was suspended over the large black hole below, as if it were part of a magic act, waiting to be disappeared into the earth.

Sophie had no idea that you could even bury someone so soon, but Ms Whitlock knew. Ms Whitlock knew everything, or at least she acted like she did. She also knew which were the top-rated funeral companies, which demanded payment upon instruction, and those that were happy to provide services by instalments – interest free. In fact, Ms Whitlock had started taking over the planning of the funeral altogether until Sophie drew the line. She was diplomatic about it, explaining that she felt it would be mentally important for her to plan the event, to help her come to terms with the reality that her father was gone. At first, she was just saying it to get rid of the woman, but when the tears came, she realised she was speaking from the heart.

Now, as the vicar mumbled words that meant nothing to her, she found herself peeking out from under the rim of her hat, allowing herself to be distracted from the reality of the moment as she looked across the churchyard to another group of mourners. They were no more than fifty yards from her father's crowd, gathered around their own coffin. They were wearing equally stoical masks of grief, broken only by the occasional squint into the freezing precipitation.

It's a good day to be in the funeral business, Sophie thought bitterly as she scanned the gathering for her counterparts. The chief mourners. They seemed to be a man with thinning dirty ginger hair plastered to his scalp and a woman who was wrestling with the wind for ownership of her impractically large black hat.

Mother? Father? Brother? Sister? Grandparent? Who are you mourning?

She felt awkward watching them in their hour of grief, yet she couldn't tear her eyes away from the strangers, a *voyeur macabre*, eagerly observing their loss in the hope that she might forget her own.

But then, wasn't that the whole point of the funereal ritual? To congregate outside no matter the weather to publicly exhibit one's grief? Cold fingers wringing. Knuckles whitening. Handkerchiefs fluttering to and from sorrowful faces like grief-hungry butterflies nibbling on the tears of the bereft.

"…though I walk through the valley of the shadow of death, I will fear no evil, for thou art with me; thy rod and thy staff, they comfort me…"

She looked up at the vicar. He was a waif of a man with thin lips and a perpetual robotic smile. His religious zeal seemed to make him impervious to the calamities of life, with that irritatingly unshakable belief that everything happens for a reason.

He had tried to give Sophie that speech when Ms Whitlock insisted that she meet with him to discuss the funeral. Ms Whitlock had cut him off, steering the conversation to the practicalities of the ceremony. Sophie was grateful to be spared from the lecture on why the calamities inflicted on humans were necessary. Why the death of her father was necessary.

It was always the same. Ms Whitlock could tug at her last nerve but always managed to redeem herself. In this case, she spared not only Sophie from the vicar and his drivel, but the vicar himself. Provoking her in her already overwhelmed emotional state, his lecture came close to triggering her to punch even a man of the cloth in the face. It would have been worth it if it meant erasing that supercilious smile of his once and for all, but Ms Whitlock's interruptions for once endowed mercy instead of irritation.

Sorry, Dad. I'm so sorry. I don't know what's wrong with me. I don't know why I'm feeling so spiteful. Well, actually, I do.

She breathed deeply as a tear slithered down her face. Or maybe it was a raindrop. It was hard to tell as the skies, like her, wept through the proceedings.

She felt bitter, resentful, hollow in ways she had never experienced, not even when her mother had left. It was the grim lottery of life; fate was picking on her once more, singling her out for the cruel and unusual pain of losing her father like this, and it made her angry. Furious. In fact, she felt so angry she could quite easily stomp over there and give Thin Lips a piece of her mind.

She looked up, flinched into the rain, and zoomed in in that dramatic way they do in the movies to those lips. She watched them move. They were talking about the cycle of life, about *ashes to ashes... dust to dust...*

Who thought that this was acceptable? Who was tasteless enough to think that it would be all right to treat the most devastating event of her life with the same conveyer belt mentality as a factory?

Two funerals on the same day at the same time? Really?

I'm sorry, Dad. I know you'd hate me thinking like this, but really... What was the man thinking? I suppose that's just it; he wasn't!

She swiped angrily at another tear.

Breathe... Remember what the doctor told you. Breathe.

Death is inevitable. Sure. But most children imagine losing their parent to natural causes, not in an accident that leaves them sandwiched between a car and a lorry.

Adverse weather conditions.

That's how the clumsy cop had begun to inform her that her dad was dead, as though that detail was so important, he felt he had to lead with it. As if it would in some way soothe her. Comfort her. It wasn't soothing or comforting. It was bloody infuriating! At least it had become so, once she had recovered from the initial shock of what she was hearing.

We're sorry but your flight's been cancelled due to adverse weather conditions.

She used that line at least once a week to inform irate passengers that their holiday plans had been stuffed up because their flight had been cancelled. But he hadn't been talking about a flight, but life as she knew it.

Sophie tuned out the production line of grief and looked across the wet stone angels and moss-riddled tombstones to the other batch of mourners and wondered what was happening over there. Was their officiant speaking the same words? Had he borrowed the same lines as that policeman? More tears slid in rivulets down her face as she wondered, merging with the raindrops clinging to her chin.

What are you mumbling to them with that same artificial empathetic frown? She wanted to know. She needed to know if the playlist over there was any better than the reality over here. She wanted to know so badly that she felt compelled to march across the wet, soggy bank to listen in and find out if there was anything about her father's funeral that was unique, that hadn't been spewed out a thousand times before with the same monotonous piety.

But the rain tapping against the rim of her hat and the squeeze of her friend's gloved hand on her numb, cold fingers brought her back to the moment. She had tried to dissociate herself from every moment since she had received that ghastly telephone call from the strange man on her dad's phone.

Is this Sophie Cooper? Are you related to Alan Cooper, driver of a Ford Mondeo, registration number…

Now, she was sitting on her side of the couch in the lounge. She had no idea how she'd even got there but at least she felt dry now. Warmer.

The room was empty, but only of the people that mattered. It was otherwise packed with strangers dressed in black.

How she hated these people. She wished they would all just piss off home. *Go home! You're not wanted here! I want to be alone.*

Her father would have reproached her for such an attitude. *Sophie! Really, where are your manners? What's the matter, my darling? This isn't like you.*

You're dead, Dad.

Stop messing about and pass me your plate. We're having your favourite: egg and soldiers.

She was in the kitchen doorway staring at the gas hob when

she came back to the moment and was already making a hasty retreat when she heard a dreaded singsong voice call her name.

Oh no.

"Sophie!" Ms Whitlock's ever-assured voice echoed around the kitchen. "There you are. Just in time."

"I really don't think she needs to hear this now," said Victoria, one of Sophie's best friends, appearing beside her with a furtive roll of the eyes.

Sophie turned once more to face the kitchen.

As the service was over and they were back indoors, it was sod's law that the sun now decided to make an appearance, its light flooding in through the kitchen window and patio doors to glint off a multicoloured selection of pots, ceramic dishes, and cellophane-wrapped fruit baskets and flowers that covered the work surfaces and island.

"Wow. Where did all of this come from?" Sophie asked, although she already had an idea.

"Yes, I was just telling Victoria that rather than sympathy cards and whatnot, I told everyone it made sense for them to bring something tangible, you know, something that you can actually eat now that you don't have anybody to cook for you." Ms Whitlock swept a hand in front of the bounty like a weather presenter.

Victoria exchanged a knowing look with her friend. "That's all very, um... American," she said.

"I've also organised all of them in the order that they need to be eaten," Ms Whitlock continued. "Homemade dishes versus the shop-bought and..." she left the sentence unfinished and pulled a disgusted face, obviously unimpressed with the presentation of some of the dishes. "I, of course, made the beef stew. All these cakes and whatnot are all well and good, but you can't exactly live off cake, can you? Marie Antoinette, you are not." There was a flicker of a smile on the woman's face, but it vanished almost as fast as it appeared. As she stood ramrod-straight in her black, button-down dress, wringing her cold-bleached hands together, she reminded Sophie of one of those Dickensian characters holding court.

"Thank you," Sophie heard herself saying as the break in Whitlock's presentation appeared to expect. "That's very kind."

"Think nothing of it. I've fit what I can into the refrigerator, but obviously there's only so much room. Again, start from the front and work your way to the back. Although, with so much food and now just you rattling around in this house, I can't see…" she trailed off, for once realising the insensitivity of her own words. "Yes, well, you have no business being back at work so soon. You should have given yourself some time. You know, to grieve. Mind you, I shouldn't wallow too much either."

"Oh, was that the door?" Victoria interrupted.

"I didn't hear anything," Ms Whitlock said.

"No. I definitely heard the doorbell. You heard that, didn't you, Sophie? You should probably answer it, Ms Whitlock. It's probably more people with more food." Victoria put an arm around her friend's back and steered her out of the kitchen.

"You're awful," Sophie said, with a giggle.

"Would you rather I left you in there with Nurse Ratched?" Victoria said in a hushed tone. "I still can't believe that, after putting up with her through all our school days, we are still stuck with her now. Headmistresses are not supposed to be for life."

"Imagine what it's like living across the street from her."

"No thanks. I've already had my nightmare for the week. I dreamt that Greenfields had burnt down. I woke up sobbing."

Sophie smiled courteously at a couple milling in the doorway, then thanked another pair who were lounging on the couch like they were at a birthday party.

If only.

She allowed herself to flirt with the thought that this was the real reason why everybody was congregated here: it was a belated birthday celebration. Her father had invited all his friends because he didn't want her to feel neglected as she often had as a child. After all, she was the introvert, the freak who had to see a head doctor because she thought her mother…

The sound of the doorbell cut through her thoughts.

"See? I told you I heard the doorbell. Underneath all of this, I'm a witch really," Victoria said, wiggling her nose, before they rerouted to the front door.

However, Janay Evans, wrapped in a flattering black flare dress, beat them to it. She looked great, Sophie thought. The dress was stylish and complimented her ample curves rather than accentuating them.

Janay had already thrown her arms around the young blonde at the door, who was wearing a long black coat over a green uniform and trainers. When they emerged from the embrace, the blonde made a sad face and opened her arms to Sophie, who allowed the girl to squeeze her for a few seconds.

"I'm so sorry, Sophie. I wanted to come to the funeral, but I was roped into an extra shift at work, and I couldn't get out of it."

Lucy Davidson was Sophie's immediate next-door neighbour. She moved in less than a year ago with her boyfriend and his Great Dane, Duke, and although Sophie and Lucy chatted regularly, and had even shared a couple of takeaways, they weren't close.

"Don't worry about it. Saving lives is much more important that saying goodbye to them," Sophie said.

"How was it? Did it go okay?" Lucy asked softly, awkwardly, seemingly unsure of the etiquette in such situations.

Sophie shrugged, equally unsure how to answer such a question. "It was okay. Quite miserable as you'd expect. I don't recommend it," she added with a faint smile.

Janay reached out and touched her friend's arm. Victoria rolled her eyes. And this is generally how it went when the two were together. Sophie always felt like she was the rope in the tug of war between them.

Sophie's best friends were both a few years her senior. It made her sad that they didn't particularly like each other and that this was often a source of tension. Victoria believed that Janay had a perpetual axe to grind with everything and everyone, that she was militant, subversive, and generally irritating, while Janay believed that Victoria paraded around with an overinflated ego and sense of entitlement that was laughable given her history. She was an obnoxious snob of the worst kind. One that had married into money rather than make it.

This was the general theme to many of their clashes. But not today. Today, they had managed to put her first, at least so far.

"It was grim and cold. But the vicar was cute," Victoria chimed in on cue.

"Yeah, if you're into that whole religious serial killer look," Janay responded with a lift of her bushy eyebrows.

They all laughed but Victoria, of course.

"How are *you* holding up, Luce?" Sophie asked, tactfully changing the subject.

"Ah, you know, one day at a time," the paramedic answered. Her smile was diminished by the sorrow in her eyes.

"I'm really sorry," Sophie said, grateful, in the nicest possible way, to be talking about somebody else's woes. "Have you heard from him?"

"Oh, you know. He only sent me twenty texts today," Lucy said, with exaggerated glumness.

"That bloke's a dick," Janay contributed bluntly.

Victoria scowled at her. "Really? We're at a wake for Christ's sake. Show some respect." Janay frowned and opened her mouth to respond, but Victoria cut her off by turning to Lucy and asking, "What are you going to do about it?"

"I know what I would do," Janay jumped in again. "I'd string him up by his—"

"Sophie!"

Sophie's heart sank.

All four women turned to see Ms Whitlock, all five foot nothing of her, standing in the doorway, face as dark as the clouds that were now casting shadows over the walls. All she needed was a black shawl and bonnet and she'd look every bit the Puritan.

Nobody dared utter a word. It was like being back at school, like they were being busted for skulking off to the back of the bicycle shed for a quick smoke, among other things.

Ms Whitlock walked up and leaned towards them, whispering discreetly, "Sophie, those people in there are here for you, to pay their respects to your father and to support you through your loss. It's very bad form for you girls to be loitering out here."

"I, um—" Sophie began.

"Sophie isn't feeling very well, Ms Whitlock," Victoria interjected.

"Is that so? What's wrong with you?" the woman demanded, automatically stepping forward and feeling her forehead as if Sophie was still at school.

"I, um—"

"She has a migraine," Lucy contributed. "Flashing lights, the works. She was out here because she was asking me for my professional opinion. I told her she should go and have a lie down or she could risk making it worse. I mean, you wouldn't want her to start vomiting all over people, would you?"

The woman observed Lucy for the longest time as if truth-detecting her eyes, and then suddenly turned to Sophie. "Well, you have been through it, haven't you?"

"Yeah, that's what I thought," Janay said, pulling a face.

"She did protest, Ms Whitlock," Victoria continued, covertly patting her friend's backside, "but I said that you were here and wouldn't mind helping me apologise to the guests after we've finished organising the kitchen."

"Well, it's still a rather poor show, but I guess one could make the necessary apologies and beg for everyone's understanding." Ms Whitlock searched everybody's eyes.

"Indeed," Janay said, but she shouldn't have bothered because the word just sounded awkward coming out of her mouth. She fidgeted with her hands. "Shall I walk you upstairs, Sophie?" Janay offered.

Sophie could only nod, such was the excruciating pain and flashing lights she wasn't experiencing. Truthfully, her head did feel tight after being out in the elements, and she even had the seedling of a headache, but nothing she thought would induce projectile vomiting.

Nonetheless, she continued with the charade and allowed Janay to accompany her up the stairs. Neither of them dared to look back to check if they were being watched. They knew they were.

The duo only allowed themselves a giggle once they were safely ensconced in Sophie's bedroom and out of earshot of their formidable warden downstairs.

"Why do you still let her talk to you like that? You're not in her school anymore," Janay said.

Sophie shrugged and shook her head. "I guess she's suffered a loss too. She was quite close to Dad. I suppose meddling is her way of coping."

Janay simply lifted her eyebrows and widened her eyes, as she did whenever something made no sense to her. "Well, now that you're up here, you may as well try to have a nap," she added. "I'll check on you in a few hours. Okay?" Janay swept a lock of hair from her friend's eyes. "I like it when you wear your hair up. You look sophisticated as well as beautiful."

Sophie rolled her eyes. "If you say so. I actually think *you* look lovely today. Stylish."

Janay grinned, patting her hair. "Yeah? Oh thanks."

They paused a few seconds then the two friends squeezed each other tightly. Then Janay left, closing the door softly behind her.

It was only now that she was alone that Sophie realised how exhausted she felt. A nap was probably a good idea if only to stop herself from thinking about the surrealism of the day.

But first she made her way to the bathroom across the landing. Instead of peeing, she spent what felt like minutes staring at her reflection in the mirror. Her father would often tell her that she looked beautiful, but she never believed it. She knew it was the kind of thing all parents said to their children, especially if they were bullied a lot.

Victoria and Janay insisted that her long hair was a *beautiful* white-blonde, but the kids at school hadn't reached the same conclusion in the playground where she was instead likened to an unpopular Harry Potter character.

You're uniquely beautiful, Sophie, her mother used to tell her. *Strikingly so.*

But Sophie didn't believe it. Certainly not today. She was sporting some seriously dark circles around her sore blue eyes. And her so-called porcelain skin that everybody went on about was a blotchy red.

She sighed, grateful to be alone and away from the strangers downstairs. It exhausted her to be around people. To be social. To behave as if everything were normal.

She opened the cabinet in front of her, retrieved a plastic bottle of pills, shook two out into the palm of her hand, and swallowed them. She ran the tap and drank greedily from it before splashing her face with cold water. Then she replaced the bottle, closed the cabinet door, opened it, and closed it again. She repeated this ritual twice more before looking at herself in the mirror, as she often did when preparing to give herself a pep talk.

What are you going to do now?

She shrugged as she watched the water drip into the basin.

Maybe I should try and dye my hair again. Go black like Vic. She looks stunning with her long black hair. Especially when she puts on heavy eyeliner.

But blondes are supposed to have all the fun. *How's that working out for ya?*

She couldn't dye her hair. She knew that. She'd tried several times with different brands. None took. She was a freak of nature.

She could feel the tears coming back. Where the hell did all this fluid keep coming from anyway? *Bloody hell!* She thought she was all cried out after a week of it. Maybe even within the first forty-eight hours. Although, it had taken her a while to get started after the initial shock of the moment. Then, once she started blubbering, she couldn't stop. The waterworks kept on springing out, sometimes delicately and at others with deep, stomach-churning convulsions.

There are people downstairs paying their respects. You should be there instead of leaving it all to your friends.

Dad's gone. You're alone now.

Her broken eyes started leaking again and she allowed the tears to flow freely, dripping into the basin like a leaky showerhead. She found herself fascinated by the way the droplets hit the enamel and exploded, like her world.

She sank back and sat on the edge of the bathtub before allowing herself to slide all the way into it, wrapping the curtain around it to create a comforting cocoon.

Maybe nobody would find her here. Not even the grief. Maybe if she sat quietly enough it might leave her alone and go torture somebody else.

As this thought was going through her mind, the door suddenly burst open, the turbulence of the act rustling the shower curtain in front of her.

"Shhh.... shhh," someone said in a loud whisper. "We need to be quiet. There's a wake going on downstairs. Someone might hear us." It was a man. Nobody she recognised.

"I'll try," giggled an unfamiliar girly voice. Sophie heard the lock turn in the door and watched as, to her horror, the shadows beyond the shower curtain moved across the small square bathroom as they created a cacophony of heavy breathing, slobbering kisses, and giggles.

They were uncomfortably close to her now. Literally inches away. The only thing separating them was the thin protective plastic veil. The thought of this made Sophie instinctively clamp a hand over her mouth and shrink further towards the back of the tub.

She wanted to scream but felt awkward, torn between revealing herself or enduring the sounds of wet kisses, the jangle of a belt, and the rustle of clothing.

She considered standing up and pulling back the curtain in a fit of rage, because, initial awkwardness aside, that's how she was feeling. She couldn't believe that these two, whoever they were, could have the audacity to do this at a funeral. Her father's funeral. On the other hand, her anger was diluted by the overwhelming sense of embarrassment she would feel to be found skulking in the bathtub, unable to explain how she came to be listening to everything they were doing like a reluctant voyeur.

"Oooh yes, do me here! Right here!" the female giggled.

"Shhhh…"

Whoever she was, she obviously thought she was starring in her own porno flick.

In my house! In my bathroom! Who the hell talks like that during sex anyway?

"Do you like me like this, baby? Yeah? Do you like me like this?" The girl spoke with a sing-song over-exaggeration that made Sophie roll her eyes in disgust. The girl's sexual companion, on the other hand, was the complete opposite. All he sounded capable of was the occasional attempt to quiet her in between his own unenthusiastic grunts.

"Yummy… yummy… yummy. You know, I had my eye on you the moment you walked through the door," the girl breathed.

"Yeah?" the man panted.

"Yeah. I was just saying to the other girls that this wake livened up when you arrived," the Marilyn Monroe wannabe giggled. "Get it? Livened up?"

Sophie stood and swished the curtain back in one angry swoop. The movement startled the duo; the girl screamed and fell into the basin, bare buttocks squishing toothpaste everywhere, while her sexual companion lost his balance and tripped, trousers around ankles, into a sitting position on the toilet.

The pair gawked at Sophie who glared back, eyes red- ringed from crying.

The girl, who Sophie estimated was about the same age as her, was vaguely familiar. It took but a moment for her to realise she was one of the waitresses from the catering company Victoria had hired.

The man, who was probably in his early thirties, wore a lazy black tie over an open white shirt. There was something familiar about him too, but she couldn't quite place him.

Sophie glowered at the girl who was still whimpering in shock, as her heavy breasts, restrained by her faded pink bra, rose and fell with her quickened breath.

Sophie was seething. "You're fired. Get out!"

The waitress pulled herself and her clothes together, stepped down from the basin and sheepishly made her way to the door. She paused and looked back at the man. "Call me?" The man smiled but under Sophie's incredulous scowl the girl turned back to the door, fiddled with the lock, yanked it open and then scuttled out, clutching her clothes to her chest.

Sophie turned her attention to the man sitting on her toilet. He held his hands up in an exaggerated defensive gesture.

Yes, she had seen that handsome face before. She remembered it because he looked American. Wholesome, in that Captain America kind of way. He had mousy blond hair and a short beard that was obviously trimmed regularly. And those lips. Not cruel and thin, but thick and kissable. At least, that's how Sophie imagined Janay would describe him.

Now, those same lips were creased into a smile. "Is it okay if I…?" He completed the sentence with a lift of his eyebrows and a gesture to his crotch. Thankfully, he was still wearing his red boxer shorts with teddy bear imprints.

"Oh…" Instinctively, Sophie turned around to give the man some privacy, but then cursed herself for doing so. This was *her* house. *He* was the one who shouldn't be in here.

"I'm sorry. I didn't know the bathtub was, um, your place," she heard him say, casually, above the chinking sound of his belt.

Sophie flared and turned to him. "Have you even noticed what's happening downstairs?"

"Yeah, of course I have. That's why I'm here."

"*That* is why you're here?"

"Yeah, of course. Why else?"

"You really need me to answer that for you?"

"What? You mean that? Her?" he said, gesturing towards the open doorway.

Sophie folded her arms and widened her eyes. He was obviously a complete moron.

"That was just some fun."

"Fun?"

"Yeah. Fun."

Sophie opened her mouth to speak but was unable to find the words. The sound that came out instead was just a whimper of a sigh.

Blue Eyes (or were they green? She couldn't work it out) cocked his head and squinted, making a show of the fact that he could not understand her incomprehensible noises.

Thankfully, a jab of anger helped her form other words instead. "Who the hell are you anyway? Why are you here? Just get out. In fact, if you leave now, you might be able to catch up with miss... miss *yummy yummy porn star.*"

He laughed. "That's funny."

She glowered.

"Okay... maybe not. I'm Christopher, by the way. Chris. I live across the street, at number nine." He moved towards her and held out his hand, but Sophie looked at it as if it was an alien's tentacle.

"I'm not shaking that. I don't know where it's been."

He shrugged, with a small casual nod of agreement, as if she might have a point, which only annoyed her more.

"Why are you here, Christopher Chris?"

"No, it's not Christopher Chris. It's Christopher *or* Chris. My second name is Darrington," he corrected. Sophie was sure he knew full well that she was mocking him but simply didn't care. "I'm here to pay my respects."

"To whom? My dad or Buxom Bimbo?"

"Um, both, I suppose."

"Oh my God. You're a pig. Just get out! I bet you didn't even know my dad; you probably waved at him once."

"So? Does that make a difference?"

Sophie stepped forward and spat through gritted teeth, "Of course it bloody does! This is my father's wake, you cold-hearted piece of...sh-shit." She faltered on the last words as that familiar lump returned to her throat. She was having palpitations now too. Her heart was hammering in her chest, eager for a chance to go over there and punch the man in the face.

She remembered him now. He did live across the road. She'd lost count of the times she'd come back from work and heard music thumping out of that place, with young men and women coming and going at all hours.

How could he even afford to live on Meadow Lane anyway? She had no idea what he did for a living.

Sophie wasn't a snob by any stretch of the imagination—that was how she was raised—but Fenfield was a tiny yet affluent suburb of the city of Cambridge, populated by lawyers, doctors, and businessmen. The houses were large, spacious, and detached, with generous gardens and views out to open fields. The road was lined with trees, manicured lawns, and governed by an active Neighbourhood Watch scheme led, unsurprisingly, by a militant Ms Whitlock. It wasn't the kind of place you would expect a bunch of young party-loving men to house share.

The man shifted away from her. Those sparkling blue (she had decided) eyes had lost their shine. "I'm sorry if you're offended by what just happened here, but I don't think your dad would have minded."

"Right, and you know this because you two were such good friends."

"Well, I wouldn't say we were best mates, but we hung out. He's been over for a few drinks and a boogie on occasion," he smiled and wiggled his hips. "Your dad could really strut his stuff."

Sophie nodded her head with mock enthusiasm. "Yeah, I bet he was over there all the time tearing up the place with the whole posse, and let's not forget the bimbos de jour."

"Well, not all the time, but often. I mean, he didn't say it or anything, but I got the feeling he felt lonely. You know, with your mum being gone and you at work all the time. We've shared more than a couple of beers out back, sitting on the tree swings you have out there." He was smiling again, as he recalled the memory.

This caught Sophie's attention. The swings were something her father installed for her. Swinging on them is something they'd often do together, often each wrapped in a blanket with a drink or a good book.

She said nothing and masked her feelings by folding her arms as if doing so would hide the thumping in her chest.

"He often talked about you, you know. How proud he was," he shrugged and rocked his head. "But also how much he wished you'd stop trying so hard to fit in and stop to enjoy life more."

"What, you mean like you?" she sneered. "Jesus, you are full of it, aren't you?"

"Sophie—"

She held up her hands. "Stop, just stop. You come in here, disrespect my dad and my home with your sex, your... Sex Olympics, and now you talk like you know us?"

"Sophie..."

"Get out."

"I really didn't mean—"

"Just get out of my house!"

"Soph—"

"Get the fuck out! NOW!"

Janay appeared in the doorway and looked at them both. "Oh my God, Soph. What's going on? What's all the shouting about?"

There was a long pause. It was quiet enough for the hushed sibilance of voices to join them from downstairs.

Christopher glanced at Janay then back at Sophie before walking up to her. With his blue eyes sad and lowered, he said, "I'm sorry for your loss," and left. Janay looked at Sophie for an explanation.

Sophie ignored his departure and looked at her friend who repeated her question. "What's going on? What happened?"

But Sophie was unable to answer. Her tears had returned, and they reduced her to a sobbing wreck once more.

3

THE BEGINNING

TUESDAY. THE WITCHING HOUR.

Her dream was different. No handsome stranger, no whirlpool of shadows, stone steps, or flickering reflections, but a river of no sound where the water didn't rush but oozed and bubbled like boiling tar.

She was standing on one side and her father was on the opposite shore. At least she sensed it was him. She could feel the comfort of his presence even though she could not decipher the blur of his outline. It seemed he had already transitioned into the haze of distant memories.

No! Dad!

DAD!

But her call went unheard, for the sound was only in her head. No matter how wide she opened her mouth, how loud she screamed, her body was unable to vocalise. She had been rendered mute, unable to traverse the chasm between them to establish a connection.

DAD! DADDY! she screamed, as her heart thudded in her chest, pumping tears of frustration to her eyes.

Then, slowly, like the sun burgeoning on dawn's horizon, she realised that the straitjacket of anxiety that was squeezing her, choking her ability to breathe, was not her own, but his. It was his blood coursing through her veins. His tension pushing inside her head. His anxiety. Not hers.

DAD?

He was moving now, running, stumbling, climbing, slipping up and down the banks of the river, searching, hunting desperately for ways to cross the bubbling blackness to get to her. To warn her.

Warn me about what, Dad?

He was waving at her now. Hands flailing wildly in the air.

I'm here! Daddy! I'm here! I'm looking at you!

He was jumping up and down in desperation. Screaming. Imploring. Yet, in the vacuum of her dream, all she could hear was the sound of her own breath, the pounding of her beating heart.

Then, suddenly, he froze, arms falling to his sides. A child standing obediently.

What? What happened? DAD? DAD! What's wrong?

That's when darkness, a gargantuan shadow of it, smothered the land. She looked up into a giant bubbling cauldron of rageful black clouds. A flotilla of darkness with edges dipped in molten lava, burning red as they funnelled towards the horizon.

Then, suddenly, the world turned crimson as a fireball streaked across the majesty of the sky. Sophie threw a hand up to her eyes to fend off the glare as the comet exploded into a mountain in the distance, catapulting dust and debris high into the atmosphere and eradiating gale force winds across the land towards her.

She knew she had but seconds before the blast would pulverise her. It was just enough time to see the silhouette of something standing there, watching her with unseeing eyes that bored into her skull with an intensity so powerful she could feel the heat burning hotter and brighter, hotter and brighter, until her chest caught fire and her skin began to blister and bubble...

Wake up!

...her lungs seared.

Wake up!

"Dad!"

Sophie Cooper jolted up into a sitting position, clutching her chest as she coughed, wheezing as she struggled to expel the dust and noxious mist fabricated by her dream yet still impeding her ability to breathe.

Calm down. Calm down and breathe properly. Remember what the doctor said. You're going to induce a panic attack otherwise. Breathe... in...out...in through your nose and out through your mouth. In through your nose and out through your mouth.

It took several minutes for her to bring her breathing back under control yet only seconds for the sadist of her mind to remind her of the one thing that wasn't just a nightmare, no matter how much she wished it to be: her father was dead.

"No," she whimpered, clutching at the ache in her chest before pushing back matted hair and rubbing and swiping at the dampness on her cheeks.

She had dreamed again, only this time it was different. For the first time since she could remember, the mysterious stranger had been replaced by her father. And she didn't need a therapist to explain that this was symptomatic of her loss.

She pushed strands of hair from her eyes and paused. The bedroom was brighter than usual. At first, she thought that someone had left a light on somewhere, but a glance out of the window revealed the full moon hanging high in a clear sky, like a cinematic spotlight.

Sophie sighed and reached over for the lamp switch but yelped when she saw a shadow standing next to the bed. It only took seconds for her to recognise the profile. She'd seen it enough times.

Dad?

She snapped on the lamp. Glorious light instantly dissolved the unknown, revealing her bedroom once more. But there was nobody there.

"Dad?" she called out to the empty room.

Nothing. Not a creak of the house. Not a dog bark in the distance. Just the rushing of blood behind her ears.

She surveyed the room. Everything was as it should be. Tourist posters of majestic cities from around the world decorated the walls. A mosaic of souvenir postcards still hung on the back of the door. All the furniture was in its place, and the walk-in wardrobe door was still closed and secured with the bolt her father had installed at her insistence many years before.

She was alone, and never had solitude weighed this heavily. "Oh God," she rasped on the sandpaper of her parched throat. *Alone.* The realisation was almost as comforting as it was depressing

She looked down to discover that she was still fully clothed with a blanket draped over her.

Where were the girls? They'd left her with the lights off. They both knew she never slept with the lights off. And yet she was alone in the house. She could sense it.

The girls had taken it in shifts to stay with her over the past week. They'd helped with funeral planning, cooking, cleaning, and generally protecting her from the solitude, so this new reality of being alone in the house was something new, and it unsettled her.

The time was 03:06. The witching hour.

She had read enough about mysticism in Western cultures to know—although Victoria was the real expert—that many believed the witching hour to be between midnight and 1:00AM when, in fact, it was between 3:00AM and 4:00AM that the spells of witches and warlocks were believed to be at their most potent.

Of course, her mind rattled off a whole trainload of reasons why she had roused at this precise moment, though none of them were good or helpful in any way. She blamed Victoria, the horror movie enthusiast. Those films often left a hideous impression on Sophie, though perhaps none as hideous as the realisation that she needed to be up for work in a few hours. She should try to get back to sleep but she knew that wasn't going to happen.

Instead, she slid out from under the covers and instantly regretted it. The wooden floor was ice cold beneath her feet. Her room was no longer a sanctuary but a refrigerator, as though she was being preserved, like dead flesh, for a purpose she did not comprehend.

Stop it! Stop.

She snapped the overhead light on, then walked over to the wardrobe, flipped on the light switch purposefully installed on the outside of the closet, hesitated a few seconds, then pulled the bolt and yanked the door open in a single action.

The hangers spaced apart at deliberate intervals swayed back and forth as if protesting being prematurely awakened from their slumber. She jumped as the light winked at her a couple of times then snatched the fleece blanket from the shelf, shoved the door shut and threw the bolt home. She repeated this process several times until she was satisfied that the door was locked before moving to the light switch. *Off. On. Off. On.* And then finally off again.

Satisfied, she wrapped the blanket around her like a cloak and tiptoed back towards her bed. She slipped her feet into her pink piggy slippers, resurrecting memories of the day they were gifted to her.

Christmas morning. *You're never too old for piggies.* This is what her father had told her with a big grin. The stab of longing was sharp, but she twisted away from it, eager to be out of the bedroom.

She reached for the door handle. As she did so, the overhead bulb flickered and died behind her.

She turned. It was okay. The unusually bright bulb she had inserted into the bedside lamp was still burning intensely. Yet when it too began to flicker, she snatched the handle and hurried out into the corridor, pulling the door shut behind her.

Thankfully, her father had installed nightlights in the hallway for her, which meant it was already lit with a supernatural blue hue. But she still felt for and hastily snapped on the overhead light switch before crossing the hallway to the bathroom. There, she felt for the light cord, tugged it on then off, then on and off again, three times, and only entered after she was satisfied that the room was empty.

Her anxiety was awake now also. So, she opened the medicine cabinet, being sure not to linger on her haunted reflection, grabbed the orange plastic vial, and shook out two of the pills. They were meant to be taken with food, but she didn't care. She needed them now. She swallowed, ran the tap, and drank generously.

When she lifted her head, she caught her reflection and half expected to see someone standing in the doorway behind her. Mercifully, it was empty.

She returned the pills to the cabinet and pushed the door shut. Then opened then shut it again two more times. Finally, satisfied that it was closed, she hurried out of the room to avoid more of the self-analysis she was prone to when confronted by her reflection.

She made her way up the hallway to the spare room where she carefully opened the door and looked inside. Even through the gloom, she could see that it was empty. She switched the light on to confirm. The bed was made. There was nobody sleeping in there.

Perplexed, she checked the boxroom. It was unlikely either of the girls would be sleeping in there, and yet, she still felt compelled to check. But it, too, was empty.

Pensively, she shuffled her way back up the corridor, fighting the urge to glance at her father's room. They wouldn't be in there. But the compulsion to see for herself was strong. She compromised with herself by knocking on the door instead, without opening it.

"Vicki? Janay?"

No answer.

She rapped on the door again. Much louder this time. She did not want to go in there. "HELLO?"

Nothing.

She bit her lip as her heart knocked in her chest once more, demanding to know why she was being so foolish. Why was she walking around the house in the dead of night rapping on the bedroom doors of dead people instead of being snugly asleep in her bed?

Don't go in there! It isn't safe. Safe? Don't look inside. There are memories lurking in there too. Don't do it! Don't. Don't!

She knew that there was no way she could leave the upstairs floor without checking. Reluctantly, she lifted her hand to the handle, snatched it away, then placed it back once more. Beads of perspiration tickled her brow as the pills slowly began to lend their support. The rectangular edge of her anxiety was now a smooth round curve.

Come on. You can do this. It's fine. Just open the door. Turn on the light. Open the door, turn on the light. Do it! Do it!

She allowed her fingers to slowly close around the handle and began to turn it when…

"Please release me, let me go, for I don't love you anymore."

Engelbert Humperdinck's sixties classic startled her. The sound was drifting up the stairs and along the corridor to her like a phantom from her past, instantly transporting her to weekends and holidays when she would often wake to this song and the aroma of baking.

Her mother was a sixties babe. Sophie had lost count of the times she'd had to endure hits from the likes of The Mamas & the Papas, The Kinks and (most cringe-inducing of all) The Troggs' "Wild Thing"; it always encouraged her father to traipse around playing air guitar, miming the words, performing the song to her mother before they'd both start dancing around the kitchen. Sophie would beg them to stop but that only prompted them to ham the whole thing up even further.

Come on little girl! Join us!

Her mother's hollow words echoed and faded in her mind as the dreadful reality that they were both gone now reasserted itself.

Her parents weren't here, yet somehow, one of their 45 vinyl discs was playing on the record player downstairs in the early hours of the morning.

Chills like an electric current rippled through her as she slowly and hesitantly made her way down the hallway.

"…for I don't love you anymore…"

She paused by the banister and peered into the gloom of the stairwell.

"Mum?"

The words just fell out, and yet, the moment they were uttered, the music eerily scratched to a halt.

"Vic?"

Silence.

"Vicki?"

Maybe that was it; maybe they were playing a practical joke on her. But she knew that they weren't, no matter how much she wanted it to be true. The girls enjoyed the occasional prank but would never be this cruel or insensitive.

She slid a hand across the wall until she felt the switch beneath her fingers. Beautiful brightness filled the stairwell. "Vicki! Janay!" she called out, leaning to the side to see as far as she could down the stairs.

Then, she listened…

Nothing. All she could hear was the sound of breathing. For one terrifying moment, she thought somebody was standing right behind her, before realising it was her own shallow breaths that were coming thick and fast. The smooth circle of her meds was wavering already.

Pull yourself together. The more you overanalyse the worse it gets. You know this.

She rolled her shoulders and took several deep breaths before descending the stairs, fast, making as much noise as she could. She had no idea why. Perhaps to scare off any would-be intruders, or maybe because she could no longer stand the sound of silence. Whatever the reason, she made it to the foot of the stairs unscathed, and immediately clicked the light on.

The entrance hallway was desolate. The atmosphere cold. Undisturbed.

At the end of the corridor, she pushed on the kitchen door. It creaked so loudly it may as well have been tied to her last nerve, compelling her to hastily reach out and click the kitchen light on too.

Empty. Surfaces gleamed. The tap dripped, dejectedly loud.

No matter how much she tried to suppress it, she could feel her anxiety crawling up her throat once more as she came to terms with the fact that she was indeed alone in the house. She'd suspected it, of course, though she had hoped it wasn't true, that the girls were down here. But they weren't, and seeing the vastness of the empty spaces for herself was overwhelming.

My phone!

She'd left it upstairs, charging on the bedside table. She would need to go back up there to get it so that she could check if...

Her train of thought was derailed once more when movement caught the corner of her eye. She whirled around and saw that it wasn't a strange presence, but the lightbulb above the stairs. It was suddenly flickering, like it belonged in one of those haunted house theme parks she hated.

She turned away, eager to avoid the mental images it might conjure, as well as the shadows it was intermittently murdering and reviving.

"Doesn't exist. Doesn't exist. Doesn't exist," she chanted to herself, as images of her childhood friend lying on the floor filled her mind, her mouth distended grotesquely wide by that creature's talons.

Reminding herself that it wasn't real—had never been real— and saying it aloud was supposed to calm her fear. That's what the doctor had taught her. But it rarely helped, and it wasn't now.

She gripped the doorframe with one hand and clutched the blanket around her as she contemplated leaving the house.

And go where?

She was safe in the light of the hallway. And yet, as soon as she thought that...

Flicker. Flicker.

She spun around and a dagger of ice jabbed at her heart. It was like boot spurs, jolting it into a gallop, as she watched the stairwell lampshade rock back and forth as if it had just been disturbed by someone. Shadows crawled up and down the walls before they were erased as the hallway, like the stairwell light before it, yielded to the dark.

Sophie Cooper screamed and stepped away until she felt the

cold wall on her back.

She looked through the blackness of the hallway to the beacon of jaundiced streetlights shining through the glass in the front door. She would have to traverse the vast expanse of darkness to get there, and anything could be stalking the shadows. Anything at all.

She turned to the kitchen instead. It was closer and the light was still glowing reassuringly bright around the gaps in the door.

She was breathing loudly again. Fast. Shallow. She recognised the signs. *You're hyperventilating. You need to calm down. Calm down. Breathe properly. Calm down.*

She slid over to the light panel on the wall while keeping her eyes on the giant black cavity of the lounge's open doorway, half expecting something to leap out of it. Then, she turned to focus on the narrow strip of light under the kitchen door but yelped and nearly tripped over herself when she saw a shadow slice through it on the opposite side.

A rat's tail of terror scuttled down her back and crawled over her skin, scaring terrified tears to her eyes. *Oh my...* There was someone in the kitchen.

Ragged breaths. Wide eyes. Body quivering. How could it be possible? She had checked the kitchen. There was nobody there. And yet, now, there was an intruder in the house, and she was defenceless and alone.

She turned and looked at the front door as her heart thundered against her ribcage like a wild animal, eager to be set free and urging her to make a run for it. *Run! Don't look back!*

She took one tentative step forward when movement caught her attention once more. No. Again, it wasn't movement, but the tell-tale flicker of the kitchen light.

Quietly, she slid her way back down the corridor, expecting to hear the stomach-churning squeal of the kitchen door as it opened behind her when –

"Il Mondo! Your love is all I need in this world…"

The sound was so loud it elicited another involuntary scream that spurred her feet into action, but the two piggies were oversized for comfort, and she tripped over the slippers and crashed to the floor.

Now, from her viewpoint on the tiled floor, she had a direct line of sight to the record player in the lounge. The light on the front of the device burned bright in the darkness in the shape of a diabolical grin as it screamed another vintage classic at her.

Like the frost coat of a winter's morning, fear enveloped her, freezing her limbs into icy shackles of paralysis. She was hyperventilating. The pressure in her head pushed at the bony confines of her skull while the engine of her thundering heart threatened to stall at any moment.

She imagined getting up. Jumping up from her position on the floor and making a run for the door. *Come on! Make a run for it. Move! Three…two…one!*

Nothing.

Again. *Three…two…one!*

To no avail.

"Il Mondo! Your love is all…"

"No. Stop!"

"… I need in this world…"

She placed her hands over her ears. "Please stop! STOP!"

And just like that, it did. The record's voice slowed to a demon-like incantation before scratching to a halt.

The only sound now was the ringing in her ears and the rasping of her breath.

It's in your head. It's all in your head. This is how it was before. Remember? You're making it all worse. Now, come on, just move!

And yet Sophie could not, for her actions were interrupted by yet another sound. One she hadn't experienced before. It started low at first but then the rumble grew in intensity and was accompanied by the peculiar sensation of floorboards shaking beneath her. The coat stand toppled over, narrowly missing her head as it crashed down. The picture frames that lined the stairs, showcasing happier times, squeaked and swung from side to side before cartwheeling down the steps in a cacophony of snapping wood and shattering glass.

Sophie threw protective hands over her head and ears while her horrified screams were drowned out by the record player as it sprang to life once more, slowly winding up to its normal speed, demonic light grinning, as other breakables jumped to their death in a loud ceramic-crashing, pot-clanging, glass-shattering din.

Sophie crawled forward at first, until she gathered enough speed and courage to jump to her feet. She half tripped and half slipped over the blanket as she raced to the front door, yanking the bolts aside and fleeing out into the freeze of the night where she skidded to a halt.

The ground outside was shaking so much that she had to put her arms out to steady herself. The normally melodic chimes hanging outside the front door jangled a dissonant tune while the family of gnomes guarding the front lawn danced back and forth before collapsing onto each other. Wheelie bins up and down the street spontaneously rolled down the lane, eventually crashing into each other and spilling their recyclable innards. Windows shattered. Roof tiles slid and smashed. The remnants of desiccated leaves on nearby trees hissed in protestation before being evicted from branches and laid to permanent rest.

Sophie could do nothing but gape at the rest of the street that was now reminiscent of the ominous opening of a disaster movie. Vehicle lights flashing. Horns blaring. Alarms wailing as dogs barked, cats yowled, and birds chirped anxiously at such a premature awakening.

The din continued for several more seconds before stopping as suddenly as it had started. It left behind only the familiar melodic tinkle of the chimes and the occasional dog bark in its wake.

Windows up and down Meadow Lane sprang to life and front doors opened as bewildered neighbours spilled out onto their driveways. All shuffled in their nightwear and makeshift wraps, cautious and confused.

Sophie watched as Ms Whitlock appeared on the doorstep of number 13 on the opposite side of the street. She was in her slippers and dressing gown and had never-before-seen rollers in her hair.

The couple at number 11 exited their home with their disgruntled baby, taking it in turns to attempt to placate the infant.

Christopher Darrington, at number 9, hurriedly left his house wearing shorts and a t-shirt, followed by two of his housemates and a couple of girls wrapped in quilts.

The Zhangs at number 8—Sophie's immediate next-door neighbours—exited their home wrapped in coats, each carrying and fussing over his or her own pet Chihuahua.

"Are you okay?" The voice startled Sophie who still had her hands raised to steady herself. It was Chris standing at the foot of her driveway, hands thrust in his pockets, shoulders hunched against the chill.

She dropped her arms and gave him a bewildered nod as a dog bark grabbed their attention.

It was Lucy, at number 12—Sophie's other immediate neighbour—pushing at her dog in an effort to stop the giant thing from leaving the house. As soon as she successfully shut him in behind the door, she crossed the front lawn and driveway to Sophie.

"Are you okay?" she asked. Sophie nodded. Then she asked the question to the rest of the street, louder this time. "Is everybody okay? Does anybody need medical attention?" The paramedic was ready although there didn't appear to be any takers, only the murmur of animated voices.

Sophie looked back at the house as a cold but gentle breeze played with her hair. The noticed that the traitorous lights were back on now and burning brightly.

"Are you sure you're all right?" Lucy asked.

Sophie turned, relieved to have some company. She swallowed and nodded. "Yeah. I think so."

"Well, that was weird," Lucy said with a nervous chuckle.

Sophie smiled and nodded. "Yeah, it's not like Cambridge is known for earthquakes."

"No. Looks like Mother Nature's finally caught up with us."

"Soph! Sophie!" It was Victoria rushing up the driveway.

"Vic!" Sophie exclaimed, relief flooding through her as they hugged. "Oh my God. Where have you been?" she demanded, emerging from the embrace. "I thought you'd gone home."

Victoria, bundled in her puffer jacket, looked at the gathering on the street and then responded distractedly, "I went for a walk. I couldn't sleep. And then I heard all the commotion."

"Oh wow!" Lucy exclaimed suddenly.

Sophie looked at her neighbour, then followed her gaze up into a star-filled sky where, despite its conspicuousness, it still took a few seconds for her to see it. When she did, her mouth fell open.

Travelling thousands of miles from Earth and yet glowing a bright pale blue, the comet was the brightest thing in the night sky.

It had arrived. Unknown to Sophie, the countdown had begun.

4

THE COUCH

TUESDAY. EARLY MORNING.

At least half an hour passed before people started to bore with the spectacle in the sky. It was then that Ms Whitlock trudged over. She told the girls that she didn't know what all the fuss was about, before adding that the sun would be up soon, and that they would all catch their death if they didn't go back inside.

Lucy took the cue and barely hung around long enough for the woman to finish her sentence before making her apologies, explaining that the dog had been playing up all evening and she wanted to check that he wasn't destroying the house.

Sophie, on the other hand—although she'd never admit to it—was grateful for the first time in her life that Ms Whitlock had inserted herself into her home. It didn't take long for her former headmistress to exorcise the house of its ickiness by immediately setting to sweeping up broken crockery and righting toppled furniture, despite Sophie's protestations.

"Resistance is futile," Victoria whispered to her as they carried out the tasks assigned to them.

"You really shouldn't leave all the lights burning like this," Ms Whitlock lectured as she snapped off switches in each room as it was tidied. "You must get into the habit of turning a light on only after the other has been extinguished unless you want an extortionate electricity bill. Remember, you're the lady of the house now. It falls on you to think of these things."

Sophie felt the empty space her father had left in her life gaping wide once more.

It took Victoria several attempts of stretching, yawning, and remarking on how Sophie needed to get up for work in a few hours before the old lady finally got the message and shuffled her slippers out of there. But not before advising Sophie, once again, that she really should consider taking some time away from *that place*. It wasn't a good fit for her, apparently, and she would be better off trying to get a role closer to home. Maybe in the city, perhaps. Or, if needed, Ms Whitlock would be happy to talk to some of her acquaintances about potential opportunities. Sophie was polite yet assertive as she declined, explaining that she was happy in her current position, that she was fine, that work had kept her busy and that's what she needed right now. "Thank you so much for coming over and for all your help tidying up," she added with her best smile, barely able to stop herself from pushing the woman out of the house.

On the plus side, by the time she had closed the door behind the old busybody, she no longer cared about record players or ghostly shadows, especially since they had indirectly already inspected all the rooms.

After hugging and kissing Victoria goodbye while reassuring her that she would be fine alone for what was left of the night,

Sophie grabbed her blanket, curled up in her father's favourite armchair and fell asleep.

Now, just a few hours – that felt like minutes – later she was in her therapist's office, sitting forward and rearranging the cushions behind her. "Sorry again about being late and thanks for the coffee. I need it," she said, still struggling to make herself comfortable.

One of the things she hated about her therapist's office was the couch. It was particularly deep, which meant that there was no way somebody of her diminutive stature of five foot and four inches could lean back comfortably without their feet dangling off the floor. It made her feel like a child, not that she didn't already. That was how she always felt whenever she came here, regressing back to the first time her father made her come, desperate to treat her adolescent night terrors.

"Of course," Doctor Albert Krauss said, observing his patient as she adjusted herself in her seat.

The doctor's accent had almost faded. Sophie had always thought he was German until she plucked up the courage to ask him one day. The psychiatrist was Austrian of a German father and, in Sophie's opinion, had aged well. He reminded her of a trendy Santa but with a much shorter beard. He was somewhere between sixty and seventy years of age with a kind round face, neat white beard, groomed grey hair, and was unafraid of conforming to the stereotype of a man his age by wearing loafers, corduroy trousers, and a shirt and cardigan. Sophie had given serious thought to buying him a pipe because he'd already mastered the furrowed brow of a studious man in perpetual contemplation.

"So, how have you been, Sophie?" Krauss asked, putting his journal down; this was an action Sophie had come to learn was the equivalent of average folk rolling up their sleeves.

She let out a nervous laugh. "Where do I start?" she asked,

opting to take off her shoes to lift her feet up onto the couch, which wasn't unusual during these sessions.

"Well, perhaps we could start with why you're feeling like you're in need of caffeine this morning," the doctor suggested with a smile.

"Well, funerals, earthquakes, creepy records, and comets in the skies mainly. Last night was strange, to say the least, which meant I didn't get much sleep."

"Indeed. As earthquakes go, it wasn't particularly remarkable, but the fact that it happened at all right here in Cambridge certainly was."

"Not remarkable? The whole house was shaking. I'd say that was pretty remarkable," she said, shifting in her seat.

"Really?" The doctor frowned.

"Yes, it knocked pictures off the wall and toppled furniture and everything," she added, sipping from her cup and rocking her head from side to side as if trying to dislodge an ache from it.

"Oh my, that does sound rather dramatic."

"Was it not the same for you?"

The doctor screwed his face up and shook his head. "No. Not really. The first I heard about it was on the news this morning."

"Well, that's weird. It felt like the house was going to fall on me," she said, taking another gulp from her mug and then setting it down on the coffee table.

The doctor lifted his eyebrows and shrugged. "Huh. Well, I'm no seismologist but I imagine the intensity of the tremor would be defined by one's proximity to the epicentre. Perhaps I simply wasn't close enough."

Sophie nodded and Krauss smiled. There was a pause while traffic rumbled down on the street beyond the window.

"Is this what you'd like to talk about today, Sophie? The earthquake?"

"Well, yes, it was really scary," she said, running her fingers over the sides of her head, feeling for bumps in her hair. She was wearing it up as she often did for work and hated the idea of bumps in the back comb.

"Of course. It's just I assumed you might want to talk about the funeral."

Sophie scowled then bit her lip. "Not particularly."

"No? Why not?"

"I just don't."

Krauss frowned and shuffled in his seat. "Sophie, I really think that—"

"I said I don't want to talk about it," she snapped.

The therapist paused, his raised eyebrows signalling his surprise at her curtness.

"Is everything okay, Sophie?" She looked at him pointedly, so he elaborated. "All right, I appreciate that everything is not okay right now, but you seem particularly… troubled this morning."

"Like I said. I didn't get much sleep last night."

"Are you sure it's just that?"

"What else would it be?"

Krauss shrugged and waited several seconds for his patient to continue, but when she contributed nothing further, he smiled. "Okay. Well, why don't you tell me what you would like to talk about today, Sophie."

"You want to talk about something?" she blurted. Krauss cocked his head as if he was going to respond but the question was rhetorical. "Why don't we talk about your couch?"

"My couch?"

"Yes. We should talk about how bloody uncomfortable it is to sit in this thing. It's too deep."

The doctor smiled in bemusement

"It's really difficult for someone like me, who doesn't have particularly long legs, to sit back comfortably. That's why I have to keep picking my feet up every time I'm here."

"Oh, well, I'm sorry about that. Would you like me to fetch you a different chair?"

"No. This one's fine. I just thought you should know, that's all."

The doctor nodded. "Okay. I acknowledge your dissatisfaction with my furnishings."

Sophie immediately clamped a hand over her mouth. "Oh… Oh, Doctor, I'm so sorry. I'm really sorry. I don't even know where that came from," she said, proceeding to smooth out those invisible bumps once more.

The doctor smiled disarmingly. "Come on now, Sophie. You know there's no need for apologies in here. It's important to me that you—"

"Express myself fully and freely, yes, I know. But still. That was rude. I'm so, so…" she cut herself off and smiled. "I, um… Dad would have been mortified to hear me talking to you like that. I sounded like a spoilt brat."

"Sophie, really, please. Don't worry about it."

"I don't know what's wrong with me. I've just been feeling so weird since last week."

"Weird?"

"Yes. You know… different."

"Different? Different how? Are you able to put that into words for me?"

Sophie thought about this for several seconds as a double decker bus stopped at the traffic lights outside. One of the passengers – a businessman – looked up from his phone and absent-mindedly gazed in through the window, interrupting the intimacy of their session.

She waited for the voyeur to rumble on his way before she spoke, as if he could hear her words. "No. Not really. I just feel different, like I've woken up from a long sleep and am just becoming aware of the world around me. It's strange. I feel…"

Krauss waited a few seconds then prompted, "You feel?"

"No, that was it. I just feel more. More aware of everything around me. I don't feel as insular. You know, less numb somehow and more sensitive."

"Emotionally?"

Sophie wrinkled her nose. "Yes, kind of. Triggered more easily by things. At work too. I mean you know how I felt when I started there. I hated the idea of being around all those people."

"Do you regret that?"

"No. No, of course not. It's the opposite now. Dad thinks…" She paused here and corrected herself. "Dad used to say that I became obsessed with work to the detriment of everything else. You know this. We discussed it."

"And you think he was wrong?"

"No. That's what I'm saying. He was right. I see that now. I mean this past week, you know, leading up to the funeral, well, it's been a completely different experience. Don't get me wrong; I still have my neuroses and rituals. I had a full-blown panic attack the other day, but it feels different now."

"Since your father's death… since your birthday?"

She shrugged, thoughtfully, as she suddenly realised that the two events were now inextricably linked forevermore.

"Sophie?"

She shook her head. "I don't know… Yes, I think so."

Krauss nodded thoughtfully before picking up his journal and scribbling something.

Sophie continued. "Do you know I nearly got into it with the vicar at the funeral?"

Krauss looked up from his notes and cocked his head. "What do you mean?"

"Well, if you can believe it, they arranged another funeral on the same day, at the same time as Dad's."

"Two funerals?"

"Yes. Two funerals at the exact same time. That's got to be bad management."

"You think there's something wrong with that?"

"Of course there is! Where's the respect? Where's the dignity? It just makes you feel like you're part of a conveyor belt system. Like cattle at a factory. Box them up and bury them. I don't think it's right. And I was ready to tell him so, but Vicki, as always, said she'd deal with it. Which I think was just her way of saying not to make a scene. Which, of course, I thought was funny coming from her," Sophie scoffed. When she noticed the doctor looking at her curiously, she added, "Well, you know what she's like. She doesn't let anybody get away with anything."

"But that's one of the things you admire about her, right?" Sophie nodded but then rocked her head. "You don't anymore?"

"I do. It's just… between her and Ms Whitlock, it can get a bit, you know, stifling sometimes," Sophie said, avoiding the doctor's gaze. But he waited for her and when she looked back, he had that equivocal look on his face. It was a look she had come to dread because it was normally the prelude to, *are you able to put that into words for me,* or his other personal favourite…

"Could you elaborate?"

"No. Not really. That's just how it feels sometimes." But the doctor was still looking at her. "What?"

"Well, I'm curious, Sophie. You just told me that ever since the funeral, you have felt different, more, how shall we say, more assertive than usual, as though the persona you normally assume when at work has kind of *spilled out* into the rest of your life. I'm paraphrasing here."

"Yes, and?"

"Well, in all the time you've been coming here, you've only ever talked about how lost you'd be without Victoria and how grateful you are to have her in your life. You said she helps and takes care of you. And Mrs Whitlock—"

"Ms," Sophie corrected. "She hates it if you call her Mrs."

The doctor held up a hand and corrected himself. "And Ms Whitlock. Well, you've always tolerated her because of your belief that she means well. We've even discussed how you might have been accepting of her controlling ways, recognising they were a potential extension of her need to mother since she doesn't have any children of her own."

"Right... so?"

"Well, this is the first time you've described both women as *stifling*. Similarly, in all the years you've been coming here, you've believed my couch to be uncomfortable and yet, you've never mentioned it until today."

"I'm sorry. I still don't follow."

"So, I'm inclined to agree with you, Sophie. Something does appear to have changed since your father's death. Since your birthday. What do you think that is?"

Sophie let out a laugh. "Well, that's your job, isn't it?"

The doctor smiled and held up his hands in a surrendering gesture. Beyond the window, a distant robotic voice and a beep announced that a truck was reversing.

"Sophie, I don't need to tell you, of all people, of the power of grief."

"Is that what you think this is? Why I feel different?"

"Not necessarily. What I am saying though is that our brains are designed and wired to function in a myriad of complex ways to keep us alive and functioning as living, breathing beings. Many of these processes are automatic, instinctive. Most often we're not even consciously aware of them. In the face of a bereavement, our bodies must continue with all those complex tasks in addition to dealing with the immense burden of loss, the side effects of which are often manifested in a variety of ways."

"So, you're saying that my newfound confidence is a side effect of my grief?"

"I am saying that I don't believe that what you're feeling is one specific thing but more a collective of things. I believe that what you're experiencing is symptomatic of the immense burdens you're having to cope with right now. Not least the loss of your father."

Sophie nodded as she internalised what was being said. Then she swallowed and her eyes misted with remembered anger as she said, "Do you know what really made me mad recently? I caught our neighbour trying to have sex with one of the waitresses from the catering company Victoria hired, you know, for the wake. *At the wake.*" The doctor shifted in his chair. "That's right. Upstairs in the bathroom. Everybody else was downstairs mourning my dead father and these two strangers snuck into the loo to have it off. Can you believe that?"

Krauss shook his head. "How did that make you feel?"

"How did it make me feel? Angry! Bloody furious!" Sophie wrung her hands together as if wringing their necks. "I mean, we'd just buried my dad and these two…" She let the words trail off as she bit her lip – eyes moist once more – and looked out of the window to the cerulean sky that was decorated with brushstrokes of white marshmallows. She wished she could fly. *Just leap out of the window, flap my wings, and soar high above all of this.*

"Strangers?" the doctor said suddenly. Sophie looked at him. "You called them strangers, but you said one of them was a neighbour."

"So?"

"Wasn't the neighbour known to you?"

She frowned. "Not really. He's some bloke who lives across the street."

"But he was at the wake. Somebody must have invited him. No?"

"Nobody invited him. He invited himself. Said he knew my

father."

"Did he?"

"I've no idea, but you're missing the point. He was in the bathroom trying to shag some bimbo while there was a wake going on. I mean, how disrespectful is that?" Sophie smoothed her hair once more.

The doctor rocked his head and sat up. "Sophie, do you remember when we discussed the complexities of the human mind and how it seeks to cope with the various stresses we encounter in life? Well, it's probably no secret to you that death is a well-known aphrodisiac." Sophie pulled a disgusted face, and the doctor lifted his hands. "No, hear me out. What I am saying is that death and sex have always been related in some way. There are many theories as to why, such as existentialism, evolution, legacy, and so forth, but my point is that different people mourn in different ways. Some eat, some drink, others yearn for physical contact."

"So, you're saying that what they did was perfectly acceptable?" Sophie bristled.

The doctor frowned. "No, Sophie. That is not what I am saying at all. I'm merely pointing out that grief affects people differently."

But Sophie wasn't listening. She had already turned away, gazing out of the window once more so that the doctor wouldn't see her chewing her lip, wouldn't sense she was holding something back. But Krauss knew her. She had been seeing him since she was a child. He knew everything there was to know about her mannerisms and that there was often more to what she was feeling that she was either struggling with or unable to articulate. He gave her a minute before prompting, "Sophie?"

"Does that explain why I felt the way I did then?" she asked without turning. Then she swallowed hard as she attempted to find the rest of the words because now that she had allowed the reality to settle in her brain, the disgust she felt was burning involuntary colour into her cheeks.

"Sophie?" Krauss prompted once more.

"I don't think for one second that those two were grieving for the loss of my father. Maybe he might have been, but she definitely wasn't. But I, um... The thing is..." Her heart throbbed at the memory, and reliving it, trying to say it out loud, was just making her feel worse.

The doctor sat forward in his chair.

She put her fingers to her lips to physically stop herself from chewing because she could taste blood in her mouth. Or perhaps she was trying to stop herself from forming the words she didn't want to speak. "I... when... after I fired the waitress, I talked to the neighbour," she began. "He's fairly young, older than me though. Probably early thirties. Blue eyes, short brown hair. But you know, someone I hadn't really looked at twice before, but... well, I felt something," she said. Her eyes were still fixed on the sky.

"Something?" the doctor prompted gently.

"A compulsion, you know. A feeling, a stirring. Something I've never felt before." She swiped at a runaway tear.

The doctor waited several seconds. "Sophie, are you saying you were attracted to him?"

She shook her head and mumbled, "No." Then, fighting back tears, she continued. "It was more than that. I... um... it was me, I... I wanted to..." She trailed off.

"You wanted to have sex with him?" the doctor suggested gently.

Sophie sniffed, trying to reinforce the dam of her resolve against the flood of further weeping. "And... and I, I felt so ashamed," she said, as inevitable tears broke through.

Doctor Krauss gave her a few minutes, allowing her to turn back, snatch tissues from the box on the coffee table and dab at her eyes.

Eventually, Krauss spoke softly. "You feel shame because you were physically attracted to this man? Why is that?"

She took a few seconds to mop up her leaky emotions with the tissue before shrugging, helplessly. "I don't know. I suppose it's because I'm sitting here going on about how disrespectful they were and all the time... I don't know, was I jealous?" She looked at Krauss expecting him to jump in. "I'm not any better than that slut," she whispered.

The doctor rocked his head.

She rolled her eyes. "Oh, of course, you don't agree."

"Well, it's not that I don't agree, but you know I'm not one for drawing comparisons, Sophie. We're all individuals and I don't think there's much to be gained from comparing ourselves to others. That said, for the sake of argument, if we were to indulge ourselves, we could start with the fact that the waitress— whoever she was, whatever her background state of mind—is not you. She's not grieving as you are. She isn't wrestling with the same challenges. Nor does she necessarily have the same sexual experiences as you. And that's because, quite simply, she isn't you," he said with a shrug. "Comparing yourself to her is no more useful than if I were to compare myself to a ballerina."

Sophie snickered and continued to dry her eyes.

"What a ghastly thought, eh? But do you understand what I'm getting at here, Sophie?" She sniffed and nodded reluctantly. "These changes in you are all signs that you are preparing to move into a new stage of your life. It is nothing to be afraid or ashamed of," the doctor said with an encouraging smile. "*Frailty, thy name is human.*"

Sophie sniffed. "I don't think that's how it goes."

"No, but I don't believe the great wordsmith, Shakespeare, would mind my minor alteration of his verse. I've always believed Hamlet got that wrong anyway," the doctor said with a wink.

"You don't think females are frail?"

"Of course not. I believe the female of the species has twice the mental strength of any man. And let's not forget the enviable, inimitable, and near omnipotent ability to give life. That's not just my opinion; these are the facts of life. Wouldn't you agree?"

Sophie shrugged.

"When the Himalayan peasant meets the he-bear in his pride, He shouts to scare the monster, who will often turn aside. But the she-bear thus accosted rends the peasant tooth and nail..."

"*...For the female of the species is more deadly than the male,*" Sophie joined in. "You're using Kipling to make your point now, Doctor?"

Krauss rocked his head and smiled. "Well, if the text fits," he said. Sitting forward once more, he added, "This is a very exciting time for you, Sophie. Time for your transition to the next phase. Time for you to realise your potential, as a woman. To fulfil your destiny, as they say."

"Yeah? Well, it doesn't feel like it. Anyway, we must be out of time by now," she said.

Krauss looked at his watch. "We still have a few more minutes."

"I've got to get to work."

"To work?"

"Yes."

"Sophie, don't you think you would benefit from some leave right now? After all, you did still go last week, against my advice, may I add."

"Why, do you think it's healthier for me to sit at home and mope?"

"I don't. But still, work, facing travellers, Sophie. We both know how much of a challenge that is for you. Especially now with this *shift* you've felt in yourself."

"I know, right? You should be happy. You're the one that

encouraged me to take this job, to push myself to get out there. Well, now, I just can't wait to. Told you I've been changing."

"Precisely. Which is exactly why I don't think you should underestimate the pressure you are under right now."

"I'm not. I just can't stay in that house, alone. I need this. It helps me to stay busy, to keep my mind on others rather than on myself."

"I appreciate that. But Sophie, in your own words, you are undergoing some kind of transformation… your self-confidence, the way you reacted to your neighbour. These developments, I feel that they warrant further exploration. Don't you?"

The doctor waited for response, but when all he received was a casual shrug and a lift of the eyebrows, he asked, "Don't you see it?"

"See what?"

"Your awakening, Sophie," he offered excitedly. "Your *sexual* awakening. Sophie, in all the years that you've been coming here you haven't once expressed an interest in anybody except the man in your recurring dream and yet now, your next-door neighbour, someone who's lived right across the street from you, for some reason has had this effect on you."

"Ew, no," Sophie protested. "You think it might be him? That he's the man I've been dreaming about? I don't think so. You haven't met him. He's a right arrogant piece of… Yeah, well no. Just no."

"Whether or not he is *the one* is not something I want us to focus on right now. What is relevant is how, just like the prince in Sleeping Beauty, *he* has managed to awaken this dormant side of you several years after puberty."

"Oh God!" Sophie held up her hands and screwed up her face in disgust. "Can we… Can we not discuss this anymore? I feel like I'm going to throw up."

"But this is good news," the doctor insisted.

"Maybe, but I don't want to talk about it anymore."

"No, Sophie, if it's okay with you, I'd like us to stay on this because I have several reasons to believe that your social anxieties, your compulsive disorders, your fear of intimacy are all intrinsically linked with your mother's departure. If we don't discuss this, I can't get to the root of what else might be inhibiting you from becoming the adult—"

"No. I said no."

"Sophie—"

"I said I don't want to talk about it anymore!" she snapped as car horns roared outside the window, followed by an almighty *crash!* of metal colliding. The impact was so strong, it vibrated through the building.

Sophie dropped her legs from her seat. The doctor jumped up from his chair and rushed over to the window.

"Oh, my goodness!"

"What happened? What's wrong?"

"There appears to have been an accident outside. A pileup at the traffic lights. Oh no. I hope nobody has gotten hurt," the doctor said, painfully, gawking out of the window.

Sophie didn't respond because, somehow, she knew that they had.

5

THE PASSENGER

TUESDAY. MID-MORNING.

Forty minutes later, Sophie was wishing she had taken the train into work. It looked like she was not only starting late, but she was also going to be late.

Like everything else, her session with Doctor Krauss felt different today. Normally, she'd come away feeling moderately better about facing the day ahead. Today, she felt marginally worse. And no matter how hard she tried to explain it to herself, she was unable to.

It no doubt wasn't helped by the crash right outside of the doctor's office, as well as the wailing sound of sirens and all the rest of the commotion that comes with an accident like that.

She had told herself to avoid looking at the scene because she knew it would be nothing but a trigger for her grief, considering what happened to her father. Yet she still couldn't help but imagine that that sound—that terrible din of shattering glass and squealing metal—was most likely the same as the last sound he had ever heard. Then, she imagined him cold and alone as he felt the life drain from his body.

These thoughts carved an ache in her chest that had worsened when she had ignored her own advice and allowed morbid curiosity to compel her to rubberneck, just like all the other onlookers, at what had happened. It seemed that a refuse truck was turning at the traffic lights and somehow ended up ploughing into one of those Smart cars. The tiny thing was unrecognisable but for its back wheels; the truck had climbed on top of it.

When a policeman had rapped on the hood of her car and gestured for her to keep moving, she did, fast, hoping to join the motorway and put some distance between her and those horrific images. But no such luck. All lanes were almost at a standstill, which meant she had nothing better to do than think. That was good in one way, she supposed. It gave her the opportunity to unpack everything that had been discussed at the morning's session and begin to process it.

Oh God. Had she really shared how she felt about her next-door neighbour with Krauss? And where did that come from anyway?

Maybe revisiting the session wasn't a good idea after all. She turned on the radio. The only topic of conversation was the fireball in the sky, with many speculating that, at its current trajectory and velocity, it was going to smash into Earth and cause a cataclysmic event never witnessed before. Others suggested that the thing was slowing down, a la *Independence Day,* which at least made her smile.

She adjusted the rear-view mirror then skipped through radio stations until she landed on the BBC with the hope of getting a more sensible perspective. Sure enough, as she tuned in one of the guests was schooling listeners on why all the scaremongering wasn't helpful, telling everyone to fact check information before sharing it. *"Easier said than done these days,"* the host retorted.

Another guest was an eminent seismologist who was invited on the show to discuss last night's so-called 'non-earthquake'. This caught Sophie's attention.

The man, with perfect English diction, began by explaining that the most common method of measuring an earthquake was the Richter scale, short for Richter magnitude scale.

"It was invented in 1935," the expert continued, *"by American Charles F. Richter. The scale has ten levels. 0 through 1.9 tremors can only be detected by a seismograph. Anything above 9 equals complete destruction. Last night's quake was barely a 2 through 2.9, where you can expect hanging objects, like lampshades, to swing a little."*

"A little?!" Sophie echoed, incredulous.

She continued listening for the next five minutes but when the show's host decided to speak to some weirdo who believed that the comet was Satan's Star of Bethlehem and that it signalled the arrival of his offspring, or some such rubbish, she shut the radio off and opened an app on her phone instead.

*"Please. Per favore. Pehr fah-**voh**-reh. Repeat after me. Pehr fah-**voh**-reh."*

"Per fa-vo-re," Sophie repeated.

"Cup. Tazza. Repeat after me. Tazza."

"Tazza!"

"Coffee. Caffè. Repeat after me. Caffè."

"Caffè!"

"Please, I would like a cup of coffee. Per favore, vorrei una tazza di caffè. Repeat after me. Per favore, vorrei una tazza di caffè."

Sophie lifted a hand off the steering wheel, pinched thumb and fingers together, then shook them up and down. "Eh! Per favore, vorrei una tazza di caffè!" Sophie said in the accent of an Italian gangster, just as her phone started ringing.

It was a video call.

Her phone was already mounted into the holder on her dashboard, so she tapped the green icon, adjusted her rear-view mirror once more and then pressed *Accept*.

"Ciao!" Sophie waved at the screen that was now showing a moving image of Janay walking through her home.

"There you are!"

"Yes, here I am. And you're video calling me, again," said Sophie through a clenched smile.

"Oh, stop complaining. You've got the prettiest face of anybody I know so why wouldn't I want to see it? Besides, you didn't reply to my texts so I thought I should get in touch, see what's going on."

Sophie gave her a pained smile. "Oh, I know. I'm sorry. It's been one hell of a morning and after last night, I was running late, and it just turned into a thing," she said.

"Oh, I know, that's why I messaged you. It's crazy. They're all acting like it's the end of the world or something," Janay said with a roll of her eyes. "We didn't feel a thing here. Which is the story of my life of course."

Sophie chuckled. "Really?"

Janay shook her head. "Yep. Slept right through it. I woke up this morning and turned on the radio only to find that everybody's losing their bloody minds."

"That's so weird," Sophie said thoughtfully, as she pushed the car into gear and crawled forward a few metres.

Janay squinted. "What, that people are already panic buying over a bloody comet?"

"Are they? No, not that," Sophie said, pulling on the handbrake once more. "No, I mean the earthquake last night. Everybody is saying that they barely noticed it. Me, the whole bloody house started shaking; I'm talking pictures falling off walls, stuff toppling over, the full experience. It was really scary."

"Oh shit, babe. That sounds awful." Janay screwed her face up into an expression of sympathy, but it instantly dissolved when she added, "Still, at least you had Cruella with you."

Sophie pushed the car into gear again and moved forward. "Well, that's another thing. I was alone at the time."

"What do you mean?"

"Well, I woke up and there was nobody there," Sophie said, checking and readjusting the rear-view mirror.

"But Vicki said she was staying with you."

"She was. She did. But she couldn't sleep so was out walking when all the excitement happened."

Janay sat down at her kitchen table and shook her head. "I knew I should have stayed but she insisted, started giving me that line about the fact I was a single mother and needed to get back for my child. It wouldn't have been a problem. You know that."

"It's fine, Janay. Honestly. Don't worry. I'm just saying that earthquake seemed much worse to me."

Janay pulled a face and leaned closer to the screen. "Well, of course it did, babe. You've been through some shitty stuff. Everything's one giant quake, ain't it? Listen, do you fancy stopping by the café today? I could…" she interrupted herself. "Wait a minute." Janay made a show of squinting into the camera. "Sophie, you're in your car!"

Sophie cocked her head. "Um, yeah, that's right, I'm in my car, and I am seriously regretting it right now because the traffic is—"

"Okay. So, let's start with that. What's with the car?"

"What do you mean?"

"I spoke to Vicki this morning, when I wasn't getting any joy texting you, and she told me you were planning on going into work today."

"Yes. So? And by the way, you know she hates anyone calling her Vicki, right?"

"Anyone but you, you mean. And don't change the subject.

Sophie, you're going into work. I thought we agreed you were going to take some time off."

"Did we? When did we do that?"

Janay rolled her eyes. "Soph…"

"Oh, come on. Everybody keeps going on about my going into work, but it's been good for me. If I stay home, I'll just go mad. Besides, I couldn't wait to get out of that place this morning. It feels different now."

"Well, of course it will, sweetheart. It's going to take some getting used to."

"No, Janay. I mean it really feels different," Sophie reiterated. She was about to elaborate when she was interrupted by a toot from the car behind. "Okay. Sorry!" There was a wide gap in front of her now, so she threw the car into gear and quickly made up the space.

When Sophie looked back at her phone, Janay was peering into the camera as if to see her friend's face more clearly, when all she would have been able to see was half of her profile and the backseat.

"What were you saying about the house?"

"I was saying that some weird stuff happened last night. It all started with a horrible nightmare I had about Dad and—"

She cut herself off here. Janay appeared to be staring at her with a puzzled expression.

"What is it? Janay?"

But her friend did not respond. Several seconds later, her image disintegrated into a myriad of jerky moving pixels, accompanied by incomprehensible snippets of her voice.

"Hello? Janay! Janay? Are you there? I think I've lost you!" Sophie yelled at her phone before glancing at the traffic ahead. It was moving now, albeit slowly.

When Sophie looked back at her phone, she could see her friend was now looking off camera, pixels reassembled. "Hello, trouble," she said happily. Moments later, the profile of a five-year-old boy appeared on screen. Janay held his face and asked, "Did you tidy up your room like I asked?"

The little boy nodded. "Uh-huh."

"Uh-huh? What does that mean again?"

"Yeah."

"Yes," his mother said. "We don't say yeah, do we?"

"Yes," the child said, correcting himself.

Sophie smiled. "You remind me of Dad," she said wistfully.

"Hey, look who Mummy's talking to," Janay said, turning to her phone. The little boy followed her gaze and peered into the camera before waving and squealing, "Aunty Sophie!"

"Hello, handsome!" Sophie responded with a big smile. "No school today?"

The boy shook his head. "Uh-uh. My teacher's at school today."

"Your teacher's at school?" Sophie asked.

Janay filled in. "It's teacher training day, isn't it, Damon?"

"Oh, I see," Sophie smiled.

"Aunty Sophie?"

"Yes, handsome?"

"Who's that?" the boy asked, pointing at the camera.

Sophie laughed, "It's me. Aunty Sophie."

The boy chuckled, then added with a big toothy grin, "Not you, silly. That man sitting behind you."

Sophie whipped her head around.

The backseat was empty.

The little boy was obviously playing a practical joke. And yet, her nerves, primed from the events of the night before, had already raked up the small hairs of her arms and scared the thump in her chest to an anxious patter. It was made worse by the sound of angry car horns. When she turned her attention back to the road in front of her, it was almost too late.

Sophie stomped on the brake with just inches to spare. She had almost ploughed into the back of the car in front.

"Shhhiit!" she hissed, clutching the steering wheel, breaths coming quick and fast as her mind spitefully fabricated images of her father's mangled body, intermingled with the most recent sights and sounds of the crash outside of the doctor's office.

She gawked at the silhouette of the driver in front who held up his hands and waved them at her questioningly. Sophie was unable to react for a moment; sweat had beaded on her forehead and the trap door of her throat had closed.

Then she heard giggling. "Aunty Sophie said a rude word!" the little boy said, pointing at the camera.

Meanwhile his panicked mother was calling to her friend, but Sophie was unable to respond. She had lost all ability to articulate anything.

6

THE MOB

TUESDAY AFTERNOON

It was midday by the time Sophie finally arrived at work. Her lateness would have normally gone down like a lead balloon with Steve and would have most likely prompted supervision. The kind where he'd take her to one side and explain that he was doing her a favour by having a chat *off the record, you know. Just to give you the heads up that I've noticed that your performance isn't quite up to scratch.* One of those intimate chats by the lockers, where he would see fit to lean into her for a close conversation of the kind that made her skin crawl.

But given that he wasn't expecting her anyway and that he clearly needed the manpower, he didn't make the fuss he normally would. Sophie was grateful. She was still reeling from her near-miss in the car.

Nothing like that had ever happened before, in the three years she had been driving. It had scared the shit out of her to the point of rendering her mute.

It had taken a middle-aged Asian man in a suit, with a thick grey beard and black eyebrows, to bring her back from her trance. He'd first made things worse by rapping on her driver side window, like some kind of bailiff, but when he noticed that the blood had drained from her face and she was hyperventilating, he seemed to recognise she was having a panic attack.

He had pulled the door open, crouched down to her level and soothed her by encouraging her to breathe slowly, explaining to her that the way she was breathing wasn't giving her body enough oxygen and causing her brain to panic. All she needed to do was *slow down. That's it. Slow down and take some deep, long breaths for me. Deep breaths. That's it.* Next, he'd placed a cool, reassuring hand on her arm and backed that up with a warm smile. Janay's panic was clear even over video call, but the man had reassured her too; her friend was going to be fine.

With the assistance of this kind stranger, Sophie had soon been well enough to resume her journey, albeit slowly, and with regular glances at the back seat. What had Damon seen?

She was still thinking about it when Katy walked into the office.

They called it that. It was more of a storage room masquerading as an office. The messy desk was a dumping place for anything no one could be bothered to file and the computer on it had seen better days. An old leather couch and a scuffed brown table in theory provided a place for agents to sit and eat their lunch. In reality, lunch was normally anything edible, wherever it could be found and whenever it could be eaten on-the-go.

As always, Katy was sporting that wild look in her eyes, like the sky had or was about to fall in. Though this morning, she would be forgiven for thinking so.

"Sophie! You're 'ere!" the girl exclaimed, as she teetered up to her in her ridiculously impractical heels.

Sophie manufactured a smile for the girl and served that up with a disarming lift of her eyebrows. "Yes. I am, Katy. And so are you," she said.

"But I thought you… that um, your dad, ya know, the um…"

"The *um* funeral was yesterday. Yes," Sophie said. "But that was yesterday. Today, I'd rather be busy here than at home staring at the dripping tap my dad said he'd fix a thousand times but never did. Is that okay? Is that all right, Katy?" Sophie's restrained questions were clearly rhetorical, yet the girl nodded.

"Good. Now, I've been through all of this with Steve, and we've already got a riot breaking out at Gate 5, so if it's all the same to you, I'd rather just get on with it."

The girl nodded again.

"Good."

They left the office and stepped onto an escalator. As they descended, Sophie said, "So, we've got a grounded flight to Majorca due to mechanical problems and we're waiting on a replacement plane. And now the passengers are kicking off with the airline. Is that right?" Sophie phrased it as a question for Katy, but it was more for her own benefit as she went through the process of fortifying herself against what was to come.

"Yeah, and they're bein' well mean," Katy whined.

"Yes, people get that way when their rest and relaxation is threatened. You should see how ugly it gets when a flight to Magaluf is cancelled," Sophie said with a lopsided smile.

The girl just blinked at her.

"That was a joke, Katy."

"Oh." The girl chuckled awkwardly.

They stepped off the escalator and Sophie hurried forward, oddly eager to get to her destination, with the girl trailing behind.

"Oh my God, Sophie. Can you believe it?" Katy said suddenly, eyes wide with interest.

Sophie looked at her colleague and then followed her gaze. She was watching a monitor, mounted high next to the *Arrivals* screen. It was beaming out a picture of a sullen-looking news anchor, before cutting to a digital graphic depicting the distance between Earth and the comet.

"It's all anybody can talk about," Katy narrated.

"Really?" Sophie said, barely interested. She just wanted to get on with her day. She'd had enough abnormal. She needed – no, she was craving – boring old normal.

"Yeah, they're speculatin' that the government knew about this thing ages ago but tried to cover it up because they didn't want nobody to know about it. Why do ya think that is?"

"Sophie… are you there?" Steve's tinny voice crackled over the radio she was holding in her hand.

"Some are sayin' that this thing is actually gonna hit us and that the government ain't sayin' anything because they don't wanna start a panic," Katy continued, eyes still glued to the monitor until she could crane her neck no longer.

Sophie lifted the radio and spoke into it. "Yes, Steve."

"Are you there yet?"

"We just left."

"Right, well you may wanna pick up the pace as it looks like things are about to seriously kick off over there."

"We're going as fast as we can, Steve. *You may* want to put a call into security."

"Security? Are you joking? That's exactly what I'm trying to avoid. It's kinda, what do they call it, counterintuitive to the whole positive experience thing, Soph. Besides, that's what you're here for, ain't it?"

Sophie was going to respond but bit her lip and instead said, "Roger that!" She signed off on the radio and turned back to Katy. "Katy, remind me again why you want this job?" she asked loudly over the din of voices, public announcements, and the sound from giant plasma screens begging for consumer attention.

The girl, who was shuffling along in quick, controlled steps to avoid toppling over as she tried to keep up, shrugged as she replied. "I don't know. It's a job, ain't it?" Sophie looked at her and cocked her head, which prompted the girl to add a whiny, "People're always so angry."

"Well, that's the whole point of the job, Katy. It's what we do. That's the challenge, to make unhappy people happy again. That's the way you need to look at it. When I first started, I was terrified of dealing with people. I really was. I was a bit like you," she said, thoughtfully.

"Really? I can't imagine you—"

"Oh yes. Much worse. I would get tongue-tied and everything, but you'll get used to it after a while and learn how to deal with people," she said, purposefully leaving out the background detail that the job was part of an exercise many years in the making.

When Sophie's mother left, her daughter refused to leave the house. She'd wait for hours, longingly gazing out of the window in the hope she might return.

Her father believed that her refusal to leave that window seat was her way of coping with the loss and that she would eventually grow out of it. She did not. Instead, things deteriorated, with Sophie exploding into violent fits of rage each time she was forced to leave the house.

And thus, his daughter was already pre-agoraphobic when Alan Cooper took the drastic step of selling up the family home and moving them to Cambridge to be closer to the specialist that had been recommended to him: Doctor Albert Krauss.

Sophie had been in his care ever since.

"Just the thought of dealing with an irate passenger used to fill me with dread, but then my dad always says that..." She stopped and corrected herself. "*Used* to say that anger is like fire." She looked at the girl as they passed yet another gate, but from the frown on her face, it was obvious she didn't get it. "It burns all clean," she added. "You see, these people are frustrated. They've spent their money to be sunning themselves on an overpopulated beach somewhere, not to be stuck in an airport. For them, every second of this time counts. You understand that, right?" The girl rocked her head. "Right?" Sophie prompted until the girl nodded. "Besides, it isn't all angry, shouty people. Look at that old lady we helped the other day. She's probably somebody's grandmother. We helped to get her home."

"Oh, yeah, right. About that. I need to talk to you about her," Katy chirped up.

"OK, what about her?"

"We've been waitin' here for over eight fuckin' hours and you can't even tell us when the next bloody flight is?"

"I want to talk to a supervisor!"

Angry voices interrupted their conversation as they arrived at Gate 5.

Sophie estimated that there were approximately one hundred people, all dressed for summer weather. Adults and children, whose spectrum of pasty-white, olive, and dark-skinned bodies told her that she was dealing with multiple nationalities, all of whom wanted to be in Spain hours ago. And yet, they were still stuck in England, where persistent black clouds hung over the airport like a thick smog, spitting occasional rain at the giant glass walls as if mocking them.

"Sir, I can assure you, we're doing everything we can to get you on the next available flight," the airline representative was saying.

"Yeah," said a burly man with thinning hair, a conspicuous black leather jacket and jowls that shook when he bellowed in a thick Estuary accent, "but you just told us there won't be another flight until tomorrow mornin'!"

"That is the next possible flight, sir," the representative, a skinny thing wearing a lot of makeup with hair scraped to the back of her head, mumbled.

"I need to be in Majorca today!" said a short lady with a thick Spanish accent. "It's my sister wedding tomorrow!"

"I can't do anything about that." The airline representative, whose name tag read Tracy, busied herself by uselessly clicking on her keyboard as the mob encircled the stand like a pack of wolves around a lonely lamb.

"Well, you better find a way then, 'adn't ya?" added the burly man. "It's your fucking job to get us onto another flight."

"Sir, please, there are children—"

"I don't give a fuck! If you did your fucking job and got us onto another plane then I wouldn't be this pissed off, would I?" the man bellowed, eyes bulging and coffee breath drifting in a noxious vapour.

"I've already told you. The quickest way to get you onto another flight is if you get the train to Gatwick and fly out of there."

"But we don't have the money to get there," said a middle-aged woman with a Scottish accent.

"And who's gonna fucking pay for that? You? Are you gonna fucking pay for us to get there?" spat the Londoner.

"Sir, I'm really going to need you to calm down and stop swearing."

"Well, are you gonna get us to Majorca tonight?"

"No. I told you."

"Why not?"

"I told you why—"

"Why not?"

"There are no seats—"

"That's not good enough."

A chorus of angry noises of approval rose from the rest of the mob.

"Sir—"

"That's not an answer. It ain't good enough, mate." The man rummaged in his pocket, pulled out a piece of paper, and thrust it at the woman behind the desk. "You see that? You see that? Do you know what it is? That's an agreement with you. I paid *you* for a service and you ain't providin' it."

"I told you. You'll need to take that up with customer service."

"You *are* customer service!" some other gangly man contributed from a distance.

"You need to write into customer service, there isn't anything I can do from here," Tracy said, abandoning her keyboard clacking and gradually backing away from her stand.

"This is a fucking joke! This airline's a joke!" someone else yelled. Next to him, an argument erupted between a group of Spanish travellers who began yelling and gesticulating at each other.

"I need to get on a flight this night!" the Spanish woman yelled.

"Look, I've already told you—"

"Not good enough. You give me ticket on another plane."

"Step away from the desk, please," Tracy said, her tone now elevated.

"Not until you give me ticket," the Spanish woman countered, going around the bench and prodding the representative with a chubby finger.

"Are you deaf? I said, I don't issue those here," Tracy retorted. "I no issue el ticketto from here!" she vocalised loudly, as if she was talking to an elderly person who was hard of hearing.

"Now you make fun on me? You make fun on me, my accent, bitch?" the Spanish woman raged.

"Well, you're not listening to me. I've already told you, there are no—" The representative didn't have a chance to finish her sentence before the woman slapped her over the head twice with a thick wad of papers that looked like her ticket wallet.

"NO! STOP THAT!" Sophie yelled as she abandoned her attempt to make her way through the crowd tactfully and pushed her way forward.

"Who the fuck are you?" said the Londoner.

Sophie snapped her head around and growled, "I'm the person who's going to get you kicked out of this airport if you carry on the way you are." Then she turned back to the representative who was holding her head as if she had been smacked with a brick. "Are you okay?" she asked.

"Yeah, I think so," Tracy said, visibly shaken. The onslaught had been going on for some time now and it appeared she had been left to deal with it alone.

"Have you called security?"

The woman shook her head.

"Do it now," Sophie ordered. Then she turned to address the mob. "Okay, hello? Excuse me, hello! Excuse me. Can I have your attention, please? Hello! Can I have your attention? EXCUSE ME! PLEASE SHUT THE HELL UP SO I CAN TELL YOU WHAT'S GOING ON!" she yelled so loudly she almost choked. She had no idea where that came from, but it seemed to do the trick.

Blazing eyes fixed on her. The mob's anger was as thick and palpable as the tension before a storm. But oddly, she wasn't nervous or afraid. She was *ready*.

Sophie had been in this situation many times before and loathed it. She hated confrontation. But today… well, today she felt different, almost as if she were spoiling for a fight. Which was ridiculous, of course. She reasoned that she must have built up some kind of tolerance to it and just hadn't realised until now.

She turned to the Spanish woman. "Hey you. If you want any chance of getting home anytime this week without spending a night in a police cell for assault, I suggest you keep your hands to yourself and start begging this lady not to press charges. Do you understand me?"

The woman opened her mouth to say something, but Sophie shot her a blistering glare. "All I want to hear from you right now is that you understand. *¿Lo entiendes?*"

The woman swallowed then followed with a reluctant nod.

"Who the 'ell are you?" It was the Londoner again and Sophie turned her sights to him next.

"I think I've already answered that question," she said, maintaining his steely gaze. She wasn't going to take any more crap from a bunch of animals because that's all these people were to her. A bunch of wild animals.

"Who's your supervisor? I want the name of your supervisor!" a spindly man yelled from the back.

"I'm busy right now but happy to provide that when I've finished talking," she responded. "And if any of you want to get to your destination anytime soon, I suggest you listen up. As my colleague already explained, the plane you were going to fly out on did not pass pre-flight checks because of a mechanical problem and, while you may hate them for it, because the airline would rather your plane not fall from the sky with you onboard, they decided instead to ground it."

There were jeers and grumbles from the crowd.

"I know," Sophie continued. "Putting your safety before getting you out of here on the first flight is rubbish, but what can I say, we're in the minority."

"Is she taking the fucking piss?" someone yelled.

"No. I'm just telling you how it is because you didn't appear to understand when my colleague told you. So, you can all be transferred onto the next flight which, as I understand it, is tomorrow morning," she looked at Tracy for confirmation and the woman nodded, "or you get on the next shuttle to Gatwick and fly out of there later tonight. Either way—"

"And who's paying for that?" someone yelled.

"—either way, it doesn't matter how much you yell and scream, you *will not* be getting on a flight today from Stansted because it simply does not exist."

"And who's gonna pay for our accommodation?"

"My colleague will be happy to hand out vouchers for meals. If you keep your receipts for any other expenses, you'll later be able to take it up with the airline's customer care department."

Another wave of disgruntlement rippled through the crowd, and she even heard the word *bitch* somewhere in the unintelligible sibilance. But this didn't deter her. "Now, if any of you are interested in rebooking onto a different flight, my colleague here will be more than happy to assist you."

With that, she stepped out from behind the desk and ventured into the crowd where she was intercepted by the angry Londoner, who blocked her path with his bulk. He was a stocky fellow, at least six-foot-something and towered over her. "Who the 'ell are you? I want the name of your boss!" he barked.

She looked up at the red swollen face and then attempted to move around the man, but he continued to block her way. "I'm Sophie Cooper," she said. "I'm one of the senior passenger experience agents here at the airport."

The Londoner, and a group of cronies behind him, scoffed and said, "You've got to be fucking shitting me. Passenger experience?"

Sophie was shaking now but she didn't know if that was still the adrenaline or the fact that she was suddenly feeling intimidated. It's like she'd used up her courage tokens for the day and was suddenly back to being her usual self. Worse, she could feel that tell-tale tickle of perspiration forming on her brow. It wouldn't be long before they spotted that.

And so, it took a deep breath and every scrap of remaining bravado for her to casually look around the mountain that was the Londoner and say, "Do you mind? I have other passengers that need my assistance."

Seconds pulled at the tension of the moment as the man looked down his very wide snout and growled, "And what if I don't want to move?"

"Then I'd 'ave to ask these gentlemen to escort you off the premises," Katy said abruptly, referring to a pair of armed police officers who were waiting nearby impassively, each donning their own disgruntled look as if someone had just interrupted their coffee break.

Eventually, after glancing at the two men, the Londoner gave Sophie a final sneer before stepping aside.

Sophie approached the two officers. "Could you please have a chat with the airline representative? She may want to report an assault."

Sophie moved away to leave the tension of the mob behind, and Katy trailed after her once more.

They were barely out of earshot before Katy's straight face creased into an enthusiastic grin. "OMG, Sophie, that was amazing! You were bloody amazing!"

Sophie let go of the breath she was holding and as much as she wanted to share the girl's enthusiasm, she couldn't because she knew exactly what was coming next.

The rest of her day carried on in pretty much the same vein.

One passenger had to have her bags offloaded from her flight because she didn't report to the gate on time. *I was at the airport the whole time!* the woman had fumed. *Yes, but you weren't at the actual gate when you were supposed to be, were you?*

Then, there was a missing five-year-old who was eventually found. A forgotten passport. Long queues at check-in that needed to be streamlined. A drunken passenger who couldn't walk straight but insisted he was fit to fly, and a pregnant lady who had to be carted off to hospital for a precautionary scan.

By late afternoon, by which time the pale sun had surrendered to a bolstered invasion of irate black clouds, Sophie had already walked ten miles, and she had the sore feet to prove it.

Still, she was thankful that she wasn't wearing Katy's heels. At one point she even felt compelled to ask the girl if she was all right in those things. The girl said that she was fine, although the grimace on her face told a different story.

Now, Sophie barely had time to return her pills to her bag, then open and shut the battered locker door three times before Steve walked in and accosted her. Ugh. She wasn't in the mood.

"Good day?" he asked, unhooking his radio from his hip with a flourish, shoving it into one of the chargers on his desk as if it were a big gun he'd been wearing strapped to his thigh all day.

"Oh, you know, the usual," she said, without looking up. She was busy swiping away several text messages from Janay and Victoria who were *just checking in on her.*

She loved them both dearly. In fact, it felt like they were the only thing she had left in the world right now. And yet, oddly, she felt like she needed a break from them too. Or more specifically, a break from being *the bereaved* for a while. Right now, she wanted to be alone to do her job. She certainly wasn't in the mood for Steve.

"The usual, eh?" Steve was standing close. Too close.

"Oh, you made me jump," she said when she turned and found him almost pressed up against her, forcing an awkward smile when his grey eyes met hers. She imagined his eyes might have once passed for dark blue several years ago, in the right light, back when his hair was dark blond and thick, not brown and thinning. She'd seen photos of younger Steve – he'd shown them to her proudly – from a time when he had abs and not the paunch of a beer belly.

The flirting began shortly after Sophie had started working there and had continued for the best part of a year, unbeknownst to her, of course. From her point of view, she had started work at the worst possible place with way too many people. Every day was a struggle just to get into the car.

But Steve had been so friendly. So understanding. He had told her that he appreciated that the job might be overwhelming at first but explained that they were a team. And that they were there to support each other. And Steve had been very supportive. A shift-change here. A day off there. Leeway on days when things had just been too much. But then there were those leaning-in intimacies, the hugging after accomplishments. And then, the kiss.

Sophie had no clue how to deal with something like that. She had frozen and simply gawked at him. He was, after all, her boss. He had been good to her. She was grateful and didn't want any trouble.

But that's exactly what she got when he leaned in to do it again a week or so later and Sophie instinctively ducked away. *That's not what I want,* she had spontaneously told him, while also trying to be tactful. He countered in a voice way too sultry to suit his masculine demeanour, *Then, what do you want?*

For you to be my boss and stop harassing me. The words were verbatim and discussed regularly with Doctor Krauss. They were the result of several frustrated weeks of dealing with her superior's unwanted advances. Krauss had insisted that she deal with it. That she had the ability to do so, she just needed to believe.

Believe?

All she believed was that she was already struggling with the role as it was and her boss's sexual overtures were doing nothing to make her feel better. Especially since she was painfully aware of the fact that Steve, beyond a monthly meeting with department heads, was the king of this small dominion. She knew that it wouldn't pay to make an enemy of him.

And yet that day, just as Krauss had foretold, she set the words that had been locked in the dark tower of her mind free, in the hope that they might deal with the situation in a professional way, as her therapist had advised.

It worked.

Or at least it did for a few months. Steve had been somewhat standoffish, sure, but she was fine with that since that's exactly how she would like to be, given half the chance.

But then he reverted to type and Sophie didn't know where to go from there. She needed the job not just for the money but for a healthier state of mind. And she couldn't tell her father at the time because he would have wanted to protect her, and that would have only made things worse.

Then, one night, out of the blue, Victoria asked what was troubling her. She told Sophie that she had noticed she hadn't been herself for a few weeks and was hoping it might be boyfriend (or girlfriend) problems, although Sophie was sure she knew full well that she was some kind of *asexual freak*. Sophie had shown no interest in anything remotely sexual in all the time they had known each other. *So, what else is it? Come on, spit it out,* Victoria had demanded with her trademark bluntness.

Reflexively, Sophie told her that everything was fine, but Victoria wasn't having any of that.

Sophie confessed.

Victoria patiently listened to her friend without interruption, and when Sophie broke down, she comforted her without judgment. It was unusual for her to stay so quietly supportive, but Sophie had very much appreciated it. It was what she needed at the time.

Only after she'd established that her friend had finished did Victoria speak. She told Sophie not to worry and that she would deal with it. When Sophie started to panic, Victoria had placed her hand over hers and asked, *Do you trust me?* When Sophie had rocked her head from side to side, Victoria dug her in the ribs. *Hey! I know I can be a bit hot-headed sometimes.*

Sometimes? Vic, any time I need a reminder of what you're capable of, all I need to do is think about Porky from that day we met at school.

I have no idea who this Vic is that you keep referring to, but she sounds like a mean bitch. My name is Victoria. Victoria Ainsworth. Her friend had given her a lopsided smile. She even relented and said that Sophie could be the only one to call her Vic, Vicki, Victoria, whatever she liked, but that she'd *rip the head off anybody else who tried.*

That was the moment that Sophie realised just how far her friend had truly come from the remedial she once knew. She admired her, for she had managed to completely turn her life around, not out of happenstance, but by dogged determination.

Porky on the other hand… Sophie had no idea what happened to him. He was probably flipping burgers somewhere.

He was a hefty oaf of a brat who, along with his posse of misfits, enjoyed nothing more than bullying new-girl Sophie. She had just moved to the area and rumours spread that she had gone crazy after her mother abandoned her and her father to go live with another man. She was so loopy, according to Porky's whispers in the playground, that she had to see a doctor on a regular basis. Otherwise, she'd go mental and start stabbing people.

Victoria, who had only just been transferred to the school that very day for reasons of her own, squared up to the boy and told him she'd tell everyone that he'd touched her inappropriately if he didn't piss off back to his pigsty. The boy had stood his ground and told her she wouldn't dare. But she held his gaze. After several seconds, he backed off and never bothered Sophie and her new friend again.

Now, over a decade later, Victoria had done it again. Sophie had no idea what exactly; Victoria refused to tell her. But she wouldn't have put it past her friend to threaten the man with visiting his home, his wife, his children.

Whatever Victoria did, the harassment stopped that same week. It was wonderful. It felt like she could breathe again.

The downside was that the man seemed to have changed. If his personality was charming and upbeat before, now it was dour and cynical. Something, Doctor Krauss explained, that was likely a side effect of being called out. He was ashamed.

Sophie shuddered.

"Are you sure you're okay?" Steve asked with peculiar concern as he leaned closer, forcing Sophie to back up against her locker.

"Yes, I'm fine. Why?"

"Well, it's just that from where I was sittin', Soph, it didn't look like you were fine," Steve said seriously. It was out with any charm and in with the severity of a discontented supervisor as those grey eyes searched hers, making her squirm inside.

"Yes, from where you were *sitting*, Steve," Sophie managed, suppressing a rising tide of anxiety.

"What's that supposed to mean?" he asked, clicking his shoulders back and thrusting his hands into his pockets.

"Nothing in particular. Just that from here, you can't tell everything that's going on out there. You know that."

"Well, that's why I rely on you lot, the CCTV, the customers, and others to keep me informed. Just like they did today."

Sophie squinted at him.

"What happened down at 5 today, Soph?"

"Well, you tell me, Steve," she said, feeling oddly bullish. "Didn't the footage show you? They were going to eat that woman alive."

"Yeah, what else is new? But that's why we have procedures. You know, rules of engagement, Soph. But you didn't handle it that way though, did you?"

"It's an airport, Steve. Not a war film. Things were getting out of hand, and I had to act."

"Out of hand, yeah. Things are always getting out of hand. People are always gettin' hot and bothered. You know this. It's what you've been trained for."

Sophie scoffed and then ducked around him. She could feel the heat of his body and it was making her skin crawl.

"What? What's that supposed to mean?" he asked, turning to her once more.

"Nothing."

"No, go on, say it."

"Nothing. It doesn't matter."

He watched her for the longest time, and she thought it was over, but then he said, "Your job isn't to make things worse, it's to diffuse situations and make sure all passengers have the best experience when usin' this airport. Now, I know you've just suffered a loss and I'm sorry for that, but, as a responsible supervisor, I did ask you if you were ready to come back to work right after your dad's funeral and you insisted—"

"Is that what you think I did down there?" she interrupted.

"What?"

"Is that what you think I did? Made things worse?"

"You tell me. I've already heard everybody else's version of what happened."

"Things were getting out of hand. I had to act. I had to be assertive," she said, standing straight as if to convince herself.

"Well, unless they've changed the bloody manual without tellin' me, last time I looked it didn't say being assertive meant shoutin' and threatenin' already irate passengers."

"I didn't shou—"

"No, you just threatened to have him escorted off the premises. Not once but twice. You even got your little sidekick in on the act. Right after I told you... right after I *specifically* told you I didn't want security involved."

"They were getting belligerent. They reduced that woman to

tears. One of them even smacked her over the head. What was I supposed to do?"

"Your job!" he yelled. The sound was so loud it bounced off the metal cabinet and rang back, making her flinch. "I want you to do your fucking job," he added with a growl, a flash of those eyes and the point of a spindly finger as he invaded her space once more.

It took Sophie a few seconds to recover from the initial shock of his outburst but eventually she came back. "I did my job," she said, gulping despite the sandpaper of her throat. Her body trembled. *No. Keep it together. Keep it together. Don't let him see you like this.*

"Well, if you think that was doing your job then maybe you 'ave come back sooner than you should've."

She glared at him, incredulous for a few seconds, as a knot tied in her throat. She blinked away the sheen that was forming over her eyes. "Is that what they're saying about me?"

He didn't respond. He didn't need to. Worse, by the way his jaw was flexing, she could tell he had more he could say about it but was choosing not to.

"Right," she said eventually. "Well, if there isn't anything else, I'm ready to get back out there and—"

"No. That won't be necessary."

"What?" She took in a ragged breath.

"I've already spoken to Katy. She is going to take over for the rest of the day."

"But Steve, I—"

"No ifs or buts," he said flatly. He took a step away from her, folding his hands over his chest. "That's my decision. Go home. Grieve your dad or whatever you need to do, and I'll have a think about where we go from here."

"Steve, please. I need this job."

"Well, you should 'ave thought about that, shouldn't you?"

"What do you mean?"

"You know what I mean."

"Steve—"

"I'm done talking about it, Soph. I suggest we leave it there for now."

She was about to say something else but thought better of it. Instead, she moved to leave but didn't get far because he stepped in front of her once more, the slits of his grey eyes boring holes into her. And that's when she was reminded. *Porky.* He reminded her of Porky. And he was stepping closer to her now, breath hot and coffee-laden, to scrutinize her face some more before eventually breathing, "I'm gonna need an official report from you about what happened. For the file. And I'll be interviewing Katy about it too."

She forced a shrug and held her head up just as her father had taught her. She attempted to swallow the lump in her throat once more before croaking, "You do whatever you think you have to do."

As she started to leave again, her supervisor raised his voice and spoke after her, "Oh, and Sophie… You should consider this an official verbal warning. I'll be following up with written confirmation in due course. You behave anything like that again and you're out, do you understand? We're in the business of 'elping people. If you can't do that then you may as well not be here."

She paused for a few beats. Then, lips trembling, she eventually managed to speak. "Is that everything?"

He took his time, then said, "Yeah. That's all for now. You're dismissed."

She hurried out of the room, down the escalator, across the perpetual bustle of the concourse, and out to her car.

7

FOR SALE

TUESDAY. EARLY EVENING.

Having spent most of the day imprisoned behind a wall of blusterous rain clouds, a recently freed sun tried its best to irradiate the land with warmth and colour, but its rays waned against the imminent onset of a wintry dusk.

Sophie pulled the car door shut, turned up the heating and took a few moments to recover from her recent encounter. She lifted her hands and looked at them. They were shaking. She had no idea if it was due to the cold or the anger that was bubbling through her like hot tar.

The anger was directed at herself, of course, for all the ways she could have dealt with Steve but had been unable to. On the other hand, the fact that she hadn't dissolved into floods of tears was perhaps an achievement in itself.

Nonetheless, the confrontation had depleted what little energy she had left, and she allowed herself to collapse over the steering wheel, tepid air hissing angrily out of the vents as if it too was frustrated by her performance.

It was then, as she leaned over, breaths coming thick and fast once more, that she noticed them. They were everywhere, as far as the eye could see.

People. Travellers. Some in vehicles, others loitering in the middle of the car park, many on wet grass verges. All were looking skywards like worshippers of an ancient god.

Sophie followed their gaze. There it was. Burning a light shade of blue in the prelude to darkness, its long tail of light streaking behind it.

The comet.

The workday had been so eventful she had completely forgotten about that thing. For others it seemed it was all they could think about; they gawked at it as if it really was the Second Coming.

But Sophie wasn't enraptured by the comet. In fact, there was something about it that gave her the creeps. It didn't even look real. It was frozen there, seemingly in the same spot, as if it were a matte painting propped against the sky and used like a movie backdrop. Maybe it was. Maybe everything that had happened over the past 24 hours was just some giant publicity stunt or manufactured by one of her hideous dreams.

But she knew this was more than a dream. The hollow in her chest reminded her of that as she shifted into gear and drove around the statues formally known as humans to get out of the car park.

On the motorway it was more of the same. Traffic was slow, but, for once, it wasn't because drivers were rubbernecking for a glimpse of an accident; instead, they were gawping at the strange celestial body, looking down on them from its perch high above.

She wanted to thump on the car horn, to yell at them, to tell them to pay attention to the road. This was exactly the kind of thing that caused accidents. The kind of thing that cost people their lives. But she knew it'd be pointless. The lemmings were captivated.

No. What she needed to focus on right now was getting home. *To what?*

The home she once knew no longer existed. She was alone now; the finality of that twisted in her gut like a rabid parasite, feeding off the little energy she had left.

Her phone beeped again, reminding her that Doctor Krauss had left a message. She wasn't in the mood for his emotionless inquisition, despite Victoria's insistence that *this may well be the one time when you're most likely to get your money's worth out of the old fart. You should lean on him more. He can help you transition.*

Transition? She didn't want to bloody transition. She wanted her father back!

Time heals all.

Not this. I'll never get over this. Just like I'll never truly get over what happened that night all those years ago.

What you thought happened, Sophie.

Doctor Krauss' cynicism echoed in her head, and she felt a flare of frustration, her anger as sudden and hot these days as sparking fire. She wondered for a split second – even though it made her feel disloyal, ungrateful – if Doctor Krauss had ever been of any help. After all, she had been seeing him all these years and yet every day was still a bloody struggle. She was tired. Sick of it. Sick of trying.

She sighed. Of course the man had helped. She was just angry after her encounter with Steve and projecting it towards someone who had been nothing but supportive all these years. He had helped her through a lot. No, this wasn't about Krauss. This was about the fact her mother had abandoned them, and she was unable to forgive her for it.

The elongated shadow talons of the trees that lined Meadow Lane reached for the car as Sophie pulled into her street. She was telling herself that she was going to need to make some changes to her whole outlook on life if she was going to make it through this. Bad things had happened, of course. But they happen to everyone. And, as difficult as it was going to be, she was going to need to try to focus on some of the more positive aspects of things, such as—

What the hell?

There was a stranger standing on her lawn. She swung the car onto the driveway, killed the engine, and stepped out.

"Um, hello? Excuse me!" she shouted, demanding the person's attention before she'd even reached him. "What are you doing?"

The skinny young man looked about the same age as her. He had brown hair, immaculately styled forward, with a flick frozen by a slick of hair product that had dried and frosted white and he was wearing a grey suit and a blue tie with brown shoes. It was an ensemble that Sophie knew offended Victoria for some reason.

He turned to her. He had a large wooden sign in one hand and a mallet in the other. "Oh, 'allo. I'm just here to get the sign up," he said.

"Sign? What sign? What are you talking about?"

He turned and showed her what he was holding. The sign was glossy chocolate brown with white lettering that read *BROWNS & CO Property Management.* Underneath, in a big bold font, were the words: FOR SALE.

Sophie forced a laugh. "I'm sorry, but you obviously have the wrong address. This is my father... my home. I live here. I've lived here most of my life. This house isn't for sale."

The young man frowned. "Nah, I don't think it's the wrong address. I checked it twice. You see, we're required to do that, you know, so that we don't make those kinds of mistakes. This is number ten, Meadow Lane, right?"

Sophie paused then said, "Um… yes, it is, but your agency obviously has the wrong information."

"Nah, that's the number that's on the listing." The young man cradled the sign in the crook of his right arm and then reached into the inside pocket of his jacket. He shook out a folded piece of paper. "Yeah, look here, see? Number ten, Meadow Lane."

Sophie suppressed a flare of irritation and calmed herself with a sigh. "Look, I don't care what your paperwork says. There's obviously been a mistake. My father owns this house and he… he died recently, so he couldn't have possibly put the house on the market."

The young man pulled an exaggerated expression of confusion which made her want to slap his face. "Says here that the property wasn't listed by tenants but by the company that owns it."

"What?"

"Yeah, here," he waggled the piece of paper at her.

Sophie had had enough. She touched her hair with both hands as if by smoothing it, she could tame the angry wild beast she felt ready to climb out from inside her. "Look, you know what, just get off my lawn."

"Well, according to this, miss, it ain't your lawn and you see, I've got a job to do. My bonus depends on how many of these I put up in a day and, well, not being funny or anyfin', but you're holding me up."

There was a rumble in Sophie's stomach. At first, she thought it was anger, but she soon realised it was something else as it grew, radiating through the rest of her body like a shockwave. She stepped forward, eyes flashing with rage. "Now listen," she seethed. "I don't give a shit how you get paid. I'm telling you, you've got the wrong house—"

"And I'm telling you, I haven't."

That was it. It was like being back in the schoolground again and Sophie Cooper wasn't having any of it. She lunged forward and grabbed the sign, but the interloping young man refused to let go and pulled it back towards him. It only made her even more determined, and thus a tug of war began.

"Get off my lawn!"

"Miss!"

"Get off!"

"No! You get off! And let me do my job."

Sophie pulled and growled through gritted teeth, but he wasn't yielding. "No... get off my property."

"It isn't your property!

"Get off!"

"No!"

"Let go!"

"NO!"

"Let go!"

"GET OFF, YOU NUTTER!" The young man shoved her backward with all his strength, sending her sprawling onto the wet grass in a crumpled heap.

"OI!" someone yelled from the other side of the street. The estate agent looked over to see a man in shorts and trainers sprinting towards them, then looked back to Sophie. She was grimacing as she held her hand to an ache in her lower back. He looked at the man again and swallowed hard.

"What's going on here?" Christopher Darrington demanded, breathlessly, as he took in the would-be sign erector and Sophie on the grass, now rubbing her arm. He hurried over and knelt beside her. "Are you okay?"

Sophie looked up into those blue eyes. His beard had been trimmed and what appeared to be concern was etched on his sweaty but handsome face. Oh God. She could smell him, pheromones fluttering off his body like a flock of butterflies taking flight.

Really? That's what you focus on now?

She pulled herself together. "I'm fine. Just wounded pride," she said, frowning as she looked around. The couple across the street at number 11 were unloading their baby and its car seat from their vehicle, making sure to have a good look at all the commotion while they did so. Next door, the Zhangs watched shamelessly from the safety of their lawn while elsewhere curtains twitched.

"Here, take my hand," Chris offered, holding it out. Sophie looked at it as if it were a red-hot poker. "Come on, it isn't a marriage proposal," he added with a smile.

Reluctantly, she took his hand. He hauled her to her feet effortlessly.

"Look, miss, I'm sorry about that," the young man began, first looking at her and then at Chris. His stance seemed to have softened now that the other guy had arrived. Chris was at least a few inches taller and, by the look of him, kept himself in great shape. "I'm just trying to do my job."

"I've already told you. You've got the wrong house," Sophie repeated with a grimace, plucking wet grass from her elbow, and then rubbing it.

"But—"

Chris stepped forward. "Mate, I think she's made herself clear, now why don't you just do one, yeah?" he said. He was serious, those blue eyes no longer soft and round but narrow and stern.

The apprentice – that's how Sophie saw him now, the male equivalent of Katy – hesitated for a few seconds and then shrugged. "Whatever, dude. If it isn't me, it's just going to be someone else," he said.

"Whatever, *dude*," Chris echoed, mocking the young man, who threw him a scowl, gathered his sign and himself, then trudged off to his car. After dumping the sign and mallet in the back of his Ford Fiesta, he climbed into the driver's seat and started the engine, glaring at them both as he drove off.

Once the car had disappeared down the street, Chris turned to the nosey neighbours. "That's all, folks!" he shouted. With slow reluctance, the onlookers returned to their own homes.

"Are you sure you're okay?" he asked.

"I'm fine," Sophie said, gingerly straightening up.

"What was all that about?" Chris asked, casually nodding at the space where the young man had stood.

"I don't know. Some stupid mix up at the estate agent's," Sophie responded, thoughtfully.

"Sure you don't need a lift to A&E or something?"

"I'm fine. Besides, don't you have some bimbo waiting for you over there?" She nodded at the house across the road.

Chris chuckled and shook his head. "You really do have a low opinion of me, don't you?"

"I don't even know you."

"Exactly," he said with a smile. "Okay, well, I'm glad you're okay. Have a good evening, Sophie." With that, he turned and walked away.

It took the guilt a few seconds to make its presence felt, aided by the last puppyish look Chris had given her as he turned away. He seemed to have mastered it, thanks to those big eyes of his. But she pushed the lingering image of them aside and instead turned towards the house.

Something was different. Over the years she had come to love her new home. The redbrick, four-bedroom detached property featured giant Georgian windows on both sides of an arched doorway, with wrinkles made of rambling roses and a full head of ivy that reminded her of one of those smiling Green Man heads.

But not today. Today, the windows looked as if they were scowling. The house looked cold. Unwelcoming. Dead. Just like her father.

She turned. "Chris?"

Her neighbour, who was already off the lawn and back on the pavement, turned to her. He must have sensed her reluctance. "Would you like me to see you safely inside?" His words were soft. Caring.

Sophie glanced up and down the street. Dusk was already pushing at twilight. It would soon be dark. Most of her neighbours appeared to have already made it home for the night. There were cars on driveways. Lights burning amber behind blinds and curtains. All only accentuated her sense of isolation, of loneliness. She couldn't imagine spending the night alone. What if the lights went out again?

She gazed at the man and was about to accept his offer when a high-pitched call from a girl across the street sliced through the moment.

"Chris!"

Sophie turned to see a ponytailed blonde she did not recognise jog out of the house on the opposite side of the street. She was dressed in an all-in-one spandex body suit and trainers and was smiling and waving.

Sophie's gaze turned into a glare. "No thanks," she said.

"Are you sure?"

"Positive."

Chris hesitated then shrugged before turning to the blonde and jogging over to her. They chuckled at something together then jogged away.

"Enjoy your run," Sophie said cynically before fishing her keys from her bag and turning to face the house once more.

8

EXISTENTIALISM

WEDNESDAY. EARLY MORNING.

"Sophie, are you with me?"

Sophie turned from the window and looked at her therapist.

"Before we start," Doctor Krauss continued, "may I ask if you would like me to fetch you another seat?"

She smiled. "No. This one's perfectly fine. Thank you. Happy to lift my feet." Oddly, this time, she was grateful to be able to retreat into the depths of the sofa. She felt more secure, more protected than she imagined she would if she were perched on the edge. Once she had pulled her legs up and found her usual spot, she put a smile on her face and asked, "Okay, where would you like to start?"

Had she been in a better headspace, she'd have known better

than to ask this man, who appeared to have the ability to read her mind, such a leading question.

"Wherever you would like, Sophie. You called me, remember? You asked for this emergency meeting. Why don't we start with whatever is troubling you?" the doctor said, putting down his notepad.

Sophie scoffed and made a show of looking at her watch. "Oh, I don't think we have enough time for that," she joked. Feeling the doctor's scrutinizing gaze, she continued. "Yes, so anyway, I really appreciate you seeing me." She wrung her fingers and looked around the room as if seeing it for the first time, scanning the bookcase as if that was where she would find her words.

Eventually she managed to go on. "It feels like it's all falling apart. Like life as I know it is unravelling. Like I'm losing control."

"Okay, Sophie. Can you elaborate for me? What do you mean by unravelling, exactly?"

She shook her head as she attempted to find the best way to explain it. "I don't know. It just seems that ever since I left here yesterday, things have been going from bad to worse."

"I'm sorry, Sophie, I'm still not following. Is this to do with what you said on the phone? About the house?"

"Yes. No. I mean yes. I mean, that's just part of it."

"Okay. Well, why don't we start with that? It must have been quite a shock for you to come home and find that man on your lawn."

"It was more than that."

"Tell me."

"It made me feel really anxious, you know? It wasn't just about the house, although the thought of someone trying to sell it from right under me is bad enough, but it just felt so definitive. Like someone was trying to put on some kind of yard sale over my father's corpse. It felt personal. Really personal. So personal that

I could have hurt that man," she added through clenched teeth while making claws of her hands.

"Hurt him? You mean physically?"

"Yes, I mean physically. As it turns out, he hurt me."

"He assaulted you?" the doctor asked quickly, his alarm clear in his voice.

"No. Not exactly. There was a bit of a tussle with the sign he was trying to put up and I ended up on my backside in the wet grass, but then Chris came over and… well, he dealt with him."

"Chris?" There was an almost imperceptible smile on the doctor's lips, like he had noticed how the mere mention of the man's name softened the way Sophie mouthed her words.

But she noticed his subtle glee. "Oh no. Don't start."

The doctor shrugged. "I didn't say anything."

"I know that look. Like a dog with a new bone."

The doctor held up his hands, surrendering. "I'm just assuming that you were *happy* that he came to your aid."

"Well, yes, at the time I was. Of course."

"And that's it?"

"That's it."

"You didn't feel anything else?"

"*No.*"

The doctor held up his hands again. Traffic rumbled on the street outside.

"Besides, he already had some bimbo on standby."

"And that upset you?"

"No. It didn't upset me. That's just how he is," she said. Then she refocussed on the therapist's expression and rolled her eyes.

"I'm not saying anything," the man protested. He shuffled in his seat. "I'm just waiting, Sophie."

"Waiting? Waiting for what?"

"For you to tell me the real reason why you wanted to see me today."

"What, some weirdo trying to sell my house from under me not dramatic enough?" she asked, mirroring the doctor's action as she resettled onto the sofa, avoiding eye contact with his truth-detecting gaze. Now that she was here, sitting in front of him in the cold light of day, she felt like she was being ridiculously overdramatic and was contemplating returning to the subject of Chris just to avoid discussing what she really came to talk about.

The doctor didn't help. He just waited.

"Do you know that someone actually died in that accident outside of here yesterday?" she asked bluntly.

The doctor nodded grimly. "Yes, I do. I heard it on the news. It's very sad."

"Isn't it horrible?"

"It is," the doctor agreed.

"No, I mean fate."

"Fate?"

"Yes. I mean, we don't know, do we? We have no clue. No idea what fate has in store for us. Don't you think that's terrifying?"

"The unknown?"

"Yes. I mean, that woman woke up in the morning, probably got ready for work, went through all her usual routines, kissed her family, and then climbed behind the steering wheel without the foggiest idea that she was drawing her last breaths before dying in that car, alone."

"Does that scare you?"

"Dying?"

"Dying alone."

Sophie nodded. "Terrifies me."

"Is it because you empathise with that woman, with what happened to her?"

"Empathise?"

"On some level, maybe? Given what happened to your

father?"

Sophie felt something twist in her empty belly as she remembered the morning of the day it had happened.

Her father had made her birthday pancakes and asked her to sit down and enjoy them with him, but she was already running late for work, and she didn't want to have to get into it with Steve. Besides, they already had plans for dinner together that evening. She'd left after giving her father a peck on the cheek. That was the last time she saw him alive.

"I didn't say that," she responded flatly, suddenly irritated with the doctor for raking up the memory.

"But were you thinking it? Unconsciously, perhaps?"

Sophie shook her head. "No. I don't think so. I don't think I became aware of it until you so very kindly brought it up just now," she said, switching the cross of her legs.

The doctor nodded. "Right. So, that wasn't the point you were trying to make?"

"No, it wasn't. What I was trying to get at was how scary it is to think that our life, our very short time on this earth, has already been predetermined by whatever cosmic shitty force is responsible for this stuff. You know, from the moment we're born all the way through to the end, but none of us know anything about it."

The doctor smiled. "Ah, existential philosophy. So that's why you came to see me today. I should warn you, I can hold my own in such debates."

Sophie smiled. "God, no thanks. Especially at this time of the morning," she sighed. "I was just wondering. I mean, you must have an opinion."

"Do I believe in fate? Happenstance? Serendipity? I'm a doctor, Sophie. I'm trained to believe in facts. Do I believe in fate? Sure, but there's no fate other than the one we make. In a nutshell, our actions invoke consequences, and those consequences ultimately shape our destiny. For example, you collect all these wonderful images of cities from around the world and yet you've visited none. Why do you think that is?"

She thought about it but could only shrug.

"Could it be that you are preparing, readying yourself for a journey you plan to take later in life perhaps?"

Sophie shrugged again. Truth is, she didn't know. She hadn't really thought about it. It just felt like a hobby to her.

A siren blared beyond the window and faded into the distance. Sophie turned as if the emergency services were coming for her.

"I'm seeing things again," she blurted, without emotion and without making eye contact with the man in front of her.

The doctor sat forward. "Seeing things?"

"Yes. At the house the other night. I think I saw something."

The doctor cocked his head. "Something?"

"I think it was Dad. And I think he was also in the backseat of my car the other day. My friend's five-year-old son, Damon, I told you about him. He saw it first."

"A five-year-old boy saw someone in the backseat of your car?"

"Oh no, don't do that."

"Do what?"

"You know what you're doing. You're trying to discredit what I'm saying."

"Sophie, you know that is not how I work. I'm just trying to make sure I've understood you. What I think I heard is that you *think* you saw someone sitting in the backseat of your car. And that you believe it was, what, the *spirit* of your dead father? And that your witness to this apparition was a five-year-old boy?"

Sophie nodded and then looked up to meet the doctor's gaze. "I saw him at the house, standing by my bed. And I think Damon saw him in the backseat of my car, sitting behind me."

"All right. What happened?"

"What do you mean, what happened?"

"After you saw him. And I don't mean to sound flippant, but

did you speak to him? Did he come home with you?"

"No, of course he didn't. You know he didn't."

"Again, Sophie. I'm just trying to understand what you are telling me."

Rain rapped at the window as if it was suddenly interested in the conversation. It had grown dark inside the doctor's office without either of them noticing until the lamplight took over the illumination of the space.

The doctor shifted in his chair. "Sophie, would it surprise you to learn that you're not the only person this week to tell me that they've been *seeing things*?" He lifted his fingers and wrapped the words in a pair of air quotes. Sophie looked at him and he nodded. "It's true. And I have to tell you that it isn't entirely surprising. The arrival of the comet," he nodded at the window, "has left a lot of people in altered states of mind, experiencing unusual thought patterns, very much the same as you are experiencing right now. Especially with all this endless talk of conspiracy theories and satanic prophesies. This unknown, like the dark, can be terrifying for a lot of people, so they look for answers, for meaning, anywhere they can find it."

"So, my friend's son is so worried about the comet, he's seeing my dead father in the backseat of my car?"

"No. You believe it was your dead father. He just saw something. Was he specific about what he saw?"

"He just asked who was sitting behind me."

"So, he was in the car with you?"

"No. We were video chatting." Sophie rolled her eyes as the doctor lifted his eyebrows. "Yes, I know what you're thinking. I told myself the same thing. But I can't shake this feeling that he was there for a reason, you know—"

"To warn you of some kind of impending doom?"

Sophie cocked her head. It was if the man had read her mind. "Well, maybe."

"Like the fire in the sky?" the doctor asked with another lift of the eyebrows. Sophie allowed her shoulders to drop and sank back in her seat. "I'm sorry, Sophie, but you can see the pattern, can't you? Your mother leaving…"

"This has nothing to do with that."

"Oh, I think it has everything to do with that."

"You know, in all these years, you still haven't managed to explain why a woman would abandon her child and her husband just like that, with no note, no nothing, never to be heard of again," she said bitterly.

"Because I didn't treat your mother, Sophie. I am treating you and what *you* believe really happened to her is all I care about."

"I know what I saw."

"You mean like you know who was sitting in the backseat of your car? We have discussed this, Sophie, haven't we? Many times. We've talked about how you rationalised your mother's abandonment as an abduction for the very reason you've just restated; you find it difficult to understand, to process, how any mother, not least your own, would wilfully abandon her child as she did. The very thought of that is hideous, grotesque to you. That's why you manifested her actions as an ugly impish demon. A demon that appeared in the dead of night and abducted her.

"We see what we want to see, and we seek to rationalise the unknown because, if we don't, it would mean we'd have to face our fear of it. So, we create ghosts and ghouls like psychological effigies because we can then validate our reactions to these terrifying things over which we have no control."

Sophie could feel the tears welling in her eyes once more. He was right. They had been here many times over the years. The conversation was as familiar as it was painful.

The rain had turned to sleet and was charging at the window. Traffic hissed and rumbled beyond the glass.

"At least we can't see that thing on days like today," she said, looking at the dark sky.

The doctor smiled. "No. We can't."

There was a long pause before Sophie eventually asked, "What's happening to me, Doctor Krauss? I mean, I seemed to be getting my crap together, but at the same time, everything else seems to be falling apart."

"What's happening to you, Sophie, is that you're underestimating just how fragile you are right now. You've been working so hard at being strong, at going out and facing your fears, that you're not allowing yourself to internalise your loss, and this is now manifesting in other ways."

"I don't think the meds are working. Maybe we should look at something else."

"Have you been experiencing side effects?"

"You mean besides my nightmares and seeing what you said isn't there?" she threw back.

"I'm talking about physical side effects, Sophie."

"Yes. My dreams are back."

"You mean the stranger? The man you're going to marry?" He spoke the last bit of that sentence with a smile that was lost on Sophie.

"Yes, but it's different now. It's moved on."

"Tell me."

"No."

The doctor cocked his head.

"Because it isn't just that," she added. "There are other dreams, dreams about my father."

"Okay. Let's talk about those."

"No. I don't want to talk about them," she said irritably.

"Why not?"

"Because you'll just try to bloody rationalise them too!" she retorted. "Like you always do! I don't want another shitty dream analysis. I just want to know what the fuck is happening to me!"

The lightbulb flickered, whined, and died, sinking the room into a gloom so dark it felt as if the day had given up and already surrendered to night. The sleet rapped on the window, demanding entry. They both looked at the dead lamp, as if attempting to bring it back to life by the power of telepathy.

Several seconds later, Sophie turned to the doctor. "I'm so sorry, Doctor Krauss. But this is exactly my point. I don't know what's wrong with me."

The doctor held up his hand and shook his head. "No apologies, Sophie."

"It's just as I explained last time. I feel like something's off. I don't feel like I'm myself anymore. It's like I'm becoming more sensitive to the world around me. Things I didn't seem to care about or was impervious to now seem to affect me more, in both good and bad ways." She said the last bit timidly, as if she were a child once more ashamed for saying a bad word.

That wasn't too far from the truth. Sophie rarely swore. Her father hadn't approved of her using bad language, which is one of the reasons why he often hadn't liked the way Victoria spoke around her, to the point where even she had learned to modify her language when visiting.

But, ever since his death… well, it just didn't seem that important anymore.

"Okay," the doctor said, offering a smile, "if I promise not to rationalise your dreams, will you describe them to me?"

9

THE CROWS

WEDNESDAY MORNING

"*Astronomers have trained powerful listening devices on the comet, formerly classified as an asteroid from a distant solar system, in the hope of picking up… well, we don't know what exactly. Darren has the details… Darren.*"

It was all anybody could talk about.

Sophie adjusted the rear-view mirror for the second time since climbing behind the steering wheel and shook her head slowly at her reflection. She was aware of the fact that she too was becoming curious now. What if the conspiracy theorists were right? What if that thing up in the sky was a sign? *What if it really signalled the end of days? The extinction of humanity and the rise of the devil's spawn or worse, the reincarnation of the Prince of Darkness himself?*

She laughed out loud. Things had certainly felt that way lately.

Anything goes. At least that appeared to be the new policy for all the media outlets. No matter the 'expert's' denomination, if the discourse involved some kind of cataclysmic event or omen of any kind, they were given their fifteen minutes of fame.

It was all ridiculous, of course. Or at least some of it was. The rest, well… it did give her pause for thought. *It* had, after all, appeared during one of the worst chapters of her life and had prompted her to question her own beliefs. Something she'd never done before.

Her parents hadn't raised her to be religious. Far from it. Sophie had no memory of ever attending church, not even the occasional midnight mass. Nothing. And they certainly never discussed religion, which was curious because, as a family, they did talk a lot. Yet religion had never been raised as a topic for discussion.

Did she believe? She wasn't sure, but she didn't think so. For her to even open her mind to the possibility of believing, she would need a clear and unequivocal response to that age-old existential question that had been asked of believers all over: *If your God truly exists, then why is there so much suffering?*

Never before had that question held so much meaning for her. After all, Alan Cooper wasn't a bad person. He worked hard and provided for his family. He never made her – or, as far as she knew, her mother – feel unloved. He was a good person.

So why?

She sighed. This was precisely why she needed to avoid social media, TV, and the radio from now on; the onslaught of debate about the comet from the perspectives of science, mysticism, Catholicism, and blah blah blah was relentless.

"…Anthropocene may be the age of humans, but that isn't necessarily a good thing. The changes that we're making are causing many a species to become extinct one hundred times faster than if we didn't exist. Not one or two, but one hundred times faster. Humans

have been around for more than 200,000 years. Our time has finally come."

"So, you truly believe that this comet is actually a Life Extinction Event?"

"Absolutely."

"But what are you basing that on? The scientific community, the data, the evidence all shows that this comet is going to miss the Earth or, worst case, burn up in our atmosphere."

"With all due respect, Alicia, that's exactly what they would want you and your listeners to believe."

"You see, it's precisely these kinds of comments that have had many professionals dub you—and I'm quoting just a few here—a quack, a scaremonger. They say that you're hellbent on causing unnecessary panic. What do you have to say to them?"

"Well, we'll soon find out who's right, won't we?"

Sophie shut the radio off, grabbed her bag and stepped out of the car. She was greeted by a bitterly cold wind that pulled at her hair and nipped at her face.

The weather had changed again, transforming the sky into inverted black and grey mountains, seemingly low enough to touch. If the radio was to be believed, during its usual interlude from the debates about that thing in the sky, there was the chance of snow.

The thought of this brought her some comfort. She liked snow. There was something about its virginal muting qualities that appealed to her. As a child, she'd go on long walks with her father that would often culminate in a trip to the park to sleigh down the hill on his old yoga mat, an impulse buy during one of his hastily abandoned health kicks. The snow activity often left them in a tangle of arms, legs, and giggles, which they'd slowly recover from by lying back and languidly creating snow angels.

Not anymore.

Cawing drew her attention to the perimeter fence. A murder

of crows watched with peculiar interest, as if they didn't see thousands of humans arrive and depart from the place daily. Their marbled black eyes swivelled as they watched her, just as they had that day at the funeral.

A shiver ran through her which she attributed to the freeze. Those clouds were certainly spectacular enough to suggest that the world was entering a new ice age. Or perhaps it was all the apocalyptic chatter she'd just listened to on the radio, the annoyance of it still clinging to her like an itchy woollen jumper.

A loud irate horn startled her, and she snapped her head around to see the bloodred bonnet of a Jaguar pulling to a sudden stop just inches away from her thigh. The driver, a lady who took power dressing way too seriously, was shaking her head disapprovingly.

Sophie hurried out of the car's path, towards the main airport entrance and the shelter of the giant pavilion, dodging people, their wheelie suitcases, and their unruly children as she went.

She was late. Again. Nearly thirty minutes. "Shit!" She cringed at the thought of Steve pulling her to one side with a roll of those raisin-sized eyes for one of his speeches, full of the subtext that, if she hadn't blabbed to her friend, life would be much easier for her. Anybody listening probably wouldn't even notice that he was making the point. But he would be. That's all he ever did. And the thought of losing her job and being confined to the haunted house of her memories, all alone, terrified her.

"Oh, I'm sorry!" Sophie said, as she collided with what she thought was a person but soon realised was a workman's ladder, right in front of the main entrance.

She looked up it to see a pair of legs clad in blue overalls. "Oh, um, excuse me…" she called out.

"Yes, love?" the man said casually, without looking her way.

"What are you doing?"

"Faulty sensor, love. Door keeps locking."

"I appreciate that, but you're not supposed to be doing maintenance at this time of the day though, are you?"

Now, the man froze and looked down with a wearied expression. "If the Guvnor says I've got to deal with the faulty door, love, I deal with the faulty door. I just go where I'm told. If you've got a problem with that, you need to talk to someone above my pay grade." The man returned his eyes to his work.

Sophie looked around. People streamed in and out of the door when it worked, but otherwise would congregate in front of it with exasperated expressions, glancing at their watches, rather than move to another entrance.

"Where's your spotter? Aren't you supposed to have a spotter with you?" Sophie called up to the ladder once more.

"Ain't no one available, love," was the man's disinterested reply.

The crowd was growing now. The murmur of their voices rapidly rose to a loud murmur before a screech sliced through the noise. Startled, Sophie turned around to see black wings as they evaded the wheels of a car.

"Shit!"

A jolt of anxiety shocked her heart into an accelerated patter.

It's okay. You're all right. Focus. Do your job. Focus on them, not on you. On them and not on you.

She took a couple of deep breaths and then addressed the crowd. "Excuse me! Excuse me!" she yelled. It had little effect, so she took the direct approach and raised her voice. "GO AROUND! THIS DOOR IS OUT OF ORDER! PLEASE GO AROUND TO THE OTHER DOORS! GO AROUND TO THE OTHER SET OF DOORS! THANK YOU!"

It cost her a few more minutes that she didn't have and the scrape of a sore throat, but the lemmings finally got the message and began to dissipate. Ironically, when there were only a few stragglers left, the door magically opened.

Sophie looked up the ladder once more. The workman shrugged. She opened her mouth to speak, but she didn't have the time and instead hurried inside where she had barely entered the building before she was intercepted by a panic-stricken Katy. "Sophie! Sophie! Oh, thank God you're 'ere."

"Morning, Katy."

"Oh yeah, morning. Listen, I've gotta problem with—"

"What's going on?" Sophie interrupted. She could hear loud voices coming from one of the airline desks, fifty or so feet away.

"That's what I'm tryin' to tell ya. Yesterday, I had to deal with some bloke who was denied boarding because he'd 'ad a skinful. He was rebooked for this morning. But what did he decide to do? He decided to celebrate being left behind by 'aving another skinful, which means the airline is denying him boarding again. They're saying they won't have 'im on any of the morning flights, that he's gonna have to wait until this afternoon, and now he's kickin' off."

"Right. Sounds like you're dealing with it," Sophie said.

"Yeah, I did, I was, I am, but I was on my own, Soph," the girl whined.

"I know, but that's how you learn, Katy. If you always have someone with you, you're never going to learn how to deal with things yourself," Sophie said, looking across at the commotion and the audience it was gathering.

"Yeah, I know. But Steve said you're supposed to supervise, but you can't do that if you're late for work all the time, now, can ya?"

Sophie turned to the girl. That's when she saw it. The rabbit-in-the-headlights innocence was gone. Instead, she was holding Sophie's gaze. The whippersnapper appeared to have found some confidence, and that could only have come from one place.

I'm countin' on you to keep an eye on her. Soph isn't herself right now. She's unreliable.

She could hear Steve's voice as if she had been present at the meeting. It would have been an intimate one, with just the two of them squeezed against the lockers no doubt, with Katy and her defenceless little girl routine as she batted those fake eyelashes, and Steve salivating in his detestable lasciviousness.

Oddly, the debate in Sophie's head was over much sooner that it normally would be. She decided against dignifying the little girl's jibe with a response but instead met her gaze with a smile. "What's the passenger's name?"

"Mr Alexa... Alexakis. Something like that," Katy said.

"Right," Sophie said. She considered reminding her of the importance of establishing the correct pronunciation of the traveller's name to facilitate a more positive discourse, but she couldn't be bothered, and wasn't sure Katy was capable of taking it in anyway. "Okay. I'm assuming he's over there?"

"Yeah. At the ticket counter."

The man's chosen airline had the biggest presence at the airport, gained by being one of the first to move in when it was first built. It meant they had a kiosk in an enviable position in the main concourse, close to the entrance.

The walk over was quiet. That was a first for Katy, for whom yapping, generally about the inane, was as important as breathing.

As was often the case with irate passengers, they could hear Mr Alexakis before they could see him. As they came closer, Sophie saw he was an otherwise thin man but for the basketball he appeared to have swallowed, that made his denim shirt bulge over his jeans. He had scraggly grey hair that was thinning on his balding scalp, which was bright red and shining with perspiration, a visual indication to Sophie – not that she needed one – that the man was unhappy.

Travellers arriving at the airport through the main entrance paused as they entered the building to look in the direction of the man's raised voice.

"Mr Alexakis?" Sophie asked with a big smile, hoping the pronunciation was correct.

The man looked her up and down with squinty dead eyes. "Are you supervisor?" he barked.

"Not exactly."

"I thought she call supervisor," the man said, rolling his eyes.

"I'm not a supervisor per se, but I am one of the senior passenger experience agents here at the airport. I'm here to try to help resolve this issue so we can get you on a flight as soon as possible. I understand you've already spoken to my colleague, Katy." Sophie nodded at the apprentice who was standing nearby.

Sophie was smiling at the man, but, inside, she was still simmering from the girl's comment. Normally, she'd be able to dismiss something so meaningless; she'd learned to after her experiences at school. But this time, and she didn't know why, she couldn't. It was probably because the words had come from Katy, of all people.

The man lifted his hands and shrugged. "I ask for supervisor, and you bring me another woman. I say I want to speak to supervisor." The man's words were heavily accented. Greek maybe? Sophie wasn't sure, but English obviously was his second language.

Sophie looked at the airline representative who spoke automatically. "I told Mr Alexakis that *I am* the supervisor. I also explained that it isn't just the airline's policy, but that it's illegal to fly while intoxicated."

The man turned on the heavily made-up woman and held up two pinched fingers, seething as he said, "And I already tell you, I not drunk. I drink last night, not this morning!"

"Mr Alexakis—"

"She cannot do job," the man said loudly, lifting exasperated hands at arriving travellers like he was spoiling for a fight. Then he turned back and added, "This is why I ask for *man* supervisor."

"Mr Alexakis," Sophie said, moving in closer to the man, who was still glaring at the airline representative, to draw him into a dialogue. The act appeared natural, but it was actually her way of establishing how intoxicated the man was. "Although you drank last night, the alcohol is still clearly in your system," she said. As she looked closely at the big-featured man with leathery olive skin, she was overwhelmed by the toxic smog of regurgitated fumes on his breath. "This is why you will not be allowed on a flight this morning."

The man ignored Sophie and turned on the airline representative again, jabbing a finger in her direction. "Then you give me refund! Give me fucking refund," the man yelled, "and I go get ticket on another plane with different airline."

More people looked in their direction as the doors opened and closed intermittently, blasting icy cold air in their direction.

Sophie noticed that the maintenance man was still out there, balancing on the ladder, and made a mental note to contact his department as soon as they were done. She considered delegating it to Katy but decided against it; she'd only have to explain safety protocols to her, and she didn't have the time or the inclination. Besides, first things first.

"Mr Alexakis," she called, touching the man's arm. "If you could please stop shouting. I'm trying—"

"WHY? Why you not want me shout? You don't want these people know how rubbish you at job?" the man bellowed, seemingly performing not just for the travellers who were entering the building but also for those milling in the vicinity. Sophie could even see a couple of people filming their every word on smart phones. "I tell you, if you no refund my money right now, I sue, I sue everyone!" the man said, holding his finger upward and revealing giant sweat patches under his arms.

"Mr Alexakis! You need to stop making a scene," Katy said, stepping forward and grabbing the man's arm in an attempt to pull it down.

"Katy!" Sophie reproached, seconds before the man snatched his arm away.

He almost lost his balance and then eyed the girl as if she were a thing from outer space. "How old are you?" he demanded.

"How old I am isn't important. What's important is that unless you stop causing a disturbance, I'm going to have to call the police."

"Katy!"

"You call police? On me?" the man questioned, his bloodshot eyes wide with incredulity before narrowing to rage. "I call police on you! On you! I call police! You steal money and now no let me fly!" he shouted.

More people paused to watch. More camera phones pointed in their direction. Then Sophie saw two men in uniform approach. She looked at Katy who gave her a shrug and a faint smile.

Sophie moved closer to her, turning her back on the men and said quietly, "You called them without telling me?"

"He's causing a disturbance."

"They all cause a disturbance until you talk to them like they're human beings. The man just wants a refund. We could have negotiated that."

"We don't have time. He's creating a scene."

"No, *you* have just created a scene," Sophie hissed through clenched teeth.

No sooner had the words left her mouth than there was an ear-piercing shriek. Sophie turned to see the man trying to shrug the two policemen off him.

"Let go! GET OFF! BASTARDS! You steal my money and now no let me fly! THEY STEAL MY MONEY! THEY STEAL YOUR MONEY!" The man looked from face to face in the crowd, for anyone who'd care to listen, repeating himself as he looked into the camera of someone's mobile phone. Several people flagrantly filmed the man's struggles while he was partly pulled and partly dragged towards the exit.

Sophie shook her head and looked at Katy. She was smiling as the man stumbled over someone's carry-on bag resting on the floor and fell into a sprawling heap, taking the officers, who were still latched on, with him.

Shirts were ripped. Bellies were exposed. There were gasps from some of the travellers and someone, somewhere, was sniggering. Mr Alexakis' ripped shirt exposed a mat of salt and pepper chest hair as he was unceremoniously dragged towards the exit by the duo of equally dishevelled cops. He repeated his protestations and spewed obscenities the whole way.

Sophie looked around and spotted what looked like the man's suitcase by the ticket counter. She checked the name tag then speedily wheeled it after them through the now functioning door, out into the bitter cold turbulence.

The weather had deteriorated. Those cloud mountains now bubbled and boiled over into curtains of sleet and snow as people hurried to and from the building, pausing only to watch or evade the struggling trio.

Nearby, the crows were still lingering, screeching, jostling as they pecked each other over the remains of a half-eaten sandwich left in the Setting Down Zone, while buses, cars, and taxis hissed back and forth over the slush of the wet tarmac.

"Hold on a minute!" Sophie called, rushing after the men. The policemen were still struggling with the disgruntled passenger who, upon impact with the fresh air, must have sobered to what was happening because he started to fight back. His broad shoulders almost successfully shed themselves of the two officers, who crashed into the maintenance ladder.

"Hey! Watch it!" called the maintenance guy, dropping his screwdriver and clinging on to the shuddering aluminium frame for dear life.

But the struggle continued.

"Oi! I'm up here!"

"WAIT! STOP!" Sophie shouted. "STOP!"

But it was too late.

Mr Alexakis yanked his arm free from one of the officers and smacked his elbow into the maintenance man's ladder, howling in pain.

The maintenance man tried to steady himself atop the wobbly aluminium frame as it threatened to topple over. It danced back and forth, back and forth, as the man held out his hands like a circus performer in an attempt to still himself. The two officers, along with a group of bystanders, could do nothing but gape upward as the man, slowly but surely, managed to regain his perch and steady himself with a big sigh of relief.

At least until a moment later, when a teenager slipped on the pavement, dropping and tripping over his overnight bag to fall against the ladder. The maintenance man toppled off of it onto Mr Alexakis, propelling him out into the middle of the road and into the path of a giant metal mountain of a bus that, with an angry blast of its horn, slammed into the man, knocking him down and driving over him. Crunched bone and squished tissue spewed out of Mr Alexakis' face like frothy crimson toothpaste.

Sophie threw her hands to her mouth. There were gasps of horror from nearby travellers and someone started screaming.

The snow was falling in blankets now, as if attempting to purify the horror, while overhead, perched on the rooftop, the crows looked on.

10

SECTION EIGHT

WEDNESDAY AFTERNOON

On the journey home, Sophie's thoughts came like the sleet and snow: forever falling but never settling. Try as she might, she was unable to process what had happened. She could not move beyond the image of Mr Alexakis lying lifeless and broken on the cold, wet tarmac.

Was this how her father died? Just the thought of it brought tears to her eyes.

She tried the radio again, but the inane banter simply made her angry. People were dead and this lot just kept on spouting rubbish.

She switched it off again, thus restarting the replay of the incident in her head. Yet each time she assembled a thought on the conveyor belt of her mind, it would instantly dissolve like the frozen rain on her windscreen.

A man was dead. A stranger. Because of her.

At least that's what Steve had barely stopped short of saying after summoning her to his office. The police had only just finished their own interrogation, as if she had personally shoved the man in front of the bus.

Squealing breaks. Crunching bones. Gurgling sounds. Screaming.

Each time she dared to allow a thought to stray beyond her boundaries of self-denial and into consciousness, a ferocious memory of what happened would pounce on it, injecting a poisonous snapshot of the man's shirt disappearing under those wheels and emerging as a mangled red mess. She doubted she would ever forget all the hideous sounds that had followed.

Steve had started their meeting with an unusually sympathetic demeanour. His voice was soft and soothing as he had asked if she needed anything, this peculiar treatment coaxing tears to the periphery of her eyes. She could so easily have fallen for him right there and then, for his kindness, his compassion. But this only intensified the impact of what came next.

He'd told her that she was being *suspended* pending an investigation into what had happened.

When she tried to argue her case, he'd held up a hand, closed his eyes, and shook his head slowly, as a parent does when they've had their fill of their insolent child's behaviour. She would have ample opportunity to share her side of the story at the hearing, he'd said, but for now, he had heard all he needed to hear from Katy.

Katy, who had refused to assist the man in any way and had instead chosen to watch events unfold from a warm safe distance inside the airport. Katy, who was ultimately the person who had pulled the pin on the tragedy grenade, only to watch it explode with horrifying consequences with barely a bat of her ridiculous eyelashes.

Steve had then asked Sophie if she needed someone to see her to her car. A threat that no doubt meant he would have arranged a security escort out of the building if she didn't go quietly.

That's when they were interrupted by a knock on the door. Katy had appeared with a blanket around her shoulders, closely followed by a paramedic.

When Steve looked up, Sophie saw his eyes widen from a troubled squint to open interest, and any thought he had for her was forgotten.

"We're done here," he threw at her dismissively. "For now. Go home and I'll be in touch." Then he jumped out of his seat and rushed over to Katy, who appeared to be visibly shaken. It was as if their roles had been reversed, as if it had been Katy who was personally traumatised by the image of the Greek traveller disappearing under the wheels of that bus.

That's when the first mental Polaroid of what that looked like had developed in her mind, propelling her up from her seat as the trio brushed past her on their way to the couch, where they carefully sat the apprentice down as if she were made of delicate crystal, the paramedic continuing to make a fuss over her.

Then, only for a second, their eyes had met. Despite the day's chaos, Sophie had already been mentally chastising herself for reading into things, for imagining what obviously wasn't there. But at that moment, she could have sworn she saw a fleeting and almost imperceptible smile on the girl's face.

Now, as she queued at the traffic lights that would take her off the main road, out of traffic and onto the quieter roads to Fenfield, she longed for her father. She ached for just one of his warm hugs. One of those ones where words were not necessary, filled with so much love.

The weather had eased up by the time she turned into Meadow Lane, where she spotted the Zhangs from next door stapling something to the trunk of one of the trees. It looked like a poster of some kind.

She waved at the elderly couple as she drove by before pulling onto the driveway where she killed the engine and engaged the handbrake.

There she sat. Motionless, she had to consciously control her breathing while her thoughts, like sadistic fingers through a photo album, replayed more snapshots of the ghastly day.

I've been suspended. I may end up out of a job. Then what am I going to do?

The corpse of the glassy-eyed Greek. Steve's severity. Katy's concealed smirk.

A different snapshot memory surprised her: the scored face of the old lady from the airport on the evening her dad had died. Maja. The amulet she had given her was supposed to ward off bad luck or something like that. A fat lot of good it had done her. But maybe it wasn't supposed to give her good luck at all. Maybe it was the opposite. Where was that thing now anyway? Sophie hadn't seen it since that day, when she'd slipped it into her pocket. And what had happened to Maja? Katy had told her that she needed to talk about the woman, and yet never did.

Katy. *Nowhere near as dumb as you made yourself out to be.*

"Oh no," she groaned when movement in the rear-view mirror caught her attention. Her ex-school headmistress was marching up the driveway with a ceramic pot in her hands.

Sophie really wasn't in the mood for the woman's judgmental gaze. And the officious rap on her car window did nothing for her already taut nerves.

Yet she smiled and pretended to be pleasantly surprised when she looked up into the wrinkled face of her neighbour. Ms Whitlock was dressed in her usual dowdy way, in a shapeless dusky pink dress that hung down to her ankles, with sensible flat shoes and a white cardigan.

Sophie pulled on the doorhandle and reluctantly stepped out of the car.

"Ms Whitlock. What a lovely surprise."

"You're early," the woman said, looking her up and down. "Is there something wrong with you? Are you feeling unwell?"

Sophie contemplated explaining but the thought turned her stomach. "It really is nice to see a friendly face, Ms Whitlock," she answered instead, before reaching back into the car to retrieve her bag from the passenger seat.

"I assumed you probably weren't feeding yourself properly, that you'd probably succumbed to that noodle-in-a-pot rubbish, so I thought I'd bring by some ratatouille." She held up the white ceramic pot as if offering a newborn. "It's still warm, but could probably do with a heat through," she added.

"Oh wow, that's very kind. Thank you," Sophie said, conjuring another grateful smile, "but I still haven't managed to start on all that other stuff you organised in the kitchen for me, which is probably going bad as we speak."

"You look tired, dear," the woman said, scrutinizing the young girl to the point of making Sophie want to hold up a hand to fend off her gaze. "Have you been staying up late again?"

"I wish it was just that," Sophie said with a sigh. "No, I haven't been sleeping that well, and then after that racket the other night..."

The woman pulled a face. "Racket?"

"You know, the earthquake, the car alarms, the dogs barking..."

"Oh, yes. All a fuss about nothing, if you ask me," the woman grumbled with a roll of the eyes.

"Well, it wasn't exactly nothing, Ms Whitlock. It was actually—"

"This ratatouille is packed with a medley of fresh vegetables, all in season, which I needn't tell you equals good vitamins. Of course, there's the usual—aubergines, peppers, and whatnot—but I like to put in a few carrots as well…"

Sophie was summoning the appropriate enthusiasm when, mercifully, the moment was interrupted by the sound of a blue Mini pulling up into the drive next door. They both watched Lucy wave as she stepped out of her car and walked over.

"Hey, Sophie," she said with a big smile which diluted when she turned to the curmudgeon standing next to her. "Oh, hello, Ms Whitlock," she added, as if she hadn't noticed her standing there.

Ms Whitlock acknowledged her with a curt nod.

Lucy turned to Sophie. "How are you bearing up?" she asked.

"Oh, you know. One day at a time." She could have unburdened herself of more details quite easily but, for some reason, she couldn't bring herself to share more in the presence of her old headmistress.

And then, as if to prove the point, "This pot used to be my mother's and my grandmother's before her. That's a testament to its quality and, of course, *its weight*," the woman said.

"Oh, of course. I'm sorry." Sophie slung her bag over her shoulder and then hastily took the pot from her neighbour. Ms Whitlock made a show of stretching her seemingly aching fingers.

There was an awkward silence, filled by the low rumble of the city in the distance, a pair of birds squabbling in a nearby tree, and an intermittent clicking sound. The trio turned in the direction of the noise.

Ms Whitlock drew in a sharp breath then demanded, "What on Earth are they doing?"

The Zhangs had made good progress up the street, Sophie thought, and were now affixing posters to trees on the opposite side of the road.

"Oh, that's right," Lucy said painfully. "The dogs."

"Dogs?" Sophie asked.

"Yeah, the Zhangs and some of the other neighbours have reported their pets missing. The Abbassis are missing a cat, and the Freemans—you know, first house as you enter the lane—are missing their Labrador. I think someone's even missing their cockatiel," Lucy said mysteriously.

"Okay... that's weird," Sophie said.

"I know, right?"

"What about your dog?"

"Oh, don't worry about him. He was at the window when I pulled up. That big oaf isn't going anywhere."

"Well, I don't care if they have missing pets or missing children, stapling posters to the trees is strictly forbidden. And they'd know that if they had bothered to read the neighbourhood watch guidelines," Ms Whitlock snapped. "The ratatouille's probably stone-cold by now. Be sure to heat it up before you eat it," the woman ordered before marching off down the driveway with a "Hello! Excuse me! Excuse me!" aimed towards the unsuspecting Zhangs.

Lucy rolled her eyes. "Blimey. She's a handful," she said. Then, as if she needed the boost, she rummaged around in the rucksack she was carrying, pulled out an e-cigarette and took a deep drag, expelling a plume of vapour into the cold air.

"Yes. She can be. She means well though," Sophie said as they watched the woman trudge down the driveway and intercept the stapling couple.

"Oh!" Lucy said, suddenly remembering. "I heard what happened at Stansted. It was all over the news. Were you there today?"

Sophie had momentarily forgotten about it. Now the knot in her stomach pulled tight once more. She didn't want to talk about it. "I was," she said reluctantly. When Lucy's eyebrows lifted inquisitively, she added, "But an investigation's ongoing so I can't really talk about it." Then she quickly changed the subject. "So, you've still got custody of Duke then?"

"Yeah, though I think he's losing his bloody mind."

Sophie cocked her head. "What do you mean?"

"Well, you know, there's a rumour going round that it's that thing," Lucy explained, nodding skywards where giant charcoal clouds scurried across a clear sky. "They're saying the comet's responsible for all the weird stuff that's been happening around here. You know, pets going missing, people losing their bloody minds."

Sophie pulled a lopsided grin. "What, you mean like aliens or something?"

Lucy laughed. "I don't know. Maybe. Anyway, the bloody dog was acting up most of the night. He'd be asleep one minute and the next he's running off into the utility room, jumping on the washing machine and growling out of the window towards your house."

"My house? Why?"

"No idea. I just couldn't get the stupid thing to calm down. As I say, at first, I thought he was barking at the comet, but then I realised that he was actually barking at your roof like there was something up there." Sophie felt a chill skitter down her spine as she instinctively looked up as if whatever it was might still be there. "But I couldn't see anything. Anyway, then I thought it might be Craig, you know, hanging around outside, because he started barking out of the lounge window. As I say, complete freak."

Sophie watched her take another puff from her device. Lucy's demeanour had changed somehow. It seemed shifty, nervous. Eyes darting back and forth. And there was a tremble in her fingers. Perhaps it was from the cold wind that had suddenly blown up out of nowhere around them, as if it were eavesdropping.

"It wasn't him though, right?" It was a rhetorical question, said more as an offer of reassurance.

"I don't think so, no."

"You've still got a protection order in force, haven't you?"

Lucy shrugged and nodded before taking another nervous drag. "Yeah, for all the difference it'll make. If he wants to come to the house, he'll come to the house and a piece of paper isn't going to stop him. He's pretty much said that, and he says he has a right to see the dog."

"Oh, Lucy," Sophie said sympathetically. It was now her turn to reach out.

Lucy smiled gratefully, and then added, "I'm thinking of moving in with my mum anyway. I mean, there's still a lease on this place but I'm not sure how much more creepy stuff I can put up with." She laughed nervously and took another drag.

Sophie laughed with her. "You mean the barking?"

"Yeah, kind of. But it isn't just that." The paramedic bit her lip as she recalled, shaking her head as if she couldn't make sense of her own thoughts. "I don't know. I can't quite explain it. It's random things, strange things."

She shifted the weight on her feet and scratched a nervous itch at the back of her neck. Then she stepped forward, as if she didn't want the hedge to hear.

"Do you ever get a feeling that you're being watched?" she asked ominously.

Sophie gave an awkward shrug like she didn't know what her neighbour was talking about, but she did. She knew exactly what she was saying because she felt that very same way the other night. That shadow under the kitchen door. Someone was in there. Or at least it felt that way.

She contemplated sharing. She contemplated telling everything, but that meant admitting it to herself. And she couldn't do that, because it was one thing to swap ghost stories now and quite another to then go back into that house alone.

Lucy observed her for a moment, as if sensing that she was withholding something, but eventually ploughed on. "I mean, the dog obviously isn't helping and last night was the final bloody straw. You know, all that staring at the ceiling like there's somebody up there. All that barking at invisible things. It's made me completely paranoid; I can't shake this feeling that there's something else in the house, you know, watching me." She paused and looked back at the house, then hunched her shoulders against the chill it gave her.

Sophie recognised the wild look in her eyes as her own.

"So anyway, I got myself so worked up last night I was going to knock on your door, to ask you if you wanted company," Lucy continued, releasing another cloud of vapour that was snatched away and carried off by the wind into the gathering gloom. "But then I noticed that you already had people round and so I didn't bother."

Sophie's heart skipped a beat. "P…people?"

"Yeah. I saw them in the back garden. I was taking the rubbish out and saw them standing there in the bloody dark. Scared me to death."

Raptor wings of anxiety fluttered in Sophie's chest, startling her heart into an uneasy thud.

"For a second there, I was ready to call the police. I mean, I thought you were being robbed or something but then I saw Victoria and just assumed they were friends of yours…" Lucy slowed to a stop here when she noticed the look on Sophie's face. "What's wrong?" she asked.

"You saw people in my house?" Sophie asked, needing confirmation, hoping she might have somehow misunderstood what she just heard.

Lucy seemed to search her thoughts for a minute but remained clear. "Yeah. In the garden."

"When?"

"Last night."

"Lucy, are you sure?"

The paramedic frowned. "Um, as sure as I can be. I mean I couldn't tell you what they looked like. As I say, they were standing out there in the dark. So it was only their outlines really, but I'm pretty sure it was two men just by their builds and the way they moved, but Victoria—"

"Lucy, I wasn't home last night," Sophie interrupted, eager to make her neighbour stop. "I made it to the front door, but I couldn't face another night alone, so I spent the night at Janay's who, as you know, lives on the other side of the city."

"Oh. Right."

"And you say you saw Vicki too?"

"Yeah. Or at least I think I did. Yes, I must have because it was the dog who alerted me to them. I picked up my mobile phone to call the police and went into the utility room to see what the dog's problem was and that's when I saw Vicki through your living room window." Lucy let out a short awkward laugh and then added, "Well, at least it was definitely someone who looked like her. Gorgeous thin body, long black hair. Oh no. Have I put my foot in it or something?"

Sophie shook her head. "No, nothing like that."

"Sophie, I—"

"Evening, ladies!"

The voice startled them, and they turned in unison to see Christopher Darrington jogging to a halt. He was wearing black shorts with a grey t-shirt that sported a large dark sweat patch down the front.

"Hey!" Lucy called with a big grin and a wave. She tracked the man's rear as he walked up to his front door, kicked off his trainers, and stepped inside.

"Ooh... Isn't he adorable?" Lucy asked dreamily.

Sophie rocked her head. "I guess. If you like that kind of

thing."

"He was the one who helped me file that order against Craig. He wouldn't take any money for it though."

"Helped you file it?" Sophie asked, distractedly. Her mind was still on the story she'd heard about strangers in her garden, about Victoria. She needed to know more as soon as Lucy stopped gushing over the next-door neighbour.

"Yeah. He's a lawyer. He said it was straightforward enough. He even came down to the station with me and everything. Lovely bloke, and bloody sexy as…"

"He's a lawyer?"

"Yeah. Didn't you know? I hear he's quite good too."

"No. I didn't know," Sophie said, numb to the current conversation.

Lucy laughed. "Bloody hell, Soph. You live opposite the man."

"Yeah, well, I've tried to steer clear of him," she said, shifting the weight of the pot into the nook of her arm. "Besides, he's not my type."

"What? You mean good-looking and brainy isn't your type?"

Sophie threw her neighbour a pointed look.

"What, Chris? Oh no, he isn't like that. He goes out on a lot of dates, yeah, but he's upfront about how he feels about serious relationships."

Sophie rolled her eyes.

"Oh no, not in that way. He's just focussed on his career, you know. He's one of those, what-do-they-call-'em? Mature students. But he is lovely. My mate went out with him a few times. She said he was the perfect gentlemen, just not interested in anything serious, you know, on account of his wife and everything."

"He's married?" Sophie exclaimed.

"Was. Childhood sweetheart and all that. Really young when

they tied the knot. It didn't last long though. Less than a year, I think."

"What happened? Did he ditch her for a schoolgirl?"

Lucy laughed. "No. I don't know the details, but I think she died. He was really cut up about it. Went off the rails a bit. Doesn't really talk about it."

There was a pause as the streetlamps responded to the burgeoning darkness.

Sophie glanced at the black lifeless eyes of the house. She was about to steer the conversation back to the whole Victoria in her living room and strangers in the garden thing when the sound of an approaching car sliced through the quiet. Its headlamps winked as it drew near before stopping at the foot of the drive.

"Oh, hello. Looks like you've got a visitor," Lucy said.

They watched as an official-looking woman in a black trouser suit and high heels left the car and clicked purposefully up the driveway towards them.

Sophie stepped forward. Her guard was instantly up and ready to defend. "Can I help you?"

The blonde, who had her hair scraped back in a no-nonsense ponytail, didn't respond but instead asked, "Are you Sophie Cooper?"

Sophie nodded. "Yes. Who wants to know?"

"And you live here?" The blonde nodded at the house, ignoring her question.

"Yes. Who are you?"

"Sophie Cooper," the woman said seriously, "you've been served." She placed a brown A4 envelope on the pot Sophie was still holding, then turned and made her way back to the car.

"Hey!" Sophie called after her. "Excuse me!" But the stranger wasn't listening. She climbed back into the vehicle, made a U-turn, and drove away as the rain began to fall.

11

SINISTER

WEDNESDAY EVENING

In the kitchen, the dark and the tempest duelled for the right to break-and-enter number 12 Meadow Lane, yet it was the wind that screeched victorious as it forced its way under the crack of the door.

The howl made Lucy look up. "Yes, Mum. Yes. I still need to work my shift because they're short-staffed, but as soon as that's done, I'll be in the car. I've already started packing so I'll be ready. Yes. Don't worry. I'll be fine. All right. See you tomorrow night. Just remember, it'll be late though so don't start panicking. Yeah. Yeah. Okay. Love you. All right. Bye."

Lucy disconnected the call and put her mobile phone down on the counter with a sigh. A second later, a thump on the glass of the patio door forced a yelp. But it was only a clump of wet leaves, hurled there by the gale, begging for sanctuary before being blown away into the unknown.

Lucy was feeling particularly jumpy after her conversation with Sophie and the storm wasn't helping any. In fact, if the weather was any better, she might have been tempted to call in sick and get an early start on her journey tomorrow. But she instantly dismissed the idea. They were already struggling as it was. How could she be so selfish?

Pull yourself together!

She fed the dog, slid into her coat, and then tentatively let him out into the garden. Frigid turbulence was busy throttling the vegetation and threatening to topple the fence.

"No, Duke! Don't run off. Stay where I can see you!" And yet it didn't take long for the hound to disappear into the dark that had devoured most of the back lawn. She considered leaving him to do his business and come back later, but then she noticed them.

Roof shingles. Smashed on the stone patio.

Shit!

She squinted upward into the dark. Raindrops spat in her face, making her cringe. She glanced at the broken shingles once more. If Duke had stood here, he could have been injured.

She hastily stepped to her left and that's when she noticed it, sitting next to the patio door. It looked like one of Duke's toy balls, and yet she didn't remember seeing this particular one before. She picked it up and held it under the overhead light. It was the size of a golf ball. Made of wood. No. Wood vine. Bound together like one of those woven baskets. And there something inside, glistening with rainwater.

What is that?

A rumbling sound caught her attention. A large plastic paint bucket, flung by the wind, rolled across the gravel and dove into the pond. Then, more movement, this time at the foot of the garden. Something was down there. Something pale. It was the dog. It had to be. And yet, this seemed... taller.

She slipped the ball into her pocket, wiped her face with the back of her coat sleeve and squinted into the precipitation now whizzing about her.

It was gone now, replaced by the ominous sound of… growling. And then barking. Loud. Aggressive. As it has been last night. "Oh Duke, come on. Don't start that rubbish."

Lucy wasn't one to spook easily, although she had only truly learned that about herself recently, now that she lived alone with nobody but a dog for company. And yet things had changed in the past week.

For example, that thing that was moving at the foot of the garden seemed to be growing bigger now. Bigger and closer. Pushing her jogging heart into a sprint.

Closer…

"Duke?"

Closer…

"Duke, is that you, boy?" Her voice was nothing more than a squeak over the elements. Then… the dog emerged from the dark and into the patio light.

She breathed a sigh of relief. "You're going to give me a bloody heart attack. Did you do your business, eh?" she asked, as if the dog was going to answer. "Come on," she said, stepping back into the sanctuary of the kitchen, "that's a good boy." She patted the animal's wet fur before promptly sliding the glass door shut and locking the tempest outside.

The relief was instant although the freeze had already taken up residence in her bones. She could not wait to get into a hot bath.

But first, she rummaged in the fridge. She performed a short celebratory dance when she found a plastic container of pasta salad from a few nights before that she'd forgotten about. She tasted it and concluded that it was perfectly fine. She was starving. Then she spotted the half bottle of wine and pulled that out too.

"Just what the doctor ordered," she said with a grin, using her foot to push the fridge door shut.

But when she turned, she yelped and almost dropped everything when she saw a pair of glowing jaundiced eyes glaring at her through the window.

It was only when she blinked and refocussed that she realised that they weren't yellow eyes at all but streetlights in the distance; they were flickering through the gnarled branches of naked trees that were themselves shaking in terror at the might of the storm.

OK.

She was feeling suitably spooked now and cursed the moment she started chatting with Sophie. Now she couldn't get the image of those shadows out of her mind. The intruders who had been standing in Sophie's garden could have been watching her the whole time.

She rushed over to the patio doors and, without looking, hastily closed the blinds. Then she double-checked all the other doors and windows before hurrying up the stairs, leaving lights burning in her wake.

In the bedroom, she switched on the speaker by her bedside table and pressed play on her mobile phone. George Michael's dulcet tones filled the room with his greatest hits, drowning out the whoosh and rumble of the storm outside. "Careless Whisper" brought a smile to her face.

She went over to the dresser and picked up a bottle of her favourite expensive perfume – used only for special occasions – and wrapped it in a jumper. She placed it in the suitcase on her bed, along with a couple of blouses and pairs of jeans.

Then she carried the speaker into the bathroom, ran a bath, adding bubbles, and went through the ritual of lighting scented candles. When the tub had filled, she toe-tested the bathwater before gingerly immersing herself into the glorious mound of foam.

The water was hot. Sublimely so. It instantly set to work

driving the cold from her bones and the stress from her muscles.

As she lay in her bliss, tuning into George Michael's silky voice as he sang the melancholy lyrics of *turn a different corner and we never would have met,* she felt sad for the passing of one of her idols, as well as the loss of the man she thought she was going to marry.

But before misery could gain a hold, she ate from the Tupperware container, washing the pasta down with some of the wine. She settled back once more to enjoy its effect on her body.

Food. Alcohol. The weight off her feet, the nourishment in her belly, the warmth of the water on her body and the massage it was giving her mind.

Orgasmic.

A few minutes later a loud rumble forced its way over the music. She allowed her eyes to spring open and survey the room. The bathroom door was shut, and nothing had changed. It was just the storm, raging against her sanctuary. She confirmed this by looking out of the small portal window that, by day, offered a view of the back garden. Now, she could barely make out the silhouettes of the trees swaying back and forth, backlit by the streetlamps.

Ugh. She thought of work and was instantly engulfed by the dread of returning to it tomorrow. God knows the kind of destruction that was taking place out there while she soaked in the bath.

Don't think about that now. Not now. Push that out of your mind.

She only had a few hours to herself before she needed to go to bed and everything started all over again. The last thing she needed to be thinking about right now was work. Instead, thanks to the deliriously pleasurable warm water and the delicate stroke of alcohol on her brain, her thoughts turned to sex. She couldn't stop herself from thinking about Craig and their best times together. Not the formulaic, functional moments driven by the need for release, but the spontaneous and creative times when they first met.

She visualised cutting the train of thought in half with a pair of gigantic shears. She hadn't pushed work aside to start thinking about him. It was infinitely worse to think about him. Surprisingly, it was still so painful.

She wiped a runaway tear from her face, telling herself it was just perspiration from the heat of the bath as she drank more wine.

Easy. You've got an early shift tomorrow. But who cares!

And, of course, George wasn't helping with his equally mournful *I can't make you love me.* The sentiment was amplified by the alcohol and the fact that she hadn't yet eaten enough to soak it up. But she was okay with that. She was fine. It was playing its part, sloshing through her bloodstream, caressing her soul, lulling her into a superficial daze.

What was that?

That sound. Faint at first. Muffled and coming from beyond the door.

She slid lower into the water, as if by doing so, the sound could be ignored. But he wasn't letting up, just like he didn't when he was having one of his fits the other night.

Shit.

She had come to love Duke very much, but it was times like this when she wondered why she had agreed to keep him. But she knew why, as much as she didn't want to admit it; she knew Craig loved Duke. In some perverse way, he was her link to him even though she knew that they would never get back together. She had more self-respect than that.

How's that working out for you? Oh, shut up!

"Okay! Okay, Duke! You can bark. Thank you for the demonstration!" she yelled to the air, as if the animal could hear her from downstairs or wherever he was.

"Shit." She kept her eyes squeezed shut, trying to stretch out her personal time for as long as possible. But something had changed. Something in the atmosphere. Something that sent a shiver through her and caused her eyes to spring open once more and look around the room.

Still empty.

And yet she had this peculiar sensation that someone had walked in there. Like there was somebody or something else occupying the space.

She sat up and scanned the room. Oddly, the candle flames were flickering back and forth, as if something had just frightened them. She squinted then rubbed her eyes as they became accustomed to the subdued lighting.

The bathroom door was still closed. The lamplight from the bedroom glowed brightly through the gap underneath.

She listened carefully.

Nothing. Just the music and silence filled in with the rumble and howl of the wind, the creak and sigh of the house.

She picked up her phone and paused the music.

Nothing. No creaky floorboards. No approaching footsteps. Just the dog's loud barks ringing up the stairs. He seemed particularly unhappy now. Frenetic. Rageful. Activated in the way dogs often were when confronted by something strange or unknown.

This unsettled her. She shifted in the tub, eyes roving around the room as water sloshed. Foam crackled and popped.

Suddenly, she became aware of her naked vulnerability in the water. The warmth was no longer soothing but chilling. And that's when she realised. The water had turned cold. In fact, the whole room was freezing. She could tell by the way the mirror was rapidly demisting. How was that even possible?

There must be a window open somewhere. Is someone breaking into the house? Is that why he's going crazy down there?

The dog was rabid now. As if straining against a chain, as if someone had approached him, daring him to attack, daring him to put his growl to action.

Louder. Angrier.

Louder… Angrier.

LOUDER… ANGRIER… then a whimper followed by…

Nothing.

The sudden and complete silence of the animal slithered icily down her spine, laying goosebumps all over her skin.

"Duke?" The word was no more than a whisper.

She thought of her mobile phone and about calling someone. Who? To say what?

The mirror lights flickered, sending a wave of fear rippling through her. The mere notion that the power might abandon her to the mercy of the dark had her gripping the sides of the bath, as if that might in some way stop the light from forsaking her.

"No," she gasped, as the music stuttered on again. Lucy turned to the wireless speaker and stared at it.

…last Chri…mas I gave you my heart but the very next day… y… g… t… way.

And then it died again.

The mirror lights flickered once more before giving up in tandem with the reassuring light strip under the door. Only the amber light of the panic-stricken candles remained, their flickering flames casting spectral shadows over the walls.

She was shivering now. Her body was the physical manifestation of both the cold and the fear that she was experiencing when… *click*. The bathroom door slowly and inexplicably drifted open, with a horror-movie-worthy, gut-wrenching creak.

"Oh… my…" she breathed, as a burst of icy cold air swept into the room and over her, first shifting and then dispelling the remnants of steam rising from the bath.

Lucy jumped to her feat, water sloshing and echoing loudly in the space as she crossed her arms over her nakedness and gaped through the doorway at the dark beyond.

"Craig?" she squeaked hopefully. He still had keys. At least she thought he did. He was supposed to return them. Did he? She couldn't remember. Her mind was as numb as her extremities.

It was silent but for the sound of her quivering breath as it fogged out in front of her.

She listened hard for the tell-tale sound of an intruder. Creaky floorboard. The rustle of clothing. Anything! But there was nothing but the rapping of rain against the window.

She waited…

…*C r a i g?*

The rasp drifted out of the blackness of the bedroom and electrocuted her with mind-freezing horror. There *was* someone in the bedroom and they were mimicking her voice. Mocking her!

"Who is that? Craig, is that you? This isn't bloody funny!" she yelled at the open doorway.

Was it Craig? It was hard to tell, the voice wasn't much more than whisp–

…*C r a i g. Is that you?* came the blood-curdling echo once more.

There was no doubt about it. There was an intruder in the house. Someone was skulking in the bedroom, waiting for her.

Tears of terror pricked her eyes as she considered what to do. She attempted to step backward, away from the door, but as soon as she moved the candles began to dance once more, as if the air had been displaced, as if someone *or something* had walked into the room.

Now, eyes wide, pupils fully dilated and darting all around, she became horrifyingly aware of the fact that she was trapped within the confines of the bath. She would have to step out –

A loud sputtering interrupted her thoughts. It was the candles again, jerking back and forth like something was breathing on them. No, nothing was breathing on them, she told herself. She was alone. And yet, she'd barely finished the thought before the candlelight was snuffed out, smothering the room in darkness.

Lucy shrieked. The sound reverberated like a siren in the empty space.

She huddled into herself. Teeth chattering, skin crawling, body trembling. "Oh G-g-god... p... please help me," she whispered under her breath, like she was at church. Lucy rarely attended church, yet that didn't stop her from promising God that she would attend every week, every day, if he just brought the lights back on and made this stop. *Please. Please... make it stop!*

And then she smelt it. Sewage. It must be bubbling out of the toilet and oozing over the floor. The pungent stench of fermenting faeces crawled up her nostrils and stung her eyes.

Hands to her mouth, she choked and gagged but forced herself to recover quickly and was once more scrutinizing the darkness with the pinpricks of light offered by the streetlamps outside.

That's when it came. The shock doubled the impact of the slap, which was so vicious it launched her out of the bathtub and onto the cold tiles. She skittered on her wet buttocks until she slammed up against the opposite wall.

She lay in a crumpled heap, mind reeling as it attempted to process what had happened. An earthquake of agony ripped through her back and rattled her skull. Her cheek was burning, her body shaking, and she had landed somewhere on the bathroom floor.

Breaths ragged, she squinted into the gloom as cold water dribbled, dripped, and tickled like insects crawling over her hair and skin.

Seconds passed. Water sloshed. The storm raged, and glass

rattled in the small window.

Get out! The voice in her head ordered. *Get out! Run!* It repeated. She realised now, slowly, as her computing faculties returned, that she could just about discern the outline of the room. This triggered her fight or flight response. *Get out of the house!* If she didn't want to die here, she needed to move. That much was swiftly and excruciatingly clear to her. *RUN!*

And so, body shuddering, breaths rasping, she folded forward, slithering across the icy wet floor, sputtering on the coppery taste of blood, dragging her naked form off the freeze of the bathroom tiles and onto the deliciously warm carpet of the hallway.

But then there was a stomp of wet feet, running, splashing on the tiles behind her, and Lucy barely had time to react when small powerful hands grabbed her from behind. No, not hands, but what felt like reedy bony claws, thick with hair. They clamped around her ankle and dragged her partially back into the freeze.

"Nooooo!" she screamed. "NOOOOOO! HELP ME! SOMEBODY HEL...P M—"

But the words were choked out of her as a weight as heavy as the world crawled and scratched its way onto her back, pushing her face into carpet, gagging her by forcing her mouth into the woolly pile. She tried to scream again but to no avail. Each time she tried to draw breath, the crude gag of fibre, dust, and carpet freshener filled her mouth.

Several desperate seconds later, she could already feel herself sinking into a hideous and helpless death. It was this realisation that fired her brain into satisfying her body's need to oxygenate. Lucy Davidson bucked and kicked with all her might to shake off the cold, hairy, fetid thing that was breathing loudly in her ears. She partially succeeded in lifting her head from the carpet gag and rapidly sucked in enough air to emit an agonised wail.

It was swiftly silenced by bony fingers on the back of her head, pushing her face back down into the carpet, restricting movement to her eyeballs which swivelled desperately as she sought to identify her attacker.

She instantly wished she hadn't. For what she saw in the gloom of the room was something so grotesque, it could only have originated from her deepest darkness nightmares, something spawned from the loins of hell.

She screamed into the carpet, stuffy air burning her face. Hotter and louder. Hotter and louder until...

Lucy Davidson awoke, partly gasping, partly gurgling, partly screaming from the bath water.

She sat up, clinging to the side of the bath as she attempted to recover. She coughed, wheezing and willing the air back into her body as the bathwater sloshed and fizzed loudly in the echo of the room.

She had fallen asleep.

"Oh God. Oh, thank you. Th...Th...Thank you... tha-thank you!" she cried. "Thank you so much. Thank you!"

She stayed that way for several minutes, shivering the tears from her eyes as she slowly recovered from her ordeal.

That was *the* worst nightmare she'd ever had because it had felt so awfully real. She could still smell that *thing* clinging to her back. And even now, in the sanctuary of her real bathroom, her eyes searched for signs of a potential intruder. There were none. She was alone.

The storm was still raging outside though, but she was safe inside. Lights blazing. Candles burning.

Eventually, as her breathing normalised, she allowed herself a deep sigh. The water was tepid now but warm enough to offer some reassurance. Along with the smooth tones of George Michael's serenade of *turn a different corner and we never would have met*, she was starting to feel much better.

But then Duke started barking.

"Okay! Okay, Duke! You can bark. Thank you for the

demonstration!" Then the music stopped, and the lights went out, plunging the room into darkness.

12

DISCOVERY

THURSDAY MORNING

Real estate in the historic city of Cambridge is so valuable that owning property anywhere near the city centre was considered prestigious. However, with video conferencing's ever-increasing popularity, that prestige fast became more of an unnecessarily expensive overhead. A fact that some traditionalists were still struggling with.

Humphries, Palmer, and Company had set up their practice in a small office block west of the city, surrounded by rows of much needed terraced homes that were privately owned but easily confused for *affordable housing*.

The waiting room was small and rectangular, with a reception desk at one end and compact leather divans at the other. It was a functional space, Sophie thought, with bare magnolia walls adorned by the occasional photograph of people in suits, smiling as they held their diplomas.

Sophie did her best to find some interest in the images, but there was only so long she could stare at them without it looking weird. Instead, she gazed out of the small window to the elements outside.

Another storm was brewing. An official one this time. Dylan, one of the first male-named storms of the season. Judging by the cyclonic funnel of blackness that was gathering over the city, he was in a foul mood. With expected winds of 80 miles per hour, travellers had been warned to expect considerable disruption.

It occurred to Sophie that being suspended might well turn out to be a blessing. Storm Dylan was part of a severe weather front that had battered the eastern coast of the United States for the best part of the month. Travel disruption in her profession meant delayed flights or, worse, cancellations.

Good luck, Katy.

Dylan spat rain at the window as a door at the other end of the room opened. Out of it came an old lady, closely followed by a tall man in black trousers and a white shirt. She couldn't quite see his face as he moved in profile then turned away towards the old lady, but Sophie got the impression he was quite young. Much younger than the men in the dated photographs in front of her.

"Remember, Mrs Gladstone, if your husband comes over, don't do anything that might compromise our case," the man said.

"I told you, it wasn't me," the old lady responded. "He's the one who started it."

"Well, pushing a suitcase down the stairs at him didn't help."

"He had it coming, the dirty cheat. I gave that man the best years of my life. A bruised wrist is far less than he deserves!"

"Mrs Gladstone…"

"Oh, all right," she said, patting the man's arm. "Only because you asked so nicely. Oh, and one other thing. I was wondering, perhaps when this is all over, if you might consider joining me for supper sometime. I make a mean lamb casserole, you know. It used to be *his* favourite."

"Mrs Gladstone, are you flirting with me again?"

"Of course I am, silly."

The man thrust his hands in his pockets. "Mrs Gladstone, come on now. We've had this conversation before. In any other circumstance, it'd be me asking you out on a date, but…"

Sophie watched him lift his left hand and show her the wedding band on his finger.

"…I'm already married, remember?"

"Oh that…" the woman said with a naughty grin. "It's just a technicality. However," she added, turning, "if you ever change your mind, you know where to find me."

"Don't worry. You'll be the first lady I call. Don't forget what I said now," he reiterated, seeing the woman to the door and opening it for her. "And be careful out there. It's getting bad out there."

Then he closed the door, turned around and Sophie's stomach lurched.

Oh shit!

She watched the man speak to the receptionist – a middle-aged woman who had poured her ample curves into a pinstripe suit and looked good with it – and then glance her way. The receptionist handed him a sheet of paper. He read it with a furrowed brow before looking her way once more.

Shit! Shit! She slunk low in her seat and then fussed with her fringe, being sure to block her face with her hand. But it wasn't long before she heard footsteps approach.

"Sophie?"

There was no escaping it. Reluctantly, she allowed her hand

to fall, and there he was, sapphire blue tie matching that twinkle in his eyes.

She straightened in her seat. "Um, C...Chris... Hi. Hello. What are you doing here?"

Christopher Darrington cocked his head and smiled. "I work here."

"You work here?"

He nodded, eyes wide. "Last time I checked."

"Oh, right."

"What are *you* doing here, neighbour?"

"I, um..." She cleared her throat as flashbacks of her meltdown in her bathroom during the wake hurtled themselves at her. "I have a meeting with Mr Palmer," she said, looking around as if the man might be hiding somewhere.

"Ah." Chris pulled a troubled face. "Mr Palmer called in sick this morning. I've been taking his meetings."

"Oh," was all she could say. "I needed to see him urgently and now..." She let the words trail off and stood up. Now she had no clue. "And now I'm going to need to find someone else."

"Well, you could. But then, I am free, and I just happen to be standing right in front of you."

"You?" she countered.

He cocked his head. "Yes, me. As abhorrent as that might sound, I am fully qualified, you know."

"I know," she said dismissively.

"You know? I didn't think you knew anything about me."

"I don't."

"And yet..." He paused then added, in mock astonishment, "Wait, you haven't been checking up on me, have you?"

"No, I have not!" she snapped, suddenly feeling hot in the airless room. Her cheeks were burning, her stomach was fluttering, and this man, with his wide smile and woody cologne, was making her feel queasy.

"Are you okay? You're looking a bit flushed."

"I'm fine," she said.

He nodded and, mercifully, took a step back. "So, would you like to come through?" He gestured towards his office.

Sophie looked at his hand, the ring on his finger, and then the doorway.

Christopher Darrington's office was as functional as the waiting room. There was a small beechwood desk. A couple of grey filing cabinets. Hanging from the same uninspired magnolia-painted back wall were his own framed diplomas and photos. Yet the place felt like a temporary office, one Sophie imagined was assigned to lawyers who were passing through. It did have a nice view though, of a small courtyard leading to other independent businesses, each with signs pinned to outer walls. Their outdoor space shared a tree as well as several brown and empty flower troughs.

"Would you like a beverage, Sophie? Tea, coffee, water?" he asked, following her in and closing the door.

"Actually, I'm fine, thanks," she said, fixing those invisible bumps in her hair and trying not to acknowledge the fact that, much to her own amazement, she enjoyed the way he spoke her name. There was something warm and calming about it. Of course, she'd never admit that to anyone.

"Are you sure I can't tempt you?" he said with a lift of his neat eyebrows.

"Maybe some water."

"Sure. Please, take a seat," he said, gesturing to the chair facing his desk, as he sat on a squeaky executive chair behind it. He reached down to a small fridge, retrieved a bottle of water, and filled the glass in front of her.

She was thirstier than she had realised and drank. Then, noticing that he was watching her with the faint trace of a supercilious grin, she felt compelled to add something to the conversation. "Well, what are the chances, eh?"

He rocked his head from side to side. "Fairly high, considering we're the closest practice to Fenfield."

"Right," she nodded. "And you work here?"

"As I said, last time I looked. I even have the diplomas to prove it," he said, nodding up at the wall behind him.

"Wow. Who would have thought?" she said with an overenthusiastic smile that she knew wasn't fooling either of them. She had to ask. She knew it was none of her business, but it was bugging her, and so the words just flew out. "And you're wearing your ring," she blurted.

He looked at his hand and then at her. "My ring?"

"Yes. You're wearing your wedding ring today, but you weren't wearing it the day of the funeral." She could have kicked herself, but she'd opened the cage now and those words had fluttered out right across the desk. There was no getting them back.

He took a few seconds, then, "No. I wasn't. How very observant of you. I wasn't wearing it that day because it was a social occasion."

"A social occasion?"

He rocked his head, realising what that sounded like, and rephrased. "I was out, socially."

His words made no sense. It was beyond her how anybody could describe a funeral as a social *occasion*. And then it occurred to her. "Oh, I see. Weddings, funerals. All fair game. All potential pick-up points. You don't want anybody to think you're still married."

"I *am* still married."

"But just when it suits you."

"Actually, Sophie, I remain *still married* three hundred and sixty-five days a year, twenty-four hours a day. And most of those are a struggle for me. But what can I say? That's my cross to bear, but thanks for reminding me. Now, is this the real reason why you came here today? To ask about my wedding ring?" He was leaning forward on the desk now. Dazzling smile still intact.

"No. Of course not."

"Right then. So shall we talk about what you really came here to discuss instead?" he asked.

She nodded, feeling suitably chastised as she remembered Lucy's words. The man sitting across from her had married his childhood sweetheart, but something happened to her. She groaned inwardly and was considering apologising when he headed her off.

"Right. So, I had a quick look at your notes..." he said, looking down at the sheet of paper in front of him. She wondered if that was his way of avoiding eye contact after she'd been so rude. "You're in luck. Property is sort of my speciality. Did you bring the letter with you?"

"Yes." She reached into her bag, pulled out the envelope, and handed it to him.

She watched his manicured hands work their way through the sheets of paper and wondered if now was a good time to say she was sorry. That she had no right to...

"Right..." the man groaned.

She sat up in her seat, readying herself for the verdict.

"This looks like pretty standard stuff, really," he explained. "It's what's known as a Section 8 notice. That is, that your landlord believes that you've broken the terms of your tenancy agreement and is seeking repossession of their property at number ten, Meadow Lane."

Sophie's body tensed. She hated the way he delivered that line. Coldly. Dispassionately. Lawyerly.

"But," he continued, "in order to issue a Section 8, the landlord needs to prove good cause. I mean, your dad will have needed to have broken the terms of the lease agreement. Did he mention anything to you about this?" He looked up at her.

She shook her head, suddenly feeling emotional. "The first I heard of it was when I was served."

"Right," the lawyer said, thoughtfully, looking down at the document once more.

"Also, you said tenancy agreement. Why?"

He looked up at her. "Well, because that's what this notice refers to."

"Yes, but that doesn't make sense. That's one of the reasons why I'm here. Dad owned the house."

"Are you sure?" He rephrased the question when she narrowed her eyes at him. "I mean, how do you know? Have you seen the deeds to the house? Mortgage statements?"

She shook her head. "No, but—"

"Then how do you know?"

She felt a stab of irritation. It was like she was being cross-examined when he was supposed to be helping her. On the other hand, she couldn't remember ever seeing a single piece of correspondence that related to ownership of the house. But then why would she? Her father would have taken care of it. Wouldn't he?

"This is ridiculous," she protested. "My father owns that house. I've lived there since I was a child. You know that. If we were renting, don't you think I'd know somehow? I mean for a start, there would have been letters or visits from the landlord, wouldn't there?"

Eyes still on the document, the lawyer shrugged and said, "I can only tell you what I see, Sophie. And, according to this, neither you nor your dad have ever owned the house. This company," he found the place in the document, "Karlson Properties does."

"But if that's true, then how did we end up living there? If Dad never owned but rented, why are they serving notice now?"

The lawyer looked up from the paper and offered another shrug. "I don't know, it doesn't go into that. All I can tell you is that this document is a notice to quit, and without seeing a copy of the actual lease or mortgage agreement, or any kind of statement that supports your position, there isn't much else I can tell you. The only thing I can assume is…" He hesitated here, naturally sensitive to the subject he was about to raise, "…is that Alan's death must have triggered some kind of clause that states that upon the leaseholder's death, the property is automatically returned to its rightful owner. Again, without seeing the actual lease I can't be sure. But it's unlikely that there'll be any provision for next of kin," he added hesitantly.

"What does that mean, no provision?" she asked.

Christopher looked at her and held her gaze. "Um, unfortunately it means that you are effectively a squatter," he said gently. "That's probably why they moved on it so quickly and were granted the Section 8."

A laugh fluttered out of her lips. "A squatter?"

"Of course, we can't know for sure without seeing a copy of the lease," he replied quickly.

"Chris, come on! A squatter?" She had an incredulous smile on her face but, inside, deep in the pit of her belly, she felt differently. It felt heavy at first, like she'd somehow swallowed a slab of stone, but this soon morphed into something else. Something darker. Something palpable and nauseating. And for a second, it felt as if she was going to vomit all over her neighbour's desk. Her neighbour? No, he was the man she had found in her bathroom that day, doing those things, while her father's wake was taking place in the room below. The same man who had just shared this ridiculous news with her.

"A squatter?" she echoed with a growl, the heavy feeling inside of her smouldering and catching fire. The ardent rageful flame burning through her veins, shaking her body.

"Sophie—"

"A squatter? In my own home?" she seethed.

"Sophie… it's just terminology," the lawyer continued apologetically. "It's not meant to—"

"A FUCKING SQUATTER?"

The hanging frames on the wall behind Chris suddenly slid from their hooks and crashed to the floor in a dissonance of smashing glass. The sound was so sudden and loud that it startled the lawyer to his feet and away from his desk. Sophie jumped to her feet too, hand clamped over her mouth which was open in a silent scream.

Diplomas, trophies, and even a family picture from the lawyer's desk lay in a shattered mess on the floor.

"What the bloody hell happened?" the man gasped.

"I don't know. Was it another earthquake?" Sophie whispered, as if to speak too loudly might trigger an aftershock.

He looked at her and then back at the twisted mess. "I didn't feel anything," the lawyer uttered.

"Are you sure?" she asked. "Maybe there was a draught from the storm."

He shook his head and looked out of the closed window. The sky was a menacing cauldron of bubbling black clouds and the tree in the courtyard was yielding back and forth to the gale, but no draught had made its way inside.

Neither of them spoke for several seconds; the room was silent but for the bluster of the weather beyond the window. A click of approaching footsteps and the knock on the door that followed broke the quiet.

"Come in," Chris said.

The receptionist appeared in the doorway. "Mr Darrington, is everything all right?" she asked, looking first at Sophie and then at her boss.

"Yes, everything's fine, thank you. Could you fetch a dustpan and brush for me? Some of the pictures have fallen off the wall." He glanced at the bare space again.

The secretary followed his gaze and her eyes widened. Then she scanned both people curiously, as if doubting what he had told her. "Of course," she nodded before retreating.

Sophie looked down and noticed that one of the photo frames had landed close to where she was standing. She bent down and retrieved it. Most of the glass was missing but for a couple of jagged shards. Underneath was a group photo of people dressed in their finery. One of the men she recognised from his picture in the waiting room, although he looked older in this image. He was dressed in a tux, holding an award, and wearing a big grin. Next to him was a beautiful young blonde in an evening gown, with her arm around his waist. And next to her, dressed in a black suit and bowtie, was Christopher Darrington. He had his arm around the blonde's waist and was grinning from ear to ear, his smile making her smile.

"Thanks," he said, taking the frame from her.

"Sure, no problem, sorry," was all she could waffle, suddenly awkward, as if she'd just been caught snooping into something personal. She felt like she probably needed to say something, but words failed her.

"Do you know where your father worked?" Christopher asked, saving her.

"I'm sorry, what?"

"Your dad. Who did he work for?" the lawyer asked, holding the frame to his side as if he couldn't bear to look at it.

It took Sophie a few seconds to engage the gears of her brain. "Um, yeah. Of course. He worked for…" The words dissolved in her mouth as the data search in her head returned zero results. She didn't know. She felt like she should, but she bloody well didn't. It just wasn't something that ever came up in conversation and, now she thought about it, Sophie's problems had taken up so much of their lives, they often didn't have the headspace to focus on anything else important. She knew he worked as some kind of logistics manager, but that was it.

Christopher noticed the confusion on her face and proceeded delicately. "What about this Karlson company? Do you know anything about them? Maybe he worked for them and was leasing the house as part of his job?"

Sophie shook her head.

"Ever hear him mention this company? In conversation or something?"

She continued shaking her head. Eyes widening as she began to internalise what this might mean about her relationship with her father.

"Ever seen any mail from them or anything like that?"

"No," she said sharply. Then, softening her stance, "Nothing." She was frustrated. Confused. How could she not know such basic stuff about her own father? And how could she have not even cared to know? What did this say about her?

She took a deep breath. "I'm sorry, Chris. It looks like I don't know anything about anything."

The lawyer hesitated and then took a step closer. "Okay, well, don't worry. I can make some enquiries for you. There's got to be something at Companies House."

"Would you? I mean, I don't really know where to start and, if this thing is real, then..." She couldn't even finish the sentence as the reality of what that meant sunk in. She was being kicking out. Where would she go?

The lawyer nodded sympathetically, then cleared his throat. "Right, so, let me make some enquiries. In the meantime, you need to go through your father's stuff. See if you can find any papers or documents of any kind. For example, I could really do with seeing a copy of a lease agreement, if it does exist, and anything else you think might help. Letters. Wage slips. Anything like that."

Sophie nodded. Just hearing someone talk about a plan made her feel better but equally guilty. She had been nothing but unkind to this man. And somehow, although she had no clue how, she felt responsible for the state of his room.

"Chris, I'm really grateful."

He shook his head. "What are neighbours for, eh?" he asked, looking into her eyes.

She smiled. "Chris, I—"

There was a knock at the door and then it opened. It was the secretary again, carrying a bin bag and a dustpan and brush. "Your next appointment is here," she said unapologetically.

"Thanks. We're finished here anyway, right?" He looked at Sophie.

She hesitated before replying, "Yes. Of course. Yes."

"I'll see you out."

They left the secretary gawking at the shattered mess and stepped out into the waiting room, where a young couple now occupied the leather divan.

"I really appreciate this," Sophie said.

"It's all part of the service," he responded with a faint smile.

"Oh, what about payment? Do I pay now? How does it work?"

"Don't worry. We can sort all of that out later," he said, thrusting his hands in his trouser pockets.

"Are you sure?"

He nodded. "Yeah. Absolutely."

"Okay. So, you'll call me if you learn anything?"

He nodded. "Yeah. And you let me know if you find something."

"I will."

And then it was back. That weirdness between them. Both suddenly finding themselves in the no man's land of hugs or handshakes. She had no idea. The result was that they just stared at each other for several seconds, long enough for the couple to stop what they were chatting about and look up.

"I'd best get going," she said, ignoring the curious eyes.

He nodded.

And then, finally, her feet turned and began to walk.

"Oh, Sophie," he called after her. When she turned back, he'd stepped closer. Close enough for her to feel the heat he was emanating. To smell that cologne. To gaze into the blue pools of his eyes. "The notes from your initial call say that you've received a letter from a firm of lawyers in London, but you didn't give any details." He spoke in almost a whisper, as if conscious the couple nearby might overhear.

She nodded. "Oh, yes, that's right. I received it yesterday right before I called. I don't think it has anything to do with this. It's just an invite to the will reading."

"In London, right? Do you have it with you?"

She shook her head. "No, sorry. Why? Do you think it might be relevant?"

"Let's not discuss it now. Can you scan it and send me a copy? Or do you remember the name of the firm?"

"Um, no. Not off the top of my head. But it was a name a bit like yours, you know, partners. I can't remember exactly, but I know they're based in The Shard."

"The Shard? That means they're expensive. Any idea why he wouldn't have chosen someone local?"

Sophie shrugged. Given the way things had been unfolding, she was beginning to think anything was possible.

"When are you due to meet with them?"

"Tomorrow."

"Okay, well, can you call me once you have? Let me know what you find out? You'll probably learn a lot from the reading."

Sophie bit her lip. "Yes. But at this stage, I'm starting to wonder if that's a good thing."

13

THE WAITING ROOM

THURSDAY AFTERNOON

Victoria Ainsworth hated the clinic on London's Harley Street. While it was a far cry from the drabness of a National Health Service waiting room, the square box still had a way of depressing her despite its classy décor, current copies of Vogue, and cheerful yet vomit-inducing panpipe music.

Luckily, she didn't have to wait long before the nurse summoned her to Doctor Sangit Kulkarni's office. In Victoria's opinion, it was an equally depressing room, made worse by the fact that the eggshell-coloured walls were plastered with brown picture frames, showcasing the eminent doctor's accomplishments. Victoria felt they were vulgar and unnecessary; the fee Doctor Kulkarni charged was enough to enlighten most to the fact he was one of the best in his field. He really did not need to parade it to all and sundry.

Despite her nervousness and the fact that she abhorred having to be there at all, she still managed to muster a smile when the man made his entrance. He wore his ubiquitous white coat and an apologetic demeanour for being detained elsewhere with another patient.

Doctor Kulkarni was a mild-mannered slip of a man. He reminded Victoria of Gandhi with his bald head, round spectacles, and obsequious manner. It bothered her that he must have been rolling in money and yet conducted himself in such a humble way, like he was doing his job because he wanted to be of service and not because he wanted to be rich.

The man had barely sat down behind his desk when Victoria piped up. "Well, here I am, Doctor. It's been nearly two months now."

"It has indeed," the fifty-something-year-old said. He spoke in a soft and cultured English accent with the occasional Asian inflection, which came – Victoria guessed, during one of the many moments of tedium – from his time spent in India, to trips back home for maa's homemade fish curry. She did not know if that was true, of course, because she'd never asked the man, nor did she care to.

Victoria had grown up in a block of flats filled with immigrants. *Stinkers* was how her mother used to refer to them, on account of the ever-present spicy *stench* that haunted the stairwell of their building like a noxious black cloud.

This particular breed of *stinker* was a far cry from the ones she'd grown up with. Those kids with their ill-fitting multi-coloured clothes were nothing like the tailored and manicured man before her. This guy looked like he visited the salon every day while her childhood neighbours seemingly failed to bathe for weeks. She knew that because of the actual *stink* she'd been exposed to many times when she fraternized with them on her endless, and some had believed desperate, quest for companionship.

She shuddered.

That was long ago. Everything is different now. Everything is different now.

Thoughts of her childhood made her stomach turn. It was a form of her own post-traumatic stress for which she needed to regularly counsel herself. In fact, such was her disdain for her origins that she would occasionally play chicken with her thoughts; she'd allow them to wander through the no man's land of her memories just so she could experience the rush of yanking them back to the present, to thoughts of her husband and her new affluent life. Her past was the sore she needed to regularly prod, to emphasise just how far she had come in contrast. *This* was her world now, and she'd rain down fury on anybody or anything that dared to mess with it.

The sound of Doctor Kulkarni clearing his throat brought her back into the present moment in his tiny office. Couldn't the man afford something more spacious than this place? He was bloody charging enough.

She didn't want to be here. She'd never wanted to be treated by *him,* but he came highly recommended and if he could solve her problem, she was prepared to endure. This is what she'd told herself the whole time she'd been coming here. The months felt like bloody years, and she resolved that he'd better have some good news today. She was sick of having to suffer those brown spindly fingers of his rummaging between her legs. As far as she was concerned, the gloves he wore were little protection against the violation.

Oh God, I'm going to puke.

"Victoria?"

"Huh?"

"Are you all right? May I bring you something? A beverage, perhaps."

"No. I'm fine. Thank you. Why do you ask?" She shifted awkwardly in her chair.

"Well, you're looking pale. And just now, it seemed as if you were somewhere else."

"No, I'm perfectly fine. I'm obviously here, not somewhere else."

He looked at her curiously, then asked, "How are you feeling, in yourself? Physically, I mean. Any discomfort?"

"No, it's all right as rain, Doctor. You should know. You examined me. Did it all look normal down there?" She lifted her eyebrows.

The doctor glanced at her, obviously unsure how to react to the question, and instead asked, "Any more abdominal cramps? Pain of any kind?"

"No, nothing."

That wasn't strictly true, but things had been better since the surgery and, in her opinion, some minor discomfort was to be expected.

Doctor Kulkarni tapped keys on his laptop, read for a few seconds and then continued. "So, yes, you do appear to be healing very well and, as you know, the surgery appeared to be successful but—"

"Wait, what? *Appear?*" She frowned. "What do you mean *appear?*"

Doctor Kulkarni sat forward in his seat, resting his elbows on the desk and making a steeple with his hands. She wanted to reach over and snap his wrists. It would be counterproductive, but she also imagined the satisfaction it would yield.

"Well, as we discussed, the surgery was to remove tissue from the lining of your womb, and this in and of itself was, as you know, successful. But you must remember, Victoria, while this could well have been the reason for your inability to conceive, there are no guarantees that it was. You'll appreciate our priority was to alleviate your discomfort."

"No," Victoria said, forcing herself to remain calm, "your priority was to treat the reason why I came to you in the first place, and that was to figure out why I can't get pregnant."

"And that is precisely what we are doing, Victoria. But these things take time."

"I don't have time!" she exploded.

There was an awkward pause as the boom of her voice filled the air between them. It was accompanied by the sound of a ringing telephone beyond the door and the traffic beyond the window.

"I don't have time," she repeated calmly.

Resuming the discussion as if he hadn't been interrupted, the doctor spoke with the same unaffected tone. "I appreciate your frustration, Victoria, but treating fertility issues is often a process and not an exact science. By that I mean that it isn't always possible to point at one specific thing. Sometimes, and often, it's a process of elimination. For example, the problem may not necessarily lie with you."

She forced a laugh, "Well, we know it can't possibly be my husband."

"I appreciate that. But if we could perhaps ask him to come in for—"

"No," she said sharply. Then, after taking a deep breath, she added, "I already told you, he's a busy man and I don't want to burden him with this. There's nothing wrong with his package, I assure you. Besides, you were the one who said it was most likely something to do with the so-called scar tissue."

There was another pause as Victoria rubbed her hands together, making patterns out of the white patches behind her skin by squeezing her fingers so tightly together they hurt.

The doctor broke the silence. "I would say that the next step, of course, if you're physically up to it, is to resume intercourse with your husband and that—"

"Done that," she said, without looking up.

"I'm sorry?"

"We've already restarted that. When he's around, of course. He's working most of the time, so we've pretty much had to fit it in whenever possible. If you know what I mean."

"When did you do that?"

"About a month ago."

"Victoria, I was very clear about—"

"Relax, Doctor. You said yourself that everything looked fine down there, didn't you?"

"That's not the point…"

Now she gave him her eyes, narrowed to slits, as she spat, "Then what IS the fucking point? Isn't the point for everything to be present and in working order? Well, it is. It bloody well is. I don't know how many times I've let him cum inside me since the surgery and I'm still not fucking pregnant, am I? Why is that, huh? Why is that, Doctor Kulkarni? I'll tell you why. This surgery that you say was a success sounds like a complete fucking failure to me."

Her eyes were wide now, desperate, roaming around the room as if looking for a solution on one of the side units, or perhaps inside the doctor's picture frames full of accomplishments, meaningless to her without the result she needed.

The doctor stifled a sigh. "Victoria. We discussed this. Fertility isn't just physical, it's also psychological. And, to me, you appear to be under a considerable amount of stress."

"Of course I fucking am! My husband wants babies. His family expects babies. They expect heirs. That's all he's banged on about since we met, and if I can't give him that, then…" She trailed off at the thought of the potential repercussions, which were even more abhorrent to her than Doctor Kulkarni was. She looked out of the tall Georgian window and allowed her thoughts to drift beyond, deep into the grey slate sky, where she envisioned images of herself falling to her knees and sobbing as her husband drove away from her. She couldn't lose him. She wouldn't. He was all she had. He was the only thing in the world that meant anything to her. She'd kill to keep him if she had to. She'd do whatever it took, no matter the warnings, no matter the risks.

"Then?" Kulkarni asked. "Please finish the thought."

Victoria hesitated. There were tears welling in her eyes. They were born of frustration but were swelling further with anger and fear. "If I don't give him children then he'll find somebody else who will," she said, without turning from the window.

The doctor's tone carried a reassuring smile. "I'm sure that isn't the case, Mrs Ainsworth. Many of my clients feel that way, but a marriage is much more than that. Besides, should we find that you are unable to conceive, there's always adoption."

Her eyes darted to him and with an angry swipe of the back of her hand, she growled, "Haven't you been fucking listening? I don't want to adopt. He doesn't. So, instead of suggesting pointless alternatives, *I* suggest you get back to earning your bloody fee!"

14

NUMBER 9

THURSDAY NIGHT

At number 9 Meadow Lane, Matthew Rowe was excited to discover that he had the house to himself. One of his roommates, Chris, was away at a conference and the other was working nightshifts. He was really looking forward to getting a decent night's sleep, instead of being awoken in the middle of it by what often sounded like zombies being pleasured in the next room.

Not that Matt didn't enjoy a good time, of course he did. But this past week, he'd experienced some bizarre erotic dreams of his own. They had left him feeling exhausted come morning – as if he'd had his very lifeforce drained from him – to the point where he was struggling to make it through his classes.

Studying to become an accountant wasn't that hard – at least it wasn't for him – but the two shifts he had to take on as a server to subsidise his income was. Especially when money was still tight. Thankfully, Chris was a top bloke when it came to paying rent on time.

After staring blankly at the refrigerator for the best part of a minute, he eventually chose to peel off the sticker from the carton of popcorn chicken that read *Alistair's – do not touch* and carry it up to his bedroom. He flicked on the overhead light and groaned.

Matt was a self-described neat freak. His bedroom was always tidy, with bed made and corners folded, an inevitable by-product of being raised under the roof of an army captain. But lately he just couldn't be arsed, much to his own discontent. His room was now well on its way to resembling Alistair's.

This pained him because Alistair was a slob. This was a subject over which the two would often clash. If Chris was good enough to let them stay in his home for minimal rent, the least they could do was keep it tidy.

Matt couldn't bear the sight and flipped the overhead light off once more. Instead, he flicked on the bedside lamp and shivered.

"What the fuck…" he breathed. The room felt like an icebox, and a simple glance across the room explained why; the window was wide open.

Who did that?

He dumped the carton on the bedside table, crossed the room and looked out onto the back garden. Visibility was limited to the overspill of light from the lounge downstairs, which was only a couple of feet into the meadow that was supposed to be the back lawn. Everything else, including the gate that led to the fields and the woodland beyond, had been swallowed up by darkness.

It was peculiarly quiet in the neighbourhood. Not a raised voice from one of the nearby houses or a hollow dog bark in the distance could be heard. What had happened to all the pets in the street? It felt odd without them. As if, like village children, they had followed the magical notes of some pipe, deep into the heart of the forest.

A chill ran through him as the cold pinched his ears. He was just about to close the window when he spotted something from the corner of his eye. Down there. On the lawn. On the boundary between light and darkness. It was the most curious thing. He had to blink a few times, refocus, just to be sure he wasn't hallucinating.

He was. Because they were gone now. He concluded that he must be so drained he had imagined it. He'd seen two pairs of shoes down there. Brogues. One brown. One black. Both straddling the light as if there were two people standing perfectly still, watching the house.

He shoved the window shut then locked it.

He swore. They'd talked about this. Boundaries. They'd agreed to stay out of each other's rooms and yet Alistair had done it again. It wouldn't be the first time the prick had invaded his space and he was sick of it. At the earliest opportunity, he was going to have it out with him.

Stay out of my room! Away from my shit! he thought, as he turned to see the packet of processed chicken meat. *Yeah. Probably should return that to the fridge.*

But he was way too tired to do that now. Instead, he shuffled into the bathroom, brushed his teeth, peed, and then contemplated having a shower. And yet, even when the shower dripped longingly for his body, he decided against it. He was just too tired.

Instead, he shut off the light, returned to the bedroom and froze: the window was wide open once more. The overhead lampshade was swinging in the chill.

What the fuck?

He looked around the room then rolled his eyes. "Not funny!" he shouted, to nowhere in particular. "Come on, guys, what did we say about staying out of each other's spaces? This isn't cool," he yelled.

Silence.

He surveyed the vicinity. He didn't hear anybody pass by. No creaking on the landing. Whoever was playing this practical joke had to be either in the wardrobe or under the bed.

He looked at the large built-in wardrobe.

"Come on, man, I'm bloody knackered and not in the mood for this shit!" he shouted irritably.

Nothing. Just curtains shifting in the cold breeze. The overhead lampshade swayed quietly back and forth, shifting circular shadows over the walls and furniture.

Matt marched forward to the wardrobe. "Dude, come on. I know you're in there. You may as well get out. You're not scaring shit!"

Nothing.

"Fine." He yanked the doors open with both hands. Hanging shirts fluttered then stilled.

The wardrobe was empty.

He turned and looked around the room. There was nothing in here but the freeze, nipping at his ears once more.

"Shit," he groaned, shoving the wardrobe doors closed and then turning and eyeing the bed. "Dude, come on. Get the fuck out from under there!"

He waited. Not a snigger. Just silence.

With a sigh, he walked over to the bed, dropped to his knees, and prepared himself for the juvenile encounter he was not in the mood to deal with. Alistair, of course. It had to be him because that packet of chicken had disappeared from the bedside table too. He was obviously being a dick about it even though he hadn't even touched the stuff. And yet...

There was nothing under the bed except a pair of dirty trainers, some scrunched up used tissues and... "What's this?"

He plucked the thing up and held it under the light.

At first, it looked like one of those small brown rubber band balls, but a closer inspection revealed that it was actually some kind of golf-ball sized basket, weaved tightly together with some kind of wood vine with – "Ow, fuck!" – fucking thorns inside.

"What the hell, dude?" Matt yelled, throwing the thing onto the bed, and jumping to his feet. He stalked across the room and pushed the window shut, once more engaging the lock. Then, he left the bedroom, went out on the landing, and yelled, "NOT FUNNY!"

Now he knew that it had to be Alistair because this was his M.O. He'd even turned the lights off in the lounge now to try to scare him. *Prick!*

He listened intently for movement, snickering or any other tell-tale sign that somebody else was home.

Nothing.

This gave him a few seconds of pause. Alistair did enjoy winding him up, but he was also obvious about it. This evening, however, it was different.

Either way, he didn't care. He was tired and sick of this shit. And, if he was perfectly honest with himself, the silence, the open window, the disappearing chicken, and that deep blackness that loitered at the foot of the stairs all conspired to send another shiver through him.

"I'm going to bed. Some of us have got to get up for work in the morning," he said, retreating to the sanctuary of his room, slamming the door behind him while once again making a mental note to put a bloody lock on his door.

Then, after turning up the radiator, he stripped down to his shorts and dove underneath the covers.

Matthew Rowe was roused from his sleep a couple of hours later to what he thought was the sound of the window opening once more. A sleepy glance across the room told him that wasn't possible since the window was still firmly shut against the winter's night. It had suspended a giant moon among the stars, like the topper on a Christmas tree, filling the bedroom with a diffused silvery spotlight.

There was silence but for the tick of the industrious radiator. It was busying itself warming the air to a blissfully snug temperature that had Matt relinquish his hold on the quilt and allow it to slide down to his chest.

He was lying on his back now, legs apart, lingering on the border of consciousness, when he felt Amy's tongue trail down his chest and loiter at the smattering of hair on his midriff.

"Amy," he mumbled. "So it was you all along," he said with a smile. "Who let you in?"

School night antics weren't exclusive to the lads. Matt wasn't as *pretty* as Christopher or as rugged as Alistair, nor did he have a body that was anywhere near as defined as either of theirs, but he held his own with the ladies. Truth be known, recently things had become a little more regular with one of his college classmates.

Amy wasn't remarkable either. She dressed conservatively, had frizzy hair that rarely escaped the confines of its ties and, with spectacles perched on the tip of her big nose, she was a bit of a nerd slash introvert.

In public.

In private, well, she was a bit of an animal. In Matt's opinion, it was true what they said about the quiet ones. In bed, Amy was the opposite of how she looked in life. She was outrageous and experimental. She derived a lot of pleasure from giving pleasure and was often kinky with it. This included the occasional unannounced midnight visit if she didn't have class the next day or an early shift.

Alistair's take was that she only did this because she wanted to keep tabs on him, to make sure he wasn't *doing the dirty* with someone else. But then, Alistair was a dick.

He tensed as Amy's cold bony fingers migrated south into his shorts. He chuckled, "Ames, your hands are bloody freezing!" And yet, they didn't have to linger long before triggering a reflexive response from him. "Hmm…" he moaned appreciatively, basking in the delirious deliciousness of the moment as he anticipated what was coming next.

He felt his underwear slide down his legs and then she began. Slow rhythmic strokes that made the quilt rise and fall, followed by the sensation of her long moist tongue coiling, ravelling and unravelling in a new and exciting way that electrified his heart into a fast and frenetic thud…

Faster…

Breath shallowing.

Closer…

Muscles clenching. Tension building. Back arching as his body sought to fulfil that primordial urge to release, to spread his seed.

Closer… faster… closer… faster.

Hot, powerful *thud-thump thud-thump* of deliciousness as sweat beaded on his forehead and he began to chew his lip… closer… closer… Then, his phone began to vibrate like an angry hornet trapped in glass, lighting up the room and sawing through the moment.

"Don't…s…t…op!" he urged, trying to ignore the grating, persistent sound drilling through the intense stillness. "D…on…t…stop…" he insisted, for he was close, so close. He reached out hastily, felt for the phone, and held it in his hand to stop the annoying sound as the release finally came in a stilted but deeply pleasurable explosion.

"Oh fuuu… Oh shit…" he cried, panting, gulping, and twitching in the aftermath.

Meanwhile the phone was still vibrating in his hand. How many times did he need to remind himself to set the bloody divert to voicemail?

After several seconds of recovery, he angrily glanced at the screen then dropped the vibrating thing onto the bed. He wiped the sweat from his forehead and breathed deeply as his heart slowed, his muscles relaxed and…

His eyes sprang open as he swallowed on a parched throat. It was now uncomfortably warm in the room. Tropical. The realisation of what he had just seen burned through his mind.

It couldn't be. How was that possible? Was it some kind of trick?

Now, fully alert, he reached down to his phone, picked it up and slowly turned it to face him as the filtered light filled the room, resurrecting voyeuristic shadows.

That's when it felt like his heart stopped.

VIDEO CALL FROM AMY ROSS
ANSWER: YES? NO?

Matthew Rowe peered over his phone's screen at the dark shape under the bed cover and then back at the screen, tapping YES.

A pixelated grainy image of Amy's face appeared, illuminated by the phone's display. "Bloody hell, Matt! Finally! It's like trying to wake the dead. Talk about killing the mood. I'm freezing my bloody tits off out here! Your door's locked and you forgot to give me your key." The video wobbled as Amy rubbed her arms and danced from foot to foot to stay warm. He wasn't sure, but he thought he caught a fleeting glimpse of his front door in the background.

"Amy?" he asked tentatively.

The all-star university student frowned. "In the freezing cold flesh…"

"Wh…where are you?" Matt continued, anxiety rising, scratching at his chest.

"Freezing my arse off outside your house, of course. Stop pissing about," she added in a loud whisper. "Come let me in now or I'm going home. I've…"

Matt tuned out of the conversation and into the sensation of his spent body under the covers. It was now cold, clammy, his erection deflated.

To his revulsion, he could still feel that cold tongue slithering around his groin and midriff. It made him want to hurl.

Slowly, heart pounding, temple throbbing, he turned the phone screen in his hand…

"Hey, what are you doing…? No time for that…"

…projecting the tiny screen light in front of him…

"Matt?"

…as he slowly peeled back the quilt and looked down.

"Matt? What… What is that?"

Its tongue slithered back in rapid retraction and its slitted eyes glinted up at him under the feeble phone light.

The humanoid creature was not of this world. It could only be something conjured from the deepest darkest pits of his worst nightmare. It was skinless, with strands of hair protruding from an otherwise bald scalp, had a hawkish nose and a long reptilian tongue that slithered greedily over a face full of serrated teeth.

"OH SHIT!" Matt screamed and turned to propel himself away.

But the creature wasn't finished collecting the seed, and now that it had been discovered, it had no choice. It opened its serrated face and bit down, just as the rest of Matthew's body hurled itself out of the bed.

The wail was so loud and piercing that Amy dropped her phone. She didn't need it anyway; the agonised screams were so loud that they were no longer being transmitted telephonically but were carried out to her from inside the house on the cold night's breeze.

15

MORGAN, THOMAS & MITCHELL

FRIDAY AFTERNOON

Sophie had never been to London's Shard before, but she had heard that it used to be Europe's tallest building. Under any other circumstance, she would have been excited to learn that her father's lawyers had an office there. But today... well, today she was already feeling out of sorts – queasy, like she'd picked up a bug or something – and the last thing she fancied doing was boarding the futuristic lift to ascend God only knew how many floors into the sky.

She looked at her hands; they were shaking. She thrust them into her coat pockets, surreptitiously breathing deeply to try to stave off the nausea as her stomach churned. But almost instantly her hands started to feel clammy, so she pulled them out with the hope of air drying them before she was obliged to shake somebody's hand.

She still couldn't believe it. This was all one gigantic case of mistaken identity. These lawyers were obviously very expensive. The location. The phone call from the snooty secretary to confirm. And that invite of thick paper with its embossed gold logo of what looked like an odd-shaped star, encircled in black. There was no way in a million years her father would have hired these people to make his will. Of course, she had tried to tell the secretary this, but she was having none of it. Well, they were about to be sorely disappointed.

The muzak stopped and a soft female voice announced that they had reached their floor. The doors swished open. Sophie pressed a hand to her belly in an effort to quell the butterflies that were swarming there.

She looked across at Victoria, grateful that her friend had insisted on coming with her. There's no way she could have made the journey on her own. Despite her suspicion that this was all one giant misunderstanding, the mere notion that this might in any way be about her father made her feel sick and dizzy with confusion.

"Are you okay?" Victoria asked as they made their way down a dimly lit corridor.

"No, not really."

"Oh, babe. Don't worry. This is just a formality. It'll be over before you know it, and I'll be with you every step of the way," she said, linking her friend's arm.

They emerged from a short corridor to a brighter space and to an immaculately groomed woman behind a futuristic white reception desk.

"We're here to see, um… Roger, isn't it…?" Victoria said, looking at Sophie for confirmation, but she was too busy gazing at the giant mirrored lettering of the firm's name, mounted on the wall behind the receptionist. "Sophie?"

"Yes, Mitchell. Roger Mitchell." She knew the name well. She'd re-read his letter numerous times, *respectfully requesting an audience at her earliest convenience.*

"Yes, Mr Mitchell is expecting you," the receptionist said. "Please take a seat," she added, gesturing to a pair of white leather and chrome chairs.

They complied as the woman picked up the phone, waited, and then began talking in a subdued tone.

Above them, a flat screen television bragged about the firm's many high-profile clients, who were *served with the utmost professionalism and discretion* from its many offices around the world.

"This can't be right, can it?" Sophie whispered.

"Stop it," Victoria replied.

"Well, it can't. Why would and how could my dad hire a firm like this to do his will when he could have chosen one in Cambridge? I mean, these days you can bloody make a will online!"

Victoria touched her friend's arm and repeated, firmly, "Stop it. You're working yourself into a state. It's a will, Sophie, not a bloody marriage. Let's just hear what the man has to say, and then we'll be out of here. I promise."

"Yes, but—"

"Sophie?" a plump middle-aged man asked, making his way towards them.

Sophie sprang to her feet as if standing to attention. "Yes. Yes. That's me."

"A real pleasure," the man said with a big smile, proffering his hand. He was well spoken. *Plummy*, Sophie thought, *very plummy.* She was surprised he was wearing a tie and not a cravat.

"I'm Victoria," said Victoria quickly, seeming to notice that her friend had lost the ability to articulate. "I'm Sophie's best friend."

"Pleasure," the man said, taking her extended hand and shaking it gently. "Would you like to come through?"

He led them away from reception through an open plan office. It featured a long wall made of glass offering an enviable view of the City of London, stitched together by the chain of the River Thames and the jewels of St Paul's Cathedral, London Bridge, the London Eye, and Big Ben.

"Oh, this view is stunning," Victoria gasped.

"Isn't it just?" Mr Mitchell smiled. "When I first came here, I couldn't stop gawking. I don't think I completed any work that day."

They followed the circle of the space before stopping off at a spacious office with glass walls and a door stencilled with the words *Roger Mitchell – Senior Partner.*

"Please take a seat," the man said, ushering his visitors to a pair of leather sofas facing each other. The friends sat on one side, the lawyer on the other. Between them, a chrome and glass coffee table held a tray of glassware and a selection of drinks.

"May I offer you a beverage?"

"Water, please," Sophie said, swallowing in anticipation.

"Me too, thank you," said Victoria, using her best posh voice.

The man broke the seal on two bottles of San Pellegrino water, poured the contents into drinking glasses and placed them in front of his guests.

"The view really is incredible," Sophie filled in nervously, as she watched London life drift forward below them.

"My favourite," Mr Mitchell contributed once again. "You know, I have to check myself sometimes, because I'm a bit of a... what do they call it..." He squinted and clicked pudgy fingers as he tried to recall.

"Anorak?" Victoria helped.

The man looked at her. "Not quite the word I was looking for but apt, nonetheless. An *anorak*. Especially when it comes to the boats. I like to watch them float back and forth up the river. It's almost hypnotic, you know. It's silly, but I like to wonder about the people on board, who they might be, why they're there. Are they celebrating a special occasion or just out on a day trip? Yes, I'm a self-confessed people watcher, I'm afraid. I think it's jolly good fun," he added with an embarrassed smile.

The man's affable demeanour went some way to calming Sophie's nerves. It was almost as if he had sensed her edginess and made the innocuous confession to put her at ease.

It was working. Although, her cynical side, the one that had been emotionally battered of late, soon reminded her that the man was still a lawyer. By the looks of it, he was a well-paid one. This could all be part of his act.

"So, Sophie…"

"Yes," she responded, as casually as she could.

"I know you spoke to my secretary, and that this," he gestured around the room "is all a bit of a shock for you."

"Just a bit, yeah. Yes," she quickly corrected herself and was instantly reminded of her father.

"Quite understandably."

"I asked her for more information, but she said she wasn't able to discuss it over the phone," Sophie said.

"Yes. I'm terribly sorry about that, but it's all part of the service, you see. You'll appreciate that we take our clients' privacy very seriously."

Sophie nodded, miffed nonetheless that she had pretty much been summoned here. But then, how much more information did she need beyond the fact that her father's surprisingly fancy lawyer wanted to see her for the reading of his last will and testament?

"So, why has my friend been summoned here?" Victoria piped up with typical bluntness.

Sophie glanced at her.

Mr Mitchell smiled with a nod. "Straight to the point. I like that. You know," he added, leaning forward in his seat, "my mother used to say that all time should be treated as if it were money." He smiled. Then, after a few seconds, he rose from his seat and gestured at a conference table at the other side of the room. "Please," he said. "Do bring your beverages with you."

The friends picked up their drinks and made their way over to a rectangular table that had room for six and took a seat on the plush leather and chrome chairs. Sophie flinched when Victoria put her glass down with a loud clang on the toughened frosted glass.

The lawyer, who had detoured to retrieve a manila folder from his desk, took a seat across from them. Without saying anything, he opened the folder and shuffled through some of the papers inside, stopping at one of them.

"So, Sophie. I can see here that you used to work as a waitress, is that correct?"

She nodded. "Yes, that's right. I was in college at the time."

"Then a sales assistant in a clothes store?"

"Yes."

"A receptionist…"

"Um, yes."

"And a theme park usher. As well as some other roles. Most lasting less than a day."

She shifted in her seat.

"Now you're working at Stansted Airport," he looked up almost as if surprised, "and have been there for some time?"

Instinctively, Sophie explained. "Yes, as a Senior Passenger Experience Agent."

"Nobody told us this was an interview," Victoria chimed in protectively.

"Oh no, of course not. I'm terribly sorry if that's how it might seem but please be reassured that it's not at all. It's just for verification purposes, to make sure this is not a case of mistaken identity, you understand. To ensure that you are indeed the person named in these documents."

"Well," Sophie said with a forced laugh, "you should have just asked me for a blood sample and had done with it."

"Yes. That would be most useful," the man said seriously.

There were a few seconds of awkward silence, punctured by the distant warble of an emergency service siren as they shared glances.

Mr Mitchell broke into a laugh. "I'm only joshing."

Sophie laughed.

"We'll just need to swab your mouth for DNA before you leave."

Sophie stopped laughing.

The man grinned. "Still joking."

Sophie resumed her stilted laughter.

Victoria clearly wasn't amused. "Why are we here?" she asked abruptly, sitting forward in her chair, and placing immaculately painted glossy black nails on the table in front of her.

The lawyer lost all trace of his lingering smile and cleared his throat. "So, just for clarity, Sophie, your full name is Sophie Cooper. Is that correct?"

Sophie nodded, eager for the man to get on with it so they could confirm this was, after all, a case of mistaken identity.

"And you were born on February 1st and have just had your twenty-first birthday. Is that correct?"

"Yes."

"And your foster parents were Alan and Elena Cooper?"

"I'm sorry, what?"

Mr Mitchell squinted. She was sitting right across from him, and he had spoken plainly, yet he repeated the question. "Your foster parents... their names were Alan and Elena Cooper, yes?"

Sophie's stomach dropped as if she was back in one of those fancy lifts and it was plummeting downward. The sensation was so potent it instantly pushed beads of perspiration to her forehead.

She hadn't misheard.

"Sophie!" It was Victoria calling to her, touching her arm. And yet all Sophie could think about was her dream. The one where she was standing on one side of the river and her father was on the other, mouthing words she couldn't hear. *Didn't want* to hear, maybe?

"Sophie!" Victoria was louder this time. She was shaking her friend who was vacantly staring into space, face ashen. It looked like she was going to pass out, or worse, puke over the frosted glass table. She prepped herself for an emergency drawback; well, she didn't want vomit all over her new Pradas. Those babies were worth the best part of a grand.

Luckily, her friend appeared to refocus once more. "Hey," Victoria said with a sigh, relief flooding through her. She shot the lawyer a glare.

"I'm so terribly sorry, Miss Cooper," Mr Mitchell said hastily. "I had no idea that you were unaware. If so, I would never have just…" He allowed the words to dissolve in his mouth. "Is there anything I can get you?"

"Yes, the door. You obviously have the wrong person," Victoria snapped.

A shadow fell over the podgy man's cheery demeanour. "Oh, I'm afraid there's no mistake. We're quite thorough in this regard."

"I'm telling you, you've got the wrong person," Victoria insisted.

"We've conducted all necessary vetting procedures," the man continued, looking at Sophie. "Miss Cooper, you are the person named in this will. The address, the date of birth, the place of birth. All the information my secretary verified before today's meeting was confirmed. Even your work history. They all match."

"Why would you even have that information?" Victoria growled with a narrowing of her eyes.

"Your father…" Mr Mitchell cleared his throat, still addressing his answers to Sophie. "Your biological father, that is, made a point of keeping in touch with your foster parents through us, to ensure your wellbeing."

Victoria's growl was matched by her scowl. "What? You mean, he—whoever he is—has been spying on her through you this whole time?"

"Well, I wouldn't call it spying, exactly," Mitchell said, "He merely maintained an interest. You know, to ensure you were being taken care of—"

"And yet, he never thought of actually making contact with her?" Victoria chided.

There was another long pause as Sophie attempted to absorb what she had learned and find the right words to articulate herself, so Victoria would stop doing all the talking for her. And yet, no matter how hard she tried to reconcile it, she could not accept what she was hearing. It was ludicrous. She would have known; her parents would have told her. The buffoon sitting in front of them was obviously mistaken. Victoria was right. He obviously had the wrong person.

Obviously.

"Come on, Vic, we're leaving," she said abruptly, standing up.

"Miss Cooper, please."

"You've got the wrong person."

"I can assure you that we don't—"

"You've got the wrong person!" she insisted, moving away from the conference table, Victoria's shoes clicking loudly behind her.

"We take our work very seriously, Miss Cooper," Mr Mitchell

added, raising his voice.

"Not seriously enough!" Sophie threw back.

"Miss Cooper!"

"Leave me alone!" She was at the door now.

"Miss Cooper, please!" the lawyer called. Realising he was losing her, he followed with an uncharacteristically desperate yell. "I have a copy of your birth certificate!"

He snatched a beige piece of paper from the file in front of him and held it up as if it were a truce flag. Whether it was enough to convince the young lady, he had no clue, but it certainly was enough to stop her in her tracks along with some of the other interns who, up until that moment, were purposefully hurrying back and forth in the corridor. It only took one glance from Mr Mitchell to send them on their merry way once more.

Victoria's gaze darted from the man in the office to her friend nearby. She felt like she should say something, but she had absolutely no idea what. The news was incredible. What could she possibly say?

Sophie was fostered. *Shit!* Even she was having a hard time coming to terms with that. In all the time she had known her, she had no clue that the life she had spent many years envying wasn't real.

Too good to be true.

The bedside stories, the family days out, the camping. The quality time with her father, swinging on those swings in the back garden. The ones he had set up for her. All fake. Those people were being paid, if not by her biological father, then by the state, to become nothing more than actors. The model parents that she had always coveted.

Victoria had always known there was something special about Sophie. She'd been told as much, but she never would have imagined this. Never.

Movement nearby yanked her out of her thoughts to see that

her friend was slowly making her way back into the lawyer's office, much to her delight. Despite everything, Victoria's curiosity was piqued.

They both re-joined the lawyer at the conference table. Victoria watched her friend take the piece of paper from the lawyer and scrutinize it. Oh, how she wanted to snatch it from her hands so she could have a good look too! But she restrained herself.

After what felt like at least a couple of minutes, she watched her friend hand the sheet of paper back to the lawyer.

"I really am very sorry. I appreciate what a terrible shock this must be for you," Mr Mitchell offered once more.

Sophie watched a helicopter follow the river. Its painted shell glinted in the sun that had temporarily escaped its imprisonment behind a moving wall of black clouds.

"Miss Cooper. If you prefer, we can reschedule..." Mr Mitchell said, quietly, trying to make eye contact with the young girl who was vacantly staring into space once more.

Eventually, her focus shifted back to him. She shook her head slowly and demanded, "Why am I here?"

Mr Mitchell hesitated, peering into the girl's blue eyes, as if trying to establish whether she was suffering from temporary amnesia. Then, he tentatively offered, "We're here to read your *biological* father's last will and testament."

Sophie nodded, understanding now. So this was not about those two strangers who had probably been paid to raise her all these years. This was about the other, newer stranger. The man whose name had been scrawled into the appropriate box on her birth certificate.

"I still have some questions. Formalities," the lawyer continued with an apologetic shrug.

Sophie nodded absentmindedly; her eyes much more interested in the city beyond the glass than the man in front of her. He was another stranger after all and, like a maniacal butcher, he was casually taking a cleaver to what was left of the bloody stump of the life she once knew.

"So, um…" he consulted the papers in front of him. "Your foster mother left when you were six years old. Is that correct?"

There was silence but for the ringing of a telephone beyond the door.

"She was taken. I mean, she left, yes," Sophie said, flatly. Victoria sighed, as if she had been holding her breath in anticipation.

"I'm sorry," Mr Mitchell probed. "She left or—"

"She's already answered. She left," Victoria cut him off.

Mr Mitchell glanced at her. "And your foster father, Alan Cooper, he passed in an automobile accident a few weeks ago?" the lawyer asked, gently.

It was less than that, but a nod, swallow and a sniff was the extent of Sophie's response. Not to hold back tears but to stop them from forming.

Victoria picked up on this, partly from her friend's stiffened posture and partly from the way she was squeezing her hand. "Look, Mr Parker…"

"Mitchell…"

"…Mitchell. My friend didn't come here to have this rubbish raked up for her. She can do that from the comfort of her home. So, if you have something you want to share, please just get to it so that I can get her out of here."

Victoria was irked. To Sophie, it would seem that her friend was being protective of her, the way she'd always been since they first met in that schoolground. Victoria was skilled at making others believe what she wanted them to believe. But really, she couldn't bear the suspense any longer. Besides, she was getting bored with all this formal rubbish. Why couldn't the man get to the bloody point? She wanted to know what was so special about her so-called friend.

Mr Mitchell looked at Victoria. "Yes, of course," he said with another of his disarming smiles. He turned his attention back to Sophie. "Miss Cooper, I'm very sorry, but for me to disclose this information to you, I'm obliged to formally ascertain that you are indeed the Sophie Cooper cited in these documents. And you'll appreciate that, in order for me to do that, I must ask the questions the verification process dictates. Please accept my sincerest apologies for any distress this may have caused you. Naturally, it is not my intention to upset you in any way."

Sophie shook her head. "I understand," she said.

The man glanced at Victoria again, who cocked her head defiantly.

Sophie, sensing that something might blow up between them, quickly confirmed the answers to his questions. "Yes, both my par…um, foster parents are gone. My foster father raised me, and he died in a road traffic incident. The truck driver was busy fiddling with his mobile phone and ploughed straight into the back of him."

"Oh…" Mr Mitchell said, as if he wasn't already aware of the detail. "How awful. And, as far as you know, you don't have any other relatives?"

Sophie shook her head. The answer to that question was almost as painful as her recent discovery, reminding her that she truly was alone in the world. "No, no relatives," she said, picking up her glass with shaky fingers and taking a gulp of water to fend off the tears that wanted to revisit, albeit for entirely different reasons now.

Mr Mitchell turned a sheet of paper in his folder, cleared his throat, reshuffled in his seat, and then looked her in the eyes once more.

"Miss Cooper…"

"Do you have to keep calling me that?" she asked.

"I'm sorry, did I pronounce it incorrectly?"

"No, but it's so bloody formal," she said. Her heart was throbbing in her chest. The tension in her skull was slowly building into a headache.

"Sophie, earlier, when I asked if you had family, you said that you did not. Is that correct?"

"Oh, for crying out loud! She's already answered that question. It's like she's being bloody cross-examined!" Victoria exploded.

Mr Mitchell closed his eyes temporarily, as if absorbing the woman's outburst and giving himself an *in with anger out with love* pep talk before proceeding. "Again, I can only apologise, but I have a process—"

"This is obviously about her biological father. Just stop dramatizing it, man, and get on with it. You've already crapped all over her day!"

Sophie looked at her friend and then back at the man in front of her. "Please, Mr Mitchell. Continue."

The man shuffled in his seat. "This will come as no surprise to you, your biological father passed recently. A Signor Alessandro DaTerra. Does that name mean anything to you?"

Sophie shook her head.

"He's Italian?" Victoria chimed in.

"Yes, from Northern Italy, to be precise."

"Italy? What about my mother?"

"There's no information here about her beyond the birth certificate, I'm afraid, but it's my understanding that she passed shortly after you were born. That's all I have. I don't have the whole genealogy or any history here. We're only privy to the essential information." He made a show of flicking through the papers in front him.

Sophie nodded and bit her lip again. She wasn't sure if she had pierced the skin or if the coppery taste in her mouth was her imagination.

"And this Signor D…D," Victoria struggled.

"DaTerra," Mr Mitchell contributed.

"Yes, him. Now he's dead too?"

Mr Mitchell paused at Victoria's candid question, then nodded. "As soon as Signor DaTerra's death was confirmed, his Italian lawyers actioned his last will and testament and retained our services to execute them," the lawyer said, delicately lifting a translucent piece of paper out of the folder.

It looked nothing like the other sheets. This one looked older, much older, and so thin that she could see through to the ornate calligraphy on the other side.

"The will confirms that the Palazzo Rosso and associated assets be bequeathed to one Sofia DaTerra, along with—"

"Wait, what? Sofia DaTerra? Is that supposed to be…" Sophie couldn't bring herself to complete the sentence.

Mr Mitchell did it for her. "You, Sofia. I believe that's you."

"Her name's Sophie," Victoria threw back.

"So my foster parents knew that this man was still alive?"

The lawyer shrugged and shook his head sadly. "I couldn't say for sure, but it would appear that way."

The information dump, the questions, the grief, and the callous realisation that each of the strangers that had contributed to her life were all gone, was simply too much for Sophie to process. Another prolonged silence followed, filled in by the rumble of a passenger jet in the distance.

"Miss Cooper?" Mr Mitchell called.

Sophie looked at him and he took his cue to proceed. "Yes, so… the Palazzo Rosso, or Red Palace, and associated assets to my daughter, Sofia DaTerra, and that—"

"What exactly is this Palazzo Rosso thing, then?" Victoria interrupted. "I'm assuming it's property of some kind. Obviously not a real palazzo, right? Just a figure of speech?" Victoria said with a scoff.

Mr Mitchell glanced at Victoria and, for the first time since they had presented themselves at the man's office, his words were not accompanied by a distinguished smile.

"Well," the lawyer continued, looking back to Sophie and then down at his folder. "I just so happen to have a photo right here."

16

THE MOURNER'S PALACE

FRIDAY AFTERNOON

S ophie hesitated before reaching over with a trembling hand and picking up the Polaroid photograph. She could barely allow her eyes to focus on it. This was her biological father's home, yet she had never seen it before in her life. Had she?

Victoria's breathing was loud as she peered over her shoulder to see a body of water, a pair of battered old speedboats, a faded white stone balustrade, green ivy, and a large pergola covered in grapevines. Towering over them was a large stone building with dark red walls and deep purple balcony shutters. There were eight of them on the facing side alone, trimmed in white. The building stood at least three storeys high and was beautifully conspicuous against the white and terracotta city behind it.

"Fuck me, that's…" Victoria exclaimed before the words dissolved in her mouth.

"…Venice, yes," Mr Mitchell finished. If he had registered the expletive, he didn't show it.

"Fuck!" Victoria said again, much louder this time. Much like how it sounded when they were children. Hearing it, after all these years, made Sophie laugh. Or perhaps it was hysteria. At this stage, it was hard to tell the difference.

"I'm terribly sorry," Victoria added, putting a hand to her lips in an attempt to restore some decorum. But she was unable to contain herself. "You've inherited a fucking villa! In Venice!" she said.

Mr Mitchell donned his trademark smile and nodded, as if he had personally bestowed the property. "Yes, just a few steps off the Grand Canal. It's not far from the Palazzo Corner, which is the seat of the Venice Prefecture," he added as if he was about to take them on a tour.

Victoria didn't seem to know what that meant, but Sophie did. She knew exactly what he was referring to as she gazed at the image in her hand.

The enormity of what the inheritance would do for Sophie's current circumstances – especially if that eviction notice was valid – was summed up by Victoria's next comment. "This place must be worth a fortune, Soph. Millions! Especially in that location. Everybody knows how much property costs in Venice. You're going to be a bloody millionaire!"

Sophie heard her friend but was still unable to absorb her words. She was still reeling from the avalanche of information that had been smashing into her for the past ten minutes.

"Sophie?"

The gaze and rosy cheeks of the man sitting across from her came into focus once more, but it was Victoria who was speaking. "Sophie, are you all right?"

Sophie nodded. But she wasn't all right. She was a thousand miles from all right.

"You couldn't make it up," she whispered, picking up the filmy sheet of paper. It was oddly smooth between her fingers. She held it up to the man whose revelations today had capsized her world. He watched her and nodded slowly, as if he could sense her anguish. And it was in that moment that Sophie realised there was something about this man. Something about his demeanour that she liked. When she searched his grey eyes, she found empathy, not professional detachment. And there was something about his chubby face that exuded kindness. She wondered if had he always been that way, or if the ravages of years spent practising the binary letter of the law had exposed his true empathetic self.

She returned the sheet of paper to the man and then instinctively threw her hands to her mouth as she tried to contain the guilty grin that had formed there. Victoria's words had finally sunk in. *Millions.*

"Am I rich, Mr Mitchell?" she asked directly, the words tumbling through her fingers.

The man smiled at her and did not speak, but simply rocked his head thoughtfully.

"You're rich! You're filthy stinking rich!" Victoria declared. "Bloody rich bitch!"

"I am!"

They both screamed at each other like inebriated university graduates then leapt to their feet, grabbing each other's hands, skipping and chanting, *"Rich! Rich! Filthy stinking rich!"*

This was followed by a spontaneous waltz around the office, gliding around the floor as if they'd already arrived in Venice and were already in their finery. People in the corridor outside paused to watch the bizarre spectacle before resuming their journey with a snicker.

Mr Mitchell let them have their crazy for a few seconds, before bringing them back to earth with a clearing of the throat.

"I'm sorry," Sophie said, breathless. "It's just, well, as you can imagine, nothing like this has ever happened to me."

Mr Mitchell nodded, smiling another of his smiles.

There was a pause as the two friends retook their seats. "So, how does this work then?" Victoria asked between recovering breaths. "What happens next?"

"Well, it's fairly straightforward," Mr Mitchell said, "*but* please don't throw anything at me when I say that there are just a few more formalities that we need to go through. For example, to return to the issue of identity verification… Sophie, did you bring your passport as we discussed?"

"Yes," she said quickly, reaching into her bag and rummaging through it.

"Splendid. I just need to document the verification and go through the details, and, of course, finish the actual reading of the will."

"Oh, of course. I'm sorry," Sophie said excitedly, handing her passport over to the man.

The lawyer studied it for a few seconds, nodded, and then, "The palazzo—" he began.

"I love that word," the overenthusiastic child that was Victoria interjected. Then, when she felt eyes on her, she added, "Sorry… sorry."

Mr Mitchell took a deep breath then continued, "The palazzo comes with a generous stipend for the exclusive upkeep and general maintenance of the property. The funds are kept in trust and will be released to your housekeeper upon presentation of three separate estimates and/or invoices derived from three separate estimates."

"H…Housekeeper?" Sophie echoed, leaning forward.

"Yes. Palazzo Rosso comes with a housekeeper and a general caretaker. Both are already appointed by the trust. Naturally, you would be consulted on any future replacements."

"So, wait, you're saying that this place comes with a fund for its upkeep as well as a housekeeper and caretaker, and that both will be paid by this trust?"

Mr Mitchell nodded. "That's exactly what I'm saying."

"What else?" Victoria asked, as if it was her name on the will. "When can we get over there to take a look? Where do we collect the key?"

"Well…" the lawyer left the sentence suspended in the air as he rose to his feet and walked over to his desk. Closely watched by the friends, he unlocked a drawer and pulled out a Federal Express package the size of a paperback book. He then returned to the conference table and placed the solid package in front of him. "The key is inside this packet," he said. Victoria reached across, but Mr Mitchell instantly placed a guarding hand over it. "I'm afraid it can *only* be opened by Miss Cooper," he said with unusual seriousness.

Victoria laughed awkwardly, irked that he had blocked her. "What difference does it make?" she grumbled.

"I'm afraid that is the will of your father," Mr Mitchell explained, eyes on Sophie. "You and only you are to open this package, and only after you have accepted the terms of the will."

"Terms? What terms? You didn't mention any terms," Victoria was quick to point out.

"Indeed. But I'm about to," Mr Mitchell responded, consulting the translucent page in front of him. "Um, forgive me, but my Latin isn't what it used to be. I have arranged an official translation which I shall include with the rest of the paperwork should you choose to proceed."

"Latin?" Victoria asked.

"Why wouldn't I choose to proceed?" asked Sophie.

Mr Mitchell didn't respond but instead continued. "I hereby bequeath Il Palazzo Rosso and all that it contains to my daughter,

Sofia Santoro DaTerra," he read aloud, nodding at Sophie without taking his eyes off the sheet, "on the strict understanding that the lady *dnec vendere ultrices accumsan oest quia quamdiu est domina vivere.*" He looked up at them both. "I'm reliably informed that means provided the lady does not lease or sell it— the property—for as long as the lady lives. Or words to that effect. It then goes on to say that the property may be bequeathed to any firstborn daughter, provided she also agrees to be bound by these terms."

Victoria laughed. "You're joking, right? Are you saying that the place can't be sold?"

"That's exactly what it says, yes."

"But that's fucking ridiculous! How can you give someone something and then tell them how to use it? Strings attached, much."

Mr Mitchell didn't respond. If he was irked that Victoria was the only person with an opinion on the matter despite the fact it had nothing to do with her, once again he did not show it.

Sophie's only response was to blink, and not because she had something in her eye, but because she had suddenly developed some kind of nervous twitch. "I'm sorry, Mr Mitchell," she finally spoke, "but I'm confused. You said that I may pass it onto my firstborn?"

"Firstborn female," he corrected.

"I don't understand. Surely, if the property's mine, it's mine to do with as I wish, no?"

Mr Mitchell shrugged awkwardly. "Under normal circumstances."

"What do you mean, normal?"

"Most wills function in that way. Others may have some binding covenants. This one, well… it's quite specific. One can only assume that this is some kind of succession tradition. A bit like a monarchy."

"Succession?"

The lawyer shifted in his seat. "Well, from what we can tell," he read from the notes in the file, "Il Palazzo Rosso was built centuries ago. It's as historical as Venice itself. And I dare say it's now viewed a bit like how we view a listed building here in England. After all, it has been home to many aristocrats, some of whom were responsible for building Venice into the city we know and love today." He looked up at her. "Technically speaking, Sophie, by inheriting this estate, you also inherit the title that comes with it."

Victoria's eyes widened. "Title?" she asked, leaning forward.

But Mr Mitchell made a point of addressing the person in front of him. "Yes. By inheriting Il Palazzo Rosso, Sophie, you would also be inheriting the title that comes with it. That of contessa."

"Contessa?" she echoed.

"He means Countess," Victoria uttered acidly.

Sophie threw her friend a look and then turned back to the man sitting across from her. That is when she felt it rising inside her.

It started slowly at first. For a second, Victoria thought Sophie was about to spit at the lawyer, but her friend's reaction soon transformed into a snigger, then a chuckle, before finally blooming into a giant belly laugh that, at least to Victoria, seemed to go on forever. She gawked at her friend. This wasn't anything like what she was expecting to hear today. And she didn't know how she felt about that.

"Coun...count...tess.... Coo... Cooper!" Sophie gasped between shudders. "Countess fucking Cooper! Ooh!" She placed a hand over her mouth, pointlessly trying to contain the expletive.

It wasn't until a minute or so later that Sophie finally managed to pull herself together, dabbing at her eyes with a tissue. "I'm... I'm sorry, Mr Mitchell, I'm really sorry, but you can hear how funny that sounds, right?"

The lawyer nodded.

The would-be countess wrinkled her nose and said, "It doesn't sound very *countessy*, does it? And that's forgetting the fact that I'm about as much countess stock as Madonna is a virgin." Mr Mitchell returned an amused smile. "Me? A countess? Oh God…" She staved off another bout of the giggles she could still feel bouncing up and down inside her, like ricocheting rubber balls begging to escape.

"Technically, you would adopt your father's name, which is more appropriate," Mr Mitchell said, in all seriousness.

"What, this Dan… Dat…"

"DaTerra."

"DaTerra? What does that even mean?"

"Forgive me, but Italian isn't my forte, if you'll excuse the pun. But I believe it means *in earth* or *from earth*. Something like that."

"Contessa Dirt?! Yeah, that'll work," Sophie said, overwhelmed by the ridiculousness of it all as she staved off yet another bout of giggles. She turned to Victoria, who simply rolled her eyes, seemingly unimpressed.

With a shrug and a reshuffle of her seat, Sophie took a steadying breath before placing her hands on the table. She needed to calmly process each point in turn if she was going to make sense of any of it. "Mr Mitchell, I'm sorry to drag this out, but just so I'm clear… I have inherited a, for want of a better expression, palace in Venice from a father I didn't even know existed. This p…palace," she struggled with the word, "comes with its own housekeeper and caretaker person, both of whom are paid by a trust set up by that long-lost biological father. Then, along with inheriting this… this…"

"Palazzo…"

"…palace thingamajig, I inherit a title. That of Countess Coo…" She broke off here for the rubber balls were still bouncing around in her belly, her laughter ready to make a comeback.

"That's correct," Mr Mitchell said seriously, seemingly oblivious to the woman's amusement.

"Uh huh. And the only downside to all of this is that I, presumably, would have to live in Venice."

Another nod from Mr Mitchell.

"And do what? I mean, how would I live? Does this place come with another… um, what did you call it… another—"

"Stipend," the lawyer helped.

"Yes, one of those. One not just for the household staff."

"I'm afraid not. Well, technically it does, but it wouldn't really be much use to you. The estate does provide your own personal stipend. A value of ten thousand lira per month—"

"Ten thousand lira? That sounds like a lot," Victoria jumped in.

"Wait, lira?" Sophie said. "I thought the Italians adopted the euro."

"Yes, they did. This document was obviously drafted a long time ago."

"A long time? Italy stopped using the lira, what, over two decades ago?"

"That doesn't make sense," Victoria joined in. "You're saying that this bloke wrote this will more than twenty years ago?"

Mr Mitchell nodded. "Given the amount, I dare say it was originally written quite some time ago indeed and subsequently revised. But yes."

"So… if it really is made up in this lira currency, how much is that worth today? Still got to be decent, right? I mean *ten thousand lira*. That sounds like a lot," Victoria reiterated.

Sophie snickered again.

"What?" Victoria looked at her friend, then at the lawyer, and then at her friend again. "What?" she repeated.

Still suppressing a chuckle, Sophie said, "Um, it's hard to say, but that's probably, what, no more than a fiver, is it?" Sophie said quizzically, as she looked at the man across from her.

Mr Mitchell nodded. "Give or take."

Victoria held up her hands. "Wait. You've inherited a palace in Venice, probably worth several million, and it comes with a salary... stipend thing... of barely a fiver *per week?*"

"Per month," Mr Mitchell corrected.

Sophie nodded, reeling in her amusement while Victoria burst into an exaggerated laugh. "Looks like you're going to have to get a job, *countess!*" The last word was spoken with emphasis before the two friends shared more laughter.

Mr Mitchell waited patiently. His gaze moved between each of the ladies in turn as they worked out their amusement with schoolgirl giggles, their chuckles laced with a litany of jokes about what exactly Sophie could afford with such a generous monthly allowance; from milk and bread to tampons, they covered it all.

Eventually, with makeup running and eyes streaming, they managed to pull themselves together once more.

"This is stupid," Victoria said, suddenly and seriously, allowing her smile to slip. "There must be a way she can sell that place. It must be worth millions. She could get herself a really nice place over here. Like ours."

The fact that Victoria was making plans with her inheritance probably should have annoyed Sophie, but it didn't. She was glad her friend was showing an interest. Supporting and sticking up for her. This whole thing was beyond surreal. Titles and stipends. She was half expecting to wake up at any moment. She would much rather have the money and use a portion of it to pay for an extravagant holiday to Venice than live there without a penny to her name.

"Mr Mitchell, there's got to be a way to sell this place," she said.

"I'm afraid not, Sophie. The will is quite specific in this

matter. It may not be sold or leased. You can only inherit to inhabit, so to speak."

"No," Victoria said empathically, shaking her head. "There's got to be a way. Once you've inherited it, it should be up to you to decide what you do with the place. I take it you have no objection to us getting a second opinion, Mr Mitchell? You see, my husband, Jonathan Ainsworth—you may have heard of him—he has connections in the city."

"Oh, by all means, please do. However, I am sure you'll find that the will is quite resolute in this matter. To this end, you should know that there is a specific provision that forbids any lien or charge against the property, or deed exchange that does not take place through the succession protocol."

Sophie squinted. "Which means?"

"Unless you inherit it, you can't own it," he said.

Victoria jumped in. "Still, we're going to get that second opinion anyway before she commits to anything, if that's okay." It was a statement not a question. "Come on, Soph," she added, standing up.

Mr Mitchell rose with them.

"Thanks for your time," Victoria said officiously, as if all the girlish silliness that took place mere minutes before never happened. She made her way to the door.

Sophie gave Mr Mitchell her hand. "Thank you so much for your time and patience with us today, Mr Mitchell. I know many of our questions and responses must have seemed juvenile. It's just, well, it's all a bit of shock," she said with a shrug.

The lawyer took her hand and cupped it gently with his other. "Please, think nothing of it, Sophie. You are most welcome. And please, my name's Roger."

"Roger. Thank you," she said earnestly.

"I am always here if you have any additional questions, and, of course, should your change your mind," he added with one of his smiles as he walked her to the door.

Sophie left the lawyer's office feeling strangely deflated. It was as if she'd just starred in her own fairy tale but hadn't gone on to live happily ever after. But it wasn't just that. It was all of it. The giant bubbling cauldron of things that she'd learned today. And none of it seemed real.

Victoria, on the other hand, was on the phone to her husband's office before they'd even reached the end of the corridor.

"He's in a meeting," she explained when she disconnected.

Sophie nodded as she snatched another glimpse of the view. Then, before they rounded the corner to reception, she felt a sudden compulsion to look back to see if Roger Mitchell, the lawyer, was still watching them.

He was.

17

NUMBER 11

FRIDAY EVENING

At number 11 Meadow Lane, Mrs Preston cussed then pulled both heavy curtains, one after the other, across the bay window, blocking out the world outside. It had taken her the best part of three hours to finally get her baby son, James, to sleep, and the police less than three minutes to wake him.

Was it really necessary to arrive in the lane with all sirens blaring? Whatever had happened to the girl at number 12 had already happened, judging by the rush of people in white jumpsuits going in and out of that house. Not much point making a racket now.

"It's all right, darling, it's all right," Debbie cooed, jiggling the baby up and down over her shoulder. But the infant was having none of it and continued screaming at the top of his lungs, drilling into her last nerve.

She smelt disgusting and was exhausted. She'd taken on both the day and night shifts yesterday so that her husband could prep and then get some sleep before his meeting today. All being well, William Preston's presentation would be a success and he would get the promotion they so badly needed, especially if they were going to continue living here on this side of Cambridge.

She had been warned, but she didn't want to listen. Having a baby in her late forties came with risks, while in vitro fertilization offered no guarantees except a hefty price tag. Especially when treated privately. That was one of the reasons they moved to Cambridge, so that they could be treated by the best, and the eventual result was their beautiful baby boy. Their pride and joy. He made it all worth it.

And yet. The reality was, pregnancy had left Debbie with a raft of health issues, not least the fact she now spent most of her days lost in a fog of depression that leached away what little energy she was able to conjure.

They had alienated the few friends they'd managed to make since moving here because Debbie no longer felt up to socialising. She either looked or felt too awful, and it was impossible to find anything decent to wear. When William suggested they have people over, she flat out refused. He knew how sensitive their son was to noise. There was no way they could have people round. Besides, she didn't have the energy to play hostess. She was irritated that he didn't realise that, especially after she was forced to fire the cleaner he'd hired after just one week because she no longer had the energy to tidy up before the woman reported for work.

It was all just too exhausting.

The result was that Debbie Preston spent most of her time on her own with her baby, who was either raging with colic or screaming with the pain of teething.

But James was worth it. He made it all worth it.

"Don't you, darling? You do, don't you?" she cooed, cringing against the shrieking as she manoeuvred the infant between arms so she could open the fridge and retrieve the gel. She made room on the small kitchen table by pushing the dirty dishes aside and then lay her son down so she could administer the medicine.

"Here we go," she chanted. "Here we go." She squeezed the tube and jolted backward when a blob of it landed on her chest. "Shit!" she hissed. The act startled the child and incited more wailing, which echoed around the room and vibrated through her skull like a fire alarm.

"Okay, come on, let Mummy put this on," she sing-songed. "Let Mummy apply this so that that you'll feel better... come on... come on," she repeated with repressed frustration. She scowled against the high-pitched siren of the baby's screams as he lay on his back, waggling arms and legs unhappily in protest at being expelled from the warm cradle of his mother's arms in favour of the cold hard table.

"Come on, now. Come on, my darling. Come on."

Ding dong.

Mrs Preston's pinky paused mid-air and her eyes flicked sideways. There was someone at the front door. Someone at the bloody front door right now of all bloody times.

She ignored it and continued with her task, pushing her finger into her son's open mouth and rubbing the gel on his tiny gums. "There we go. There we go. This will make you feel so much better. So much better for Mummy. So much better so you'll stop scream—"

Ding dong.

And yet the wailing showed no sign of abating. If anything, the shock of the cold gel in the baby's mouth only renewed its discontent.

Bang! Bang! Bang! Thumping on the front door now. Whoever it was had obviously tired of getting no satisfaction by ringing the bell, so they had taken to pounding on the front door instead.

"Fuck off!" Debbie hissed, her words lost among the baby's cries. She snatched the baby up from the table but, in her haste, knocked one of the dishes, smashing it loudly on the floor. "Shit!" She left the kitchen with the disgruntled infant tucked under one arm and hunted around the living room. It had to be there somewhere. She was in the living room when she last texted her husband.

Bang! Bang!

Ding dong. Ding dong.

"Where was I?" she mused under her breath, as she tossed around and rummaged behind sofa cushions before finally spotting the phone on the coffee table.

She grabbed it, awkwardly juggling the baby while attempting to tap out words on the screen. Eventually, she succeeded in typing the search:

Dealing with screaming baby.

Lots of impractical results appeared. 'Give him or her to a family member to deal with.' Chance would be a fine thing. The other useless suggestions were of no help either. Swaddling, swinging, shushing… None of that worked. 'Take time out. Leave the baby for a while. Avoid shaken baby syndrome.'

No. No. No. Oh no no no.

She had no idea why, but ever since the screaming had started, that nefarious thought – shaken baby, shaken baby, the phrase itself like a rattle – kept forming in her mind. And she hated herself for it. Of course, she could never even contemplate anything like that.

She threw the phone onto the sofa as if it had just burned her and stepped away from it.

Bang! Bang! Ding dong.

"WHAT?" she hissed, yanking the front door open. Two uniformed policemen stood in front of her with inquisitive looks on their faces as they took in first the screaming infant tucked in the nook of her arm and then her.

Behind them, two patrol cars were parked diagonally across the street. Yellow police tape fluttered in a bitter cold wind. Blue lights flickered and licked through trees and over buildings.

"Evenin', madam. Sorry to be persistent, only we heard the baby cryin'. Just wanted to check that everything was okay. Is... everything okay?" the older of the two coppers asked as his breath fogged out in front of him before dissolving into the night.

Debbie Preston could feel the man's eyes roving over her, could sense his colleague looking around her and into the house.

She tucked strands of lank brown hair behind her ears, fiddled with the top buttons of her dress for fear that her ample bosom might be on display, then attempted to stand up straight.

"Everything's fine," she said curtly. "But as you can see, I've literally got my hands full. What do you want?"

The cops glanced at each other and then back at the woman before them. The look wasn't lost on Debbie, and it annoyed her. The older officer hesitated a few seconds before finally getting to it. "Well, as you may have noticed, there's been an incident across the street and—"

"The girl at number twelve? Yes, I noticed," she interrupted, trying to hurry him along so she could close the door. It was bloody freezing. She shuffled the baby into both arms and proceeded to jiggle him. He clearly wasn't enjoying the cold either, to the point that even his screams were trying to escape far into the dark.

"Actually, madam... can you tell me if there's anybody else in the house with you?"

She frowned. "Why do you need to know that? No, there's nobody else in the house. I'm alone. My husband's at work. What's this about? If it's about number twelve, I'm afraid I don't know anything."

The policemen exchanged looks again. "Well, it's not just your neighbour across the street we wanted to talk about but your neighbours next door at number nine." He nodded in that direction.

"The boys? Oh, we don't have anything to do with them," she said quickly.

"Still, would it be all right if we came in for a quick chat?"

"Chat? About what?"

"We just want to ask you a few questions, that's all."

"What kind of questions?"

"Well, first, we need to confirm some details, such as your name, if that's all right—"

Debbie shook her head. "It's Preston. Debbie Preston. And does it look like it's bloody all right?" she grumbled, holding her child in front of her.

"I appreciate that, madam, but these are serious incidents," the younger cop suddenly piped up, "and for your own safety we'd like to—"

But the baby was still screaming, and Debbie had had enough. "I'm sorry, you're going to have to come back," she said, retreating inside and using her bare foot to close the door.

"Mrs Preston, it's really important that we—"

But the young officer's words were cut short when the door slammed shut in his face. Frustrated by the woman's attitude, he was about to knock again but his senior stopped him. "What?"

"Have you got kids?"

"Bit early for that," the younger one said with a grin, "and after seeing that—"

"Yeah, well until you do, you won't know why knocking on that door again right now is tantamount to asking for a stabbing." He cocked his head. "Come on. We'll come back later. Maybe when the husband's home."

Inside the house, Debbie turned away from the door and was

surprised to still feel the cold on her face. She glanced at the thermostat. It was still turned up high. Then she looked through the lounge to the kitchen and frowned.

The back door was wide open, a dirty tea towel flapping in the chill.

Did she leave the door open and forget? But no, she couldn't have. She had had no reason to go into the back garden, and yet…

Baby still crying, drool dripping onto her bare arm, Debbie stepped forward. She paused when she realised it was now dark in the lounge but for the dull light spilling in from the kitchen and the flickering blue that flashed in through the bay window, bouncing off the walls.

She gaped for a few stupefied seconds, unconsciously jiggling the baby as she tried to work out what was different… That was it! The lamp was off. And the… the curtains were open!

But she was sure she had closed them. She had been at the window, investigating the commotion, when she'd pulled them shut in irritation. Hadn't she? It was hard to think with the baby's shrill cries drilling through her eardrums.

Was she losing her mind? Is this what it was like? Had motherhood finally driven her insane? It was perfectly plausible. She's considered it many times before. She was self-aware enough to know that she was barely the shadow of her former self since becoming a mother.

Yet it didn't matter. Her son was worth it. "Aren't you, my lovely? Aren't you?" But the baby rewarded her with renewed discontent. Face hot and creased.

"Let's get you some more of that gel," she said flatly through the noise, as if she were no longer hearing it.

She stepped forward and yelped when she felt something prick her foot. At first, she thought it might be one of the toys her son had thrown to the floor in response to her attempted placations, but when she bent down to pick it up, she could just about tell that it was not.

She moved into the kitchen light and held the thing up to the bulb. Odd. She'd never seen this toy before. It looked like a tiny ball. One of those traditional organic ones. About the size of a golf ball. Made of natural wood. No, not wood... vine? It looked like wood vine weaved together. She didn't recognise it. William must have bought it and forgotten to mention it, and...

Oh shit!

She suddenly realised the baby had stopped crying. Oh my... the baby has stopped crying!

Like her, he appeared transfixed by the ball. His face was still red, blotchy, aggravated, and tearstained, but his eyes sparkled, and his lips creased into a faint smile as he ogled the thing.

"Oh, you like this?" she asked. "Do you like it?" The baby's smile broadened. "Of all your toys, you like this shitty little thing? That's great. That's no problem. No problem," she repeated in an animated voice as a shiver scuttled over her.

"Brrrrr..." She walked over to the open back door and instinctively peered into the gloom. She wasn't sure what she was expecting to see but there was nothing there but darkness. Although there appeared to be some commotion next door where those boys lived. There were flashlights bobbing around the back garden, the general buzz of people talking in hushed tones, and the crackle of radio chatter. None of it interested her and all of it represented a threat to the fragile peace that had finally settled inside her home, so she hurried back inside, closing the door behind her.

Yes, she was behaving unneighbourly, but who gave a shit? These were desperate times.

"Brrrrrrrrr," she said loudly, allowing her lips to quiver for the amusement of her son. "Brrrrrrrrr...!"

"A bbr... A bbrr... bbr," was his fascinated response.

"Blimey, who would have thought that an ugly piece of vine was the solution to—"

Debbie interrupted herself when she scrutinized the ball more closely. To her dismay, she now noticed that the vine was actually weaved around a clump of vicious thorns.

"Oh!" she cried. They were obviously what had pricked her earlier. She reacted impulsively and threw the ball to the floor. It didn't roll, despite its shape, but fell with a loud plop like one of those big spiders from the ceiling.

Instantly, the baby started screaming.

"Oh no! No! No! No! Shhhh… Shh…" Without even thinking twice, Debbie Preston crouched down, retrieved the ugly thing, and offered it up to her infant. And, to her amazement, he stopped crying once more. He even reached out to touch it.

Debbie shook her head. "No, no touch. You want this? You really want this? But it's dangerous, darling. Really dangerous." Yet the baby was determined to touch it with his clumsy chubby fingers. "Fine… fine. If it'll keep you amused long enough for Mummy to take a shower, then I'm all for it. Yes? Yes?"

The baby appeared to be bamboozled by the object and that was good enough for her. Without delay, she shifted the baby to her hip and climbed the stairs.

In the nursery, she placed her son in his carrycot and the thing at his feet, just out of reach. Perfect. Not only was he entranced by it, but the position would keep him busy as he tried to reach it. His tiny would-be sit-ups brought a smile to her face.

Oh, the relief was orgasmic. The quiet was as palpable as the freeze that had made itself at home in the now peaceful building. Debbie shivered and smiled in anticipation of the sensation of hot water cascading over her body.

Sod William. Her husband obviously wasn't planning on coming home anytime soon. As with everything else, she needed to sort this. She needed to take control. And she was.

She pulled a hat onto her son's head and packed out the carrycot with a warm baby blanket, pulling and clicking the safety strap over it. Then she made sure the ugly ball thing was returned to the cot but positioned down far enough that her baby couldn't reach it.

She paused as her son's face contorted, and for one horrifying moment she thought he was going to start whinging again, but concluded it was just wind. That, or he was doing something she was going to have to clean later.

"You're a little stinker. A little stinker, eh? You're Mummy's little stinker, aren't you? Mummy's little stinker." She wiped snot from her son's face with the back of her sleeve and welcomed fresh waves of love for him. It had felt like the baby's heart-wrenching wailing had been doing its best to drive a wedge between them. That could never happen. She knew that. At least, she did now, now that the mind fog was clearing. But in those moments, those desperate moments, when she had those awful thoughts, those disgusting thoughts, everything felt so different.

Ugh. She felt unworthy.

"I love you, my baby," she said, placing a gentle hand on her son's chest, bridging her love to him. "Now, Mummy's going to get some clothes. You just wait here, okay?" She spoke the words, but she was confident that her son wasn't going anywhere. He was perfectly fine in his cot, strapped in and seemingly entertained by that thing. She made a mental note to give William a mouthful when he came home for bringing it into the house. It was all well and good, going organic and everything, but it was pretty irresponsible to give their child a toy made with bloody thorns.

I mean, what the hell was he thinking? If he was even thinking at all. And you know what? No matter what bloody happened today at his meeting, things need to change from now on. There are two of us in this marriage, two parents. I am not alone, and I shouldn't be made to feel that way.

That's how she'd been feeling of late. Although, if she was fair, it was only because her husband had been working so hard. First, it was so they could have their beautiful little boy and then so they could keep the house and provide for him. But still, they needed to talk.

She pulled one of her dresses out from the wardrobe and a pair of thick tights from the chest of drawers. She hadn't worn the dress in a while, opting instead for practical sweatpants and fleeces. But now, she was suddenly feeling better. Her mental fog appeared to be clearing by the second, leaving her space to be reminded of the person she used to be, and she wanted to dress accordingly.

Back in the bathroom, she checked on her son. He was still trying to perform sit-ups despite the fleece and the fact that he was strapped down into the cot. His perseverance was as adorable as it was amusing and, for the first time in a long time, Debbie Preston allowed herself to giggle.

"You're so cute! Yes, you are. Yes, you are" she smiled, realising that her resident headache was also subsiding.

She swished the curtain aside and ran the shower until it started to steam in the cold room. Then, as she stripped, she watched her little boy struggle with those sit-ups even as his eyelids began to droop.

Debbie chuckled. "Be good," she said with one last look before stepping inside the bath and pulling the shower curtain closed once more.

The hot water set to work immediately, massaging her neck, back, and shoulders. It was sublime. And for a minute or so she simply enjoyed it that way. Then, she peeked around the curtain. Sure enough, the baby was nodding off.

She glanced at the ball thing. She didn't want to, given how useful it had been, but she planned to throw it out as soon as she was out of the shower. Of course, she needed to find a replacement first, but that thing was too dangerous, and she didn't want it around her son.

But for now, she focussed on the task in hand, lathering the loofah and running it over her body, washing away her stench. As she did so she felt so much bloody better, she could sing.

A quick check beyond the curtain showed her son was asleep now. It was wonderful. So bloody wonderful! All she needed to hope for now was that the bloody bastard police didn't decide to blast their sirens again.

She felt warmer now. So much better, confidently lathering shampoo into her hair as the steam rose, taking her spirits with it. Shampoo had never smelt this good, and Debbie was –

SLAM!

One of the doors. Out in the hallway. At least that's what it sounded like. Then the bathroom door creaked and a draught crept into the bathroom, rustling the shower curtain.

Finally.

"Will! I'm in the shower!" she called, as loudly as she dared, before continuing to massage the lather into her scalp and rub away the dregs of that headache.

Seconds sluiced by before she heard the bathroom door creak again. She opened her eyes, squinting through the foam and wrinkled plastic curtain to see the outline of her husband standing in the doorway.

"I can see you, you know, but shhhhh… I've only just managed to get him to sleep," she said in a loud whisper over the sound of the hissing water. "He's been a nightmare all day," she continued, closing her eyes to rinse the suds from her hair and face. When she reopened them, her husband was still watching her, quietly.

"Oi, you little pervert," she said with a giggle. "How did it go today?" She held her face up to the cascading water one last time. But when there was no reply, she scowled, rubbed water from her face and peeked out from the curtain. "Hey. Why aren't you answer—"

The words drowned in her throat. There was nobody standing in the doorway.

"William?"

When she looked down, she was surprised to find her baby wide awake once more. "Oh hello, handsome, are you awake already? Are you awake already, my little boy? What are you looking at? What are you looking at, eh?"

The baby was no longer fixated on the thing in his cot but by something else on the other side of the bathroom. And yet, when Debbie Preston turned to follow her son's gaze, the overhead light flickered and died, killing both the light and the whir of the extractor fan.

"Oh shit… William?" she called over the hiss and gurgle of the water, but there was no response. She shut the water off. "Will?" She waited.

Drip…drip…gurgle. Drip…drip…gurgle.

"Will?"

Seconds drifted by.

"This isn't funny. And I'm definitely not in the mood."

Nothing.

Drip. Drip. Gurgle.

And then, just as that familiar claw of anxiety started to scratch at her throat, the light came on and the noisy fan whirred back to life, startling her. "Oh shit!"

When she looked down, her son was watching her, nonplussed, feet gently kicking under the blanket.

"William?" Debbie called out of the door.

Silence, but for the fan, unusually loud in the echo of the space.

Had she imagined it? When did you last eat? She was unable to answer her own question. She couldn't remember and now she was imagining things.

Leaving the shower and wrapping towels around her body and hair, Debbie Preston stepped out onto the landing and called down the stairs. "Will? Are you home?" But there was no reply.

The house was empty. She could feel it.

She grabbed her son and hurried back into the bedroom where, with the carrycot now sitting on the carpet by the bed, she dried herself in front of the wardrobe mirror, being sure to avoid looking at her naked body.

She dressed quickly before brushing her hair. As she did so, she noticed that her son's reflection was watching hers. "Are you looking at me? Are you watching Mummy?" she asked with a big smile.

She was feeling so much better, despite that icky feeling on the landing just now. She might even cook tonight. Nothing fancy. Maybe some pasta. It would be nice for her husband to come home to a hot cooked meal. It had been a while. Time permitting, she'd lay the table nicely too so that they could eat together. Take their time. Maybe even talk.

"What do you think? Eh? Spaghetti?" she asked her son's reflection. When he didn't react, she put on a big giant voice. "Spa-ghe-tti," she growled deeply yet softly. She knew he liked that voice as it sounded like Daddy's.

Yet the baby's reflection continued to ignore her. She turned to look at him. It was only then that she realised, based on his line of sight, that the infant hadn't been looking at her but towards the top of the wardrobe.

"Oh no, you're not doing that. You're not fooling Mummy," she said with a grin. And yet, she couldn't resist the urge to look up there. Just to be sure. Slowly, she turned and lifted her gaze.

There was nothing there. Nothing. She chuckled as relief flooded through her. "See? Nothing there."

Debbie turned back to the mirror and resumed styling her hair. When she glanced at her son, she saw that he wasn't looking at the top of the wardrobe anymore but that his attention had been drawn to something else.

That toy. It was no longer at the foot of her baby's carrycot but sat on the carpet next to the bed. She rolled her eyes as she bent to retrieve it. "Oh you," she said with a smile. "Did you do that? Did you kick that out of your—"

The rest of her words were cut short when the lights flickered. Off. On. Off. On. Off… Debbie Preston's blood froze in her veins. For there, under the bed, just inches away from her son, a pair of narrow slanted eyes glinted in the darkness.

William Preston had barely made it through the front door before he was rushed forward by his wife's bloodcurdling scream.

He dropped his rucksack and the flowers he was carrying and raced up the stairs, taking two at a time.

He paused before entering the bedroom to process what he was seeing. The empty bed with discarded bath towel. The upturned bedside lamp burning bright. His wife on the floor in the corner of the room, hands clamped to her face, crying hysterically. Nearby, their son's carrycot sat empty.

He rushed to her. "Oh shit! Debbie! Debbie! What's wrong? What happened? Debbie? Debbie? Answer me! Debbie! ANSWER ME! Where's James? Debbie? Where's James?" But she wasn't responding.

William rushed out, checked the bathroom. Nothing but a dripping showerhead. He rushed back. "Debbie! Debbie? What happened? Where's James, Debbie? Where's our son?" He shook his wife's shoulders, desperate to see her face. "DEBBIE! Where's James? Where's our son?" he yelled. "Where's our son?"

Eventually, Debbie Preston focussed on her husband and, with eyes full of terror, wailed, "It took him! It took him!"

18

BARREN

FRIDAY. LATE EVENING.

After her meeting with Christopher Darrington, Sophie had turned the house upside down in her attempt to find the property deeds, or documents of any kind that might go some way to explaining the predicament she was in. But she found nothing except a couple of utility bills in one of the kitchen drawers. It was as if the place had been cleared out. The thought only made her brain ache even more. Had it always been like this? Maybe her father simply didn't feel the need to leave that stuff lying about the place. Maybe he scanned everything and filed it away on a computer.

You are fostered, she kept telling herself. *Fostered, not adopted,* which, to her, was a crucial distinction. How did that even make sense? Why would anyone foster a child into adulthood and not just go the whole way through to adoption? Was there something wrong with her? She couldn't have been that bad. Could she? No, of course not. Otherwise, they would have handed her back years ago.

She thought about Christmas mornings, birthdays, holidays in Devon. The fun, the laughter and, yes, the love. She had felt loved by these people. Loved by that man as if she was his own flesh and blood.

But she wasn't.

Her name was Sofia DaTerra. Contessa Sofia DaTerra. *Countess Sofia from Earth? Really?*

"Sophie!"

She turned and her best friend's face came into focus. They were both rocking back and forth in their seats as the train clattered loudly through an expanse of black ploughed fields and withered grassy verges.

Rush hour wasn't even over yet darkness was already settling in. It reminded Sophie how much she hated short winter days. Even the moon was readying to assume its throne in a clear winter's sky amid a constellation of early stars that winked like diamonds as they made their way through the shadows. And yet even this spectacle was upstaged by the comet. That *thing* was like a giant cosmic starting gun that had signalled the beginning of the end of Sophie Cooper's life as she knew it.

"Are you all right?" Victoria asked. "You seem miles away."

"Everything I've known was a lie, Vic," Sophie said flatly.

"Oh, babe," was Victoria's commiserating response as she turned toward her friend and placed a reassuring hand on her arm. "It wasn't a lie. It still happened, and you are still you. The same lightweight who can't handle her drink. The same boring good Samaritan that can't walk past a bloody homeless person without giving them her last penny and sometimes even food meant for your own bloody mouth." She followed that with a roll of the eyes and a smile.

But Sophie didn't feel like smiling. "Maybe. But it still doesn't change the fact that those people lied to me."

Victoria thought about this before shaking her head sympathetically. "Well, they must have had their reasons, Soph. Maybe they thought they'd be hurting you more by telling you. I suppose your dad never thought it'd end like this."

"And what about her? What about my so-called mum?" Sophie asked acidly.

"Maybe that's one of the reasons why she left," Victoria offered.

Sophie looked at her friend for the longest time. That was just it though, wasn't it? To her mind, Elena Cooper didn't abandon her family. She was taken. *Sophie, remember what the doctor told you. It's a slippery slope.*

"The fact that they took you in in the first place has got to mean something, right?" Victoria continued. "You know that I would have cut off an arm just to have experienced what it was like growing up in your house."

Sophie nodded. Vicki had had a much harsher upbringing for sure. She knew this and had often witnessed it throughout their childhood. The alcoholism. The abuse. The cliché probably stung Victoria even more than what she had endured.

Her friend never cared for labels, not unless she was affixing them onto others, and she certainly didn't have time for any of that self-indulgent *woe is me* shit. *If you've been wronged, then you put it right.* She wasn't a victim. She was a survivor, and that wasn't because she posted a hashtag to social media, it was because she left her pity party behind years ago and worked hard to make something of herself. To become someone else.

Perspective. Victoria had often brought that to their friendship, and she was doing it again right now. Those strangers may have withheld the truth, but they had also made sure that she had never wanted for anything and that, artificially or not, she had always felt loved.

And yet, "Don't you think it's odd though?" Sophie asked.

"What?"

"That he didn't tell me?"

"Why's it odd?"

"Well, he... they were my foster parents. Their responsibility, at least in theory, was temporary. Why wouldn't they just tell me?"

Victoria thought about the question and then shrugged. "As I said, maybe they didn't want to hurt you."

"Well, if they had told me as a child, I probably wouldn't have thought anything of it."

"I think you're doing that oversimplification thing again."

"You think?"

"Yeah. I mean, put yourself in their situation. When's a good time to tell your kid that they're fostered? Over breakfast? In the bath?"

Sophie shook her head, dubious. "I suppose so," she said. Several seconds clattered by as she allowed herself to be temporarily lost in thought until... "But don't you think it's a bit—"

"Oh, for Christ's sake, Soph!" Victoria snapped. "Give it a fucking rest, will you?" She turned away from her friend and looked out of the window. "Jesus Christ. You've done nothing but go on about it since we left that place."

Sophie looked around to see if anybody else had witnessed the outburst, but none of the zombies that filled the carriage were paying them any attention. Some were asleep, others were gormlessly peering into their mobile devices as if entranced by the blue glow. The only person who seemed interested was a teenager with ear buds in. He smiled at her then sat back, manspreading, before closing his eyes and allowing his head to loll from side to side with the motion of the carriage.

Sophie turned back to her friend who was still gazing out of the window. Okay. So this felt better. This was more like the usual dynamic between them. Victoria troubled by something and Sophie the consoler, the maker of better.

It was often this way.

As teenagers, unsurprisingly, the dramas were of the heart, generally focussed on disastrous dates with boys Victoria had prematurely declared *the one*. They weren't. They were just hormonal teenagers doing what they were biologically programmed to do. But Victoria… well, it never seemed like she understood that. She only saw what she wanted to see. It became a syndrome. The more she seemed to hunger for love, the more she allowed herself to be used for sex. The more she allowed herself to be used, the worse her reputation became. She was soon viewed as nothing but an *easy lay*. Sophie even remembered one boy commenting that she was only good enough for weed and a fuck if you had nothing better to do, especially if there was no footy on TV.

Victoria saw her worth not only as a prospective girlfriend but as a human plummet. As such, she sought affection in the backseats of cars, in alleyways and public toilets, but was seldom invited home.

Sophie, in comparison, spent her life fantasizing about one man: the man of her dreams. Literally. He was a recurring dream that began shortly after she hit her teens. His face was always obscured but he became someone she hungered for, nonetheless. It was a premonition she believed she should take seriously. *Kindred spirits are not bound by the body, but by the mind. Your mind already knows. Now you just need to find him. Don't ever settle for anything less.* She had read this as a teenager, and it had stayed with her, reinforced somewhat by some of Victoria's incessant cautionary tales.

Besides, she'd never truly understood all the fuss. As children, boys were smelly. As teenagers, they were immature and smelly, and as adults… well, she just never felt interested in that way. Never felt those compulsions, those urges for a man or a woman. At least not until the day of her father's funeral. That day in the bathroom.

Doctor Krauss had explained that it was a side effect of the trauma she had sustained as a child. A repressed fear of abandonment born out of the fact that she was abandoned by her mother, and thus she was repulsed by the very idea of intimacy for fear of being hurt. He told her that her feelings were transitional and would change over time. When she least expected it, those urges would awaken, and she would know that her time had come.

And it made sense.

Is that what was happening to her now? Was Christopher the one?

Ugh.

She shuddered as she watched the glow of amber-lit streets, and the angular silhouettes of buildings appear in the distance.

Sophie turned to her friend and gently touched her arm. "Vic?"

Seconds rattled by. Then, "Jonathan's having an affair," Victoria uttered.

The words were spoken so quietly they were almost lost in the din. Sophie spoke to her friend's reflection in the window. "What did you say?"

"I think Jonathan's seeing someone else."

"No," Sophie whispered in astonishment. "Why would you think that? How do you know?"

"Oh, you know. Texts. Work. Showers."

"What?"

There was a long pause that was shattered by the rush and blur of a train travelling on the opposite track. It exploded past them, startling Sophie, but Victoria didn't even flinch.

"He just keeps receiving loads of texts," she said. "He's always working late, and then... then he often comes home, smelling freshly showered."

Sophie waited several seconds for more damning information, but there was none.

"Is that it?" she asked with a smile. "Is that all you have? He receives texts, works a lot, and smells fresh?"

Victoria finally turned to face her. Face blotchy. Eyeliner smudged. She had been crying. Sophie hadn't witnessed that in a long time. *Crying was for wimps,* Victoria had declared many years before. This was bad.

"Vicki," she began, but her friend cut her off.

"You don't understand. The text messages are always written out of my eyeline. The phone calls are always explained away as work and taken in private. And it bloody stands to reason that you don't come back from work smelling better than when you left. He's showering somewhere else."

"Oh Vic, come on. Have you even talked to him about it?"

"No, of course I fucking haven't!"

A lady with white hair, in the seat in front, made a show of turning to look at them.

"What are you looking at?" Victoria growled. "Turn around and mind your own business. Go on!"

"Vicki, stop," Sophie whispered, looking around them. Then, after waiting a few seconds for the moment of tension to pass, she continued in a hushed tone. "There's probably some perfectly reasonable explanation, Vic."

"What if there isn't? Do you think he's just going to confess?" She was shaking now, something else Sophie didn't remember witnessing perhaps ever before.

"My God, Vicki. You're really worried," Sophie said, squeezing her friend's arm.

"I can't lose him, Soph. I can't," she said, quickly and seriously. "He's all I have."

Sophie pulled her friend into a hug and carefully stroked her hair while ensuring she wasn't messing it. Victoria hated that. "Don't be silly, you doughnut. You're blowing this out of proportion. You're not going to lose him, and besides, you're not alone. You've got me."

There was a pause, filled in by the squeak of the cabin and the clatter of steel followed by the *ding dong* of a bell announcing the next station.

Victoria spoke from her muffled position against her friend's coat. "Only until you go and collect your crown as Countess whatsit."

Sophie chuckled and broke the embrace. "Dirt, you mean. Before I collect my crown as Countess Dirt. What was it? Of dirt. From dirt? I don't know."

Victoria laughed. "God, I must look the pits," she said.

Sophie was shaking her head. "No, you don't. You look beautiful as always… just… with panda eyes."

Victoria scoffed. "So much for permanent application. Do you know how much I spent on this stuff? Now it's all down my bloody face. I look like one of those warriors."

"That's because you are," Sophie said softly, eyes misting. She'd always been in awe of Victoria ever since the day they first met, when she'd stood up to that bully. This, her love for the man that gave her the one thing she'd craved all those years, was her only weakness. "I'm sorry," Sophie said, feeling the strength of her friend's pain even though she couldn't empathise with it. Something else to discuss at her next session.

"Oh shit, it isn't that bad, is it?" Victoria asked, looking at herself in the window's reflection then reaching for her bag. As she did, she noticed the squinty eyes of the white-haired lady observing them through the headrests.

"Woman, seriously? If you don't turn around, I'm going to poke those beady eyes out with my useless eyeliner."

The woman scowled but turned to face forward.

Sophie continued as if her friend hadn't just threatened a fellow passenger. "I'm so sorry, Vic. I've been too bloody self-absorbed lately to even ask how you've been," she said.

"Shit, girl. Your so-called parents were lying arseholes, you've been suspended from your job—which, by the way, normally means you'll be sacked or forced to resign—and you're about to be made homeless. I think you've deserved some time focussing on yourself," Victoria said dismissively.

"And there she is," Sophie said with a forced laugh, applying fingers to her would-be leaky eyes.

They both allowed themselves some time to sift through thoughts as the train rolled to a stop. A trio of seemingly carefree teenage girls stood and left the train in a cloud of enviable giggles.

A gust of fresh frosty air rushed in like a harassed housemaid, eager to purify the cabin, before the doors beeped and closed once more.

As the train resumed its journey so did the conversation.

"He plays squash," Sophie said, suddenly.

"What?"

"Jonathan plays squash, doesn't he? That's how he manages to keep fit and maintain that gorgeous body you love so much, right?"

"Yeah. I thought it might be that, but he doesn't play squash all the time."

"No, he doesn't. But he does play other sports, Vic, hence the showers. Come on. Why would he want to stray when he has you?" Sophie gave her an encouraging smile that faded when she noticed the look on her friend's face. She didn't know what it meant, but it was clear that she hadn't told her everything.

"What?"

Victoria shook her head but didn't speak. She was busy staring at the back of the white-haired lady's head, presumably wondering if the old bag was listening to their every word.

"Vic, what aren't you telling me?" Sophie demanded, leaning forward, and twisting her friend's face to make eye contact.

Victoria bit her lip then turned away from her once more, shaking her head as if struggling to keep the beast of her words from escaping the confines of her mouth.

This wasn't lost on Sophie, who was unnerved to see her friend like this. "Vic? What's the matter? Talk to me."

She did. But the words were such a whisper that they were lost over the clank and din of the train. "What was that?" Sophie asked.

"I'm damaged," Victoria repeated, turning but keeping her face bowed.

Sophie forced a laugh. "Yeah, well, we already know that," she said, stopping when she realised her friend wasn't sharing her amusement. "What?" she repeated. "For crying out loud, please look at me. What's wrong? You're starting to worry me."

"The next station is…"

Victoria was about to speak but stopped when she heard the announcement. The train began to slow.

The white-haired woman gathered her belongings, rustling bags and zipping up her coat in readiness for exposure to the elements. Once the train stopped, she stood up with a turn to give Victoria one final glance.

Victoria stuck her tongue out. "Try not to slip and fall out there, won't you?" she said with a fake smile.

The woman shook her head with disdain as she hustled out of the carriage and into the night, breath fogging out in front of her.

Cold, fresh air filled the cabin once more as they waited in silence. It was subliminally accepted by the both of them that if the train stopped so did their conversation. It was an unconscious policy, but necessary for privacy given that there were still a couple of suited men, as well as earphones guy, sharing the carriage with them.

The doors beeped and the train resumed its journey.

"I can't have babies," Victoria said miserably. "There's something wrong with me."

The news hit Sophie like a hammer. She knew how badly, desperately, her friend wanted to be a mother, but she had just assumed she was holding out for the right time. They often joked about how Victoria had only married her husband for his money while he had only married her to bear his children. It seemed like good banter, until now.

"I've been seeing my doctor for a while now. And it just isn't looking good. I can't seem to get pregnant," Victoria continued, still avoiding eye contact with her friend. "The damage…" She trailed off here, as though realising she might end up sharing more than she wanted to.

But Sophie was hanging on her friend's every word. "Damage? What damage?" she asked in a whisper, as if the men in suits across the aisle and three seats down might be interested.

Victoria hesitated and then said, "It doesn't matter. The bottom line is, I don't think I can give Jonathan kids."

"Does he know?"

"No," Victoria said sharply, as if the mere mention of it might beam the information to him. "And you can't breathe a word, Soph," she added quickly, desperately.

"Of course, of course. You know I wouldn't," Sophie reassured her. "How long have you known?"

"Not long."

"Are you going to tell him?"

Victoria scoffed. "And send him screaming for the hills? No way. You know his parents. They hate me as it is already! But they're pretty much royalty, Soph. You know that. Having children isn't a choice, it's a fucking duty!"

"You need to tell him, Vic. He has the right to know."

"What?! You're supposed to be on my side." The comment was sudden and so loud, it prompted a glance from one of the men.

Sophie looked at him, smiled apologetically and then turned back to her friend. "I *am* on your side. Of course I am," she whispered, as low as she could, as the lights of Cambridge city came into view. "But if you hide something as big as this from him now, it's only going to make things worse further down the line. I know that, after today."

"The next station is Cambridge. This train terminates here."

And so did the conversation as they alighted and found a taxi that took them back to Fenfield, where neither woman was prepared for what awaited.

19

THE DEVIL'S WORK

FRIDAY NIGHT

Detective Inspector Patricia King was in a foul mood. She'd pulled extended shifts all week and hadn't long been home when her mobile rang. It was her boss, who made no apology because these were extraordinary times. They were overstretched and she was needed at a serious crime scene in one of the city's outer areas.

Another one?

She'd had a full bloody week of *serious* crime scenes, each and every one shittier than the last. They all reminded her how depraved so-called civilised humans could be. That was why, no matter how much she loved her job, she had been looking forward to some down time. If it was anyone else on the phone, she would have chewed them out, but the Chief Super wasn't just her boss, he was a friend.

He had supported her promotions through the ranks during

her fifteen years in the force, despite the fact most of them had proved challenging. Not because Patricia wasn't capable – her appraisals were second to none – but simply because she was an unusually attractive female who also happened to be black. The assumption used to be that she bed-hopped her way through her promotions, until it then became about the colour of her skin. It used to infuriate her how her hard work and dedication to duty was reduced to the fitness of her body or the sapphire of her eyes. Then it frustrated her how her achievements were perceived as a woke box-ticking exercise that left no one willing to truly communicate with her, and her colleagues, mainly men, often deferring to her for fear of being tarred a racist as soon as any debate gained some heat.

In her opinion, all these so-called *movements* were doing nothing but stoking the fires of racism. They fostered a *them and us* mentality and perpetuated senses of entitlement to various degrees that were all, nonetheless, odious.

Which is why now, at the pinnacle of her career, she'd learned to not give a shit about the opinions of anyone other than those who mattered. It was an outlook that had served her well, albeit with some side effects; after barely three years of marriage, she was now party to an acrimonious divorce on the grounds of her husband being a militant prick.

Fenfield was much closer to the city than she remembered, more of an outskirt suburb than the satellite village she had thought it to be. The car had barely warmed up by the time she was turning into Meadow Lane, past trees that had been stripped of their summer beauty and autumn fire. The houses were large with relatively expensive cars parked out front. It was the kind of place people retired to when they were done selling their souls for a six-figure salary.

Onlookers, media trucks, and reporters swarming in jerky movements under the flickering lights of the two patrol cars blocking the street forced her to bring her vehicle to a rolling stop.

She swore and stepped out. She was wearing her jeans instead of her trouser suit, trainers instead of her black shoes, and was wrapped up in a coat that she usually considered too shabby for work. She'd topped the look with a black baseball cap with POLICE stamped on the front of it, for no other reason than it was the first thing she had been able to find. She'd already let her long wavy hair down when she got the call and was too tired to do anything with it.

But now, as reporters thrusted microphones and questions at her, she realised her mistake.

"Are you in charge?"

"Can you tell us your name?"

"What can you tell us about what's happening here?"

"I just got here. Excuse me. I've just got here," she said with a detached and professional smile, as she made her way through the crowd. "Just got here."

By the time she reached the yellow police tape that was fluttering in the chill, it felt more like the finish line to a race.

There were a couple of ambulances on the other side of the boundary, as well as two vans, more patrol cars, more uniforms, and several SOCO, that one reporter was already explaining into her camera meant Scenes of Crime Officers.

Jesus. No wonder we're overstretched.

She flashed her ID at the two officers who were repelling onlookers, and, only because she needed to, spoke to one of them.

"Where am I going?" she asked irritably. There was so much activity it was hard to tell.

"Depends which crime scene you're after, guv," the older of the two cops responded.

DI King frowned. "*Which* crime scene?"

Number 12 Meadow Lane felt colder inside than the world

outside. King had barely stepped through the door when she barked, "All right, what do we know?" Her question was directed at nobody in particular as she made her way down the dimly lit hallway.

The scene reminded her of one of those bad movies, where investigators stumbled about in the dark by phone light instead of turning on the overheads or a lamp. That's what they would normally do at a crime scene, whatever Hollywood would have people believe. In this case it was officers with flashlights, so her eyeroll was lost in the gloom.

"Has anybody even tried turning on a bloody light?" She reached for the switch on the wall with a gloved hand. The gloves were a gift from her soon to be ex-husband and about the only thing she was keeping from him, mostly out of practicality until she got a chance to buy a new pair for herself. Her hand paused when she stepped on something that crunched underfoot. "What the…?"

"It's glass. All of the lightbulbs have been smashed," said a faceless voice from the gloom.

"All of them?"

"Yep. Every single one."

King rolled her eyes again. "Well, has anybody thought about getting some mobile lights in here, for crying out loud?"

"Yeah, they should be here soon," the voice said, this time from over her right shoulder, startling her.

"You know, sneaking up on people like that is a good way of getting yourself a punch in the face," she grumbled.

"Sorry, guv," the voice said. "Wasn't intentional."

King couldn't see the man's face, but she was sure there was a smile in those words. "Yeah? Well, you may want to check that. Where am I going?" she asked, rooting around in her pocket for her phone before remembering she'd left it in the car. "Shit."

A phone light appeared out of the darkness, the beam leading to the stairs. "Up the stairs, left into the bedroom, then left again into the ensuite," the voice spoke once more. It had a faint lilt of an accent. Yorkshire, maybe. She wasn't sure.

"What's with all the activity in the back garden then?" she asked, looking down the long space that must be the corridor to the lights bobbing around at the rear of the property.

"One of them is out there. But the worst of it is upstairs."

"One of them? Didn't anybody think to mention that there are several victims? Might that be useful information to pass on to me?" She shot the man a look on reflex, but it was lost in the gloom.

"It's a dog. Great Dane. We think it tried to put up a fight and lost. Half of its neck is missing," he said grimly.

"Missing?" King asked.

"Torn out. And I mean torn. Like it was just ripped away."

They started up the stairs, following the shard of light as the faceless narrator continued. "The human victim is up here. Her name is Lucy Davidson. She's a 28-year-old paramedic, working out of Addenbrooke's Hospital. She was due at her mum's in Newcastle late last night. When she didn't show, her mum got worried and called it in."

"Late last night?" King repeated.

"Yeah. At first, her ma thought she had to wait before reporting it, that twenty-four-hour bollocks, but after getting no joy calling her mobile, she called us late morning. We managed to get a pair of uniforms out here this afternoon. They didn't find nowt wrong until a neighbour reported the dog."

"And she lived alone, except for the dog?"

"Only recently. She used to live here with her boyfriend until he moved out. Right now, he's a person of interest since she had a PO against him."

"A protective order? Abusive?"

"Sometimes."

"What do we know about him?"

"Craig Wheeler, thirty-five. He's in sales. Tractor parts. Bit of a wide boy according to some of the neighbours. Flashy motor and all that."

"Get a car over to his house. I'd like to talk to him."

"Already done that."

"What about preliminary on the body—"

"Bodies."

"Bodies," she repeated tersely as she stopped on the landing.

"You should know that it's pretty bad," the voice said gravely.

King turned to the silhouette. "Worse than murder? In what way?" she asked seriously.

The voice hesitated and then said, "It's unusual. Cruel and unusual."

"Cruel and unusual?" she echoed, snatching the phone from the man's hand and shining it in his face. "Who the bloody hell are you anyway, and what are you doing at my crime scene?"

The light revealed a man in a shirt and tie, with a square jaw and crew cut. Even though a hand blocked part of his face as he fended off the glare of the light, she could tell by the smoothness of his skin that he was probably still in his late twenties.

"Jesus," she hissed.

"I'm DS Butler, guv."

"Who?"

"Your new partner."

King rolled her eyes again and tossed the phone back to him, the beam flipping a few times before it was finally caught. "You must be bloody joking! How old are you?"

"Twenty-nine, guv."

"Bloody hell. And stop calling me that," she said irritably. "I asked for a new partner, not a bloody schoolkid," she lamented. "Jesus Christ."

She walked forward. "Has anybody got any—"

She was interrupted by Butler's hand appearing out of the dark. It was holding a neatly folded coverall. She unravelled the white jumpsuit and stepped into it while Butler shone a helpful light for her.

Suddenly, there was commotion downstairs as an officer entered the house, clanging and bumping portable lamps up the stairs and onto the landing, before finally plugging them in and switching them on.

The overspill of light bounced off the walls, partially illuminating the bedroom they were standing in. King could see her new partner properly now. He looked even younger than his years and, by the way his suit was clinging to his body as he stepped into his own white jumpsuit, she couldn't help but conclude that he too was a CrossFit fanatic. And just like that she was reminded of her husband.

She shook her head, then barked, "Tell him we need a couple of those up here. There's not much point only lighting up the hallway when the crime scene's in here, is there?"

The DS complied and called down the stairs as King zipped up her jumpsuit and gingerly made her way forward into the bedroom. It was steeped in shadows but for the phone light of a policeman who was seemingly doing nothing but guarding an empty bed. He nodded at her, but she didn't acknowledge him. Instead, she started to make her way towards the bathroom, stopping when something caught her attention under the roving beam of light.

"What the…" she breathed. Visible words seemed to float on the air around her before melting into the obscurity of the gloom. It was as if the circle of light was birthing them as it travelled up and over the walls.

"Aim that over here," King ordered. The officer trained his phone light to the space she was pointing to in front of her. The word was clear in places and faded in others, seemingly stencilled all over the walls and ceiling. Hundreds, maybe thousands of times.

"Have you ever seen anything like it?" Butler asked as he sidled up behind her, an action that was in no way helping him to ingratiate himself.

King took a step sideways and a few seconds to identify the pungent odour in the air. It smelt like sulphur and public toilets.

She sniffed, trying to clear the acrid stench from her nose. "I've seen all sorts, especially this week," she said, "but nothing like this."

"And we haven't even seen the main attraction yet," a deep voice, out of breath, said from behind them.

They turned in unison as Butler trained his light at the sound's origin.

"Hey, Arthur," King said. "Nice of you to join us." Then she turned to Butler. "Make sure you get some pictures of this," she said, nodding at the walls.

"Yeah, I've already asked the snapper to—"

"I meant with your phone," she interrupted.

Butler squinted as if he was going to say something more, but instead he nodded and went about carrying out the order.

King made her way over to the pathologist. He was a short, plump, balding man wearing a white jumpsuit stretched over his belly.

"Sorry. I got here as soon as I could," the man said breathlessly. "It's been one hell of a week. It's like the world's gone mad."

"Tell me about it," King groaned. "I've lost count of the nut jobs that have blamed that comet."

The doctor looked at her. "You look tired, Patricia," he said with a soft and careful articulation.

"Wow, thanks."

"Don't mention it. Who's your new boyfriend?"

King sighed. "You already know who it is, Arthur. Don't pretend."

The doctor snickered. "Blimey, Patricia. They're getting younger by the day."

"You know you can be quite inappropriate sometimes."

"Just sometimes? Oh, come on. It's common knowledge that you've missed having a partner. Word is that you were so excited about the prospect that you were unable to choose one, so he was chosen for you." The grin on the pathologist's face was almost lost in the shadows but this banter wasn't unfamiliar to King. Arthur was one of the very few people she allowed to indulge in it.

Still, "The *word* should mind its own bloody business," she said, her eyes on her new partner who was now on the opposite side of the room. They watched Butler frame and then snap photos on his phone, the flash from the device intermittently revealing the black markings, like a swarm of insects, all around them.

"Oh," the doctor said appreciatively, lifting his eyebrows. "Despite the ill-fitting onesie, I'd say they've chosen rather well."

"Yeah? Well, I can't say for sure, but something tells me you're not his type."

"Story of my life," the man said with a forlorn sigh. "Oh, and I was sorry to hear that you weren't able to work things out with... well you know, he who must not be named."

"You *hear* a lot, don't you?" she said.

"Occupational hazard, I'm afraid. Workplace rumour mill and all that."

"Well, did you *hear* about this? Any thoughts? As much as I know you'd rather discuss the implosion of my marriage." She aimed light at the walls.

The doctor shook his head. "Not yet, except I can tell you that the wording looks like Latin," he said.

"It *is* Latin," Butler agreed from across the room, as he framed one of the clearer iterations then tapped the shutter button on his phone. The flash fired, revealing the scrawled word. V E N I T.

"Doc?" King asked.

"I'm afraid my Latin rusted away a few centuries ago," the man said.

"It means *coming* or *he is coming* from the word *venire*, which means *to come*," Butler jumped in once more.

King and the pathologist exchanged looks.

"Not just a pretty face, eh?" Arthur said, before sighing deeply and pulling on a pair of gloves. Then he turned to face whatever awaited in the bathroom. As he moved towards it, his plastic-clad feet made a squelchy, spongy sound. King tried to follow his gaze as he looked down, despite the shadows. "You know, Detective, it would be really useful if we could get some light in—"

The doctor was interrupted by a clanging and tolling sound. It was accompanied by footsteps on carpeted stairs as the breathless officer noisily made his way up to them and lumbered into the room.

"Where do you want this?" he asked the room at large.

Butler turned to intercept him. "Anywhere over there will do. Thanks."

After rummaging around for what felt like an age to an already aggravated King, the policeman finally pushed the plug home and flipped the switch. The instant transformation from night into day revealed the true horror of the scene.

It took several seconds for King to become accustomed to the glare. When she had, it became clear that the wall and ceiling marks hadn't been stamped or stencilled on at all. They appeared to be burned or seared, deep into the magnolia, and what they had first thought was black ink was in fact singed crimson blood. The same blood had washed over the white tiles of the bathroom and onto the oatmeal carpet of the bedroom, where it had been absorbed, dying it red.

"Jesus Christ," the officer who had just fetched the lights uttered, staring past the DI and the pathologist to the bathroom beyond.

King and the doctor glanced at the man and then at each other before turning to follow his gaze.

The bathroom was still imbued with shadows but the overspill from the LED light was enough to reveal a grotesque tableau of a naked female, sprawled in a partially filled bath. Her arms were snapped at the elbows and twisted into a gruesome articulation that had them pointing upward while her forearms dangled forward. The only thing connecting them was a thin strip of pallid skin. Her head was slumped back, partially submerged under the water. Wet hair was slicked against her deathly pale face as glassy, filmy eyes stared, vacantly, at the tiled ceiling.

Like her arms, her legs appeared to have been snapped at the joints, thighs forced apart. Her right leg dangled over the side of the bath by a fleshy tether.

"Can we get some fucking light in here, please?" It was the softly spoken doctor. In all the years she had known the man, King had never heard him swear like this at a crime scene. "Sorry," he added. "Been a long week."

The copper who was still clutching one of the lights in his hand appeared to be in a trance, so Butler sprang into action. He startled the man by tapping him on the shoulder before telling him to go and get some air. They wouldn't want him stomping all over the scene anyway.

Butler moved carefully around the soaked carpet, homed in on a socket, plugged the lamp in, and angled it at the doorway. The light projected giant shadows of King and the doctor onto the bathroom walls, adding voyeuristic spectators to the scene.

King turned around. "Thanks, Detective, we'll take it from here. You can finish taking statements from each and every one of the neighbours. Somebody must have seen or heard something."

Butler frowned and stepped forward. "What? I've been assigned to this case and—"

"Now please, Detective."

Butler gawked at her, jaw muscle clenching, but King was unaffected. She maintained his gaze until the young man shook his head then turned, mumbling something about bullshit.

King turned back to the bathroom. The doctor was already taking a closer look at the body under the new light.

"Making friends already?" he asked without looking up. Although the room was now awash with light, he was carefully training a small flashlight over the body. King didn't respond. "Well, I think I can safely confirm that she's dead," he said grimly, glancing up at her.

"Arthur… what the hell?" King asked, with quiet astonishment.

"I haven't seen anything like it before," the doctor said, shaking his head. "At least not here in Cambridge. In Africa, yes, all too often, but here…" He left the sentence unfinished. "What exactly do we know about her?"

"She lived alone. Recently separated from her boyfriend."

"Unlikely to be relevant," the pathologist said, panning his light over the dark water in the tub. "This kind of mutilation," he narrated, "it doesn't exactly smack of an impulsive crime of passion. It's something else. Something more premeditated." He looked up at her again, as if to suggest that she might want to start there.

King took in a long, sad breath. "You're thinking FGM?"

The doctor cocked his head, his eyes still roving over the body. "Technically, it is some form of female genital mutilation, but it's atypical."

"How so?"

"Well, there are four types of FGM," he said, gesturing between the legs of the body as if it were a scientific mannequin and not a formerly living, breathing human being. As he did so, King flinched, but inwardly, as was her style. She had seen a lot during her service, but nothing quite like this.

"Type 1," the doctor continued, "is where the clitoris has been completely removed or cut in half. Type 2 again includes removal of the clitoris, but also the inner lip, otherwise known as the *labia minora*. Type 3 is where everything is removed and what remains is stitched together, leaving just enough of a gap for the passage of menstrual flow and urine. Type 4 is referred to as unclassified. This is when other damage has been done, such as when the clitoris has been pierced or corrosive material has been injected into the vagina—"

"Jesus Christ, Arthur!" King complained with a grimace.

The doctor looked at her, nonplussed, as if she'd just interrupted his recital of his weekly grocery list.

"Okay. Maybe that was a bit too much detail, but you did ask. On the other hand, Pat, isn't this precisely the problem? Just because people don't like hearing about this stuff, it doesn't mean it doesn't happen. It does and, as you know, it's only by bringing light to these things that we can—"

"Yeah, all right, no need to get on your soap box. You're starting to sound like my ex. Let's stick to what is going on here. Are you saying that this doesn't fit any of those categories?"

The doctor looked up and nodded. "I can't say for sure before I've had a chance to properly examine the body but in three years I spent over there, I never saw anything like this. FGM, yes, but the rest of the body. The way it's been discarded…"

"Not staged?"

"No. There's no particular design to this. The body just appears to have been discarded here. And, with that trendy wallpaper out there, I'm inclined to think that it may well be post some kind of a ritual. Of course, I'll know more once I've conducted the post-mortem and had the bathwater analysed. Could you please make sure some moron doesn't come in here and pull the plug? I had that happen a few weeks back. The idiot quite literally flushed all the evidence down the drain."

King nodded. "What exactly do you think is in the water? Why's it that colour? Is that blood?" She was referring to the brownish discolouration that made it look like stagnant dishwater.

The doctor glanced at it. "Blood, I'd say. And judging from the ripeness of the smell, faeces too. Given the trauma, it's highly likely that she soiled herself when it happened."

Someone's daughter. King recited this thought in her head every time she attended a crime scene. What was just another day at the office for her was *someone's son. Someone's mother. Someone's father.* The silent mantra helped her stay anchored to the nuance of human emotions. It was a technique finally suggested to her by one of the force's psychologists following the complaints that had been made about her over the years for being, among other things, *cold, blunt, harsh,* and *unsympathetic.*

King had always subscribed to the idea that families would much rather she focus on doing her job than dispensing inane sympathy. In her opinion, kind words were pointless. The only comfort came from justice or, in some cases, retribution, although she'd never say that last bit out loud.

DI Patricia King had barely made it out of the house at number 12 Meadow Lane when she was accosted by DS Butler. She felt the urge to roll her eyes again because she knew what was coming next but concluded that would probably only make him worse. She might as well let the guy vent. Apparently, that was supposed to make people feel better.

"You do realise that I'm a fully qualified detective, right? I've even got one of those certificates and a shiny badge to prove it. In fact, not unlike you, I pretty much graduated top of my class. And in case you've forgotten what that was like, that actually means I was smarter than most of my peers."

"You know, you don't need to recite your CV to me. You've already got the gig. The fact that you're here at all means that somebody in their infinite wisdom thinks you have something to…" King cut herself off when an inhuman shriek interrupted her. "What's going on over there?" she asked.

"Number eleven," Butler explained, as they both looked over to see a bereft female collapse into the arms of a suited man in front of two uniformed officers. "They're the abduction. Six-month-old baby taken from inside his home, apparently. At least, that's the story according to his mother. She says that her baby was taken by some kind of creature."

"Really?"

Butler nodded. "A DI Spencer is heading that."

"Oh" is all King could say.

"You know him?"

"Know of him." They both watched as the woman was escorted to one of the waiting ambulances, barely able to put one foot in front of the other, such was her distress.

"And the other?" King asked.

Butler nodded to the house next door where a young male and female were chatting animatedly to two officers. "This is next door to the last one. Number nine. House share, three males. Apparently, um…" Butler cleared his throat. "This appears to be a sex game gone wrong. Somehow, and it's still unclear how, the girlfriend managed to bite off her boyfriend's penis."

King squinted at her colleague. For one fleeting moment she thought he was having her on.

He wasn't and he continued. "The girlfriend denies it though. She says that she never made it inside the house because the door was locked, and that she only entered the building when she heard his screams by smashing the glass in the back door."

"What does the boyfriend say?"

"Not much. He's still touch and go. In intensive care. Lost a lot of blood. Prognosis isn't good." Butler raised his eyebrows.

King mused on this. "Make sure we get full witness statements and that these are copied to all of the SIOs."

"Already in progress."

King nodded. It was highly likely these events were linked, so it made sense to have just one senior investigating officer overseeing the whole thing. She made a note to discuss this with her boss. With a bit of luck she might be able to offload this crazy to someone else. Chance would be a fine thing.

She allowed her gaze to fall back on the house they'd just left, before noticing the one next door. In stark contrast to the rest of the street, all the windows were black. "What's that, number thirteen?" she asked, moving in that direction.

Butler followed. "Number ten, actually."

"Who does the Range Rover belong to?" She was referring to the black SUV parked on the drive.

Butler didn't even consult his notes. "It's registered to a Victoria Ainsworth. She was seen by neighbours arriving this morning and then leaving with a Sophie Cooper, her best friend, in a cab. Yes, we've contacted her husband. Yes, we've tried her mobile and no, she isn't answering. He says they were in London today so it could just be she has no signal or her phone's dead. Yes, we're looking for them and yes, we've even gone as far as deeming them person or persons of interest, given that Sophie Cooper lives just next door to number twelve. Oh, and I can also walk and chew gum at the same time," he added sarcastically.

King nodded then pulled a face at the added irrelevant piece of information. Then she watched how a taxi was forced to stop, as she had been, further down the road due to congestion near the police cordon.

Sophie was the first to spot the blue lights as the taxi made its way down Meadow Lane. Curiously, she leaned forward and then arched her neck to get a better view. Although she couldn't see much, the flutter in her gut told her something was wrong.

"What's goin' on here then?" said the taxi driver, as if verbalising her thoughts.

As one, the two women strained against their seatbelts to look out of the front window where two patrol cars slowly came into view.

"This is as far as I can go," the taxi driver said, squinting at all the commotion.

Sophie unbuckled herself and stepped out into the wintry freeze. It nipped at her cheeks and tugged at her hair as she pushed her way through the crowd. She only stopped at the police cordon where she was promptly intercepted by two officers in fluorescent jackets.

"Sorry, miss," one said, breath fogging out in front of him. "This area's off limits."

"But I live here," she said, pointing at her house.

"What number?"

"Ten. What's happened? Can you tell me what's happened?" she asked anxiously, her stomach churning in anticipation of the response.

The policeman consulted his notepad. "What's your name?"

"Cooper. Sophie Cooper," she said, instantly reminded of her day. *No, it's not. It's some Italian name you can't even remember!*

"Wait here," the cop said. He turned his back to her and talked into the radio affixed to his chest.

Sophie gawked at Lucy's house. It was ablaze with light, tinged in a periodical pearlescent blue that bounced and rolled off the nearby buildings, transforming night into a surreal underwatery day.

The scene was as chaotic as it was scary. The crowd behind her were mumbling and jostling for a better view.

Her immediate thought was that something had happened to Ms Whitlock.

"Um, excuse me! How much of the road do you need exactly?" Sophie heard Victoria's scathing tone before she felt her touch her arm. "Oh, what the hell is going on?" she gasped, hunching into her coat, just stopping short of jogging on the spot to fight the cold.

"I don't know," Sophie responded distractedly, taking in the scene, nodding at a familiar face. She was about to ask what had happened when...

"Okay. You can go through," the officer said, turning to her and making an arch of the tape so that she could pass under it.

"What happened here?" Sophie repeated.

"The DI will speak with you."

"The D what?"

"Just go and see that lady over there," the officer said, pointing at King, who was already making her way towards them, Butler by her side.

"Wait for me!" Victoria said, teetering over.

"Who are you?" the officer asked.

"I'm with her."

"Do you live here?"

"Pretty much."

"Sorry, unless you actually live here, I—"

"I'm with her," Victoria said seriously, shooting the man one of her worst glares. "That's my car over there. Look, on her drive." She pointed.

"She's with me," Sophie corroborated.

"And you are...?"

"I'm Victoria. Victoria Ainsworth."

After hesitating a few more seconds, the cop finally made an arch of the tape for her too, and she stepped under it.

Heart pounding, pulse racing, Sophie hurried forward. Something was wrong. Something was very wrong. Worse, the police, the people she had come to loathe ever since she received that phone call that night at work, were everywhere, and they were making her feel worse. Much worse. Nauseated.

"Sophie Cooper?" asked the DI.

Sophie nodded because she was unable to form words right now.

"Are you Sophie?" the detective repeated.

"Yes, I'm Sophie Cooper."

"You live at number ten?"

Sophie nodded impatiently. "Yes. What's happened?"

"I'm DI Patricia King."

"Are you in charge?" Victoria asked, joining them.

King observed her. "I'm the senior investigating officer, yes. And you are?"

"What happened here, miss senior investigating officer?" Victoria replied curtly. "My friend has asked enough times now."

King glanced at the house next door where SOCO personnel were still milling in and out. "Your neighbour at number twelve—"

Sophie had already followed her gaze and drew in a sharp breath. "Lucy?" Her eyes pricked with immediate tears. "Has something happened to her?"

"I'm afraid so."

"What? Is she all right? Is she okay?"

The DI looked at her. *Somebody's friend. Somebody's neighbour.* She was preparing a suitable response when…

"What happened?" Victoria demanded.

"I'd rather not talk about that just yet," King said.

"Well, we would. Tell us. We have a right to know."

"I'm sorry, who are you again?"

"Please…" Sophie said, instinctively reaching out to the woman, not wanting this to escalate into something else.

The DI hesitated and nodded before asking, "Do you have somewhere else you can stay tonight?"

20

GREENFIELDS

LATER FRIDAY NIGHT

Sophie was surprised to discover how relieved she was to leave Fenfield behind. The further Victoria drove them out of the lights and into the darkness of the countryside, the better she felt.

She was still unable to process exactly what the detective had told her about Lucy. Despite the fact that the woman had refused to go into any detail, it was obvious that something horrific had happened. This renewed the hollow ache of bereavement in her chest. The two may not have been close friends, but Sophie still felt the loss.

Sophie's friendship circle was small. As a child this wasn't by choice. In fact, shortly after moving to Fenfield, she had longed for the companionship that might help her fill the void left behind by her mother. But as word spread about her past and her frequent visits to Doctor Krauss, so did the schoolground bullying, and she retreated into herself until she met Victoria. She was like a breath of fresh air. She was everything Sophie wasn't. Tough, fearless, independent. Yet broken, just like her.

Janay on the other hand was different. She had her own schoolground battle scars and, because of her pregnancy, was forced to grow up quickly. She certainly wasn't as wild as Victoria, but she was warm, wise, sassy, and funny with it. They met shortly after Victoria had ditched her at the café where Janay worked as waitress to chase after one of her ill-fated romances. When Janay found Sophie sitting alone in one of the booths, they struck up a conversation about the pros and cons of friendship. Like Victoria, Janay was several years older than Sophie, yet they discovered that they had much in common. They were soon ensconced in deep conversation before Janay's boss was forced to put an end to it.

It was shortly afterwards that Sophie concluded that these two people were all the companionship she'd ever need in her life. Her yin and yang of friends.

Shit! Janay! Janay had left multiple messages throughout the day and now Sophie even had a couple of missed calls from her. But with everything that had happened, she'd been unable to respond. She made a mental note to do so as soon as she was settled in.

Their destination was less than a thirty-minute drive out of the Cambridge suburbs, on windy roads through moonlit fields and woodland. Victoria swung the Range Rover onto a short, gravelled drive under naked branches of wintry trees. Sophie knew they were the skeletons of the lush canopy that bloomed there in the spring, their green just a memory for now as they emerged into a forecourt in front of Greenfields.

The three-bedroom hexagonal building of wood, metal, and glass was the brainchild of controversial and eminent architect,

Franz Mult. Mult had built his reputation on being the dissident of architects. He designed buildings that would either delight or disgust, such as the phalanx-like office block proposed for Cambridge City Centre, along with the vagina-shaped arts centre that celebrated the accomplishments of women through the ages.

Victoria had fallen in love with Greenfields the moment she clapped eyes on it, telling Jonathan that the place spoke to her.

The estate agent did an excellent job of highlighting both the building's history as well as its unique characteristics. Each of the six hexagons of the building were divided into a functional living space: kitchen, dining room, lounge with mini cinema, study, utility room, and playroom. Each featured walls made of stone and double-glazed glass, offering spectacular views of the surrounding woodland. But the most stunning feature of the building was its centrepiece island aviary. It featured living trees, a pond, birds, and there was even room for a collection of exotic fish.

Just off the aviary, floating stairs led to the first floor and three spacious bedrooms, each with its own full-sized bathroom.

Outside, a series of outbuildings could easily be converted into stables, the pretty blonde agent had suggested after Victoria let slip that she loved trees and animals, horses especially.

The tour had ended in one of the bedrooms, in front of a giant picture window that overlooked the acre or so field of the back lawn. Victoria had looked at her new husband. Words had not been necessary. He had known exactly what she was thinking and couldn't deny her. Besides, Jonathan may not have gushed like his wife – that wasn't his style – but it didn't mean he wasn't impressed with the place. He hadn't seen anything like it before either. Victoria knew that had excited him. Especially when thoughts turned to friends, clients, and general entertaining.

Jonathan Ainsworth was of the House of Ainsworth, Buckinghamshire, aristocrats of the worst kind with very distant links to the British royal family. This detail was never far from any discourse.

They had met in a London club, although Jonathan had told his mother a different story. He was instantly smitten with Victoria. She had humility absent from the other girls in his circle, most of whom he said bore a tedious sense of entitlement.

Victoria wasn't like that. She appreciated the simplest things in life, and Jonathan seemed to enjoy nothing more than pleasing her. Besides, he had been eager to escape Buckinghamshire and the clutches of his mother who, if she had her way, would have them make a home and raise a family on one of the Ainsworth estates.

And so, after ordering a battery of surveys on Greenfields and an investigation into the building's history, receiving nothing but positive reports, they made an offer. They moved in six weeks later. Within a couple of months, the outbuildings were converted, and they took delivery of two Cleveland Bay rescue horses, Star and Moon, as well as one black and white Shire they called Samson, inspired by his lusciously long black mane and fluffy white boots. Victoria's pride and joy.

Victoria's dream had been realised. She had moved far enough away to disassociate herself from her past, but not so far that she couldn't parade all that she had become as Mrs Jonathan Ainsworth.

That was two years ago, and the Ainsworths were as in love today as they were back then.

At least, that's how Victoria had felt until recently, when the maid had selfishly failed to report for duty because she allegedly had a fever. This meant that it fell on her to pick up around the house and run errands, which included collecting Jonathan's suits from the dry cleaners. There, the Asian man, who kept her waiting much longer than she would have liked, had handed over Jonathan's suits along with a department store brand of used lip gloss. Apparently, he had found the thing in the inside pocket of the suit jacket and assumed it was hers. It was not. And, as far as she knew, her husband did not use lip gloss.

When she returned home, she placed the pink, glittery vial on the kitchen counter and stared at it for the best part of an hour as all kinds of thoughts, like an ugly oil slick, slithered through her mind. She had even sniffed the thing for possible clues, but there were none. The act was as ridiculous as she was desperate.

She agonised for the rest of the day as to whether she should raise the subject with her husband. That thing was innocuous enough but, like a weapon of mass destruction, it had the ability to destroy everything. And so, she chose to say nothing. To forget she ever laid eyes on it. Then, after cursing and spitting on it, she buried it in the back garden, mumbling unintelligible words as she did so.

As for nosy Mr Lee at the dry cleaners, she reported him for making inappropriate comments during her visit that, quote, *made her feel uncomfortable*. He was fired.

That was a month ago.

Now, as they drove onto the forecourt, triggering the security lights and revealing the empty parking spaces, Victoria saw that her husband wasn't home. Her heart sank. And yet, she managed a bright, "Well, here we are. Home sweet home."

"Are you sure Jonathan won't mind me staying?" Sophie asked, eyeing the house through the windscreen as if she were afraid of it.

Victoria frowned. "Why would he mind? This place is so big, we won't even know you're here," she added with a wink. Yet Victoria noticed her friend's faint smile. "Look, I know everything feels like shit right now because it has been shit for you, but—"

"It isn't just that."

"No?"

"No."

"Then, what is it?"

Sophie frowned. "Vic, Lucy is dead. By the sounds of it murdered, probably by her ex. You've got to admit, some really weird and scary stuff has happened on Meadow Lane over the last few nights."

Victoria scoffed. "So?"

"So? What do you mean *so*?"

"Well, you don't know those people. And it's not like Lucy was your best friend or anything, was she? I am, Sophie," she said, reaching out and touching her friend's arm.

Sophie drew in a breath to speak but then wasn't quite sure how to articulate it. No. She wasn't best friends with Lucy, but they were neighbours, and Victoria knew her too. They had shared several girls' nights together and yet she seemed completely unaffected by all of it.

"Look. I get it. It's horrible scary stuff, of course I get it. But Soph, you're my friend. My priority is you. And this isn't the end, you know. This is just the beginning. Destiny has plans for you. Many delicious plans. You'll see."

Sophie squinted at her. "*Delicious plans?* What are you, a fortune teller?"

"Didn't you know? Now, come on," Victoria said, pulling on the door handle and stepping out into the night.

That was Victoria's way. She'd always had a knack for perking Sophie up, even at her worst moments. *Teflon* is how she would refer to herself; no matter what life threw at her; she'd just let it slide off with a smile. It was both inspirational and scary to Sophie, who believed everybody had their breaking point. She shuddered to think what might happen if Victoria ever reached hers.

For Sophie, however, there was no coming back from this. No Teflon magic was going to make the last few weeks disappear.

She followed her friend out into the night as a biting wind attempted to sink its teeth into her, but she was impervious now, much more affected by the fresh, mossy scent that rode it like a wild stallion. She breathed deeply as all around them the naked trees hummed like tenors under the direction of the wind.

"Wow," Sophie said thoughtfully. "I'd forgotten just how disconnected you are from the city out here."

"I know. Brilliant, isn't it? It's one of the things I love most about this place. I love it so much I could fuck it!" Vicki said with an exaggerated clench of her teeth.

Sophie squinted at her and laughed. "You're mental, you are. You know that, right?"

"I've been told," she said, linking her friend's arm. "But can't you feel it though, Soph?" Victoria asked with a big sigh.

"Feel what?"

"Nature! In the earth, the trees, the wind. It's all around us, crackling with life. It's like an electric current." Victoria held her belly. "Flowing right through you."

Sophie eyed her friend seriously for a few seconds before erupting with laughter and wagging a finger at her. "Ah, you almost got me then! Almost!"

Victoria rolled her eyes. "Heathen. Oh well, I tried. Come on, let's go inside. I'm so excited you're here!"

"Crackling with life?" Sophie mocked with a giggle before stopping so abruptly Victoria bounced into her.

"What?" Victoria followed her friend's gaze up into the starlit sky.

There, like a queen among her glittering minions, the comet appeared to shimmer.

"I hate that thing," Sophie said with disgust.

"The comet? Why?"

Sophie mused then shook her head. "I don't even know. What I do know is that everything turned to crap the moment it arrived."

"Right," Vicki said slowly, as if her friend was losing her mind. "And you say that I'm mental."

"No, I'm serious. Ever since that thing arrived…" she paused here, unable to find more words to explain it.

"Yep. Okay. Time to get you some vino," Victoria said, tugging at her friend and steering her towards the entrance.

Inside, Victoria had barely closed the door behind them before the hallway light came on.

"Don't you find that creepy?"

"What? The lights?"

"Yeah, the way they seem to have a mind of their own."

Victoria frowned. "They don't have a mind of their own, you doughnut. They're motion activated. They sense movement and do their job. Which is more than I can say for a lot of people I know."

Victoria's shoes clacked loudly on the marble floor as they passed by the aviary, where the lights remained off for the comfort of its feathered inhabitants, and the floating stairs to the next floor. They used to be made of brick and plaster, but Victoria had had them replaced with solid wood sourced from local trees.

Sophie took in the space as if she were seeing the building for the first time, though she wasn't, of course. She had been here many times before. Mostly for highbrow social events for strangers with a lot of money, such as the Ainsworths' friends. More specifically, Jonathan's friends, though they were rapidly adopted by Victoria.

Victoria had known the moment she saw him that Jonathan Ainsworth had always been popular. At school he was the preppy guy who was smart, played sports with the lads, and could hold a conversation with anyone, including his teachers, about an array of topics. He matured into a handsome Clark Kent of a thirty-something-year-old man, with a neat demeanour, thick black spectacles, and a cultured articulation. The fact that he spent most of his time at schools away from home had afforded him an altogether different kind of wealth, that of life experiences. He didn't enjoy talking about class or his family or relying on them for anything. Jonathan worked hard to forge his own career and make his own money in trading. Some business magazines used to refer to him as the perfect bachelor, though it was a title coined by his own family, Victoria had later learned. One squandered, in his mother's opinion, on the likes of someone like her.

How on Earth did my son end up with you? Did you hex him or something?

"Vic!"

"What?"

"Are you all right? You spaced out there."

"Yeah. Yes. I'm fine. Fine."

"You sure?" Sophie asked.

"Yes, sure."

"I asked if Jonathan was at work," Sophie said as they walked into the kitchen.

Victoria pulled a pained face. "Yeah, yes. He sent me a text, saying he was going to be late, but that he'd be getting the next train back from London." She was lying because she was already regretting her overshare with Sophie. She was fine sharing anything else, just not that. Not cracks in her marriage. That was hers. That was personal.

Truth was, she hadn't heard from her husband, and she was actually starting to worry, for multiple reasons.

"Ugh. I don't know how he does it," Sophie said, cupping her hands to her face in an attempt to see out of the glass panel of the balcony door.

"What? The commute?" Victoria asked, retrieving wine from the rack and placing two glasses on the counter. When she noticed her friend peering into the dark through the glass, she touched a wall panel. Instantly, the balcony was revealed, its steps leading down to a giant patio and then, like a runway coming into view, a sprawling manicured paddock framed by woodland.

"Shit," Sophie whispered. "I forget how big your back garden is."

Victoria smiled as she poured wine into the glasses. "So, how are you feeling? Want to watch a film or something? Or would you prefer to take this bottle and some snacks with you into a hot bath?"

Sophie grimaced as she thought about where they police had said they'd found Lucy. "Not really in the mood for a bath, but a shower would be nice. Do you mind?"

"Of course not. Me casa is your casa and all that shit," Victoria said with a grin, clinking her friend's glass.

They sipped their drinks and then Sophie remembered. "Speaking of *casa*. Did you come round the house the other night?"

Victoria cocked her head. "What do you mean?"

"The other night. What was it, Tuesday? I was at Janay's. Lucy said that she saw you at mine.

"Did she?"

"Yeah. She said she saw you downstairs in the living room. She said she wasn't sure but that she'd seen other people there too."

"Really?"

"Yes," Sophie said, stepping closer and eyeing her friend with mock suspicion. "You said you were going to be away. You're not secretly having parties at my house, are you?" she said with an exaggerated lift on an eyebrow.

Victoria thought about this for a few seconds then smiled. "As clever as you know I am, Soph, even I can't be in two places at the same time, can I?" she asked before taking a sip from her glass.

21

MOONLIGHT

FRIDAY NIGHT

Thirty minutes later, Sophie was installed in one of the guest bedrooms.

Victoria had carried a tray to her room with snacks, wine, and a bottle of water. Then she had rummaged in her closet for spare clothes for her friend to sleep in, as well as a change that she could wear in the morning since, on police advice, they had left Meadow Lane without so much as a glance back. At least for the night.

Sophie was fine with that. There's no way she could have stayed in the house alone after what she had just learned. The detective may not have said much but what little she did share, about dead dogs and dead neighbours, was enough to put her off ever going back.

When she'd asked about potential suspects, the police didn't say much about that either, only that they were *following any and all leads*, which just sounded like their stock answer. It naturally wasn't good enough for Victoria, who had made it clear that there could only be one suspect. He used to live with her and had a history of violence.

Sophie wasn't sure. Lucy's ex wasn't the nicest guy in the world, but murder? And he was supposed to love that dog more than he loved her.

Finding clothes wasn't too difficult for the two friends who were similar in size and stature, although Victoria, who was fanatical about keeping the weight off, was somewhat thinner. Unhealthily so, some would say. She attributed her thinness to the fresh country air and early morning runs in the woods. She managed to find a couple of old shirts she'd worn once, some new underwear she didn't like, and jeans that were too big for her. Once she'd given them to Sophie, Victoria hugged her friend and left, closing the door behind her.

Alone, Sophie collapsed onto the bed. Marauding thoughts and memories stomped across her mind like wild animals, each sniffing, scraping, and vying for attention. Everything that had happened on Meadow Lane over just the past few nights. That strange stuff at the house. The missing baby. The boy next door. Was it all connected? It had to be. And what about Lucy, and that stuff she had told her about people being at the house? Was she mistaken? She certainly appeared to be when it came to Vicki, who insisted that she was out of town that night. And what about her and her husband? Could Jonathan really have been cheating on her? They seemed so in love.

Her mind was relentless. Thoughts gushed through her like an endless torrent of water she was unable to shut off.

She considered calling Doctor Krauss to talk things through. He had a knack for helping her arrange her thoughts in such a way that she could process them more clearly and therefore feel much better. He was, after all, skilled at that, good at helping her see things for how they really were rather than how her mind was presenting them to her.

But then he also had a way of making her feel as if she was losing control, making each of her thoughts lose the substance she had attached to them. Maybe he was right. After all, she did imagine that her mother had been devoured by some kind of demon.

NO!

She launched herself off the bed, as if she could leave her quarrelling thoughts behind, picked up the glass of wine, and gingerly sipped on it as she peered out of the picture window to see what was out there. Although she couldn't explain it, she felt the skin-prickling sensation of being watched. Which she knew was ridiculous, because Greenfields was out in the middle of nowhere.

Yet, she stepped back from the window. The persistent inky blackness was making her feel worse. She'd forgotten just how tangible the dark was out here.

She made her way into the ensuite. It was spacious and luxuriously decorated, with black marble floors that winked a constellation of colours under the spotlights and grey tiles with flecks of white. There was a large granite basin overlooked by an ornate gold Gothic mirror, a large walk-in shower, and even an ostentatious chaise longue of crushed red velvet.

Trust Vicki.

The thought made her smile, but it disappeared the moment she spotted the bath, standing on gold claw feet on its own podium in the centre of the room.

She turned away from it as her mind conjured a series of gory images that she reassured herself must be worse than how they'd really found Lucy's body.

And yet, despite its lonely appearance in the centre of the room, its rapidly building suds and steamy breath were nonetheless inviting.

Victoria had ignored her protestations and taken the trouble to run the bath, as well as light a series of black and white pillar candles carved with unintelligible hieroglyphics that meant nothing to Sophie. They looked good though, even if the scene did look more like something out of a satanic temple than a bathroom, but then that was classic Victoria. And, oddly, there was something comforting in the strangeness, as though it were familiar on some unconscious or symbolic level. And that was something she needed right now, a little familiar comfort.

She set the wine down on the stand next to the tub and then dipped her finger in the bathwater. It was the perfect temperature, and the giant bath was already almost full. She reached over and turned the two gold claw taps until the sound of running water gave way to the rickety creak of the skylight directly overhead as the rumble of the wind pulled at it, demanding to be let inside.

Sophie began to unbutton her blouse but paused when she caught her reflection in the black picture window. By day it offered a spectacular view of the fields and woodland and yet now, by night, it only reminded her of how tired she looked. No, not tired. Haggard. She allowed her vision to blur, focussing from her reflection to the inky blackness of the glass instead. After a while, it appeared to quiver and bend to the will of the wind pressing on it like a tidal wave of ink, threatening to smash its way through and drown her in its murky goo.

She turned away, rubbing at the ache in her neck and then rocking her head from side to side to crick away the tension that had built there. The tension, she realised, was made worse by the fact that she didn't feel comfortable undressing in a room with no blinds or frosted glass.

You're in the middle of nowhere.

Still. She didn't like the idea of being spotlighted inside while out there, loitering in the darkness, anything or anyone could be…

She pulled the bands from her hair and allowed it to spill freely to her shoulders. She looked rough. At least she thought she did, and yet her beauty wasn't a stranger to her. She had received a fair amount of attention and flattery over the years but had never given it any significance.

Until recently.

She returned to the bedroom to pick up her phone when she noticed that the door was open. She frowned as she recalled the memory of Victoria pulling it shut on her way out earlier. She did. She was sure of it.

And yet…

She scanned the room. The walk-in wardrobe. Under the bed. Behind the door.

Stop it.

She walked over to the door and popped her head out onto the landing. Nothing but the creak and sigh of the house's resistance to the elements outside.

"Vic?" The word was barely a whisper.

The night lights glowed a subtle amber in their attempt to make the house appear cosy, yet it felt empty.

She retreated into the bedroom and checked the door for a lock. There wasn't one, so she satisfied herself with making sure the catch was engaged. It was. She retrieved her mobile phone from her bag and returned to the bathroom once more, closing the door behind her.

Drip. Plop. Drip. Plop. The bath taps beckoned with a watery serenade accompanied by the innocent *fizz* and *pop* of the suds. She looked around the room. It was empty, obviously. And yet something felt off.

She walked over to the bath and peered at her reflection in a sud-free section. Above her, the tiles blinked under the flickering candlelight.

There's nothing wrong with this place. It's you. Just have a soak. Get some rest.

It made perfect sense. But then she saw Lucy's lifeless glassy eyes looking over her shoulder and the vision startled her.

"Nope. I'm sorry, I can't." She plunged a hand into the bath, resisting the urge to snatch it back at the thought of something grabbing her, and then yanked the plug.

The drain rumbled loudly as if protesting her action, as the atmosphere in the room seemed to shift and morph into anticlimactic disappointment.

All in your mind. You should probably lay off the...

She didn't finish the thought because that's when she noticed. The sight of it ran a chill so powerful through her body, it made her rebutton her blouse.

The wine glass, it was... empty. But it couldn't be. She distinctly remembered Victoria filling it almost to the brim. She was sure of it. It nearly spilt over the sides. They laughed. She'd had to take a sip and then another and then another, and yet...

It was almost full when I set it down. I didn't drink it all. Did I?

She surveyed the room once more, as if someone could be hiding behind the bath towel or perhaps inside the toilet bowl. Yet again, even though she could see the space was empty, she couldn't shake the sensation that she was being watched. She instinctively rubbed at her arms where it felt like an army of invisible ants were busy erecting goosebumps all over her skin. She hastily attempted to rub the sensation away.

Drip! Plop! Gurgle! Drip! Plop! Gurgle!

She yelped at the sound of the ravenous drain devouring the bathwater and then again when her phone started vibrating.

"Shit!" she hissed, turning the device over and then smiling at the image of Janay's chubby face and protruding tongue.

"Oh hello," she said apologetically. Gratefully.

"Bloody hell, there you are!" Janay complained.

"Oh, I know, I'm so sorry. I saw your messages. I meant to call you back and I was about to, but today has been so full on, like you wouldn't believe, and…" Sophie lowered her voice, "and my phone was still on vibrate from today's meeting."

"Why are you whispering?"

"I'm not whispering."

"Yeah, you are. Are you with someone?"

"Yes, he's lying on the bed right now with a rose in his teeth."

"A rose? Girl, you've been watching way too many romcoms. You need to watch yourself some porn."

Sophie giggled. "You're awful. I was lowering my voice because there's a loud echo in here."

"Oh, so you *are* at Cruella's? Sorry, I mean *Victoria's*." She added the last bit with a plummy accent.

Sophie smiled. "You guessed that from an echoey bathroom?"

"No. I know she was with you today. I assumed you'd be round there after what's happened. My God! Have you been home? Did you hear the news? I sent you like a thousand messages!"

"I know. I'm sorry. That's why I brought my phone in here, so I could call you back."

"Uh huh. So, how did it go? Are you okay?"

Sophie sighed. "Well…"

The two friends spoke for the next half hour as Sophie filled Janay in on the day's events, from the truth about her parents through to the police presence outside her home. When she was finished, they shared a very long silence, where the only sound was the rumble of the window and that now familiar creak of the skylight above.

"Are you still there?" Janay asked eventually.

"I'm here."

"So, what's the plan? Shack up with Cruella for the rest of your life or emigrate?"

"I really don't know."

"Wait. You're not seriously thinking about leaving the country and living in that place, are you?"

"There are worse things."

"Yeah, like being separated from everything and everyone you know!"

"You can visit."

"Sophie!"

Sophie forced a nervous laugh. She had no idea what she was talking about. Flirting with the idea of upping sticks and moving to a palace in a foreign land certainly sounded romantic, but the reality would be a completely different thing. Janay had a point.

"Hello?"

"I don't know what I'm going to do, Janay. All of this is making my brain hurt. Anyway, pretty soon the decision's going to be made for me. I'm going to be homeless. And even if I wasn't, from what I've heard so far, I'm not sure I will ever want to go back to Meadow Lane. Besides, the place has changed now. It doesn't feel like home anymore. Everything I knew there was a lie."

"Oh, Sophie. I'm sorry..." is all Janay could muster. She wished her place was bigger. But she lived in a small two-bedroom flat with her son. She loved having Sophie stay but the practicality of that was a different story. And with the best will in the world, she knew there was only so long Sophie would want to sleep on the couch. Victoria on the other hand... *Miss Money Bags* had plenty, thanks to her husband.

"Well, if you do decide to emigrate, just make sure you take me with you. I could do with a break from my job. My boss is well and truly getting on my tits!"

Sophie laughed. "Everybody gets on your tits!"

"Yeah, you may have a point. Do you know that this morning I was—"

"Shh...."

"What?"

Sophie stared at the door handle. Was it her imagination? She could have sworn she saw it rattle. No. Not rattle but move. It moved as if someone had placed their hand on the other side and was turning it.

"Soph... what's going on?"

"Hold on a sec. Just a sec," she whispered. She placed the phone to her chest and called out. "Hello? Vic?"

Silence. Just the wind buffeting the house.

"Vicki? Is that you?"

Nothing.

"Sophie?"

Rap! Rap! Tap!

She whirled around to look at the window. Bony shadows were tapping on the glass.

"Sophie? Speak to me! What's happening?" Janay's tinny voice insisted.

"I don't know... I think someone..." She let the sentence dry in her mouth when the spotlights dimmed overhead, drawing in the walls, animating shadows until the blue hue of her phone's screen scared them back.

Someone was out there. She could hear the faint scuffle and swish of feet on carpet.

"Vicki!" she called loudly, her voice reverberating around her.

"Sophie?"

Sophie lifted the phone and spoke into it without putting it to her ear.

"I think someone's outside the bathroom door," she whispered loudly.

Tap tap!

Her head snapped up to the skylight once more. Tree branches swished and scratched as they danced in a moonlit breeze, their twisted talons reaching out and tapping on the glass.

"Vicki!" she yelled. If she was out there, then she wanted her to come to her aid.

Nothing.

"Janay, I'm going to have to call you—"

But her friend was already gone. The device's screen was dead. She slapped it desperately.

Nothing.

Then the rattling door handle squealed at her. She yelped back as shivers, like cockroach legs, scuttled down her back, forcing her to step cautiously backward.

"Vic…Vicki, is that you?"

Silence but for the rumbling wind.

"Vicki? This isn't funny."

Vicki! Vicki…Vicki…

The muffled sound from beyond the door dragged a claw of terror down Sophie's spine. Somebody was out there, and they were… mimicking her voice. It sounded just like her but with different intonations. Impersonating. Mocking.

"Vic! This isn't funny! You've scared the crap out of me!"

Vic…Vic…This isn't funny… Isn't funny… Isn't funny.

She was trembling. It was cold in the bathroom, but she knew that it was fear that was shaking her body now. Heart throbbing in her chest. Breaths thin and fast. She recognised this. It was the prelude to a panic attack, which was silly. It was just Victoria having a laugh. And yet somehow, she knew it wasn't.

Creak. Rattle. Click.

Someone was turning the door handle, the latch finally giving way to allow the door to slowly drift open. A sudden gust of winter's breath instantly extinguished the life from every candle, plunging the room into darkness.

Then she heard it. Subtle at first but growing louder with each wheezing sigh. The sound of wind being sucked in through tight nostrils then whistling as it was exhaled, filling the room with a fetid stench that burned her eyes. The smell instantly resurrected the zombie memories of her childhood.

She stepped back further, into the walk-in shower.

It was looking for her. Moving through the darkness, displacing the air in the room as it made its way forward, talons clicking loudly on the tiled floor.

She looked hopefully towards the window and then up at the skylight. Maybe she could climb out, call for Victoria. But she instantly wished she hadn't. From behind the glass, she saw a pair of giant black eyes staring back at her. Cold. Unblinking inside of an enormous white face. It shrieked. She screamed.

Sophie Cooper awoke with a start to find herself lying on the bed in the guest room at Greenfields. Bedside lamp burning bright beside her. Door firmly shut.

She sat up and groaned at the ache in her arms and legs. The cold had settled in there. She shivered then leaned forward and drew the red bed throw around her body.

Beside her, the tray of nibbles remained untouched.

It was 3:15AM.

The bathroom light was on, fan whirring. Sophie shuffled over to turn it off but paused in the doorway. The bathtub was still full of water and the wineglass sat empty on the nearby stand. She ran her hands through her hair as she wandered through the sleep fog of her brain to retrieve the memory.

As if it might help, she crossed the bathroom to the tub and peered into the now clear water. She had no memory of taking a bath. She looked at herself; she was still wearing her clothes.

She tentatively looked at her dishevelled reflection, resisting the urge to look over her shoulder. There was nothing there anyway. She was alone. She must have downed that glass at some point and decided not to take a bath. Either way, she was too tired to try to work it out right now, so she plunged her hand into the freezing water and pulled the plug. Instantly, the slurp and gurgle began as she spotted something submerged in there, at the opposite end of the tub. She couldn't be sure, but the thought of it dropped a stone into the pit of her stomach. "Oh no."

But it was true. She reached in, pulled her mobile phone out and turned it over in her hand.

"Shit," she hissed as she tried to wake the dripping thing that had been reduced to a useless glass and metal slate. It was dead.

Sighing, she stood, walked to the door, turned the light off, and… that's when she realised. There was no obsessive compulsion. No need to turn it off and on again. No urge to tap it three times. Nothing. She simply snapped the light off and was ready to leave, when a bright white light caught her attention.

It was the security light outside. This side of the house looked onto the forecourt and to the trees beyond. Was somebody out there at this time of night?

She crossed the room and looked out. His and hers Range Rovers were motionless on the driveway. Trees swayed back and forth in the wind. Jagged silhouettes drifted across a full moon, and there on the periphery, between the front lawn and the woods, was the fluttering white shape of a person.

At first, it could have quite easily been mistaken for a stereotypical ghostly caricature of a person wearing a white sheet and prancing around the garden. But that was before Sophie rubbed her eyes, blinked, and refocussed. There was no mistaking it. It wasn't a ghost but a person. Someone dressed in a white ankle-length nightgown. And, although she couldn't be sure, it appeared as if that person had long flowing black hair trailing behind her.

"Vicki?" she whispered to herself, rubbing her eyes once more. Yet when she blinked and refocussed, the apparition had vanished, swallowed up by the trees.

"Shit!" Victoria was sleepwalking. She used to do it as a child. It had happened numerous times during sleepovers. It freaked Sophie out the first time, but her father taught her how to deal with it. *Don't interfere or try to wake her, simply guide her back to her bed.*

Sophie had no idea what Victoria had done with her coat, so she drew the throw around herself before hurrying down the stairs and then out into the night.

The ice moon was high and already busy illuminating the land's glittering layer of frost, transforming night's blackness into a supernatural silvery hue. It made Sophie's ingress to the woods much easier than she'd expected.

However, it wasn't long before a flutter of wings startled her into pulling part of the fleece blanket over her head. When she emerged, it was with some trepidation. She may well have strayed beyond the confines of her bravery, she realised. She was just contemplating the shame of turning back when a cry reached for her on the wind. Short and sharp, it sounded like someone screaming, but when it happened again several seconds later, she concluded that it must be a fox. She'd heard a fox before. It had to be a fox, because anything else would have her turn around and run back to the sanctuary of her room.

Snap! Crackle! Twigs and leaves disturbed in the hollows of the woods.

Vicki?

She moved forward with purpose now, pushing aside her reservations along with the thought of the wild animals she was sure must be roaming in the night all around her. She dodged the occasional bramble and ducked to avoid the twisted claws of curious trees.

Another loud flutter of wings made her yelp, and she looked up to see a dark shape with a white face glide over her and settle on the branch of a nearby tree. It hooted loudly and received an almost immediate response from somewhere else deep in the night, adding to the etherealness of the landscape. Then, as she worked to free herself from the thorny overfamiliar fingers of a bush, she heard more rustling and snapping up ahead.

Aided by the supernatural moonshine, she followed the dirt path for what felt like the best part of five minutes, before another flap of wings, a squeak, and a squeal had her ducking for cover once more.

Her heart engine was thumping now, as it wound the spool that pulled on the tension in her body. She was already regretting going out there and considered turning back once again, but the thought of her friend kept her there. She told herself to get a grip, but another cry, seconds later, had her reconsidering her own pep talk, for it was different this time. Louder. Shrill.

Vicki?

Was she hurt? Her thoughts, like the galloping thump in her chest, were gathering pace now as she raced through all kinds of unspeakable scenarios, and she had to resist the urge to scream, to call her friend's name for fear of…

Of what? Anything and everything out here.

With a deep breath, she stepped forward, eager now to get this reluctant adventure done with so that she could get herself and her friend back into the security and warmth of the house.

Rustle! Snap! Somewhere in the distance. She ignored it. *Snap! Rustle!* She still wasn't listening, but then she heard it again and it froze the blood in her veins. That cry. It definitely was *not* a fox. And it wasn't Victoria either. The pitch, it was different. It sounded like something else. It sounded like… a baby?

That was ridiculous, of course. *What would a baby be doing out here in the middle of the woods, in the dead of… Shit!* Yes. It definitely sounded like an unhappy baby. Its disgruntled cries rang through the still of the trees.

She continued forward. Faster yet still cautious. She had no idea what awaited her out there.

Turn back now and pretend that you were never out here. Never crazy enough to run into the bloody woods with only a throw wrapped around you like one of those Gothic literary heroines!

The gale obviously agreed because it was humming through the naked woodland with an ominous, ghostly drone, and on it rode the sound of something else. Something that didn't make sense yet sounded so familiar.

Susurrus.

There were people out there. A group of them by the sounds of it. Talking. No, not talking. Harmonising. Murmuring indistinct words that floated on the wind and fell around her like hot embers.

She could smell it now, over the earthy moss, the sweetness of sandalwood and cedar, the dampness of the night's frost. Woodsmoke. It was unmistakable, as was the red glow through the trees. Not early dawn but a fire.

Who the hell would start a fire in the middle of the woods, in the dead of night?

She moved closer, slowly, cautiously, as she clutched the red fleece to her quivering body with numbed, white-knuckled fingers. She ducked behind the occasional tree for fear of being seen. *By whom? By what?* It didn't matter. The terror that constricted her breaths was so powerful it both paralysed her in her cowardness and propelled her interest.

The woodsmoke was much stronger now and stung her eyes, the hisses that accompanied it louder. She was close. Close enough to see what looked like the edge of the trees, the rim of the woodland floor glowing red. Her heart skipped a beat as her eyes followed the white flutter of Victoria's nightgown as she disappeared over the horizon, but not before she took one furtive look behind her, hair floating in the wind.

Sophie threw her body behind a tree and into a carpet of

desiccated leaves that hissed and crackled at the disturbance. Her reaction was instinctive because, suddenly, she no longer felt like she was *rescuing* her friend from her unconscious stroll but intruding, prying on something intimate and personal.

And now Victoria had seen her. She had bloody seen her, and Sophie would have to explain herself. She would have to explain why she was spying on her, why she was following her in the dead of night through the woods. She would just tell the truth. The truth should be good enough. Then why did it feel like it wouldn't be?

Any second now, she was going to hear the snap and scuffle of footsteps walking up to her, Victoria looking down on her and demanding answers. She braced herself and waited. She kept her head down and waited…

And waited.

But the sound never came. What did was that unmistakable sound of a wailing baby. Yes. It was definitely a baby. Out there, in the freezing cold. And judging by its high-pitched and strangulated cry, it was a newborn. Just like the one that had been abducted from the Prestons' across the street.

No!

The sound of its anguished cries must have tugged at something in Sophie because it compelled her to stop hiding and act. To leave the sanctuary of that tree trunk and look.

She did. She lifted her head and cautiously peered around the bark at the flickering orange ridge up ahead.

The path was empty. Nobody was coming for her.

She stood and rubbed the cold dank moss from her hands and readjusted the throw around her body. Then, she cautiously stepped forward once more.

The cries grew louder with each step, as did the unintelligible murmuring, rising with the smoke high into the trees.

Closer…

Harmonising. Baby screaming.

Closer…

Chanting. Baby crying.

Closer…

Droning. Baby wailing.

Closer.

She was less than ten feet from the ridge. The flickering orange and red glow was now painting the trees with light and shadows.

Don't go, a voice told her. *Don't look or nothing will ever be the same. Don't go. Don't look. Don't go. Don't look. Nothing will be the same.*

But she couldn't help herself. The baby's heart-wrenching cry was all around her now, encircling her, no longer one but many, calling, beckoning, eliciting a yearning deep inside her own womb that she could not ignore.

She was five feet away from the ridge now. Just five feet, between her and what she hoped was a figment of her overactive imagination.

And yet she could now feel the heat on her face and see the tip of the flames. They were so high it appeared as if the forest floor was breathing fire. But then, as she reached the ridge, she could see how the ground fell away to reveal a large crater in the earth. Surrounding it, like warriors around a castle, were a series of giant trees with wide trunks, towering high into the star-filled sky as if reaching for the comet that burned brightly overhead.

The bonfire snapped, crackled, and burned eagerly at the centre of the crater. It roared over the buzzing of whispers that slowly metamorphosised once more, now a loud incantation to rival the sounds of the wailing infant.

Now, through the quivering heatwave of flames, Sophie could clearly see that chanting those incantations was a group of women. Ten, maybe more. Naked bodies of all shapes and sizes, their pale white skin gleamed iridescently under the moon and firelight. Arms entwined, they formed a semicircle around the blaze as they swayed from side to side, as if readying to perform some bizarre nude folk dance. And, as much as the vision remained incomprehensible to Sophie, the worst part was that she thought she recognised some of the faces. Not least that of her childhood friend, who had abandoned her white shift to reveal her slim body and pert breasts as she joined the circle of arms. And then there was her, breasts hanging, folds of loose skin wiggling, and that ubiquitous tangle of white hair, normally harnessed into a plaited bun atop her head but tonight hanging low over her buttocks. Her old headmistress, Ms Whitlock.

This isn't happening. This isn't real. I'm dreaming this. This isn't real. This isn't real.

But the heart-breaking screams of the baby were real enough to slap Sophie around the face, spurring her to continue on, to act.

Yet she'd barely taken a step forward when suddenly, mercifully, the crying ceased, as if the baby sensed her anguish and chose to torment her no more.

Sophie drew a sharp breath at the suddenness of the silence. It was soon followed by collective sighs of contentment then giggling from the gathering, before becoming another dissonant murmur that gradually intensified as the group turned to the flames. They lifted their arms, offered their bodies to them, then stepped back, before repeating the motion: arms up, bodies forward, step back, arms down. Up down. Up down. The group moved as one. Lifting their heads to the sky then bowing. Lifting then bowing. Lifting then bowing, before stopping suddenly to link arms and sway from side to side once more, all the while murmuring words that Sophie did not understand.

Then, from behind the chain of undulating flesh, Ms Whitlock appeared once again, white hair floating in the cold wind.

She had her back to Sophie and the fire and was carrying something in one hand as she moved in front of each group member. It prompted a change in each one of them as they switched from the collective chant to a peculiar animalistic howl that flew on the wind, thrusting and twisting a dagger of horror into Sophie's gut. She threw both hands to her mouth to stifle the scream that was attempting to flee from her lips, as she wished she had fled, back to the house.

She could see it now, through the dancing flames of the roaring fire, the new dark glisten on the face of the first of the naked forms Ms Whitlock passed. Then the next and then the next. Sophie could only gawk in a bewildered stupor as one by one each member of the congregation, including her friend, broke their union of arms to smear the black sticky slick from their faces over the rest of their bodies, before breaking into exulted laughter as they kissed and caressed each other.

The cackling continued faster and louder, faster and louder, until it also became part of a new bizarre incantation. It saw the flames hiss, crackle, and shift in such liquid and undulating ways that even Sophie found herself entranced by them, for the fire appeared to slither, ebb, and flow – up, down, backward, forward, and sideways – as if it were a living entity bound only by the shackles of its wooden origin.

Then she saw. It was, of course, all part of the grotesque nightmare she was having because these fantastical occurrences were impossible. They were the fruit of her beleaguered mind, fables handed down from century to century that had no basis in modern day realities. And yet the bitter cold that was slowly devouring Sophie's extremities did its best to convince her that what she was seeing was in fact true, that she wasn't dreaming, and that those cackling naked women who had painted themselves with the unimaginable were now levitating beyond the bonfire, several feet above the ground.

It was at this point that her mind could bear no more and sought to wake her from her nightmare with a scream. Seconds later, she realised that it was she who was screaming, the sound startling winged creatures into flight and silencing the grotesque spectacle before her.

Sophie Cooper dropped the blanket and ran. She ran as fast as her feet would carry her and never looked back.

22

SEKHMET THE POWERFUL

SATURDAY MORNING

She couldn't see him, but she knew he was there, watching her from the other side of the room. She longed for him to move closer, near enough for her to smell his skin, feel his heat, hear the thud of his heart. When she sensed him approach, her whole body began to tingle with tantric anticipation. It felt as if she had waited years, maybe centuries, for this moment and now, finally, it had come.

He was close. He had climbed the stone steps and pushed through the throng of people just to be near her. Just a few more seconds now. A few more steps and he would be in the light, in the bright shining light, and she would finally be able to gaze upon him. Taste the vision of him.

Rhythmic steam train of her heart thundering.

Closer.

Pulse quickening. Lips hungering.

Closer.

Moments now. Seconds.

Oh, she could hear him! Soft subtle sighs. *In and out.*

Closer… One more step.

Breathing and neighing. *Breathing and neighing.*

Neighing. Neighing!

Bird chorus. Sunshine.

Sophie's eyes flickered open. The dregs of her dream instantly dissolving into overwhelming disappointment. *NO!* It couldn't be a dream. It felt so different this time. It felt so real. *He* felt *so* real.

Until he wasn't. All essence of him rapidly evaporated into the haze of the morning sunshine that had flooded her room.

It took Sophie several seconds to get her bearings. There were no clanging bins, loud banter from the refuse collectors. No door slam and engine start of next door's car. Just the allegory of crows cawing, birds singing, and, somewhere beyond the glass, the sound of horses whinnying.

She looked at the giant wardrobe, the solid wood dresser, and the general minimalism with which the space had been decorated. She felt the Egyptian cotton sheets on her skin, the downy quilt warming her body, and the softness of the pillow under her head.

It was true. She had spent the night at Greenfields, Victoria's home out in the sticks and what felt like a million miles from civilisation.

She yawned and stretched, indulging in the warmth of the covers for a few seconds longer before reluctantly hauling herself up into a sitting position.

Through the wall of glass, the sky was a pale blue. The trees seemed close enough to touch.

Despite the distraction of her new surroundings, it didn't take long for her mind to crank up its rusty conveyor belt of bad memories and she groaned inwardly.

She'd had other dreams too. Strange dreams. Yet they felt so real. The heat of the flames. The bite of the cold air. The sound of wailing and chanting. The worst kind of dream. But it felt so distant now, in the cold late of day.

Thank God. The thought of Ms Whitlock naked... Gross!

She abandoned the bed and padded over to the picture window, where she watched squirrels and birds scamper and flutter to and from branches as if they were wildlife at a zoo.

And yet, as lovely as the sight was, she allowed herself to reflect on something she had been ignoring ever since her arrival; she didn't like Greenfields. There. She admitted it to herself. It wasn't that she didn't like the look of the place – what was there not to like? – but it was more to do with the feeling that came with it. The building had had an effect on her from the moment she walked through the door. Oddly, she didn't remember feeling this way any of the other times she'd visited, but this time... something felt different. She felt like Gretel inside the proverbial house of sweets.

It made no sense. Victoria was her best friend. And yet... that stuff in the bathroom and...

"Oh shit."

The memory of the night before made her heart skip. Somehow, even though she had no idea how, she had totally *bricked* her phone. Somehow, she had dropped it into the bathwater and left it to soak there for God knows how long while she slept.

Bad sleep. Bad dreams. She needed to leave Greenfields, of that she was sure. But how? She was disconnected from the rest of the world with no insurance for a new phone. She would have to buy another one but was painfully aware of the fact that she had been suspended from her job. She knew what that meant. Her time at the airport was over. And for once, it wasn't by choice. She would have to find another job. And what would she do in the meantime? The house was in the process of being repossessed for reasons that had also began to tweet at the periphery of her mind. *Foster parents. Real parents.*

She sighed, pushing hair off her face as she watched a grey squirrel scamper onto one of the tree branches, pause to eyeball her, and then resume its journey.

If you can't see the beauty in all of this, then there's definitely something wrong with you.

She gradually became aware of her reflection in the glass and realised that she wasn't completely impervious to it; the squirrel had made her smile. She traded the smile for a startled frown when she saw two giant almond-shaped green eyes staring back at her in the reflection. She was wearing Victoria's oversized nightshirt, the green eyes adorning the black cotton.

Vicki.

As a teenager, Victoria had always been a bit of a goth. Dark eyeshadow, pentagrams, black magic. She was obsessed with that stuff, unlike Sophie. The whole idea of black magic gave her the creeps.

I bet she wouldn't be seen dead in this thing now, though.

Is that what happened last night? Did she see the silly shirt Victoria had given her to wear and dream all of that, influenced by her memories of Victoria's past interests? Really? Was it that simple?

The simplest explanations are all too often the most plausible.

Doctor Krauss had a habit of being in her head even when he wasn't. But did he have a point?

She needed time to think. Time to get her head straight. She'd make up some excuse. Use the house phone to call a cab or something and then, as soon as possible, she'd ring Doctor Krauss. He would know what to do.

She made her way out of the bedroom and down the stairs, bare feet slapping on the hardwood as she went.

She paused halfway down the hallway when she was overcome

by a peculiar sensation. The wood floor was sole-tinglingly warm, but not in an underfloor heating kind of way. It was more as if it were subtly... vibrating. The effect was slight but powerful enough for Sophie to notice it the moment she stepped off the stairs. It was unlike anything she had ever experienced before.

She leaned on the wall as the sensation came at intervals, like small lapping waves on a lake. Warm pulsations travelled through the balls of her feet, up her shins, her thighs, between her legs and... Oh, the sensation was odd yet peculiarly sublime. Ripples of deliciousness lingered and then travelled through her extremities.

The sound of somebody giggling made her look up and down the hallway, half expecting to see Victoria. But there was nobody there.

When it happened again moments later, she realised that it was her. *She* was the one giggling, like a mischievous little girl. For several seconds she wondered what was wrong with her until she realised that it was because of the hum. The warm vibration seemed to pulsate through the very walls of the building. The delicate electrical current pleasantly *tickling* her in sensitive places.

A new kind of underfloor heating?

She smiled to herself and waited several more seconds, pretending to look back to admire the aviary as the sensation continued to surge through her.

She watched the miniature colourful birds hover and flutter to and from the trees, hues blurring, as the fountain pumped frothy sparkling water over a smooth collection of stones into a small lagoon of exotic fish, who basked lazily in the sunlight cascading in through the glass ceiling. It was a sight to behold and one that, like the pulse before it, brought more smiles to her face.

After several seconds, the sensation eased enough for her to resume her journey down the hallway. When she reached the kitchen door, she was greeted by the sound of a female newscaster who, not surprisingly, was talking about the comet and the world's reaction to it. Apparently, levels of crime were up as well as a rash of particularly cruel and unusual cases, the definition of which was being explained as Sophie entered the room.

The kitchen looked completely different by daylight. The proverbial heart of the home was open plan. Work surfaces were arranged in a semicircle overlooking the breakfast table and chairs which were set out in front of the glass wall. Outside the glass, the patio led to views of the lawn that seemed to roll endlessly westward towards more trees.

It didn't always look like this. Much of it was Victoria's design. She insisted that the heart of their home be remodelled so that it faced due west. Sophie assumed it was because she romanticised sitting outside at dusk, wrapped in a blanket with the man of her life.

The same man whose backside Sophie could not help but admire in his tight suit trousers. Jonathan was a bit of a fitness freak and it showed.

No wonder Vic's obsessed with you.

Where the hell did that come from? Stop it!

On cue, the man turned to her. His short black hair was combed to one side and his blue eyes practically sparkled behind vintage black-rimmed spectacles. He was wearing a blue shirt, navy suit, and matching tie. He was immaculately turned out. Like one of those photo models posing in a catalogue as he fed bread to the toaster.

"Good morning," he said cheerfully. "I didn't wake you, did I?" He motioned to the small TV on the counter.

"Good morning." Sophie shook her head. "Oh no, of course not."

"Coffee?" he suggested brightly.

"Yes, please," she said, walking forward and taking a seat at the breakfast bar, pulling down the large t-shirt as far as it would go to protect her modesty.

She watched her friend's husband move over to the coffee pot and admired his chiselled jaw. He had a broad nose that looked like it may have been broken at some point – probably while playing rugby – nestled above a neat smattering of manicured stubble. She could see why Vicki adored him. He was handsome, but not in a typical kind of way. In a traditional, vintage way. Cufflinks. Braces. He was cool, a bit like Cary Grant and…

What the hell is wrong with me? Stop it!

She shook her head in an effort to dispel these ridiculous observations about a man whose physical appearance she'd barely noticed before, and looked in the opposite direction, out of the window. But only moments later, she turned back and watched as he poured filtered coffee into a cup, placed it on a saucer, and then pushed it in front of her, the cloud of his cologne mingling with the steam rising from the cup.

"There you go. Would you like some toast? I've just put some bread in."

Sophie was going to refuse because she churlishly didn't want to accept food nor eat in front this man, but then she told herself to stop being silly, so she nodded. "Yes, please. That would be nice," she said.

He busied himself placing more sliced bread in the toaster while she distracted herself with the television. A man with wiry white hair was giving an interview. A caption along the bottom of the screen identified him as a *Professor Emeritus of Folklore and Ancient Prophecies*, while behind him the image flicked through a slideshow of amateur pictures of a comet that had been called Sekhmet, which, according to another caption, meant *the powerful one*.

"Did you sleep okay?" Jonathan asked.

"Yes, thanks. Like a log," she lied, without taking her eyes off the screen. Not because she was particularly interested, but because she wanted to avoid eye contact with him. She was worried he might read her mind and see all the new and inappropriate thoughts that she didn't seem to be able to stop herself from thinking.

"Have you been following this?" he asked when he noticed her interest in the television.

Sophie shook her head.

"It's incredible. They think that the recent spike in crime actually has something to do with that thing. Something to do with the weather and the way different barometric pressures affect people's brains. People are losing their shit over it. It's crazy. It's like it's the end of the world or something." He shook his head in disbelief. "And this guy is practically spoon-feeding hysteria to people, spouting rubbish about ancient prophecies and the uprising of *the one,*" he said, lifting his eyebrows and making air quotation marks with his fingers.

"The one?" she asked.

"Yeah. You know. The Prince of Darkness. Ruler of the underworld. Apparently, this comet, the first of its kind in however many years, is supposed to be some kind of omen that signals the rebirth of his offspring so that he *or she* might fulfil his will on this earth, I think they said, or some such crap. That and, oh, the end of the world in a few days. Blah blah blah."

Jonathan leaned against the counter and took a sip from his coffee, causing his muscular biceps to push on the cotton of his shirt. Then he turned to her, those blue eyes shimmering in the early morning sunlight. Sophie had to resist checking if she'd spilt something on herself, feeling exposed in the spotlight of his gaze. Then, to her relief, she realised he was looking at her nightshirt because he was smiling at it.

Suddenly, she felt underdressed but tried to act casual. She pinned her legs closer together because, try as she might to dispel it, the vibration was still pulsating embarrassingly between her thighs.

"I'm sorry, Sophie. I'm going on like a bloody idiot. How about you? How are you doing?" he asked delicately.

"I, um…" She cleared her throat. Her mouth felt dry. Parched. She had no idea what was going on. There was just something about this morning. Something about *him*. "Oh, you know, one day at a time," she said, stalling as she thought of a better way to answer and taking a sip from her cup.

"Well, that's the best way to take it," he said with a comforting smile.

He held her gaze for a few seconds then put down his cup and stepped towards her. It only made things worse; she felt a burning in her cheeks that she hoped he could not see.

"Sophie…" he began, her name soft on his lips. "I'm sure Victoria has already told you this, but in case she hasn't, I need you to know that you are most welcome here. You can stay for as long as you need. Please don't ever feel that you're intruding in any way because you aren't. We have plenty of room." He gestured to the space with a look of mock embarrassment on his face but a gleam of pride in his eye. "And, quite frankly, I think Victoria could do with the company," he added thoughtfully, retreating to take a sip from his cup. Then he fished the toast from the toaster and placed it on a small plate before sliding it, the butter dish, and a knife in front of her. "Would you like some jam or anything? Marmalade?"

"Oh no, this is fine, thanks."

They absent-mindedly watched the animated chatter on screen for a few seconds until Sophie remembered the conversation with Victoria on the train yesterday. She decided she would attempt to verbally investigate Jonathan, not least because it might help her forget the odd reaction she was having to him.

She took a bite from her toast, choosing her words carefully before asking, "What did you mean by that?"

"Sorry?" His eyes were still on the screen. He was obviously more interested in the interview than he had first let on.

"You said you think Victoria could use the company. Has something happened?"

He turned with one brow furrowed behind his glasses as he batted those long lashes at her. She hadn't noticed them before either, but she saw now how they made his face look warmer, softer.

"Well, you're her best friend. Technically, you've known her longer than I have and probably better than I do. But lately, well, I don't know. She seems different. You know… preoccupied. Like she's on edge or something. But when I ask her, she keeps saying that everything's fine."

Sophie scowled then added a deliberate shake of the head, as if she had no idea what he was talking about, hoping that he might share more.

He hesitated, as if contemplating whether it was wise to confide in his wife's best friend, before eventually continuing. "I can't really put it into words exactly. It's more of a feeling. But, well, she's always understood me. What I do, the way my business works… you know, that I need to wine and dine clients as part of the job. But lately…" He trailed off as if digesting his own words before taking a sip from his cup.

"Lately?" Sophie prompted.

He smiled and shook his head. "Nah, I'm sorry. I shouldn't be boring you with this."

"No, please. I'm interested. Really."

He looked at her thoughtfully. "I don't know. She just seems uptight. She always seems to be asking questions about where I am and who I'm with."

Sophie smiled when she realised; she wasn't the only person on a fishing expedition. "Are you asking me if she thinks you've been cheating on her?" she asked.

He forced a laugh. "Well, I'm not sure I'd quite have drawn that conclusion, but I suppose, if it fits…" He paused then looked into her eyes once more, as if searching for the answer there. "Does she?" he asked with a swallow, bobbing his prominent Adam's apple.

Seconds ticked by. Birds chirped.

"…and we're just going to interrupt that interview to bring you some breaking news. The helicopter of billionaire property tycoon, businessman, and philanthropist, Nathaniel Karlson, has crashed. Mr Karlson was in Abu Dhabi on his way to the opening of one of his so-called mega hotels when the accident happened. An investigation is under way. Nathaniel Karlson is succeeded by his thirty-year-old only son, Samael Karlson. Our correspondent, John Waterhouse, has the story."

"The prime minister has said that he is shocked and deeply saddened by the loss of one of his closest friends. Nathaniel Karlson's friendship with the prime minister began during their time at Eton together and went relatively unnoticed until Karlson made the headlines not long ago when he successfully outbid multiple Chinese competitors for the rights for Karlson Communications to lead the building of the 5G network across the UK.

"Karlson Enterprises was also instrumental in the building and procurement of the Nightingale hospitals at the height of the coronavirus pandemic, which sparked major controversy given the businessman's close ties with the prime minister.

"Karlson was one of the world's richest men with a diverse portfolio of public and private companies across the globe. His son, Samael Karlson, is also no stranger to business, having joined the board of the Karlson Group at the tender age of eighteen. Now, at the age of thirty, he is expected not only to inherit his father's fortune but to succeed him as the head of one of the world's most successful corporations…"

"Do you follow the business news?" Jonathan asked.

For reasons unknown to her, Sophie was unable to take her eyes off the screen. She was particularly interested in the black and white photo of a young man with short black hair and large sunglasses who –

"Sophie?" Jonathan interrupted.

She refocussed her eyes on the man in front of her, but her mind remained distracted by that name and the images of those men on screen. She had never seen them before but that name, Karlson, sounded so familiar.

"No, not really," she said. "I'm sorry. Just the crash. Dying like that must be a horrible way to go." She felt her lip quiver and her eyes start to glisten as she was suddenly reminded of her father.

She fanned herself with a flap of her hand. It wasn't an action she was known to perform – she'd never really been a dainty girl – but she needed to do something to stop herself from dissolving into floods of tears in front of this man.

"I'm so sorry. I don't know what's come over me."

"Hey, hey…" In one action, Jonathan bounded across to her and cradled her to his chest.

She wished he hadn't because the kindness, the human contact, only made her feel worse. Vulnerable. Emotional.

"You don't need to apologise," he cooed, muscular arms encircling her, fresh scent drugging her. She was instantly reminded of her dream and could not resist breathing him in. His aroma was rich, woody. But not just his cologne. His own scent. His heat. It stirred something in her. Something she didn't even recognise. Something primordial. Animal. And even through her tears, she could feel it surging through her like a herd of wild horses, her thundering heart galloping and her emotions gushing in tandem with the pulse throbbing in her veins.

She looked up into those blue eyes and wanted to possess him. She imagined fingers searching. Tongues tasting. Bodies…

"What the fuck is going on here then?"

Victoria walked into the room, her long black hair swishing like one of her horses' manes as she took in the scene of her friend sitting on a breakfast stool in her old t-shirt with her husband's arms around her, as he gazed into her eyes.

The union dissolved instantly.

"Morning, babe," she said, moving over to her husband, placing a hand on his midriff, and standing on tiptoes to kiss him on the lips. When it was over, she looked at them both expectantly.

Sophie and Jonathan exchanged glances. Sophie wiped her eyes, lost for words.

"So?" Victoria asked, hands on hips.

"Victoria, I, we—" Jonathan began.

"Well?" Victoria prompted. Then, breaking into a smile, she added, "I'm just messing with ya," before frowning once more. "Were you having a moment, babe?"

Jonathan released the breath he was holding, looked at their guest.

"Yes. I was," Sophie nodded. "We'd just been watching—"

"Oh no," Victoria complained. "I've just realised you're wearing a suit. I thought you said you were working from home today?"

"I was but now I have a couple of meetings in the city. But I should be back early afternoon-ish."

"Right. Well, I know what that means."

"No, I promise I'll be back. And we can have dinner together," he said. "We can eat out if you want. Anywhere you like. My treat." He looked at both women eagerly.

Victoria made a face. "Oh well, if you insist. I've got somewhere I need to be at lunchtime anyway."

"Oh right. Anything exciting?" Jonathan asked casually,

thrusting his hands into his pockets.

"Don't worry, darling. You'll find out all about it soon enough."

"Okay, be like that. I know where you're going anyway," he said, pulling his wife to him and looking into her eyes.

"Oh yeah?"

"Yes." He hesitated dramatically before adding with a smile, "You're taking Sophie shopping."

Victoria laughed. "Sophie hates shopping."

He turned to her and asked, "You do?"

Sophie rocked her head and was about to answer, but Victoria jumped in. "Yes, she does. Besides, she hasn't even showered yet. Have you, babe? Can't go anywhere looking like that, can you?" She abandoned her husband and turned to her friend. "Soph, babe. You all right? You're looking a bit worse for wear. Did you sleep all right?" She walked over and placed a hand on her forehead. "You're looking a bit flushed."

"I'm fine," Sophie said, though the intensity in Victoria's eyes before her words, like a knife jab to a sandbag, released a trickle of hideous memories of the night before. *The lights dying. The darkness. The presence beyond the door.* And then what she believed she saw in the woods. "Um, actually, Vic, did you come to my room last night?" she asked, the words spilling from her mouth before she had a chance to catch them.

"You know I did," Victoria chortled, stroking her friend's hair.

"No. I mean after you left."

"After I left?"

Victoria frowned then glanced at her husband. Sophie noticed the look and qualified her question. "It's just... I, um... It's just I thought I heard someone come back to my room a bit later."

Victoria shook her head. "No, babe. With all that excitement yesterday, I went to bed not long after you and was out for the count until this morning. What about you, darling?" she asked, turning to Jonathan.

He held up his hands and shook his head. "No, I came to bed as soon as I got back, and the next thing I heard was the alarm. You know me, I sleep like the dead."

"Oh" is all Sophie could say.

Victoria exchanged glances with her husband once more, then turning back to her friend, asked, "Why? Did something happen?" Her eyes were full of eager interest.

There was a long pause. Wood pigeons cooed as Sophie considered her response. She glanced at Jonathan. For some reason she didn't want him thinking she was a nut job. She might have had a franker discussion with Victoria if he wasn't there, but right now, she felt awkward. Foolish. She imagined what Krauss would say and groaned inwardly.

What do you think is most likely, Sophie? That you saw those things or that it was an expression of your subconscious, brought on by the immense emotional turmoil you're dealing with right now?

And when was the last time she'd taken her pills? She couldn't even remember.

"Sophie?"

"Oh no. I just had the strangest dreams last night, that's all, and to top it off I dropped my phone in the bath and totally bricked it."

"Oh no! That's rubbish. Is it insured?" Victoria asked.

"I don't think so. I need to ring and ask."

"Oh well, don't worry, I can drive you back to the city if you need to get a new one or something. In the meantime, just use the house phone if you need to make calls."

There was an awkward few seconds, filled in by the distant call of a cuckoo, before Jonathan said, "Well, I best get on with work. I need to send some emails before I go to my meetings." He kissed his wife and smiled at Sophie before leaving the room.

"So?" Victoria said as soon as her husband was gone. "I see

you've already got breakfast. Why don't you finish that, have a shower, and get dressed? I've got stuff I need to do in the barn. Feed the babies and all that. Then maybe we can go for a walk if you're up for it? You know, get some fresh air." Victoria smiled sweetly at her friend.

Sophie nodded reluctantly. The last place she wanted to go was back into the woods, even during daytime. "Sounds great," she said, forcing a smile until she caught herself doing it. Why had this become so difficult? This was her best friend. She'd stayed here several times before. And yet this time... everything felt different. Awkward. Like they were strangers.

And what was all that Jonathan stuff about? She cringed inwardly. To make things worse, Victoria was still looking at her, lips curved down in a serious expression as she stepped towards her. Sophie's heart inexplicably switched gears.

"Look, Soph. I know everything must feel strange right now. Your mind must be on overload, imagining all sorts of crazy shit. Especially now that you're on your own, away from all your stuff. But I... we," she corrected, looking over her shoulder as if her husband was still standing there, "we really want you to feel at home here, for as long as you need." She placed a hand on her friend's shoulder.

The sincerity in her voice summoned a lump to Sophie's throat as the emotional pain that she'd been suppressing threatened to make a reappearance. Victoria recognised it. And yet, rather than put her arms around her friend, she settled for patting her arm.

"Thank you," Sophie uttered.

Victoria shrugged and retreated to the island where, without looking at her friend she said, "Now, why don't you go get that shower while I clean up in here?"

23

FEEDING TIME

LATER SATURDAY MORNING

Sophie's heart was still thumping as she made her way up the stairs. She couldn't be sure but there was something about Victoria's words that felt more like a warning than an invitation.

Oh God! I'm being paranoid.

But are you? She saw that thing between you and her husband! She saw you last night! You're being ridiculous. Pull yourself together. Ring Doctor Krauss.

I can't. I have no phone and…

Her thoughts were decapitated by what she was seeing in front of her. She had just returned to her bedroom. The bed was already made and the red throw that she had clutched to her body last night was back, neatly folded at the foot of the bed once more.

Oh God…

She felt her legs go weak. She didn't imagine it. She was sure of it. She had dropped the throw in the woods.

Or you fell asleep and dreamt the whole thing.

It felt as if her head was going to explode. She had no evidence of anything that had taken place the night before, just fuzzy memories.

She pushed the door shut and examined herself in the mirror. When that wasn't enough, she pulled the t-shirt off her body and inspected it. Maybe there was a hole in it. A tear perhaps from catching on a bramble. But she could see nothing.

Stop it! Stop!

I didn't imagine that stuff.

No? You didn't imagine your mother being eaten by a demon either.

She grabbed one of the pillows, pressed it to her face and screamed into it. Again. And again. Until her face was hot, clammy with perspiration, wet with tears. And then, suddenly, a moment of clarity. None of this was helping. She was going to drive herself insane. She needed to get out. Get away from Greenfields. If only to gather her thoughts and get a second opinion.

Then bloody do it, Sophie! Take action!

One hour later, she was showered, dressed, and had made her way back downstairs once more.

The *pulse* felt different now. It was still there but, mercifully, it did not seem as potent. It was almost as if she was becoming accustomed to it. Although there had been moments in the shower when her mind drifted back to what happened in the kitchen with Jonathan. Coupled with her nakedness and the water's warmth, it was enough to scare her out of the cascade and into the fresh clothes Victoria had picked especially for her the evening before. It was a simple combination of jeans, t-shirt, and sweater. It was something Victoria would normally turn her nose up at, but Sophie was happy to dress plainly.

In the meantime, eager to avoid any further interaction with Jonathan, she tiptoed her way down the corridor towards the back door.

The study was in one corner of the building's hexagons, on the opposite side to the kitchen. If she was careful, she could make it out okay without Jonathan noticing. At least, that would have been the plan if he hadn't been coming in the front door as she was trying to escape out the back.

"Sophie?"

Shit. She wanted to keep walking, but she knew she'd never get away with pretending she hadn't heard him. So, reluctantly, she came to a stop and turned.

"Oh, um… hi," she fumbled, touching her freshly brushed and blow-dried hair which was hanging neatly around her shoulders. "I… I was just looking for Vic."

He nodded down the corridor. "I think she's feeding the horses," he said.

His blue eyes were glowing with something she couldn't interpret. Sympathy, perhaps? Shame? She wasn't sure.

"Jonathan, about earlier…" He cocked his head expectantly. She had no idea what to say so she blurted, "Um… thank you."

He nodded and smiled at her.

With that, she turned and hurried through the kitchen to the sliding glass doors, out into the sunshine, down the steps, and through the grass toward the stable.

As soon as she reached a blind spot and she was confident she couldn't be seen, she stopped, doubled over, and drew in deep lungs of air. It was tangy, cold, fresh, and delicious.

That's it. Keep breathing. Yes. It was working. *Breathe.*

She remained that way for a minute or so, waiting for her heart to slow, her breaths to normalise. *You're fine. Breathe. Breathe.*

She sighed. The early morning sun was winter weak yet warm enough to melt the anxiety that was attempting to scale up her chest. *You're fine. You're fine now.*

Like much since she had arrived last night, it was peculiar. She felt as if she'd just escaped from some kind of airless chamber and was finally able to draw breath. Mercifully, that thrum that had been continuously stimulating her senses ever since she descended the stairs had also ceased, returning control of her body to her, and giving her back some headspace in which she sought to recapture clarity.

She looked at the house. Whatever it was, it was definitely coming from inside the building, and she was relieved to be free of it.

She sighed once more. Spirit levels elevating.

The stable was the only thing left untouched by Victoria's grand designs. The weatherworn barn of wood and stone was still holding strong although the interior space had been converted into a long corridor with pens on either side in the style of a traditional American ranch. With a few extra touches, of course. Such as a couple of decorative yet original wagon wheels hanging above both the front and rear exits, as well as two neat rows of authentic vintage oil lanterns hanging outside of each of the pens. They had only been used once shortly after they had been acquired at auction, and just as a test.

The stable, as Victoria now referred to it, was less than half the size of the house yet big enough to hold ten horses, although she was content with just three, for now.

Victoria's babies.

When Sophie entered the stable, the first thing that greeted her was Samson's stare. Victoria's favourite Shire observed her with glossy black eyes as she made her way over to pet him.

"Hey, handsome. How are you?" she asked with singsong affection. "Where's Mummy then? Do you know where Mummy is?"

The horse simply nodded at her touch as if responding to her question. That's when she noticed the braiding. It was an ornate, sophisticated crisscross pattern that had turned the horse's head of hair into a series of black and white diamond shapes. It was a beautifully symmetrical weave of a kind she had never seen before. She had no idea that Victoria had taken to braiding. She had always talked of how proud she was of the mane's length and how much she enjoyed brushing it to see how far it extended over the horse's muscular body. She called it his strength and beauty. Hence his name.

These random thoughts flitted through Sophie's head as she gently stroked the animal, until she heard what she thought was Victoria's voice.

At first, she thought she had imagined it, so she paused and listened carefully. Crows cawed. Wood pigeons cooed, and yes, beyond the occasional woosh and rumble of the wind, the chomp and rustle of the other horses, she concluded that it *was* Victoria's voice. It just sounded different. It was affected, in that very same tone people use to infantilise children.

"Vicki?" she called tentatively.

At the opposite end of the barn, Victoria froze, eyeballs swivelling sideways with animalistic interest. There was an intruder in the barn.

She waited.

Birds tweeted. A woodpecker knocked. The wind breathed through the eaves.

Nothing.

After several seconds, she resumed her activity, gazing down to her breast and cooing once more in a language that was alien to most human ears. But not to the creature. It too had paused at the sound of the intruder and was now watching her with unblinking, bulbous black eyes until, eventually, encouraged by the human, it continued.

"Vic?" Sophie stepped forward. As she approached a pen at the opposite end of the stable, the sound of her friend's voice grew louder, though she was still unable to decipher exactly what she was saying.

She was feet away from the wooden gate now. Her friend's singsong voice drifted to her from the other side.

She stepped closer as clouds rolled overhead, dimming the light as a sudden belligerent gale swept through the barn, clanging lanterns and conjuring dust devils of hay. The whirl instantly reminding Sophie of last night's supernatural dance around that campfire.

Cautiously, she stepped onto her toes and peered over the gate where her friend's black body warmer came into sight. She was sitting in the straw, hunched over something with her back to her.

"Vic?"

She waited.

"Vicki?"

Still nothing.

"Vic!" she yelled.

Slowly, Victoria turned to face her friend. Sophie couldn't help but feel as if she had interrupted something. Something personal. Intimate.

Then she saw the straw lift and fall as something scampered underneath it, running under the wood partition and into the next pen.

"Oh shit!" Sophie cried out, instinctively jumping away from the gate.

When she looked back seconds later, Victoria was staring at her. "Oh, hello to you too," she said cheerfully.

"Oh shit. Did you see that?" Sophie demanded, looking around the pen, half expecting that *thing*, whatever it was, to come scuttling back.

But there was nothing. Victoria was alone.

"See what?"

"I don't know. Under the straw! It was right next to you! Didn't you see that?" Sophie asked, pointing.

Victoria cocked her head. "What do you mean?"

Sophie frowned. "Just now. It was right next to you."

Victoria shook her head, calm. "I didn't see anything."

"It was just…" Sophie paused. Victoria was watching her curiously, like she thought she had taken leave of her senses. "Never mind," she said testily. She was done. "I called you. You didn't answer"

"I didn't hear you."

Sophie frowned, then forced a smile, eyes darting around in case whatever that scuttling thing was decided to make a return visit. "Who were you talking to?" she asked.

"What?"

"You were just talking to someone. Weren't you? I heard you."

Victoria shook her head. "Um, no. Just me here, and the babies."

"But I just heard you. You were talking to…" she heard herself again. "It sounded like you were talking to someone."

"No. Just little ol' me," she said, standing up and brushing the straw off her jeans.

"What's that?" Sophie asked suddenly.

"What?" Victoria looked at herself.

Sophie pointed at her friend's chest where a wet patch appeared to be growing underneath her light blue sweater.

Victoria shook her head and shrugged. "I've no idea. I was trying to get it out. That's probably what you heard. Me, swearing." She followed that up with a roll of the eyes. Then, "Did you need something?"

Sophie was still scanning the pen. At this stage, even she had no idea why. But surely, she didn't imagine it?

"No. I was just looking for you," she said distractedly.

"Well, you found me," Victoria responded with another smile, gesturing to the gate. Her friend was blocking her path.

"Oh, sorry," Sophie said, stepping aside.

Victoria left the pen, closed the gate behind her and made her way towards the exit. When she noticed that Sophie wasn't following, she stopped. "Are you coming?" she asked over her shoulder.

With one last look at the empty pen, Sophie turned and followed her friend outside. The weather was taking a turn for the worse. An invasion of dark clouds had occupied the sky and blindfolded the sun, sinking the land into a premature gloom while their ally, the wintry wind, celebrated triumphantly by blowing the two friends' hair about their faces.

"So, do you fancy that walk now, before it starts chucking it down?" Victoria asked, squinting into the wind.

Sophie shrugged. "Actually, Vic, that's why I was looking for you. Something has come up."

"Something?"

"Yeah. I... um... I need to go into the city. Something to do with the house. The lease thing. I just heard." Sophie shifted her weight awkwardly from one foot to the other.

"Oh? I thought you said you bricked your phone."

"Um... I have. I did. I just remembered that I agreed to meet... um, Chris Darrington, you know." She shook her head, minimising the importance of her words.

"Your neighbour?"

"Yeah. Yes."

"But I thought you didn't like him. I thought you said that he was a creep, and that all he ever thinks about is—"

"As a lawyer, Vic. Blimey. I don't want to sleep with him. He's just acting as my lawyer," Sophie jumped in.

Victoria nodded. "Right. But I told you that Jonathan knows plenty of lawyers. You should have just asked."

"I know, Vic. Yes. But I received that notice and I panicked and—"

"You decided to go to your neighbour? What's the matter with you?"

"No, Vic," Sophie said quickly, struggling to retain her composure. "I didn't go to him. He just happened to work there."

"Bit of a coincidence, don't you think?"

"It was. Look, Vic, I just have a meeting with him, all right?"

"On a Saturday? Well, he's committed, I'll give you that."

"Yeah. And, as you know, I need to sort out my phone too, but I need to go to a shop to do that," she added, forcing a nervous smile because even she realised that she was trying too hard. Rambling. But the words just fell out of her mouth.

There was a pause. Victoria grabbed a clump of hair that the wind had just blown over her face and tucked it behind her ear before looking at her friend, violet eyes glowing in the low light. "Oh, for fuck's sake, Soph. This is me you're talking to. You don't have to pretend, you know."

"What do you mean?"

"You know what I mean. You don't have to be all embarrassed about it."

It was Sophie's turn to brush the hair from her face, which was convenient because it meant that she could momentarily mask her reaction. "Sorry, I don't know what you mean."

"I saw the way you were looking at him. I'm not a fucking idiot, you know."

Sophie swallowed hard. She knew exactly what her friend was talking about and had a choice; deny it or come clean. Instead, she shook her head and babbled. "It wasn't what it looked like, Vic. You know I would never—"

Victoria let out a short laugh. "I know that, you doughnut!" she said with a big grin.

"You do?" Sophie let out a sigh of relief and smiled.

"Of course I bloody do! Come on, Soph, this is my husband we're talking about. We both know that he wouldn't look twice at someone like you. You know that, right?" Victoria said with a scoff.

Sophie's smile evaporated.

"It's hardly surprising though, is it? That it should take my fella to blow away the cobwebs from that dusty unopened sarcophagus between your legs. Right?"

Victoria was grinning with her mouth but certainly not her eyes. They had narrowed to menacing slits.

In all the years they had known each other, Sophie had never been on the receiving end of her friend's ire, nor did she ever wish to be. They had fallen out, sure, but the discord didn't normally last long. Sophie was under no doubt about how fiercely protective Victoria was of her marriage and woe betide anybody who dared to interfere with it. And yet...

The two friends held each other's gaze for the longest time as the wind blew about them, goading them for a fight.

Crows cawed, birds tweeted, and horses chomped, until the sound of nature was suddenly upstaged by the faint pop and scrunch of tyres on gravel. The car could not have arrived at a more appropriate time, sounding its horn like the bell at the end of a match, shattering the tension between the two friends.

Victoria glanced at the house and then back at her friend.

"I called a taxi," Sophie anticipated.

"You did? Why?" she asked, seemingly as disappointed as she was surprised, as if she hadn't just shared those words with her friend.

"As I said, I need to get to the city."

"Right. When will you be back?"

"I'm not sure," Sophie stated, still reeling from her friend's comments.

"Will you be back for dinner? Jonathan said he would take us out, remember?"

"I don't know. I'll see how I get on."

Sophie braced herself for what might be coming next, but instead her friend suddenly put a smile back on her face and said, "Okay. Well, let me know."

With that, Sophie nodded and walked away. At the corner of the house, she turned once more to see if her friend was still watching her.

She was.

24

FAMILIAR

SATURDAY. NOON.

Her hands were shaking, and they felt clammy inside her gloves. The urge to take them off to air them was strong but she resisted. She knew why. This wasn't just about nerves, but fear. As much as she tried to deny it to herself, she was afraid. She was about to do something that she'd been explicitly forbidden from doing.

But she was unable to resist. Like repaired power cables, the current of Mother Earth had been restored and was surging through her, like an appliance with an outlet waiting to fulfil its purpose.

Or some such shit. She hadn't quite thought her excuse through yet, but she would worry about that later. Right now, she needed to focus on the task in hand. Everything was going to be just fine. All she was going to do was make contact. That's it. Nothing more. She wanted… no, she needed to understand why.

And yes, of course she realised that this was a distraction. That, at least for them, it went beyond the scope of her purpose. Truth be told, she had accepted that.

But then the investigator delivered his report. Dates. Times. Places. Including this one. All of it laid out in cold, dispassionate paragraphs of black and white text, complete with full technicolour photos.

How could she not react to that?

Oh yes, of course she had a word with herself. She concluded that she had every right to pursue this because she'd bloody earned it. She had given of herself unreservedly to this shitty so-called cause. She had done everything asked of her, performed her role like the dutiful servant she had sworn to be, and now she was taking a little something for herself. Surely no one, not even he whose name must not be spoken, would begrudge her that.

Besides, she wasn't planning on staying long. Not long at all. Just a quick visit. A quick chat and she'd be back to work before anyone noticed, attempting to repair the damage her jealous tongue might have caused this morning.

Then, once she was through with all this shit and had ascended to her rightful place, she planned to deal with the others. Each and every one of them. And she would take her time. Oh fuck, would she take her time. But now, she needed to focus. She had a house call to make.

The flat on the opposite side of the city was tucked away from the main road, behind a TGI Fridays. It was a new development consisting of a square of four luxury apartments and included a generous self-contained courtyard enclosed in high walls, an electronic gate, and state of the art security. It was certainly a far cry from student accommodation and somewhere Victoria could only have dreamed of living as a child. But now that she was married to Jonathan, who adored her, this place was well within her means. This was a useful detail in her little scheme.

Of course, she had to play this card very carefully, since the woman – whom she had just discovered was actually a few years older than her – had met her at least a couple of times before.

She was the agent who had shown them around Greenfields. The attentive one who kept calling, updating them regularly, stopping by both before and after the sale to ingratiate herself. Initially, Victoria had believed that she was just great at her job and excellent at customer care, until she started to suspect that such care did not extend to her but was exclusive to her husband.

So, she reasoned with herself, she had to be careful, cool-headed, and *not* let her emotions get the better of her. This was a *contact only* mission.

She had scouted the area already and could see that her quarry was already waiting behind the gate, hunching her shoulders and teetering around in cheap heels that were way too young for her age. What was she? Late thirties? Early forties? Is that what her husband saw in her? A motherly prostitute in heels?

Focus!

She walked down the street in her own designer shoes, making a great display of how laden down she was with her bounty of shopping bags as she passed the giant billboard advertising the luxury apartments, and then the gate itself.

She wasn't paying attention to her but was busy fiddling with her mobile phone. Probably texting someone. She felt a sudden scrape of irritation. Was she texting him? She brushed the thought aside because now she'd need to use a direct approach to get the bitch's attention.

"Gemma?" she asked, cocking her head and peeking through the bars of the gate.

Surprisingly, the woman wasn't wearing anywhere near as much makeup as she remembered. If she was honest with herself, the vibrancy of those blue eyes and the sheen on that blonde hair meant the agent looked better than she had expected. Radiant, even. The thought stung more than she expected it to, like grazed skin.

The agent looked up and squinted equivocally at her. "Can I help?"

"It's me, Mrs Ainsworth. You helped us buy Greenfields? You know, Jonathan's wife," she said sweetly, dropping her bags and removing her unnecessary sunglasses.

The woman broke into a smile. "Oh, of course, Mrs Ainsworth. How… how are you?"

"Oh, I'm absolutely fine, thank you," Victoria said with her plummiest voice, sounding much older than her years. "How are you?"

"Oh, I'm good. I'm really good, thanks."

Victoria nodded through the bars. "Are you working?"

"Oh, always," the woman said with a smile.

Victoria made a show of admiring the property beyond the gate. "I've always wondered what they'd end up doing with this place. It looks stunning. I bet it's lovely on the inside."

"Yeah, they're really nice properties."

"I wouldn't mind taking a look, actually."

"Oh, you're looking for somewhere to stay?"

It seemed that the woman was getting her hopes up. Her porcelain skin, that Victoria wanted to take time peeling from her flesh, flushed with an excited pink. Did she think Victoria was planning on leaving Greenfields and her husband?

"Oh no, not for me, for my, um… sister."

"I didn't know you had a sister," Gemma said, as if they knew each other of old.

Well, that would be because you don't know anything about me. You only know what he told you.

"Oh yes, I've got three of them for my sins. Jan… Janay, the eldest, would love a place like this. She lives in a… well, you know, not the nicest place. Terrible décor. She could probably do with moving somewhere like this. As I mentioned, if it isn't too much trouble, I would love to take a look. Would that be possible?"

The agent looked at her watch. "Unfortunately, I already have a showing. In fact, she seems to be running late, which means there's a good chance she'll be here any second."

Victoria made a disappointed face. "Oh, really? What a shame. I know my sister's looking for somewhere that's a quick buy. You know, somewhere she can just move in. For the right price, of course."

The agent bit her lip, looked around, and then shifted her weight from one foot to the other. She continued hunching her shoulders against the cold like she was in fucking Siberia, her neck practically disappearing into the lapels of the big coat she was wearing. It irritated Victoria. She didn't know why; that was the kind of rubbish Whitlock would get pissed off about, not her. *Don't slouch. Stand straight!* But then she realised that it wasn't that. It was just a side effect of everything else, including the way she stood there, clutching her big folder and her mobile phone with gloved hands, as if trying to look important or something.

Gemma's hesitation went on for far too long, so Victoria prompted her on, adding, "Well, you're right. Who am I to barge in like this when you already have a showing with somebody else? I saw a property with another agent on the other side of town, so I'll ask them if they have something similar. It was lovely to see you again, Gemma," she said, conjuring another of her best smiles before moving to pick up her bags.

"No, wait," the agent said. "You're right. You're already here. I doubt there'll be a big problem with me showing you around." She clicked her way to the side of the gate and pressed a button. Instantly, there was a clanging sound and the gates shuddered open with a loud hum.

"Are you sure?" Victoria asked, pausing.

"Oh yeah, it won't be a problem. If my showing arrives, they'll ring the bell."

"Oh, that's very kind of you," Victoria said sweetly, picking up her bags and following the woman through the gate to the small courtyard.

"This is the courtyard, though it's not quite yet finished. They'll be some trees here and this hole will be a nice pond," the agent narrated.

Corporate prisoners might appreciate the distraction, Victoria thought, but it didn't appeal to her.

Then they were climbing metal steps, each clanging like a loud bell under the agent's heel. It made Victoria want to reach up, grab the woman's coat, and yank her backward, then casually step aside to see her smash and twist onto the steps below. She could. It's not as if the place was overlooked or anything. And with it being the weekend, there were no workers around. All she had to do was reach out…

No. That wasn't why she was here. She was here on a strictly exploratory mission. Nothing else. She had promised herself. Anything else risked the wrath of the others.

A wail from the woman in front cut through her thoughts and she glanced up, hoping that her hostess might have opened a vein on a rusty screw someone had left carelessly poking out from the railing.

No such luck.

"What's the matter? What's wrong?" Victoria asked with as much interest as she could muster.

The woman was leaning back onto the railing, holding a hand to her chest as if to still the lump of ice Victoria imagined she must have for a heart. She appeared to be on the verge of hyperventilating.

Victoria looked at her horror-stricken face, drank it in, and then glanced at the drop behind the railing.

Nah, not high enough to break a leg or that pretty little skull of hers. Not for certain anyway.

She followed the woman's gaze. She was pointing at the mezzanine that led to the front door of the first apartment.

"I think I saw a rat!" she cried.

"Where? I can't see anything," Victoria said coolly.

"It was there! It ran around the corner."

"Oh, it's fine. I'm sure it's more scared of you than you are of it," Victoria said dismissively.

After several seconds, the woman appeared to get a grip of her emotions and allowed herself a nervous laugh. "Of course. I... um," she smoothed her hair and her coat with a reassuring hand and shrugged herself together. She suddenly seemed to remember why they were here. "I'm sorry. I'm so sorry. I just, I... um, well, it's most unusual to see those things here and um, I hate rats," she said, realising her overreaction.

"You do? Oh, they're harmless," Victoria said with a big smile. "Until they bite, of course! Grrr!" She made claws of her manicured nails and held them up at the woman, bearing white teeth as if she were a rodent.

The agent looked at her, hesitated, and then burst out laughing.

Then, after several seconds, "Anyway... moving on," she finally said, taking the last step up to the mezzanine.

Victoria kept a grin on her face until the estate agent had turned her back to her once more before allowing it to slip. She had no idea why she was even here. What was she hoping to achieve exactly?

At the glossy red door, the agent swiped a key card and the lock clicked open. "The apartment is fully kitted out with all the latest technology. It's a true smart home. That lock can even be opened using a biometric app on a mobile phone," she said, pushing on the door handle and opening the door for her would-be buyer. "You know, in case you forget to take your key card with you."

"Wow, that's really swish," Victoria said, trying her best to sound impressed before accepting the woman's invite to step through the front door.

It smelt odd inside. A mixture of new carpet and fresh paint. The air was thick with it.

"Ooh, I love the smell of new carpet," the agent said enthusiastically.

Victoria wanted to gag as she dropped her shopping bags by the front door, retaining only her shoulder bag.

"But we'll leave the door open to let some fresh air in," she added, shoes clacking into a small entrance lobby made of faux grey marble tiles.

"Wow, they look like the real thing," Victoria marvelled.

"They're brilliant, aren't they? I was showing a potential tenant around the other day, and she couldn't tell the difference. She believed they were real. You obviously know your tiles, Mrs Ainsworth."

Victoria smiled when the woman looked at her. It wasn't difficult. She'd spent most of her pubescent life either going without or settling for fake things. And then most of her adult life avoiding them.

"So, what kind of tenants have you seen so far?" she asked, moving further into the lobby.

"Oh, we get all sorts," the woman said. "Couples, single men… you know, execs either coming from abroad or here on temporary assignment."

"Single men? What, no married men?" The words just fell out of Victoria's mouth as she casually opened one of the doors. It led to an empty lounge with an oatmeal carpet and a large window overlooking the courtyard.

Shit.

The agent hesitated, puzzled by the question, but did a fairly good job at masking any kind of reaction. "Um, well," was all she said, as she scratched a sudden itch on her neck. That same slender thing that had most likely felt the brush of her husband's lips. A mental Polaroid of what that must have looked like appeared in Victoria's head, closely followed by one of her walking over there and ripping it open with her bare teeth.

"…so yeah, I have seen the odd gentlemen around. You know, the odd divorcée."

"Divorcé."

"I'm sorry?"

"Divorcé. A man is a divorcé, and a woman is a divorcée."

"Oh, is that right?"

"Yes." Victoria observed her for the longest time. Peering into those small blue eyes of hers, scrutinizing them for a sign. Anything that might reveal that she did indeed bring Jonathan here. Maybe she'd exposed that body to him on the brand-new shit-smelling carpet.

"Shall we take a look at the rest of the place?" the agent asked.

Victoria realised she was still staring. "Oh, of course."

They moved back out into the corridor and then into a small but functional kitchen. "What about you, Gemma? Have you ever thought of moving into somewhere like this? You know, with your boyfriend?" Victoria asked suddenly.

The agent laughed. "Me? In somewhere like this? No. Not quite my thing or price bracket."

"Really?"

"Yeah. And I don't have a boyfriend. Well, I kind of do but we're not quite ready to move in with each other."

"No? How come?" Victoria asked, pulling open a drawer and then watching it close itself slowly.

The agent forced a smile, clearly unsure how to respond. After several awkward seconds, she cleared her throat. "Well, he's still in a relationship right now, you know. Trying to get out of it."

"Really?"

"Yeah."

"Must be frustrating for you."

The agent rocked her head. "Yeah, kind of," she said. "She's one of those jealous types, you know. Can't let go even though she knows it's over."

Victoria looked at that face again, studying the woman. She seemed older now under the artificial light in the house. There were lines around those eyes. Definite crow's feet. Not laughter lines. And was this bitch onto her? Sassing her back? A needle of something she didn't quite recognise jabbed at her.

"Maybe she doesn't know it's over," she suggested through tight lips.

"No, she knows," the agent said.

"How can you be so sure?" Victoria asked, and when the agent hesitated, she filled in the blank. "Did he tell you that?"

The agent looked at her, her eyes flicking back and forth like she was struggling with something. Eventually, she stepped back out into the corridor and asked, "Would you like to see the rest of the apartment? Only I have a limited amount of time. No doubt my next appointment will be here soon. She might be waiting out there right now."

She wasn't. Victoria was the woman who made the appointment. "I thought you said she would ring the bell," she said, opening another door to reveal a decently sized box bedroom.

"Yeah, but that thing has been known to be temperamental. You know, teething problems and all that."

Victoria forced a laugh. "You're not doing a great job at selling the place, are you? First you point out a rat and then you're talking about things not working. Anyone would think you didn't want to sell the place, Gemma."

"Oh no, no, it ain't that. Just I… well, you know, there's a process. Management are sticklers for following protocol."

She was nervous now. Victoria knew the moment she spoke about married men that she would pick up on it. That was stupid. *Stupid! Now she's gone into defensive mode.*

Oh well. She pulled the bedroom door shut with a sudden slam that startled the woman, prompting yet another of those nervous laughs. Victoria found them really irritating but no doubt her husband found them endearing. Perhaps even sexy. On the plus side, the image of her startled, almost frightened face was delicious.

They were looking at each other again, eye to eye as they were both the same height. The woman had obviously dragged her lipstick over those thin lips of hers because they were smudgy around the edges. *Why do some women do that?* She never would understand why anybody would want to go out with a wonky lip line. *If you're going to put lipstick on, make the effort. It only takes a few minutes longer to apply a decent lip balm and to reduce any ugly crevices. Draw a lip line with a decent pencil and fill in with lipstick from the centre outwards. It's bloody simple.* She wasn't wearing foundation though. She obviously didn't need it. *Bitch.*

"Oh, I haven't seen the master bedroom yet. It's the most important place in the home after the kitchen, right?" Victoria said. She didn't wait for a response. "Oh, what am I saying? You're not married, are you?" she added, pushing past the woman and walking down the hallway.

The last door on the right revealed another spacious room with a built-in wardrobe and more of that noncommittal oatmeal carpet. She stepped inside and made a show of looking around, sliding open the mirrored wardrobe and inspecting the space.

Gemma hurried in after her. "I really need to see to my next appointment," she said suddenly.

Victoria didn't respond. Instead, she walked across the room as if the woman wasn't even there, into the bathroom where the overhead light came on automatically, prompting an extractor fan to whir to life. The windowless and characterless room had to have been designed by a man, she thought.

After casually swiping and tapping on her mobile phone for several seconds, the agent followed Victoria to the bathroom door. "Mrs Ainsworth, I'm sorry, but I really need to—"

"No problem. I've seen everything I need to see here," she said imperiously, turning back towards the hallway, handbag swinging off her slender shoulder until it slid down her arm and crashed to the floor, vomiting its contents.

"Oh shit," Victoria hissed, crouching down.

The woman watched her collect her phone, makeup case, keys, and a packet of tissues from the floor before she seemed to break out of her trance and offered to help.

She crouched down amazingly well considering the tight skirt she was wearing, although she did wobble from side to side a little.

"Are you okay?" Victoria found herself asking.

"Oh yeah. I'm fine. Just a bit nauseous, you know," she said casually.

Victoria cocked her head. "Nauseous?"

"Yeah." The estate agent looked like she was going to explain further but seemingly changed her mind.

Several dramatic seconds of silence followed as the sound of the city drifted through the open door and down the hallway.

"You're pregnant?" Victoria gasped. The rouge in the woman's cheeks and the awkward smile that followed was her only reply, but she may as well have shoved a dagger into Victoria's heart for the difference it made. "How long?" she uttered.

The estate agent didn't respond. Instead, she changed the subject by homing in on a small cylindrical object on the floor. It was the size of a disposable lighter. Scarlet red in colour with four black ridges. She picked it up. "Oh, this is pretty," she said, holding out the thing to hand it back to its owner.

Victoria was still reeling from what she had just learned. She kept telling herself that there could easily be other explanations, that this didn't necessarily mean what she was suspecting. After all, he wouldn't do that to her. He loved her. This woman was *not* carrying her husband's child. *Come on. You know she's a slut.* It's obvious that this abomination was from the seed of some other sad wretch of a man. It couldn't possibly be his. It couldn't be Jonathan's!

And yet, Victoria knew. She had no idea how, but she could sense it, feel it twisting inside her gut as if it were she carrying the slithering parasite.

So now she had a choice. Leave now. Take some time. Consider her options. Or she could choose the other path. The one she kept struggling with yet kept coming back to. The one that almost certainly would spell her own demise.

And yet, "Do you like it?" she asked, eyeing the object in the estate agent's hand.

Don't do this! LEAVE!

"Oh yeah, it's lovely. What is it?"

Victoria smiled. "It's a perfume diffuser."

"It's very pretty," said the agent, still attempting to hand it back to her.

Victoria closed her eyes and swallowed down the hammering in her chest that was telling her to stop.

Then she reopened them. "Try it," she urged, delicately licking her lips and tasting the cherry flavour of her specially made lip sealant.

"Oh no, I couldn't," the woman said, shaking her head.

"No, please. You'll love it. It's my favourite perfume and I know it'd suit you. It would suit you really well," she said.

"You think? Who's it by?"

Victoria hesitated while the rational side of her mind screamed at her, attempting to make her see reason so she would take herself out of this situation now. "It's an exclusive boutique fragrance. I made it myself."

"No!" The woman looked at her. Eyes wide. "Really?"

Victoria nodded, licking that specially made sealant once more. "Really. I have my own perfumery at home. You should see the stuff I get up to. All sorts of herbs and spices. Potions and spells." She followed that up with a giggle and a smile. "Go ahead," she said eagerly. "Press on the black ridges. Right there with two fingers."

The woman looked at the object and studied it.

"That's right. Just there," Victoria pointed.

The woman placed her fingers on the corners of the device and held it up to her. "Like this?"

"That's exactly it. Just like that," Victoria said, sliding her tongue over her lips with the casualness of a snake. "Now, press hard and breathe in. I promise you, it's a fragrance like no other."

The woman squinted like she was unsure where exactly the fragrance would spritz from, and she didn't want to inadvertently spray it into her eyes. She closed them and then squeezed the sides of the device as instructed. Victoria turned away as a mist filled the space between the two women, shimmering in the light like glitter. Then, the estate agent breathed in through her nose.

Having heard the woman draw the deep breath, Victoria turned back to find that her eyes were still shut and there was a smile on those badly painted lips.

"Ooh… you're right. It smells divine," she enthused, breathing in what was left of the scent. "It smells a bit like one of those sweets. You know, those old ones. Do you know the ones I mean?" she asked, opening her eyes to find Mrs Ainsworth standing over her.

"Yes, I know exactly what you mean," Victoria said with a wry smile.

"I can't remember what they're called. Oh yeah, um, Parma Viol...cor, bit strong though," the woman interrupted herself, swallowing and then clearing her throat. "Ooh, sorry." She repeated the process over and over in an attempt to dislodge the taste that had coated the back of her tonsils. It suddenly felt as if something was growing there. A disgustingly furry early-morning mouth.

"Are you all right?" Victoria asked casually. "Still feeling nauseous?"

"No. Um, I'm fine," the woman said, holding a hand to her neck. "Just feels like I've got some of it at the back of my throat."

"Really? Maybe some water will help."

"Yes, good... um, ah..." she coughed, "good... idea."

Victoria moved to help her up, but the woman twisted on her heel and lost her balance.

"Wow, are you sure you're okay?"

"Yeah, just, my... uh hum... uh... legs feel like..." She cleared her throat, touching it gingerly with her hand, and then cleared it again. "I just..." She was finding it hard to speak. "I..."

More coughing and spluttering followed as the agent wobbled on her feet once more. Her eyes began to bulge as she attempted to suck in air through the restricted passageway of her throat that felt as if it was swelling shut.

"I... I...." She stumbled towards the bathroom, heels clacking and scuffing loudly on the bathroom tiles as she staggered and partially fell onto the basin. The automatic lights sprang to life, highlighting the red veins that were popping in the whites of the woman's eyes.

Victoria followed her to the bathroom doorway, folded her arms and leaned on the doorframe. She watched the pathetic thing gasp, splutter, and hyperventilate as she both attempted to breathe and drink the water now hissing out of the tap.

The stupefied estate agent gawked at the reflection of the woman's casual demeanour behind her. "I... I... something's happening... ambulance," she croaked.

Victoria smiled then pulled a pained expression. "I'm afraid it's too late for that," she said calmly. As she watched, the woman's heeled foot buckled beneath her, dropping her face into the basin as she collapsed to the floor.

"You see, many years ago, they used to burn women like me. Women who spent their lives worshipping the incredible power of nature. Back then, the heathens didn't know any better so if one of us herbalists slipped a little something in someone's drink and then held up our hands, like this..."

The agent had managed to flip over onto her backside and was now leaning up against the cold tiled wall, breaths coming woefully quick and sharp. Victoria pointed a finger at the woman as if casting a spell on her.

"...then it would be easy to believe that they had the power of magic or even telekinesis when, in reality," she shrugged, "I don't. Well, not yet anyway. You see, I wasn't born with the 'gift', which means I don't have any natural powers per se, but I do know enough about mixing up a good batch and its antidote. You know, in case of emergencies." She licked her lips. "Enough to make a whore like you suffer anyway. And trust me, you're going to suffer," she added with a menacing growl.

The bewildered woman's eyes bulged in terror, blood trickling from a gash in her chin as she gradually lost sensation in her limbs. It felt as if she was being bound by invisible ties. As if her whole body was being squeezed by an invisible force, pushing the air from her lungs.

She tried to scream, call for help, but all that came out was a mouse-like squeak. This amused Victoria and she laughed as the basin filled with water and dribbled over the sides, leaking to the floor.

"Now, I could stand here and tell you why this is happening to you, but I get the feeling you already know that. In fact, I got the feeling you worked it out the moment we met at the gate, didn't you? Go on, confess, Gemma. You rumbled me the second I asked to have a look around, but you weren't sure, were you?" she asked with a knowing smile. But the only reply was the hissing and frothing sound of water filling the basin, pouring over the sides, dribbling onto the woman's skirt, and sluicing forward on the floor.

Gemma tried to move but her limbs had become as heavy as lead. The only parts of her that still moved freely were her eyeballs, rolling around in their veiny sockets as she attempted to process the terror of what was happening to her.

"Don't worry. You won't completely stop breathing. Not yet anyway. We still have a few more minutes. And nothing nasty is happening to you on the inside or anything. Your lungs aren't putrefying, your heart isn't rotting, nothing gross like that," Victoria reassured as the woman's stifled hyperventilation grew in intensity. "In fact, you may be interested to learn that the famous philosopher, Socrates, is rumoured to have suffered the same fate as you. He too was poisoned by conium, known to the uninitiated as hemlock. Did you know that just a few leaves are enough to kill a human? Again, don't worry. The potion I prepared doesn't have nearly enough to kill you.

"You see, what you're experiencing is what doctors refer to as *ascending muscular paralysis.* Which is a posh way of saying it paralyses the legs first." She pointed to the woman's bare legs; one was still propped up in an arch while the other was sprawled out beside her. A red shoe, scuffed in places, was now discarded to one side, its heel symbolically snapped. "Then, it travels through your groin, up your stomach, and to your chest."

She paused here. Closed her eyes and bit her lip. The sight of the woman's ample breasts protruding from underneath her blouse nauseated her because it conjured snapshots of her husband's lips on them.

After a brief pause, she swallowed hard and resumed her speech with a forced smile. "And it's here where the magic, if you excuse the pun, really happens. You see, the plant's toxin literally paralyses your muscles and what is the heart if not one giant muscle?"

"P...p...pl..." Gemma attempted to speak, but she was unable to shape the words in her mouth. No matter how furiously her mind screamed them, her body refused to act.

Victoria carefully stepped forward. The water had covered the white tiles and was dribbling toward the bedroom carpet now. "What was that? I'm afraid you're going to have to annunciate. But then, I guess that's what he saw in you. A bit of rough, eh?"

"P...p...ple..."

Victoria put a hand to her ear and scowled. "I still can't hear you. What is that? Please? Pleasure? Plastic? Which is probably what those things are made of, right?" She nodded at the stricken woman's breasts. "Oh, for crying out loud. Do you know that it's bitches like you that give the rest of us girls a bad name?"

She squatted close to the estate agent as the tap continued to hiss loudly above her as if echoing her thoughts.

Victoria bit her lip. She wanted to scream, yell at the bitch, but also did not want to attract any unnecessary attention.

"Oh, and just in case you're hoping your booking might show to rescue you," she said, making a sad face, "that's not going to happen. It was me who called your office. So, just in case you were worrying, don't. We have plenty of time." She rocked her head from side to side, thoughtfully. "Well, not too much, actually. I have somewhere else I'm supposed to be. I told *my* husband that I wouldn't be long."

The woman was shaking now. It was a faint movement. Of the head, primarily, as the cold water enveloped her legs and soaked into her skirt, travelling up the rest of her body.

"Ple...ple..."

"Save it!" Victoria shrieked, the rage transforming her dimples into long dark gouges that travelled up her face, narrowing her eyes. "Nobody cares about your supplications. Nobody is listening to you here. You tried to steal my world from me. You selfishly put your grimy little fingers over the only thing I care about and you need to understand that that is not acceptable. YOU need to be taught a lesson. You can't go round taking what isn't yours, you can't go round ruining other people's lives and you certainly cannot..." The words froze in her mouth as if they were tangible things. Large stones rammed down her throat, making her gag, making her want to spew.

She breathed, swallowing the vitriol, and then cricked her shoulders before allowing her eyes to roam over the pathetic thing sitting in the water, legs akimbo, white knickers on show.

And then she had an idea. A wonderful idea. A deliciously wicked idea. One that made her whistle. But it wasn't a tune. It was more like a call one uses to summon a pet.

Seconds dribbled by. Water gushed. Gemma struggled for breath as the world outside continued about its business before it – the *thing* – appeared at the door's threshold.

The first part to come into Gemma's view was its long snout, bobbing up and down and from side to side as it sniffed for danger. Then, its whiskers – quivering minute balancing poles – as it jerked its head around to allow its bulbous black eyes to survey the room.

Victoria smiled. "There you are," she added as she stood up, causing the water to slosh underfoot. Then she turned back to the traumatised woman on the floor. Much to her delight, her eyes had widened further at the sight of the rodent, which had now cautiously stepped into the water as if eager to take a bath. Its long tail floated behind it like a conjoined reptile.

Snuffling, panicked sounds came from the woman now as her eyeballs flicked every which way, willing her body to take her there. But it wouldn't. No matter how hard Gemma Hind willed her limbs to move in her head, they obstinately failed to respond. It was as if they didn't even belong to her anymore. Like she had faded away and all that remained was her consciousness and the blue eyes that Jonathan had complimented on so many occasions, both watching the *thing* part scurry and part float towards her.

She screamed so loud that her temples throbbed, but the only sound that came out was a muffled whimper, as if her open mouth was gagged by some unseen muzzle.

"Ah, see, he likes you," Victoria said, wearing an affectionate smile as she watched the rat first sniff then jump onto the woman's bare foot.

Gemma felt its claws scrape across her skin. The revulsion produced a lump in her throat and pumped horrified tears to her eyes.

"You see, Gems," Victoria began in a casual singsong voice, "it's like this. Even if I could get over the fact that you've put your filthy claws all over my man, I can't get over the fact that you've got that thing inside you. That was supposed to be his and mine. MINE!"

The rodent scrambled over the paralysed human's breasts, black nose twitching, eyes glinting with predatory purpose.

Victoria stepped forward and squatted once more. Her face wasn't far from the whore who had led her husband astray, and it was without pity that she watched the tears streak down her blotchy face as the sewer dweller crawled up her chest. Then, in a sinister humanistic trait, it turned to look at its master, whiskers quivering with eager anticipation. After several seconds, Victoria smiled. "I bet you can't guess what I've asked my little pet to do to you, can you?"

The agent's only response was to flick her horrified eyeballs back and forth from the creature on her chest to the demented woman crouched before her.

Seconds washed by as Victoria savoured the moment. Eventually she said, "You really don't want to know." With that she stood up, splashing her way back to the door.

Gemma's horrified screams were nothing but muffled gags as she smelt the foul creature scratching her chin, heard it sniffing her face.

Then came Victoria's fatal words. "*Do it.*"

Without hesitation, the rat thrust its head into its victim's partially opened mouth. Then it proceeded to stuff the rest of its body in behind it. When the gap proved too small, it used its sharp claws to gouge purchase anchors out of the soft flesh of the women's cheeks as it scrambled inside, forcing the host's gag reflex to action. But the creature was strong and persistent. It pushed, scratched, wiggled, and chewed to crawl its way to the back of its victim's throat, where it slithered into the moist folds of her vocal cords.

Victoria watched with a smile as the rat forced its whole body into the woman's mouth. The same mouth that had been all over her husband, now gaping wide in an unnaturally grotesque distension as the furry rear and reptilian-like appendage dangled out like a hideous intestinal worm.

The gagging and squelching sound upstaged the running and frothing of water for a few seconds as Gemma's vessel of a body spasmed in response to the beast's frenzied assault. It burrowed and chewed its way down her gullet, until its tail could be seen no more.

25

THE CUPPA

SATURDAY AFTERNOON

The Cuppa was a small café five minutes from Cambridge City Centre. It was ensconced down an alleyway that smelt of cinnamon and the sweet malty aroma of baking bread.

Despite its discreet location, each of the eatery's ten tables was occupied, including the one by the window with a view of the Senate House, a neoclassical building that was formerly the meeting place for the university's council of the senate. It had since been relegated to hosting degree ceremonies and on-location political television shows.

Sophie and Janay were sitting opposite each other, nursing mugs of hot chocolate. Janay still wore her green apron that sported a giant gold teacup on the front.

"Okay," she began, "you have thirty official minutes, but most likely less. Generally, until Attila over there starts whining." She waved at her boss who was busy taking money from customers in exchange for artificial smiles.

"I didn't know his name was Attila," Sophie said.

"It isn't. That's just his nickname. So, what's going on? Why have you already left Castle Ainsworth?"

Sophie took a sip from her mug then shook her head. "I don't know. I just needed to get out of there."

"Okay. I'm listening."

"Oh, it's nothing specific," Sophie said, playing it down, clueless how to tackle the subject.

"Soph, babe, you've been there one night, and you've already ran away. Now, given Cruella's personality, most people, including me, would find that perfectly understandable, but you…" She left the sentence unfinished and waited for her friend to fill in the blank. But when she didn't take her cue, she added, "Soph? Come on. Jokes aside, what's going on?" Her tone was attentive and serious. So serious, she put her mug down.

Sophie looked around the room, finding comfort in both the old song playing on the radio and the dissonant babble of the other diners. It meant nobody was listening to them. Why would they? And yet, she couldn't shrug the feeling they were being watched again. That *she* was watching and listening to their every word, and any second now there was going to be a loud rap on the other side of the window, where she would find her friend glaring back at her.

Oh wow. Things were worse than she thought.

"Sophie?"

She looked at her friend and slowly shook her head. "I've really no clue. But you know when something doesn't feel right? You know, off?"

Janay pulled a face indicating that she was *kind of* following but that it really depended on where her friend was going with this.

"Well, I've been feeling like that for a while now." Sophie shrugged as if trying to shake a chill. "Nothing feels like it used to anymore, Janay. *I* don't feel like I used to. It's like… like I'm losing myself. Like I'm no longer me." Sophie swallowed the lump in her throat and blinked back tears of frustration.

Janay slid a chubby hand across the table and smiled. "Soph, given what you've been through in the last month, of course things are going to feel off," she said sympathetically.

But Sophie didn't respond to her friend's touch. Instead, she scanned the room again as if looking for someone. "It isn't just that."

"Then what is it?"

Sophie shook her head. "That's just it. I don't know. I'm just having those weird dreams again and then this morning…" She trailed off, unsure how to articulate the words.

"What? This morning, what?"

"It doesn't matter."

"Soph, I'm your best friend, especially now you've fallen out with Posh Spice, but I can't help if you don't talk to me." She shrugged then added, "That and I want to know what the fuck happened. Tell me!"

A senior couple sharing a slice of cake at the next table looked over. Janay smiled sweetly at them then turned back to her friend.

"It's nothing. I've just not been feeling right."

"Yeah, you've said that. But you're going to need to be a bit more specific, darling."

Sophie sighed. "I don't really know where or how to start. Stuff that happened last night, or whatever that thing was with Jonathan this morning, or—"

Janay's eyes widened. "Wait, what… Jonathan? Start with that, of course. Lead with that! Wait, you two didn't… you know… did ya?" she whispered, eyes bulging out of their sockets.

Sophie looked around and then hissed, "No, of course not. It wasn't like that."

"Phew," Janay said, holding a hand to her ample chest. "Because that's just asking for an arse kicking. That bitch is fanatical when it comes to her bloke." And then, "Hang on a minute. When you say *it wasn't like that,* how was it exactly?" Janay asked with a cock of the head.

"It's nothing, really. Just this morning it felt like we had a moment, that's all."

Janay lifted her partially drawn on eyebrows. "Come again. A moment? Define *a moment.*"

"It was nothing. I was upset, he put his arms around me and…"

"And?"

"He… I… I just felt something. Something I have never felt before with anybody. Well, almost… now that I think about it—"

Janay interrupted her friend's babbling. "Not just *anybody,* your friend's husband. Shit, Soph!" Janay calmed the alarmed look on her face with a slurp from her cup.

"Relax, nothing happened. We didn't do anything. Not even a kiss. He just had his arms around me when Vic walked in."

"Holy shit!" Janay hissed loudly before noticing that the same elderly couple were staring once more. "Sorry," she whispered.

"I told you. Nothing happened. The point is that I've never felt like… that," Sophie said, delivering the last part of the sentence in a hushed tone, eager not to share the intimate details of her life with the other diners. "Not even around him before now."

"Well, newsflash, Soph! It's really common. It's called being horny!" Janay said loudly. This time it was two teenage boys sitting behind Sophie who stopped their conversation to look over and smile. "Please. How old are you exactly?" Janay asked, giving them a disappointed scowl before turning back to Sophie. "Shit.

No wonder you got out of there. Healthy choice, by the way. So, what, did she confront you or something?"

"No, not exactly. We barely talked about it."

"Really?"

"Yes. It was weird. She didn't say much, but what she did say was more than enough."

"What did she say?"

Sophie shook her head as she recalled the look in her friend's eyes. "Enough to make me think that it's best I don't go back. Can I crash at yours again tonight?"

"You know you can, but don't change the subject."

"I'll tell you everything later when we don't have a whole café hanging on our every word." Sophie forced a smile and shook her head.

The sound of a smashing glass startled everybody. All eyes turned to the server behind the counter who cheered, making most people laugh except the owner, a thin Asian man with a balding head of jet-black hair who looked in Janay's direction and tapped his wrist. "Hey, it's barely been five minutes," she said, tapping her own watchless wrist. "See what I mean?" she said as she turned back to Sophie then took a sip of her beverage. "Okay, well, as you can see, my minutes are numbered, babe, which means you've got a limited amount of time to tell me what's really bugging you besides your early-morning grope with Clark Kent."

Sophie knew that the words were said in jest but all they did was make her cringe. Pushing a lock of hair from her eyes she said, "What's to say, Jan? Apart from the fact that my life as I knew it was a lie. I have no money, I'm most likely going to lose my job, I've already lost one of my friends and, it would appear, my mind. No, strike that. I think I lost that years ago and just didn't realise until now. Oh, and I'm probably going to end up sleeping on your couch for the rest of my days."

Janay made a show of thinking about that. "Yeah. Does sound

shitty," she said, clucking her tongue.

"Maybe I should take that trip after all."

"A trip away?" Janay asked, eyes wide with excitement once more. "Where? I'm down," she said. She lifted a hand to shield her mouth and rolled her eyes as she added in a loud whisper, "Anything to get away from these fucking customers!"

But the couple next to them heard and scowled at her. "Not you," she said quickly with a sweet smile. "Definitely not you. Anyway, Soph, where are you thinking? North or South? Hey, I've got a mate who's been banging on at me about this cottage she keeps renting up in Yorkshire... I could ask her—"

"No, Janay. Not England," Sophie interrupted.

"Okay, what? Like Costa del Sol or something?"

"No, not Spain either. Italy."

"Yeah, Italy," she said with a chortle. Then, realising, "Wait, what? You're not seriously considering that, are ya?"

"Why not?"

"Because Sophie, and I'm no bloody expert, but I think that the last bloody thing you should be doing right now is making major life-changing decisions."

"But that's just it, Jan. My life has already changed. *I* have changed. This would be the only decision that isn't being made for me," Sophie countered, looking around the room.

Janay followed her friend's gaze. "Okay, so now I'm officially worried. You keep looking around the room like you're a bloody spy and are expecting to be drugged and carted off or something. Now, what's really going on? What really happened at that place?"

"I don't know. Things."

"Things? What kind of things?"

"Weird things."

"Weird things? Soph—"

"Jan, I can't even explain it."

"Try," Janay prompted, sitting back in her seat, folding her arms expectantly.

"Janay!" It was her boss again.

"In a minute!" she snapped. "See? Attila's already on the warpath. Now tell me," she insisted, eyes wide with expectation.

Sophie hesitated, but she needed perspective, and she knew that the only person, of all people, who could provide that was sitting across from her right now.

So, she leaned forward and in a fast hushed tone she gave her friend a synopsised version of everything that happened the night before, leaving nothing out.

Janay listened without interruption, with nothing but the occasional widening of the eyes, an infrequent scowl, and energised shifts in her seat.

Eventually, Sophie sat back, feeling both unburdened and strangely vulnerable when the door slamming shut behind the couple who had sat two tables down from them caught her attention. Then, she slowly tuned back into the background music, the general hubbub of the café, and refocussed on her friend. "Yes, I know what it sounds like," she said. "I've been going through it in my head over and over. It sounds bloody crazy!"

Janay reached across the table, touched her friend's arm, and said seriously, "Sophie. You are my best friend and I love you dearly, but…" She blew air out of her mouth. "…I don't really know how to unpack all of that. I mean, you said it yourself. You've been struggling lately, you know, with losing your dad and everything. I mean, as I say, I'm not a shrink. I don't have the first clue, but Sophie, when you tell me that Cruella is taking…" she said in a hushed tone, leaning in "…midnight walks to some kind of… what, witches' coven? Then…" she interrupted herself. "Actually no, wait. Ignore me. That makes sense. That makes perfect sense to me."

Sophie rolled her eyes.

"Well, you can't blame me for trying to make light of this shit. But Soph… Sacrifices? Really?"

"I know, I know. I could hear it as I was telling you. It's just insane. I am insane. I have finally lost it."

"No, stop it. Don't say that." Janay jumped in. "Don't. I mean it. I mean I made a joke because, well, it's just icky, uncomfortable stuff and I don't really have a smart remark to make about it. But…" She sighed. "Well, maybe it is time to go see your doctor. *Not* because I think you're a few sandwiches short of a picnic but because I think he'd do much better at dealing with this stuff than me."

Sophie nodded, her face falling, heavy with disappointment. "So, you don't believe—"

"No, don't finish that sentence. I *do* believe that *you* believe you saw that stuff. I do believe that."

"But you don't believe that it was real?"

Janay screwed her face up. "Well, if I'm perfectly honest, Soph, it is kind of like what you said happened to your mum. Which, *in your own words,* you said was how your mind dealt with what happened. I'm wondering if, maybe, you know, just maybe, this might be like that only with, you know, your dad and everything."

Sophie nodded and was about to respond when she stopped herself and looked up.

Janay followed her gaze. "What…?"

Behind the dissonance of babble and chatter, behind the chinking of cutlery and the hissing of the coffee machine, the radio had switched from golden oldies to a news report.

"*…still investigating the disappearance of a six-month-old boy. The infant, who has not been named, is believed to have been abducted from his home in Meadow Lane, Fenfield, yesterday. Simon Baker has the details…*"

The two women exchanged looks just as the door opened and

the sound of the city rushed in. "Oh shit," Janay said. "I forgot to tell you."

"Tell me what…?" Sophie asked, but it was too late. When she followed Janay's line of sight, she saw Christopher Darrington making his way towards them.

Janay whistled under her breath. "Wow, I have to say he is looking fine today," she whispered dreamily.

"Chris, what a surprise," Sophie said, shooting her friend a look.

Janay, finally taking her eyes off the man, said, "Yes, sorry. Sophie, I meant to tell you before we got distracted gossiping and all that, but Chris has been looking for you. Yeah." She said with a wide smile. "He said he's been leaving messages on your dead phone but didn't hear back, obviously, so when he was in here this morning, I told him that you were coming over and that he should come back later and—"

"JANAY!" It was her boss again.

"And that's my cue. See you tonight then. Chris, it was delicious seeing you again." She gave the man a flirtatious wink and her friend a kiss on the cheek before leaving them. "All right, customers," she said, raising her voice, "the wait is over. Janay is back in the house serving pastries and delicious beverages with a sunshiny smile! Let me hear it!" There was light applause before it was absorbed into the babble of voices once more.

Sophie looked at the man standing before her. He did look good today, in jeans, black shirt, and coat.

"I'm sorry to barge in on the both of you like this," he said with a smile. His voice sounded deeper today. Softer. "I've been leaving messages."

"Yes. Sorry. Phone problems."

"That's right," Janay said.

They both stood awkwardly for a while, not knowing whether Chris should join her at her table or… "Shall we go outside?" she suggested. "It's a bit loud in here."

"Sure." He stepped aside, allowing her to collect her things, then led them out. As Sophie followed, she smiled as Janay pointed at his backside appreciatively, then passionately kissed the back of her own hand. When one of the customers gave her a funny look, she shrugged and said, "It's all right. It's just my girlfriend."

Sophie was relieved to be back outside in the fresh air and out of earshot of the café's crowd. She could finally breathe once more.

"So, what happened to your phone?" Chris asked, cobalt eyes sparkling in the afternoon sun.

"Oh, I dropped it… in the bath."

"Oh. That's not good."

"No, it wasn't. On the other hand, I've discovered that it's oddly liberating," she said with a smile.

He tilted his head. "Yeah?"

"Yeah."

"I might give that a try."

She nodded. "I highly recommend it."

"Do you have a backup?"

She laughed. "No."

"Do you even care?"

She nodded eagerly. "Yes, of course. At least I think so." But then she thought about it. "Actually, no. I don't. I think I might get a new one. You know, with a totally new phone number."

"Yeah?"

"Yeah. I'm going to be a rebel."

"I like your style," he said with that big smile of his.

"So, what do think?"

"About what?"

"Fancy walking me over to the shop to get a new phone?"

"Well, that depends."

"On what?"

"On whether or not I'll be the first person to get your new number."

Sophie laughed, and rather annoyingly, felt the heat rise to her cheeks. She started forward in the hope that he might not have noticed.

They walked back up the alleyway and emerged onto the main thoroughfare, where more people walked while others glided by on bicycles.

"So, you wanted to talk to me?" she asked.

"Oh yeah," Chris said, thrusting his hands into his coat pockets. "I've made some enquires, you know, about the company that owns your father's house…"

Father? So much had changed since she visited the lawyer's office, and she considered interrupting when she heard him say, "…the company that leases your home, and a whole bunch of other properties around the world, is held by a larger organisation which is itself held by an even larger multinational. And, it wasn't easy, but I've managed to confirm that this multinational is owned by an even larger conglomerate. Karlson, Inc." There was a pause as they moved around a trio of tourists gathered around a map. "I'm assuming that doesn't mean anything to you?" he asked. Sophie shook her head. "It's one of the biggest companies in the world, Sophie. I mean this monolith is the company behind the companies. British Petroleum, HSBC, AstraZeneca. They're just some of the companies these people have an interest in."

Sophie shrugged. "I'm sorry, Chris. I'm not sure what that means exactly."

"It means that this is the very company that's making headlines right now. Karlson Senior just died in a crash. It's been all over the news. The man's an old school friend of the prime minister."

Sophie remembered the bulletin on TV. Then she

immediately pictured Jonathan leaning against the counter. "Oh right. Yes. I think I remember seeing something this morning. But, well, if this company is that big then there's nothing mysterious about them owning a titchy little house on the outskirts of Cambridge, is there? They probably have a whole real estate thing going on that owns houses all over."

"No, nothing mysterious when you look at it like that. But Sophie..." He stopped walking and looked at her so she would follow suit. "They were not leasing the house *to* your father. They were leasing it *for* him," Chris said, carefully emphasising the distinction.

Still, Sophie frowned. She had no idea what he was suggesting and wasn't even sure she cared anymore. All he was doing was reinforcing everything she'd learned over the past few days. That there wasn't much left for her here anymore.

"Chris, I really appreciate everything you've done for me so far. I really do, but, well, things have changed for me."

"Changed? What's happened?"

"Well, the reading..."

"Oh right, how did it go?"

She looked up into those now cerulean eyes of his and almost had to look away. He was gazing down at her in such a way that stole the breath from her lips and quickened the thud in her chest. That look made her feel like she was the only girl left in the world. Like nothing else mattered to him but her. Not the truck reversing, or the people flowing around them like a shoal of migrating fish. Not the market callers in the distance. And – she was certain now – nobody had ever made her feel this way before.

She clutched his arm and imagined herself diving into the pools of his eyes. Imagined the scraping sound of her fingers on his stubbly jawline. Yearned for those smiling thick lips. To kiss them. Taste them if only just once. And she could feel herself lifting onto her toes so she could bring herself closer to him.

"Chris…" she breathed. Their faces just inches from each other… "Are you *the one*?"

He frowned at her.

And that's when she realised. She'd spoken the words aloud, and suddenly her vision changed to something else.

Chris screaming in agony… Flesh tearing from his body… The world on fire…

Sophie snatched her hand away. "I've got to go," she said suddenly.

"Go? Go where?"

"I've got to go," was all she could say, cheeks burning red.

"Okay, but the shop's that way," he shouted after her. "Sophie!"

But Sophie Cooper wasn't listening. She just ran as fast as her feet would take her.

26

THE TRUTH

MONDAY AFTERNOON

Victoria was brushing Samson when she heard the car pull up at the front of the house. Her hearing was just one of her senses that had been heightened since they moved out to the woods. She didn't believe it was any kind of divine magical power but more of a sensitivity to mechanical vibration.

She had no idea who it might be since she wasn't expecting anybody, but then Jonathan had been working from home. It might have something to do with him.

It was the second day of him working from home with no visits to either London or Cambridge. Coincidentally, this began after her tour of that apartment. And this pleased her. It pleased her very much.

Jonathan was in his study when he heard the door chime. He had just finished dialling Gemma's number for what felt like the hundredth time. His stomach was in knots. Neck taut with tension. She hadn't returned any of his calls or messages which was unlike her. At one stage, he had felt so desperate he had taken a risk and removed his second mobile phone from its hiding place in the locked drawer of his office and brought it home. He'd been calling her ever since, but nothing.

He'd even driven over to her house – a cosy two-bedroom terrace in one of the small villages orbiting the city – something he was loath to do because of his paranoia that somebody might see them. *Nobody cares,* Gemma had reassured him. But he cared. He cared very much. There was something about his wife that made him think she had eyes everywhere.

This meant that most of his meetings with Gemma had to take place at his flat in London which was a ball-ache, but he often had business in the capital and Gemma often worked out of her agency's office there. He felt much safer in London since Victoria didn't even know about the apartment. It was leased in his company's name.

He placed the mobile phone in the bottom drawer of his desk and locked it. Then, bare feet slapping on the oak floor, he made his way to the front door and pulled it open to find two strangers, with an air of authority about them, staring back at him.

The black woman with long wavy hair and rather attractive sapphire eyes was dressed in a navy-blue trouser suit. Her partner, a white male with a crew cut and the posture of someone who was on military parade, was in a black suit. It was obvious who they were and the sight of them pulled at the knot in Jonathan's stomach.

"Yes?"

"Mr Ainsworth?" the woman asked.

"Yes."

She held up an identification badge. Her colleague mirrored the act. "I'm Detective Inspector King from Cambridgeshire police. This is my colleague, DS Butler. We'd like to speak with you if that's okay."

Jonathan swallowed but it did little to smooth the sandpaper that was the back of his throat. "What's this about?" he managed to croak.

"Is it okay if we come in?" King asked.

Jonathan hesitated and looked around the driveway, as if checking to make sure none of the non-existent neighbours were watching, then stepped aside.

His guests glanced around the place and then at each other. Jonathan knew what they were thinking, and he was fine with that. He'd worked hard for his money, which was more than he could say for some other people he knew. *Besides, having money isn't what makes you a piece of shit. Cheating on your wife does,* he told himself.

"Nice place," Butler said appreciatively as he took in the aviary.

"Thanks," Jonathan replied, as casually as his nerves would allow.

"Is your wife home, Mr Ainsworth?" King asked.

"Why? Is it her you've come to see?"

"Well, actually, we would like to talk to the both of you. Just not at the same time," King said flatly.

Jonathan observed her for a few seconds but then answered. "Yes. She is. She's out back in the barn."

There was an uncomfortable silence as the trio exchanged glances before Jonathan pushed with, "So, are you going to tell me what this is about? Do I need to call my lawyer or something?"

"I don't know. Do you?" King asked seriously.

Jonathan frowned, unsure what to make of that.

Butler jumped in. "Is there anywhere we can talk more

privately, Mr Ainsworth?" he asked.

Jonathan glanced at King, still simmering from her remark, but then, "Of course. My study is just through here," he said, leading the way.

He ushered them into a spacious room with a giant picture window view of the front lawn. The space was tastefully yet conservatively furnished. Desk and chair. Wall unit adorned by various sports trophies. Framed diplomas and smiling photos hanging from the wall.

"Please," Jonathan said, pointing to a small couch set to one side of the room as he took a seat behind the safety of his desk.

The two detectives looked at the seat and then each other. It was snug but they managed to wedge themselves in without it looking too comical. Both were sitting closer than either of them would like.

"So, what can I do for you?" Jonathan asked.

Butler managed to extricate a notepad from the inside pocket of his jacket and poised himself to take notes while King spoke. "Mr Ainsworth, do you know a Gemma Hind?"

Jonathan clasped his trembling hands together and fixed them on the desk in front of him. Then he made a show of thinking about the question, before casually answering. "Um, the name seems familiar, yes. Um, yes, she was our estate agent. She helped us find this place," he said, looking around the room.

"When was that?"

"Oh, um, I can't remember. My wife would no doubt be able to give you the exact date, but me… I think it was a couple of years back."

"And is that the last time you saw Miss Hind?"

There was a long pause. Birds tweeted beyond the glass. Jonathan swallowed. He suspected that they already had the answer. He didn't want to be caught in a lie… "Um." He looked at his trembling hands and then hid them behind the desk.

"Mr Ainsworth, would it help jog your memory if I told you that we're in possession of Miss Hind's phone records?" King said, suppressing a sigh.

The businessman looked up. "Has something happened to her?" he whispered.

King had already clocked the man's demeanour – shifty eyes, fidgety hands, sweaty brow – and, given the evidence so far, she'd already formed a theory about the nature of the man's relationship with the estate agent. She knew it the moment she clapped eyes on that smiling picture of him on his website, in the *London Metro*'s article for the paper's entrepreneur of the year, and then seen it again at the front door. Those handsome well-groomed features and bright white teeth were unmistakably described by Gemma's neighbours.

King nodded, "I'm afraid so."

Jonathan made an odd throaty sigh as the news knifed and then turned in his gut, as he attempted to quieten the storm of anxiety that had been gathering in his chest since the detectives arrived.

Something had happened to Gemma. The woman who, he now realised, he loved perhaps more than his wife.

"I love my wife," he quickly whimpered, the words pushing on his lips and then scampering out of his mouth. "I know that's going to be hard for you two to comprehend. I know you'll have already formed your own opinions of me. The cliché. The rich arsehole who can't keep it in his trousers, but it wasn't like that," he blurted. "It isn't like that," he affirmed. A tear dove from his eye and was absorbed into the blotter on his desk.

"Well, if the cap fits…" King said.

Butler looked at her and then at the man behind the desk and stated clearly, "We're not here to judge, Mr Ainsworth. Just to find out the truth."

King, on the other hand, had witnessed this scene many times.

She'd even been through one of her own. Infidelity and crimes of passion were no secret to her. She was done with that shit.

They were still waiting on the official report, but the preliminary take was that Gemma Hind's death was in no way caused by an accident as the flood in the bathroom might have suggested, but by something else. Something much more horrific. Something that had been rammed down her throat with such force it dislocated her jaw.

"What happened to her?" Jonathan asked, tentatively.

"We're not really at liberty to say. You'll appreciate that the investigation is ongoing," King said, observing the man with beautiful eyes but ugly indifference.

"But she's... she's... d...dead?" he asked, eyes brimming with futile hope.

"Yes."

"Oh Jesus..." He turned away from them to look out of the window, to the haze of the cold winter sun that was busy coaxing colour from the land. He thought of Gemma and how he would never experience this with her again. That's when the tears began to fall.

"Mr Ainsworth," King prompted.

"Is there any way we can do this another time?" he asked, lip quivering, voice breaking with emotion.

"I'm afraid not, Mr Ainsworth," King said to the back of the man's head. "We really need a statement from you, as you and your wife were most likely the last two people to see Miss Hind al—"

"Wait, what? My wife?" Jonathan interrupted, spinning in his chair to look at the two bearers of this unbearable news. "What's she got to do with this?" he demanded, wiping his face with his shirt sleeve.

"Mr Ainsworth, we need you to focus on answering *our* questions for now, and—"

"Tell me!" he insisted. "What's this got to do with my wife?"

King exchanged glances with Butler and then turned to the distressed man in front of her. He looked nothing like the confident and dominating businessman from the photograph she had seen. Instead, he seemed reduced to a love-stricken teen.

"We have reason to believe that your wife may have been the last person to see Miss Hind alive," King said.

"My wife?" Jonathan echoed once more, eyes large behind his designer spectacles.

"Mr Ainsworth, I really need you to take a few breaths and try to calm yourself down," King said firmly, sensing the man's agitation.

"Calm down?" the man asked through sighs. "Does my wife know? Does she know about me and Gemma?"

"Mr Ainsworth—"

"Does she know?" he yelled.

King closed her eyes. She could also feel her partner tensing next to her, as if prepping for a confrontation, so she spoke up. "We don't know."

"And are you here to tell her?" Jonathan demanded.

"Not unless we have to."

"Please... please don't tell her... please don't tell her," he supplicated, tears bubbling in his eyes once more. "Please."

"Mr Ainsworth—"

"Please don't tell her. I promise. I'll tell you everything you want to know, just please don't tell her," he begged. He held trembling outstretched hands out in front him, wedding band glinting on his finger. "Please, please, please, promise me, please."

King sighed. "No guarantees, but we obviously won't disclose anything unless its pivotal to the investigation."

Jonathan released the breath he was holding.

"But I recommend that you tell your wife as soon as possible, because, in my experience, these things have a way of getting out."

For the next fifteen minutes, Jonathan Ainsworth answered, as best he could, all the questions put to him by the two detectives. When did he last communicate with Gemma? How did he normally contact her? The entrepreneur corroborated what the detectives had already supposed; he used a cheap burner phone which he kept locked in his drawer at work. The burner phone's number was the same number that had called and texted Gemma multiple times in the last twenty-four hours without reply. He also confirmed that he hadn't seen Gemma for a few days and that as soon as she didn't respond, he suspected something was amiss.

When King told him that she had no more questions for now, he attempted to establish how exactly they believed his wife might be able to help them. King wasn't sharing.

That's when the trio then exited the house through the patio doors, into the sunshine and that ever-present chilly breeze.

Victoria was unknotting the freshly woven plaits from Samson's mane and swearing under her breath when the light in the stable dimmed. At first, she thought it was gathering clouds, but she soon sensed that it was something else. Or, more specifically, someone else, and they were blocking her light.

"Victoria?" It was Jonathan.

She turned to see her husband, unusually casual in jeans and a partially unbuttoned blue shirt. Next to him was the black woman she recognised from the other night. She looked smarter today, albeit still a mess in that off-the-peg wrinkled rag.

"Mrs Ainsworth," the woman acknowledged with a nod of the head.

"Detective," Victoria said cheerily, without stopping what she was doing. "I wasn't expecting you." It was her way of saying that she didn't care much for unwelcome guests.

Noticing that the woman wasn't going to stop brushing the horse's newly tangled mane, the detective and her sidekick ventured into the barn, with Jonathan trailing curiously behind.

"We'd like to ask you a few questions if that's okay, Mrs Ainsworth."

"Detective," Victoria began without giving the woman her eyes, "I've already told you everything I know about Lucy. I didn't really know—"

"This isn't about Lucy Davidson," the detective interrupted.

Victoria paused brushing. "No? Then what's this about?" she asked, resuming what she was doing as if she had no idea why they were there. But she knew all right. She just didn't understand how they did.

"Do you know a Gemma Hind?" the detective asked.

Victoria stifled a roll of the eyes. Of course she knew her, but she naturally had to play down just how well. More's the pity; she'd happily revel in what she had done if she could.

She stole a glance at her husband who was skulking behind the two cops, eagerly awaiting her reply. "Um, the name does sound familiar, yes," she finally said without looking up.

"Are you saying you don't remember the name?" King asked.

"Um, no, I just said that I recognised it," she responded, shooting the woman a glance while rigorously brushing the animal's mane. The scrape echoed loudly around them.

"Mrs Ainsworth, do you think you could stop doing that for a moment?" the sidekick asked. She was clearly already irritating him.

"Why?"

"Because we want to talk to you," King responded.

"You *are* talking to me," Victoria said with a grimace. "I need to get these knots out."

Scrape... scrape...

"Mrs Ainsworth."

Scrape... scrape...

"Mrs Ainsworth!"

"What?" Victoria snapped, finally stopping and looking up. She was aggravated. These two were encroaching on her time. Worse, they were invading it with talk of *her*. She thought she'd dealt with that once and for all and yet... "I told you the name sounded familiar."

"Well, it should. You husband told us she was the agent involved in helping you buy this property," Sidekick said. "Is that correct?"

Victoria made a show of thinking about it. "Oh yes, her. Nice woman. Bit ditzy if you ask me," she said with a shrug and a glance at her husband. His mouth was slackened, his forehead creased in the way it always did when he was concentrating. What was he thinking about? Her? The thought of that annoyed Victoria almost as much as these two standing in her barn. "What about her?" she asked with repressed irritation.

"Have you spoken to Miss Hind lately?" King asked.

"Lately?"

"Yes. Say, within the last week or so."

"No. Why would I?"

"Are you sure about that?" Sidekick asked.

Victoria looked at him and concluded that he wasn't so offensive to the eye. He clearly had a kind of post-pubescent enthusiasm for his new career, hence the short back and sides of light brown hair which was undoubtedly ginger as a child. She bet he had been called a few names. Probably why he decided to be a policeman. Reclaim some of that power. Although, she doubted he was going to accomplish that, even with the serious knot on that blue tie he'd put together with that suit. That chequered pattern did his wanting-to-be-taken-seriously eagerness no favours. But she could change that. All she needed was some time with him and she would have his look completely reinvented.

And I'm not even going to get started on her.

She was staring at him now as she wondered what he might look like under those clothes. What underwear he might be wearing. Hipsters, no doubt. Then she wondered about the quality of his seed. Its level of potency and what expression he would have on his face at the precise moment it was   harvested —

"Mrs Ainsworth?" King said, interrupting her trance.

"Am I sure? Do you think I'd forget something like that?" she said casually.

"That's what we're trying to establish," King said.

Victoria was bored now. "No. I haven't spoken to her. Not since she assisted us with this place." She turned to her husband's eager scrutiny. "How about you, babe? Have you seen or spoken to her lately?" she asked with a lopsided smile.

"Mrs Ainsworth, if you don't mind, we've already spoken to your husband," King piped up.

"And? What did he tell you?"

She was still holding her husband's gaze, but she noticed the two detectives exchange glances through the corner of her eye, and she knew she was pushing her luck. She knew that if she pushed them too far, there was a good chance they'd give her that line about finishing the chat down at the station and she wasn't interested in that because it would mean finding a whole new practical outfit and she wasn't in the mood.

"Look Mrs Ainsworth," the young specimen began. "We can always do this down at—"

"No, not interested."

"What?"

"In finishing this chat down at the station. I've already told you what I know. I haven't spoken to that woman in ages, Detective. How many ways do you want me to say it?" she asked, looking at her husband once more. He was sweating now. Could he be any more obvious? It was pathetic. His legs were probably quivering.

Poor baby.

She went from wanting to separate his beautiful head from his body to wanting to fuck him, then to wanting to fuck the young detective and make him watch in the space of a few seconds, but, in the end, she settled for the two intruders pissing off back from whence they came so she could sit her husband down for a serious chat. They could get through this. Together. Now that the problem had been removed.

"Well, that's odd," King said.

Oh crap. Is she still talking? "What is, Detective?" she asked without masking the fact that she was now thoroughly bored with their presence.

"That you should say that you haven't spoken to her."

"Really? Why's that?"

"Because her office seems to believe that she met with you."

Victoria could feel her husband's eyes on her. "Oh?"

Sidekick jumped in next. Yes, she was loath to admit it to herself, but there was something about his broody disapproval of her that she found bloody well sexy. Disappointingly, he didn't play into the fantasy and instead knocked the bravado out of her, temporarily of course, when he said, "Where were you Saturday around lunchtime, Mrs Ainsworth?"

"Would that be twelve or one because some people do the whole continental thing and others—"

"Do you think this is funny, Mrs Ainsworth?" King asked.

"No. It's actually quite tedious. You asked me a question. It was vague and I need clarification."

"Around *noon,*" Butler said impatiently.

Victoria screwed her face up like she was recalling. "Um, I was here, of course."

"Are you sure about that?"

Victoria smiled. "Yes, Detective. I'm sure."

"Huh," the man said, nodding.

"Huh? What does that mean? Huh?"

"I think what the detective is trying to say," King continued, "is that he finds that odd, because the receptionist at Miss Hind's firm said that she sent them a message saying that her appointment was a no-show and that instead she was now showing around a Mrs Ainsworth."

Victoria racked her brains, but she didn't remember the woman using her phone. Or did she? And then it occurred to her. Of course, when she was looking around the bathroom. She had followed her in. She was fiddling with her phone.

Shit. "Right, and?" she asked nonchalantly.

"Well, can you explain that?"

"Explain what?" she asked, baffled. Then after a few seconds of everybody's eyes on her she added, with a forced laugh, "What? You think that was me?" She frowned, then smiled. "Detectives. Are you seriously suggesting that we're the only Ainsworths in the country?"

"So, you're saying that she wasn't referring to you?" King asked.

"Of course that's what I'm saying. Why would I be looking at a flat?"

The detectives exchanged glances. Jonathan was looking at her.

"What?" she asked, as if they were all in on some kind of private joke.

"How did you know it was a flat?" King asked.

"What?"

"How did you know that the appointment was to see a flat?"

Double shit. "Well, you mentioned it, didn't you?"

The detectives looked at each other. King shook her head. "No. We didn't mention it."

"Well, it's hardly a bloody leap. She's an estate agent for crying out loud."

Fuck. Schoolgirl error. You're playing with fire.

"Look, I've already told you. I haven't seen her since we bought this place and even if I had, I'd have no reason not to tell you, would I?" Then addressing her husband, she added, "Would I, babe?"

Jonathan said nothing. There was another uncomfortably long silence. Samson was obviously feeling neglected because first he nickered and then he nuzzled her. She petted the animal distractedly before pretending to wonder why they all had looks like smacked arses.

"What?"

"Miss Hind is dead," King announced. "Still want to make jokes?"

Victoria frowned. "Oh. Right. Okay. Well, that's terrible. But, um, what does that have to do with us?"

Then, it appeared that Samson had more to say with a sudden whinny.

Victoria rolled her eyes. "What? I'm a heartless bitch because I'm not shocked and appalled by her death? People die every day, *Detectives*. Nobody cries for them. I barely knew this woman." There was another pause. Crows cawed. "Anything else?"

"Well, as explained, her office seems to think you were the last person to see her alive."

"No. You said her office told you that a *Mrs Ainsworth* was the last person to see her alive. That could have been anybody. It certainly wasn't me. Again, why would I need more property? We're more than happy here. Aren't we, babe?" she added, smiling at her husband.

He nodded and, finally buoyed by his wife's confidence, cleared his throat and spoke up. "Look, Detectives. My company does a lot of work with building contractors, and I've been on enough new sites to know that most of them are monitored by security and CCTV. Whoever met with Miss Hind would have been caught on camera. Wouldn't they?"

King nodded but it was Butler who spoke. "Yeah, that's exactly what we thought," he said. "But unfortunately, we aren't able to look at the footage from the surveillance cameras."

"Why not?"

"They weren't working at the time."

"No?" Victoria chirped up.

"No."

"Why's that?"

"Well, believe it or not, because of rodents."

"Rodents?" Jonathan asked.

"Yes," King said with a sigh. "Some kind of a rodent chewed cleanly through some of the wires."

"Oh, well fancy that," Victoria said with a lift of her thin eyebrows.

Jonathan closed his eyes and pictured a smiling image of Gemma. He held it tightly, before swallowing hard, and croaking, "Well, Detectives, I think we've been more than forthcoming with our answers. As my wife has already explained, there's no reason for her to be looking at more property. And um, I don't know who Miss Hind must have been referring to, but it couldn't have been her," he said decisively.

King nodded but it was obvious that she suspected something. What, exactly, was unclear.

"Now, will that be all?" Jonathan asked. "Or should I call my lawyer?"

Victoria had to perform a double take. What was that? Did she just witness a flash of her old husband? Was his grieving over already?

"That's everything. *For now*," King said. "We really appreciate your time."

Victoria drank in another sexy scowl from the young detective before the duo turned to leave.

Interestingly, the moment passed as soon as she looked away from them and back at her husband. Now that the image of his weakness – the simpering face, the downcast eyes – had diluted, his sexiness was once more fanning the flames of her desire. She added to that the mental image of the terror on that estate agent's face moments before her demise, and it was this delicious snapshot that she would replay over and over as they made love.

27

THE SUMMONS

TUESDAY. EARLY HOURS.

Dawn's darkest prelude was transformed into daylight at intervals by a giant silvery moon duelling with a battalion of thunderous rainclouds. It aided her ingress into the woods and her journey to her rendezvous. The air was frostlike and yet thunder rumbled in the skies overhead like distant canon fire.

Most would fear this hour but not her, not anymore. Not since that fateful night many years before. Now, the woodland was her playground, the trees her family. This, outside of the arms of her husband, was her favourite place to be.

She smiled at the thought of him. They had made love multiple times. Angry at first, as she overcame the stinging reality that that whore had possessed him in such a way to have used his precious seed for her own selfish purposes, but she had now put an end to that. And she used that mental replay to amplify her pleasure during their lovemaking. And it was delectable. Sublime.

Now, in the fresh of night she could still smell him on her, feel the power of his seed burgeoning inside her. This time it was going to happen. She knew it. She had seen to it and the mere thought of that made her deliriously happy.

She just had to get this meet over and done with, so she could hurry back to him.

At the giant tree, she stepped down into the concave space. To the average bystander, it was just a leaf-carpeted clearing in the middle of the woods, but then the moon, momentarily released from its cumulonimbus blindfold, acted as a spotlight onto the ritual circle.

She waited.

A fox cried into the night. Second later, another responded.

Then she felt it. It was almost undetectable at first, but it slowly grew in intensity. It started as a warm embrace, shaking off the chill that was clinging to her hair and skin and replacing it with long, warm strands of pure golden energy. Like blood through arteries, it travelled the tree roots, the earth, and then through each and every living organism in the woods until it became the very air itself, tickling senses, caressing extremities. It was invigorating, empowering, nourishing, and Victoria had learned to welcome it. It was the essence of life itself, humming through her like an electric current.

Beside her, the rat squeaked and sniffed the air. Its whiskers bobbed up and down with the movement of its long snout. Then it whimpered and scampered behind Victoria's boot as the sound of beating wings pierced the air and a giant shadow swooped over the circle to land on a branch in a nearby tree. An owl, with a ghostly white face and expressionless round eyes, shook its wings then recomposed itself as it took up its position over proceedings.

Then came the sound of snapping twigs and rustling leaves as two shadows moved forward and joined her in the circle. Two old hags appropriately dressed in what appeared to be multi-layered wraps of grey rags.

"You're late," Victoria grumbled, using her best authoritative voice.

"Non serviamus tibi," croaked one of the old women who, if Victoria recalled correctly, was a middle-aged stick of a checkout clerk by day.

"How many times have I got to tell you? I don't speak that Latin shit," she hissed through gritted teeth.

"She said, she doesn't subserve to you, child."

To them, she was their High Priestess; to the rest of the world, she was known as Ms Whitlock, former school headmistress and general neighbourhood busybody. The old maiden, who was normally dressed conservatively with hair neatly plaited atop her head, was now wrapped in a long crimson cloak, her silvery mane spilling over it like cascading water in the moonlight.

Thunder rumbled.

"You've been busy," Whitlock said, thrusting hands into the folds of her wrap.

Victoria felt her heart skip. Did they already know what she'd done? "What do you mean?"

"You've alienated your charge."

"It's not the first time we've fallen out."

"Not like this."

"Like what?"

"You've made it personal with your groundless accusations."

"You're still getting what you want, aren't you?"

Whitlock frowned and cocked her head. "Speak plainly," she ordered.

"Well, you want her out of the country, don't you? Italy, of all places. A contessa, no less. You kept that bloody quiet, didn't you?"

"We don't answer to you."

"No. But a little heads up would have been useful."

"Useful how?"

"In helping me do my job. In helping her make her decision."

Whitlock scoffed. "Her *decision,* as you call it, was preordained long before you even came to be. It's her purpose. Yours was to stay close and observe, not alienate her. Especially since by doing so you would dissolve your usefulness."

"I *have* been watching her," Victoria retorted through clenched teeth. "You try spending hours with that simpering idiot. It's soul destroying. She's pathetic."

"Blasphemantes!" one of the hags whispered.

"Conflictatus!" echoed the other.

Victoria glared at them. They must be at least two hundred years old. They disgusted her. Almost as much as that pet cockroach. One of them insisted on carrying it around on her shoulder like a fucking brooch. She could see that thing's shiny arse from where she was standing, and it made her want to gag. What kind of familiar is that anyway? Gross.

"They think you're insolent," Whitlock continued. "That you've become a liability and allowed yourself to become distracted by trivialities."

Victoria bit her lip. "I assume you're referring to my marriage?" She turned to the old hags and pointed an angry finger at them. "My fucking marriage isn't trivial to me!"

"And yet it is to the cause," countered Whitlock, stone-faced.

Victoria was about to respond but thought better of it. She knew how rapidly this could go wrong for her. Instead, she reeled in her disdain and offered, "I didn't ask for much… and, well…"

The hags whispered to themselves.

Whitlock let out a short cackle. "What? Are you thinking of filing a formal complaint?"

Victoria shook her head. "No. I, um… Well…"

"Speak, child!"

"I made a pact!"

"A pact?" Whitlock echoed with mild amusement, like the former headmistress she was.

"Blasphemantes!" one of the hags hissed.

"Indignus!" the other echoed. "Auditorium!" the other croaked. Then they both cackled.

A smile crept across Whitlock's thin lips. "We could arrange an audience if you so wish. However, as you know, those things don't tend to end well."

Victoria glanced at the hags and then, withdrawing her emotions the best she could, she threw out, "I just asked for two things!"

"And that's exactly what you received."

"No! No, it isn't," Victoria yelled loudly, as tears pricked at her eyes.

"Vengeance. Love. These are the things you asked for, were they not?

"Yes, but he was… is fucking someone else!" Victoria blurted. "He even gave his seed *to her!*"

"Dissatisfied males stray, it's a truth as old as time," Whitlock said with a disinterested shrug.

"He isn't dissatisfied!" Victoria yelled again, her voice ringing out in the still of the night.

"No?"

The hags whispered and then laughed among themselves.

"You old bitches. I should roast you alive!"

"Insolentia!" one hissed back.

"Indignus!" followed the other.

"Enough!" Whitlock yelled angrily, sharing a glare with her sisters. Then, crossing her hands in front of her, she spoke, softly and calmly. "You asked for vengeance; that is exactly what you received. You asked for love; that is what you have enjoyed. What you did not ask for and what can never be gifted is command of free will. Your husband's free will to fornicate with another woman is his choice and his alone."

"Liberum arbitrium!" one of the hags sneered.

The other hissed and then they both spat together.

Victoria's tears broke free. "But I love him!" she sobbed. "I can't lose him and I'm definitely *not* sharing him with anyone, ever!" she added resolutely.

The hags cackled at the sight of the wretched girl's weakness and spat once again in her direction. The green phlegm landed in splodges at her feet, causing the rat to take cover behind a nearby log.

Thunder rumbled again as the moon momentarily disappeared and a sudden gale moaned through the trees. Victoria's statement had caught the High Priestess' attention. She scowled. "You are not a true breed. As such, you have already been warned against practising the arts. It is strictly forbidden. Do you understand?"

Victoria hesitated.

"Answer me!" the woman growled. The hags' distracted murmurings ceased.

"I understand."

"You've already proven yourself as sloppy, bordering on the unworthy…"

"Indignus!" one of the hags echoed.

"Such practices would only draw attention and our purpose is far greater than you—"

Victoria's snigger interrupted the woman mid-sentence. The hags whispered. One of them began petting the mouse on her shoulder like she was settling in to watch a show.

"Am I amusing you?" Whitlock asked curiously.

Victoria stifled another chuckle. "Well, you lecture me about drawing attention when you let loose those things on that street, and here at Greenfields! I swear, if they touch my horses again, I'm going to fucking shoot them in the head. And what they did to that girl and her dog... It's disgusting. Fucking barbaric. Yeah, you've definitely managed to stay below the radar there. And what about the boy next door? You keep letting those things harvest seed for you and look what happened. You talk about sloppy..."

"Silence..."

"...Oh yeah, you're doing a fantastic job at—"

"I said silence!" Whitlock screeched, forcing the hags to huddle together, the owl to flutter on its perch, and Victoria to take a step backward.

Moonlight returned, casting dark shadows under Whitlock's eyes and turning them into bottomless cavities as the frigid wind played with her hair. "I'm going to indulge you by repeating myself, to ensure there is no ambiguity here. Your sorrow for the barrenness of your womb and your dramas of unrequited love are of no importance to the ritual that has already begun and *must* be fulfilled. Do you understand?"

Victoria hesitated, partly because she did not want to acknowledge the hateful woman's words, but also because of the lump in her throat.

"Answer!"

"I understand."

"Furthermore, if it is discovered that you have in any way strayed from your remit, despite our previous warnings, the consequences will be of a kind you couldn't imagine even in your deepest darkest nightmare. Am I making myself clear to you?"

Thunder filled in the momentary silence as drizzle began to whizz around them.

"Am I making myself *clear*?" Whitlock repeated through gritted teeth.

"Crystal clear," Victoria responded, with all the disdain she could muster.

"Very good," she said. "See that I am not disappointed. We've all had just about enough of your insolence."

"Insolentia!" the hags whispered and then sniggered.

Victoria stared at them, eyes brimming with hatred as she blocked thoughts of watching their skin melt from their withered, leathery flesh. Then she looked at the woman in front of her, concealing other thoughts from her mind. The ones that would see all these bitches burn.

28

THE BINDING

TUESDAY. BEFORE THE DAWN.

By the time Victoria made it back home, the moon had surrendered to the marauding rainclouds and their ally, the northerly gale. Together, they wasted no time pelting the land with rain.

The chill was pinching her cheeks by the time she rushed through the front door and shoved it shut behind her. It was weird, like the foul weather had whipped itself out of nowhere.

When she moved forward, she noticed the lights hadn't come on. So she moved again. Still nothing. After that, she tapped the wall panel a couple of times. No response. Just that howling wind, raging around the building, hurling rain like pellets at the windows.

She felt a chill scuttle down her spine as rivulet shadows cast by the battery-powered nightlights wriggled down walls and across furniture.

That's when she felt it. It was nothing specific. Just a feeling. A dread in her gut. Something wasn't right. She was about to climb the stairs to her bedroom when…

BANG! BANG! BANG!

She spun around to the front door. It was the early hours of the morning. She waited. Surely, she must have just imagined that.

BANG! BANG! BANG!

"WHO IS IT?" she called, her voice so loud and hollow in the hallway that it panicked the birds in the aviary awake. Or was it something else spooking them? Either way, their shrieks scratched at her last nerve.

BANG! BANG! BANG!

"WHO IS IT?" she repeated irritably.

But the only response was drumming rain and the growling gale as it stalked the perimeter of the building, hunting for her.

Slowly, she approached the front door and gingerly placed her eye to the spy hole, but the view was limited in the darkness.

With a deep sigh, she stepped back, extended her arm, and then yanked the door open.

Thunder cracked. Lightning illuminated the woods as well as the sheets of water falling out of the sky. She squinted up into a freeze that stole the breath from her.

There was nobody here. *Then who was banging on the front door?* She asked herself the question, but she suspected she already knew the answer. That's why she quickly reversed back into the house while snatching a glimpse at the driveway. Both cars were still there. The view momentarily filled her with relief until she glanced down.

Victoria had never been one to scream. Not since that night all those years before in the very woods she now called her own.

After that night, after they had taken it in turns with her, after she had made her pact and had her retribution, she vowed that nobody would ever make her scream again.

Until now. Victoria Ainsworth could do nothing but gawk at the wet object at her feet as that long-lost stranger called fear reintroduced itself by shunting a spike of terror into her spine.

The ball of vine, shaped like a golf ball with thorns for a heart, was a well-known calling card. One she had used herself before but was confident she would never receive. And yet, there the thing was, sitting outside her front door soaked in rainwater, staring up at her like an ugly disconnected eyeball.

She slowly stepped back across the threshold of the front door as the rain continued to hiss, patter, and spit in perfect synchrony with the pounding in her chest.

"YOU DON'T SCARE ME!" she raged out into the tempest as it washed over her.

She waited for a response, but none came. Then she yelled, at no one in particular, "I did everything that was asked of me. Everything! I just took one thing for myself, that's all. Just one fucking thing! That isn't too much to ask. Is it? I can manage her, I promise. Just like I have all these years. You just need to trust me. Nothing's changed. NOTHING!"

She waited for a response. But none came.

She looked down at the door's threshold. She was standing just across it, on the inside of the house. She thought about Jonathan. *Please be in here with me. Please.* He would be safe inside the house. Safe with her. She had seen to that.

"You know you can't touch me in here! Why do you think I remodelled this whole place?" she asked with a trace of a smile. "You stupid bitches. What do you think I've been learning all this time? This whole house is protected, but then you already know that, otherwise you'd be in here already."

Seconds washed by. The absence of any kind of response one

way or another was unnerving her. Worse was that she couldn't hear her husband's approaching footsteps, asking what all the noise was about. Why was that? She'd left him in the house.

"Jonathan?" she called over her shoulder, desperately trying to mask any trace of panic in her voice. "Jonathan?"

Nothing.

She left the door and half raced, half stumbled up the stairs, calling his name. Still, there was no response. But she really felt her heart switch gears when she entered the bedroom; the bed was empty.

"Oh no," she cried, throwing hands to her hair, pushing it back then rubbing her face. "JONATHAN! JONATHAN! Answer me!"

She looked at the bedstands. Both phones were charging. He had to be in the house.

She rushed over to grab her phone and checked it for obvious messages but there were none. She tapped again and the flashlight sprang to life.

She used the light beam to make her way down the stairs once more, calling her husband's name as she went.

She knew now. She knew why they had summoned her to the woods. It was a delaying tactic. A distraction. But from what?

Bitches. But she'd make them pay. They were all going to pay.

She rushed back to the front door once more, being sure not to cross the threshold, and called out into the night. "You think you can scare me? How's this for scary, huh? Do you know who I'm calling? I'm going to scupper your precious plans and then let's see how you answer for that!" She tapped her phone. There was ringing on the line. "It's ringing!"

"Hi, you've reached Sophie. I can't get to the phone but please leave me a message and I'll get back to you as soon as I can. Have a fantastic day!"

"Sophie, it's Victoria! Please hear me out. I'm sorry. I'm so sorry about how I behaved but this isn't about that, Soph. I promise. This is much more important. I need to talk to you *urgently*. Please, Soph, call me right back. It's about Venice. Whatever you do, DON'T GO! Sophie! DON'T GO! PLEASE! YOU'RE IN DANGER! Call me and I'll explain. I promise I will explain everything."

"To leave your message, hang up. To re-record your message, please press 1."

Victoria smiled to herself. "See how much attention that's going to draw, you stupid bitches!" she laughed. No, it was a cackle. Her own cackle that she was immensely proud of. And Victoria was still cackling when she heard the sound.

It wasn't obvious at first. It was just background noise. An instrument of the meteorological cacophony. But after a while it became much clearer and instantly wiped the smile from her face.

The barn door was creaking open then slamming shut. *Creaking open then slamming shut.* The way it always did if it was left unsecured. *Unlocked.*

"No," she whispered under her breath. "Oh no. Please, no."

She hurried down the corridor into the kitchen and looked out of the glass doors. It was true. From this angle, she could see part of the barn, and – to her horror – that the lights were on.

No!

It couldn't be. Jonathan had no reason to go out there. He rarely did. The only time he would venture out there was when he was looking for... HER!

J o n... J o n a t h a n... J o n! H e l p... Jon...h e l p me, the voice that began as a loud whisper called from the open doorway. A voice that sounded like hers but wasn't.

It sounded like one of those things was in the house.

Slowly, with shivers of terror washing over her, Victoria moved back to the hallway and looked to the open door as part of a tail slithered out of sight.

"NO!" she screamed. "NO!" Without even thinking, she ran to the patio doors, pried them apart, and threw herself out into the rainstorm once more.

She half stepped, half slipped down the wet wooden steps, almost losing her balance as she did so.

"JON! JONATHAN! JON!" she called as she sprinted, slid, and tripped through the wet grass, the elements tugging at her sodden hair.

Eventually, she reached the barn door. It was still slowly swinging back and forth, freezing her in her tracks as she caught glimpses of the interior beyond the doorway.

She could see that the oil lanterns were lit, illuminating the space with a warm flickering light.

Door close. Slam!

Door open. There was straw scattered all over the floor.

Door close. Slam!

Door open. Victoria grabbed it and held it from slamming once more.

Inside, perched high on one of the rafters, the white-faced owl watched with its same dispassionate eyes as the human tentatively entered the barn.

"Jonathan?" Victoria called. But there was no response. Just the ubiquitous drum and hiss of the rain. "JONATHAN!" she yelled, desperate now, as she moved further inside the building, willing her husband to respond. But the only sound came from Samson; the horse whinnied unhappily as if she had just disturbed his sleep.

And so, without taking her eyes off the rest of the building, she walked up to his pen and started petting him. "Hey. It's all right. It's okay," she said softly, stroking the horse's head. But rather than lean into her hand as usual, the animal nodded up and down as if trying to headbutt her away. "It's okay, baby. It's all right." But the horse wouldn't be soothed. Something was agitating him, and he started to kick at the door to his pen.

"Easy, boy! Easy!" Victoria cooed as she reached over to stroke the animal's back, but it lifted its powerful neck so abruptly that it knocked her backward, off her feet, crashing into a heap of straw.

The shock of the impact stunned Victoria for several seconds. Then, "What's wrong with you?" she demanded, sitting up as the horse continued to whinny, rocking its head up and down, digging at the floor with his front hoof, kicking at the gate. He was definitely riled. She never saw him like this, which only fuelled her fear that someone or some*thing* had interfered with the normally gentle giant.

She looked around the barn. The other two horses stared impassively from their pens. The light from the lamps was dim, which meant that there were deep shadows in the rafters and corners, but otherwise the place seemed empty. They were alone. And yet it didn't feel that way. It felt as if she was being watched.

She hauled herself onto her feet, cringing at the sharp twinge of pain in her coccyx, and unconsciously brushed her hands on her clothes. They felt dirty. Sticky.

She turned the palms up, studied them and drew in a sharp breath. There was a dark sticky substance on her right hand and although its colour wasn't clear under the gold light, its viscosity was unmistakable.

Blood.

She looked at the horse. It appeared to have stopped stomping but was still puffing, nostrils flaring, black marble eyes observing her with alarm.

"Samson?" She retrieved her phone from the floor. The light was still on, so she trained it over the horse's face, its long neck and then its body. "Oh no," she cried. "No." The horse's mane had been braided again. This meant *it* or they had been in here. Could still be lurking deep in the shadows.

Rage bubbled through her. "You little fuckers! Where are you?" she demanded, sweeping the light around the barn. "Where are you?" she screamed.

Hammering rain. Howling wind. Rumbling thunder.

She turned back to the horse, shining the light over him once more until she spotted that one side of the horse's neck glistened. "Oh, what have they done to you, my baby? What have they done to you?" She pulled the gate bolt aside. Immediately the horse started rearing, huffing, puffing, and whinnying once more.

"Easy boy. Easy. Let Mummy see. Let Mummy see what they've done to you. Let Mummy see." But the horse wasn't interested and backed away from her, head bobbing up and down once more, eyes flashing. Hooves lifting and smashing to the floor. *Lifting and smashing! Lifting and smashing!*

But Victoria wasn't dissuaded. She entered the pen slowly, pulling the gate shut behind her.

"Hey... it's me. It's me..." she said, calmly reaching out for the horse's head. But the animal twisted away, hooves digging, muscles flexing, tail swishing.

Victoria took a step back for fear that the horse might bring its two-thousand-pound muscular body stomping down on her foot. As she did so, the light beam from her phone glinted off something on the floor. Something tangled in the straw. She redirected the light to it and lead dropped into the pit of her stomach.

Eyeglasses.

She slowly moved forward and, wary of the frantic animal just a few feet away, reached down and plucked the glasses up before holding them under the light. The frame was twisted and one of the lenses smashed but there was no mistaking it; they were Jonathan's.

But Victoria had no time to react. Out of the corner of her eye, under the light beam, she could see a dark glistening trail.

She followed it to a pool of blood then to a black shoe, a socked foot, a leg, and then a tableau that could only have been conjured straight from her *deepest darkest nightmare*. The corpse of what was once her beautiful husband lay slumped against the manure-spattered wall, one leg twisted beneath, arms folded backward. And there, resting on his blood-soaked shirt like a broken piece of a human puppet was his grotesquely extended jaw. His handsome face no longer recognisable in the ugly bloodied cavity with dead eyes that it had become.

Victoria threw a hand to her mouth to stifle the grief-stricken scream, but her body was too shocked to produce it. She stepped back into the corner of the pen where the shadows stirred and shifted. She barely had a chance to glance backward and register the two malevolent eyes when the horse reared up once more with an unnatural squeal. It towered over her, three times her height, and she just about had time to raise defensive arms before they were both snapped by the thunderous hooves of the giant animal. She opened her mouth to wail in agony but all that came out was an incredulous grunt as her legs buckled beneath her and she collapsed onto herself. Her energy knocked from her body, she turned her gaze to look up as what felt like the weight of the world itself smashed down onto her shoulder, sledgehammering her further into the floor. As she tried to breathe through the surging pain, the giant crashed through the door of its pen and bolted out the barn.

It took several minutes for Victoria Ainsworth to slither her broken body out of the pen, leaving a drag of crimson straw in her wake, before coming to an abrupt stop as she sputtered and frothed blood from her mouth. Then she lay still. Eyes beseeching. Life ebbing.

Above, high in the rafters, the owl watched with its usual indifference until the storm calmed outside. Then it jumped down from its perch, extended its wings to their full length, and swooped through the barn, knocking down each and every lantern from its mooring. They crashed to the barn floor, spilling flames and oil into the straw. It followed Samson into the night, soaring to a safe distance in a nearby tree.

The fire grew, languidly at first. It was as if it were a living being, taking its time to ensure that Victoria could witness the destruction of the rest of her world before her lifeforce was expelled from its shell. Then its flames took on an energy of their own, licking at wood columns and struts before devouring the rest of the building, until there was nothing left but the roar of the inferno and the screams of the animals trapped inside it.

ﾃ

EPILOGUE

TUESDAY MORNING

Sophie rode the lift. It wasn't to meet with Doctor Krauss as she had agreed with Janay the night before, but Roger Mitchell of MORGAN, THOMAS & MITCHELL.

Sophie had taken the weekend to carefully consider her options but, to her mind, this should not preclude exploring the further detail of her inheritance. She told herself that this was just a chat and that it didn't mean anything, though that passed over the fact she was doing this in secret. There had to be a reason for that. If she was being honest with herself, as much as she loved Janay, she knew her friend's intentions were not entirely selfless. They were best friends and she no doubt had a vested interest in her staying in England, as conceited as that made her feel.

But Sophie had to do this, otherwise she'd spend the rest of her life wondering. Of this she was sure.

To her surprise, Roger Mitchell was waiting for her when the doors swished open. As always, he looked immaculately turned out, sporting a blue pinstripe suit with pink bowtie.

Sophie had no idea why, but the sight of the man brought a smile to her face. There was, after all, something attractive about him, in that distinguished older gentleman kind of way, of course.

"Good morning, Sophie."

"Good morning," she smiled.

"Would you like to follow me through?"

"Of course."

The events in Meadow Lane were still leading evening news bulletins and Janay had insisted on watching all of them. The police were scaling up the search into the disappearance of the Prestons' baby as well as the investigations into the other bizarre occurrences in Meadow Lane, one of which was being treated as a homicide. There had been the usual appeal for witnesses as well as the announcement that the street had been designated as off limits to anybody who wasn't a resident. There was much speculation about what had happened, as well as a whole bizarre spinoff segment about how, despite what most would expect, property values in the street would soar.

But Sophie no longer considered herself a resident of Meadow Lane. She now felt alienated from the place and not just because of recent events. She had felt that way ever since she discovered the truth about her parents. It all became clear to her when she watched those reports. It felt as if someone had thrown a switch, giving her a sudden moment of clarity.

She was never going back there.

Not even to collect her things. She wanted – no, she needed – to start anew. And she wasn't sure, no matter how hard she tried to explain it, that Janay would understand.

And so here she was, reclaiming some control over her life. That had to start with ignoring all outside influences. No Krauss, no friends – at least not for now – and definitely no more mainstream news or social media. This was something that she needed to tackle herself. Alone.

This time she didn't walk but strode through the open plan office like she had serious business here, taking in that view as she did so. She was reminded of Vicki and how they had shared a look upon first seeing it.

She missed her friend. Victoria would no doubt have a completely different spin on all of this. For all her faults, Vicki was much more of a pragmatist than Janay, who was probably the more emotional of the three. Vicki had put that down to the fact that she had a son. Apparently, motherhood changed you, or so she had been told.

Sophie had decided that she was going to make things right with Vicki. They'd fallen out many times before over the years, as all friends did, and had always managed to work it out. Admittedly, things had never been this weird between them, but Sophie concluded that this was mainly her fault. She was going through a lot right now and her head was all over the place.

At least it had been. Now, Sophie had never felt more lucid, more in control of herself as she did at this moment. Terrified, of course, by all the uncertainty, but for the first time in as long as she could remember, she didn't feel incapacitated by some irrational thought. This was evidenced by the fact that her obsessive-compulsive urges and her need for persistent self-assurance had all but dissolved. And she felt good about that. She felt bloody fantastic! As if she'd been liberated from her demons.

Of course, if the man she'd known as her father was here, he'd say, *This is one of your most wonderful traits, Sophie. Your ability to bounce back from the things that hurt you.* Whether it was fallouts with friends or disagreements with parents, Sophie rarely sulked or harboured resentment. Hours, sometimes minutes later, she'd simply bounce back as if nothing had happened. Oddly, she hadn't ever truly believed that.

Until now.

"You look well, Sophie," the lawyer said, ushering her into his office. "It's a real pleasure to have you back."

Sophie smiled but couldn't return the pleasantry. She suddenly didn't feel well. She felt sick to her stomach. Now that she was back here everything was starting to feel serious once more.

Mr Mitchell gestured to the same seat she had occupied during her previous visit. The emptiness of the seat next to her tinged the moment with sadness. But she had already resolved to reconnect with Victoria and would. As soon as she had decided where her future would lead her.

The lawyer sat opposite. His usual direct eye contact was unnerving. Last time it was endearing. It made her feel important. This time it just felt like he was expecting her to say something specific. To lead the meeting.

"May I offer you a beverage?" he asked as if reading her mind.

"Thank you," she croaked and then promptly cleared her throat.

"Water?"

She nodded. The lawyer fetched a small bottle of San Pellegrino from the chiller. He opened it then placed it with a drinking glass in front of her.

"Thanks." She poured the water and drank with great thirst.

"Better?" he asked with a warm smile.

"Yes, thank you."

There was silence but for a phone ringing somewhere in the next office.

"So, what can I do for you, Sophie?" Mr Mitchell asked as if they hadn't spoken before.

Where do I start? She supposed he could begin by telling her why the hell, in the space of a few weeks, her life had completed imploded. Or maybe he could unravel what this whole thing was with the man next door, a man that she had barely clapped eyes on in all the time she had lived on her street yet suddenly couldn't stop thinking about. Someone who was friends with her father, whoever he actually was. Someone who had the most bizarre effect on her.

It wasn't love. It couldn't be just that. Sophie knew she was naïve when it came to affairs of the heart but the thing with Chris, it was something else. Something more. And that moment they had on the street? Well, that was something else entirely. It was an omen. A bad one. At least that's how it felt to her.

Are you the one?

Oh, every time she replayed that in her mind it made her cringe. That confused look on his face had said it all. He probably thought she was a complete nut job.

She did feel bad for leaving him like that though, without so much as an explanation. She had thought about sending him a text but realised she didn't have his number. Or a phone. And as for that company who owned the house, they were welcome to it!

No more thinking about him, about any of it! Argh!

"I've come to claim my inheritance," she declared, perhaps a tad more forcefully than she had intended. It wasn't an entirely accurate statement, but it would do for now.

The lawyer's eyebrows lifted as if he was surprised. As if there might be some other reason for her visit. "Oh, I see."

"It is still available, right? I mean nobody else has claimed it or something?" she asked, straightening in her seat. "No long-lost brothers or sisters I don't know about that you forgot to mention last time? I wouldn't be surprised at this point," she said with a nervous chuckle. "There aren't, are there?" she added seriously.

The lawyer smiled. "May I ask what changed your mind?"

The obvious answer was right on the tip of her tongue. That she didn't really have anywhere else to go. Or stay, apart from her friend's lumpy second-hand couch. She didn't have a job anymore; she had accepted that. It was obvious that they were building a case to fire her, but she planned to pre-empt that with a resignation letter anyway. It was time to move on.

"It's time for a change," she said.

Mr Mitchell nodded slowly. "And you're now able to accept the terms of the will?"

Sophie thought about this. "What, you mean leave everything I know to become a countess or *countessa*—contessa, whatever the word is—in Italy? Um, yeah, kind of." She was chuckling again like the mad person this whole thing had reduced her to.

Roger Mitchell, the friendly lawyer, appeared to uncharacteristically lose his smile. He leaned forward and said, "Sophie, I'd be remiss if I didn't ascertain that you are not in any way unclear about what it is exactly that you are committing to."

Sophie was taken aback by the change in the lawyer's demeanour. "You make it sound like I'm going to prison or something."

The lawyer observed her for several unnerving seconds before finally speaking. "The role of contessa is for life, Sophie. It isn't like one of your other roles. You can't simply resign."

Sophie swallowed a pang of irritation. She understood that he was doing his job, but still. It felt like he was having a dig.

She shrugged. "I understand. Of course, I understand. I'm not an idiot," she snapped. "I'm sorry. I'm sorry. I don't mean to take it out on you. But Roger, what other choice do I have, really?" she asked as tears pricked her eyes. "I don't have anything left," she added, wrestling with a sudden bout of emotion.

The lawyer said nothing. He simply rose from his seat, walked over to his desk drawer, and pulled out that familiar FedEx packet. Then, retaking his seat, he said, "Sophie, becoming Contessa Sofia DaTerra of Palazzo Rosso isn't just about inheritance. It's a duty. Some say it's a calling. It is a position that you should not take lightly."

"Okay, I get it. No resigning once I've been crowned Queen," she said.

The lawyer rocked his head and returned the dregs of a smile to his face. "Okay. It's not quite a coronation, but... well, you get the point. Now, remember, you will not be able to—"

"Sell, lease, or sublease. I know." She wanted to scoot past this bit. She already felt bad about her dastardly plan to take on the place only to try to sell it later.

"It's my duty to inform you that the trust will ensure you don't," he said, creepily, as if he had just read her mind. "Now, there are some formalities that we'll need to go through. Nothing too arduous. Things such as the *permesso di soggiorno.*"

"What's that?"

"As a non-EU national, you will not be allowed to stay in Italy longer than three months without their equivalent of a visa." When Sophie pulled a face, the lawyer quickly added, "Don't worry. I will walk you through all of that. I already have the papers ready."

"Am I that predictable?" she asked with a bite of the lip.

The lawyer smiled and shrugged. "We just like to be prepared," he said softly.

"What if this is my destiny?" she asked eagerly. Then added, "But what if it isn't?"

Mr Mitchell held the packet up to her. Then, holding her gaze he said, "At this point, your fate is in your hands. Open *only* if you wish to commit to the terms of the will."

The man's ominous words froze the scene for a few seconds. Footsteps clicked outside. Voices murmured. A helicopter buzzed in the distance.

Sophie took the packet from the man. "Wow. It's heavy. What else is in here?" she asked.

"We're not permitted to open it. But as far as I know, it is just the key," the lawyer said, eyeing the packet.

Sophie felt the weight a little longer before looking at the red *tear here* strip.

It was time to decide.

MALEFIC

BOOK 2 OF THE SINISTER SERIES
Sophie Cooper makes her decision, but nothing can prepare her for what happens next.

COMING WINTER 2022 - ORDER NOW!

If you enjoyed

SINISTER

Please leave an Amazon / Goodreads rating
so that others may enjoy it also.

Generally, only a fraction of satisfied readers will leave
a rating, so yours really will make a difference.

THANK YOU.

Subscribe to the blog, mailing list, or follow on social media for the latest news, special chapter previews and exclusive giveaways.

VISIT
www.tonymarturano.com

JOIN THE MAILING LIST
visit www.tonymarturano.com,
click on contact and subscriptions.

LIKE THE FACEBOOK PAGE
facebook.com/tonymarturano.author

BROWSE INSTAGRAM
instagram.com/marturanotony

FOLLOW ON TWITTER
twitter.com/tmarturano

or google tony marturano

ACKNOWLEDGEMENTS

I'm so very grateful to everyone at a Different Angle, who has supported me throughout this book's journey, from manuscript to print. A special thanks to the following who have actively contributed to its realisation.

THE CURSED FOCUS/READER'S GROUP
My heartfelt thanks to all members of the Sinister reader's group, for giving so generously of their time and opinions!

(In no particular order)
Francesca Marturano-Pratt – Anna Pratt – Renee Owens –
Lisa Hall – – Cheryl Green

MY WONDERFUL NEW EDITORS
Nicola, for helping me shape the story into the best that it can be.
Sydney, for that all-important attention to detail.

Welcome aboard!

YOU, THE READER
If you're reading this book, there's a good chance you bought it. I'm obviously very grateful for that.

Thank you!

On the other hand, if you borrowed from or were gifted this book by somebody else, even better! It means they thought it was good enough to pass on.